THE DWELLING-PLACE OF LIGHT

THE MACMILLAN COMPANY
NEW YORK · BOSTON · CHICAGO · DALLAS
ATLANTA · SAN FRANCISCO

MACMILLAN & CO., LIMITED
LONDON · BOMBAY · CALCUTTA
MELBOURNE

THE MACMILLAN CO. OF CANADA, LTD.
TORONTO

"I—I CAME HERE TO—TO KILL YOU—ONLY I CAN'T DO IT."

Norwood Press
J. S. Cushing Co. — Berwick & Smith Co.
Norwood, Mass., U.S.A.

THE DWELLING-PLACE
OF LIGHT

BY

WINSTON CHURCHILL

AUTHOR OF " THE INSIDE OF THE CUP," " A FAR COUNTRY,
" THE CRISIS," " RICHARD CARVEL," ETC.

Mr. Winston Churchill has been moved to
picture the rapidly changing conditions of
American social and industrial life in a
story of great earnestness and power.

40098

New York

THE MACMILLAN COMPANY

1917

" Where is the way to the dwelling-place of light ? "

THE DWELLING–PLACE OF LIGHT

THE DWELLING–PLACE OF LIGHT

CHAPTER I

1

In this modern industrial civilization of which we are sometimes wont to boast, a certain glacier-like process may be observed. The bewildered, the helpless — and there are many — are torn from the parent rock, crushed, rolled smooth, and left stranded in strange places. Thus was Edward Bumpus severed and rolled from the ancestral ledge, from the firm granite of seemingly stable and lasting things, into shifting shale; surrounded by fragments of cliffs from distant lands he had never seen. Thus, at five and fifty, he found himself gate-keeper of the leviathan Chippering Mill in the city of Hampton.

That the polyglot, smoky settlement sprawling on both sides of an historic river should be a part of his native New England seemed at times to be a hideous dream; nor could he comprehend what had happened to him, and to the world of order and standards and religious sanctions into which he had been born. His had been a life of relinquishments. For a long time he had clung to the institution he had been taught to believe was the rock of ages, the Congregational Church, finally to abandon it; even that assuming a form fantastic and unreal, as embodied in the edifice three blocks distant from Fillmore Street which he had attended for a brief time, some ten years before, after his arrival in Hampton. The building, indeed, was symbolic of a decadent and bewildered Puritanism in its pathetic attempt to keep

abreast with the age, to compromise with anarchy, merely
achieving a nondescript medley of rounded, knob-like
towers covered with mulberry-stained shingles. And the
minister was sensational and dramatic. He looked like an
actor, he aroused in Edward Bumpus an inherent prejudice
that condemned the stage. Half a block from this tabernacle stood a Roman Catholic Church, prosperous, brazen,
serene, flaunting an eternal permanence amidst the chaos
which had succeeded permanence!

There were, to be sure, other Protestant churches where
Edward Bumpus and his wife might have gone. One in
particular, which he passed on his way to the mill, with its
terraced steeple and classic façade, preserved all the outward
semblance of the old Order that once had seemed so endur-
ing and secure. He hesitated to join the decorous and
dwindling congregation, — the remains of a social stratum
from which he had been pried loose; and — more irony —
this street, called Warren, of arching elms and white-gabled
houses, was now the abiding place of those prosperous
Irish who had moved thither from the tenements and ruled
the city.

On just such a street in the once thriving New England
village of Dolton had Edward been born. In Dolton Bumpus was once a name of names, rooted there since the seventeenth century, and if you had cared to listen he would
have told you, in a dialect precise but colloquial, the history
of a family that by right of priority and service should have
been destined to inherit the land, but whose descendants
were preserved to see it delivered to the alien. The God
of Cotton Mather and Jonathan Edwards had been tried
in the balance and found wanting. Edward could never
understand this; or why the Universe, so long static and
immutable, had suddenly begun to move. He had always
been prudent, but in spite of youthful "advantages," of an

education, so called, from a sectarian college on a hill, he had never been taught that, while prudence may prosper in a static world, it is a futile virtue in a dynamic one. Experience even had been powerless to impress this upon him. For more than twenty years after leaving college he had clung to a clerkship in a Dolton mercantile establishment before he felt justified in marrying Hannah, the daughter of Elmer Wench, when the mercantile establishment amalgamated with a rival — and Edward's services were no longer required. During the succession of precarious places with decreasing salaries he had subsequently held a terrified sense of economic pressure had gradually crept over him, presently growing strong enough, after two girls had arrived, to compel the abridgment of the family. . . . It would be painful to record in detail the cracking-off process, the slipping into shale, the rolling, the ending up in Hampton, where Edward had now for some dozen years been keeper of one of the gates in the frowning brick wall bordering the canal, — a position obtained for him by a compassionate but not too prudent childhood friend who had risen in life and knew the agent of the Chippering Mill, Mr. Claude Ditmar. Thus had virtue failed to hold its own.

One might have thought in all these years he had sat within the gates staring at the brick row of the company's boarding houses on the opposite bank of the canal that reflection might have brought a certain degree of enlightenment. It was not so. The fog of Edward's bewilderment never cleared, and the unformed question was ever clamouring for an answer — how had it happened? Job's cry. How had it happened to an honest and virtuous man, the days of whose forebears had been long in the land which the Lord their God had given them? Inherently American, though lacking the saving quality of push that had been the making of men like Ditmar, he never ceased

to regard with resentment and distrust the hordes of foreigners trooping between the pillars, though he refrained
from expressing these sentiments in public; a bent, broad
shouldered, silent man of that unmistakable physiognomy
which, in the seventeenth century, almost wholly deserted
the old England for the new. The ancestral features were
there, the lips — covered by a grizzled moustache — moulded
for the precise formation that emphasizes such syllables as
el, the hooked nose and sallow cheeks, the grizzled brows
and grey eyes drawn down at the corners. But for all its
ancestral strength of feature, it was a face from which will
had been extracted, and lacked the fire and fanaticism, the
indomitable hardness it should have proclaimed, and which
have been so characteristically embodied in Mr. St. Gau-
dens's statue of the Puritan. His clothes were slightly
shabby, but always neat.

Little as one might have guessed it, however, what may
be called a certain transmuted enthusiasm was alive in him.
He had a hobby almost amounting to an obsession, not uncommon amongst Americans who have slipped downward in
the social scale. It was the Bumpus Family in America.
He collected documents about his ancestors and relations, he
wrote letters with a fine, painful penmanship on a ruled
block he bought at Hartshorne's drug store to distant Bumpuses in Kansas and Illinois and Michigan, common descendants of Ebenezer, the original immigrant, of Dolton. Many
of these western kinsmen answered : not so the magisterial
Bumpus who lived in Boston on the water side of Beacon,
whom likewise he had ventured to address, — to the indignation and disgust of his elder daughter, Janet.

"Why are you so proud of Ebenezer?" she demanded
once, scornfully.

"Why? Aren't we descended from him?"

"How many generations?"

"Seven," said Edward, promptly, emphasizing the last syllable.

Janet was quick at figures. She made a mental calculation.

"Well, you've got one hundred and twenty-seven other ancestors of Ebenezer's time, haven't you?"

Edward was a little surprised. He had never thought of this, but his ardour for Ebenezer remained undampened. Genealogy — his own — had become his religion, and instead of going to church he spent his Sunday mornings poring over papers of various degrees of discolouration, making careful notes on the ruled block.

This consciousness of his descent from good American stock that had somehow been deprived of its heritage, while a grievance to him, was also a comfort. It had a compensating side, in spite of the lack of sympathy of his daughters and his wife. Hannah Bumpus took the situation more grimly: she was a logical projection in a new environment of the religious fatalism of ancestors whose God was a God of vengeance. She did not concern herself as to what all this vengeance was about; life was a trap into which all mortals walked sooner or later, and her particular trap had a treadmill, — a round of household duties she kept whirling with an energy that might have made their fortunes if she had been the head of the family. It is bad to be a fatalist unless one has an incontrovertible belief in one's destiny, — which Hannah had not. But she kept the little flat with its worn furniture, — which had known so many journeys — as clean as a merchant ship of old Salem, and when it was scoured and dusted to her satisfaction she would sally forth to Bonnaccossi's grocery and provision store on the corner to do her bargaining in competition with the Italian housewives of the neighborhood. She was wont, indeed, to pause outside for a moment, her quick

eye encompassing the coloured prints of red and yellow
jellies cast in rounded moulds, decked with slices of orange,
the gaudy boxes of cereals and buckwheat flour, the "Brook-
field" eggs in packages. Significant, this modern package
system, of an era of flats with little storage space. She
took in at a glance the blue lettered placard announcing
the current price of butterine, and walked around to the
other side of the store, on Holmes Street, where the beef
and bacon hung, where the sidewalk stands were filled, in
the autumn, with cranberries, apples, cabbages, and spinach.

With little outer complaint she had adapted herself to
the constantly lowering levels to which her husband had
dropped, and if she hoped that in Fillmore Street they had
reached bottom, she did not say so. Her unbetrayed regret
was for the loss of what she would have called "respecta-
bility"; and the giving up, long ago, in the little city which
had been their home, of the servant girl had been the first
wrench. Until they came to Hampton they had always
lived in *houses*, and her adaptation to a flat had been hard
— a flat without a parlour. Hannah Bumpus regarded
a parlour as necessary to a respectable family as a wedding
ring to a virtuous woman. Janet and Lise would be growing
up, there would be young men, and no place to see them
save the sidewalks. The fear that haunted her came true,
and she never was reconciled. The two girls went to the
public schools, and afterwards, inevitably, to work, and
it seemed to be a part of her punishment for the sins of her
forefathers that she had no more control over them than
if they had been boarders; while she looked on helplessly,
they did what they pleased; Janet, whom she never understood, was almost as much a source of apprehension as Lise,
who became part and parcel of all Hannah deemed reprehen-
sible in this new America which she refused to recognize
and acknowledge as her own country.

To send them through the public schools had been a struggle. Hannah used to lie awake nights wondering what would happen if Edward became sick. It worried her that they never saved any money : try as she would to cut the expenses down, there was a limit of decency ; New England thrift, hitherto justly celebrated, was put to shame by that which the foreigners displayed, and which would have delighted the souls of gentlemen of the Manchester school. Every once in a while there rose up before her fabulous instances of this thrift, of Italians and Jews who, ignorant emigrants, had entered the mills only a few years before they, the Bumpuses, had come to Hampton, and were now independent property owners. Still rankling in Hannah's memory was a day when Lise had returned from school, dark and mutinous, with a tale of such a family. One of the younger children was a classmate.

"They live on Jordan Street in a *house*, and Laura has roller skates. I don't see why I can't."

This was one of the occasions on which Hannah had given vent to her indignation. Lise was fourteen. Her open rebellion was less annoying than Janet's silent reproach, but at least she had something to take hold of.

"Well, Lise," she said, shifting the saucepan to another part of the stove, "I guess if your father and I had put both you girls in the mills and crowded into one room and cooked in a corner, and lived on onions and macaroni, and put four boarders each in the other rooms, I guess we could have had a house, too. We can start in right now, if you're willing."

But Lise had only looked darker.

"I don't see why father can't make money — other men do."

"Isn't he working as hard as he can to send you to school, and give you a chance?"

"I don't want that kind of a chance. There's Sadie Howard at school — she don't have to work. She liked me before she found out where I lived. . . ."

There was an element of selfishness in Hannah's mania for keeping busy, for doing all their housework and cooking herself. She could not bear to have her daughters interfere; perhaps she did not want to give herself time to think. Her affection for Edward, such as it was, her loyalty to him, was the logical result of a conviction ingrained in early youth that marriage was an indissoluble bond; a point of view, once having a religious sanction, no less powerful now that — all unconsciously — it had deteriorated into a superstition. Hannah, being a fatalist, was not religious. The beliefs of other days, when she had donned her best dress and gone to church on Sundays, had simply lapsed and left — habits. No new beliefs had taken their place. . . .

Even after Janet and Lise had gone to work the household never seemed to gain that margin of safety for which Hannah yearned. Always, when they were on the verge of putting something by, some untoward need or accident seemed to arise on purpose to swallow it up: Edward, for instance, had been forced to buy a new overcoat, the linoleum on the dining-room floor must be renewed, and Lise had had a spell of sickness, losing her position in a flower shop. Afterwards, when she became a saleslady in the *Bagatelle*, that flamboyant department store in Faber Street, she earned four dollars and a half a week. Two of these were supposed to go into the common fund, but there were clothes to buy; Lise loved finery, and Hannah had not every week the heart to insist. Even when, on an occasional Saturday night the girl somewhat consciously and defiantly flung down the money on the dining-room table she pretended not to notice it. But Janet, who was earning six dollars as a stenographer in the office of the Chippering Mill, regularly gave half of hers.

The girls could have made more money as operatives, but strangely enough in the Bumpus family social hopes were not yet extinct.

2

Sharply, rudely, the cold stillness of the winter mornings was broken by agitating waves of sound, penetrating the souls of sleepers. Janet would stir, her mind still lingering on some dream, soon to fade into the inexpressible, in which she had been near to the fulfilment of a heart's desire. Each morning, as the clamour grew louder, there was an interval of bewilderment, of revulsion, until the realization came of mill bells swinging in high cupolas above the river, — one rousing another. She could even distinguish the bells: the deep-toned, penetrating one belonged to the Patuxent Mill, over on the west side, while the Arundel had a high, ominous reverberation like a fire bell. When at last the clangings had ceased she would lie listening to the overtones throbbing in the air, high and low, high and low; lie shrinking, awaiting the second summons that never failed to terrify, the siren of the Chippering Mill, — to her the cry of an insistent, hungry monster demanding its daily food, the symbol of a stern, ugly, and unrelenting necessity.

Beside her in the bed she could feel the soft body of her younger sister cuddling up to her in fright. In such rare moments as this her heart melted towards Lise, and she would fling a protecting arm about her. A sense of Lise's need of protection invaded her, a sharp conviction, like a pang, that Lise was destined to wander: Janet was never so conscious of the feeling as in this dark hour, though it came to her at other times, when they were not quarreling. Quarreling seemed to be the normal reaction between them.

It was Janet, presently, who would get up, shivering, close the window, and light the gas, revealing the room which the two girls shared together. Against the middle of one wall was the bed, opposite this a travel-dented walnut bureau with a marble top, with an oval mirror into which were stuck numerous magazine portraits of the masculine and feminine talent adorning the American stage, a preponderance of the music hall variety. There were pictures of other artists whom the recondite would have recognized as "movie" stars, amazing yet veridic stories of whose wealth Lise read in the daily press : all possessed limousines — an infallible proof, to Lise, of the measure of artistic greatness. Between one of these movie millionaires and an ex-legitimate lady who now found vaudeville profitable was wedged the likeness of a popular idol whose connection with the footlights would doubtless be contingent upon a triumphant acquittal at the hands of a jury of her countrymen, and whose trial for murder, in Chicago, was chronicled daily in thousands of newspapers and followed by Lise with breathless interest and sympathy. She was wont to stare at this lady while dressing and exclaim : —

"Say, I hope they put it all over that district attorney !"

To such sentiments, though deeply felt by her sister, Janet remained cold, though she was, as will be seen, capable of enthusiasms. Lise was a truer daughter of her time and country in that she had the national contempt for law, was imbued with the American hero-worship of criminals that caused the bombardment of Cora Wellman's jail with candy, fruit and flowers and impassioned letters. Janet recalled there had been others before Mrs. Wellman, caught within the meshes of the law, who had incited in her sister a similar partisanship.

It was Lise who had given the note of ornamentation to the bedroom. Against the cheap faded lilac and gold wall-paper were tacked photo-engravings that had taken the younger sister's fancy: a young man and woman, clad in scanty bathing suits, seated side by side in a careening sail boat, — the work of a popular illustrator whose manly and womanly "types" had become national ideals. There were other drawings, if not all by the same hand, at least by the same school; one, sketched in bold strokes, of a dinner party in a stately neo-classic dining-room, the table laden with flowers and silver, the bare-throated women with jewels. A more critical eye than Lise's, gazing upon this portrayal of the Valhalla of success, might have detected in the young men, immaculate in evening dress, a certain effort to feel at home, to converse naturally, which their square jaws and square shoulders belied. This was no doubt the fault of the artist's models, who had failed to live up to the part. At any rate, the sight of these young gods of leisure, the contemplation of the stolid butler and plush footmen in the background never failed to make Lise's heart beat faster.

On the marble of the bureau amidst a litter of toilet articles, and bought by Lise for a quarter at the *Bagatelle* bargain counter, was an oval photograph frame from which the silver wash had begun to rub off, and the band of purple velvet inside the metal had whitened. The frame always contained the current object of Lise's affections, though the exhibits — as Janet said — were subject to change without notice. The Adonis who now reigned had black hair cut in the prevailing Hampton fashion, very long in front and hanging down over his eyes like a Scottish terrier's; very long behind, too, but ending suddenly, shaved in a careful curve at the neck and around the ears. It had almost the appearance of a Japanese wig. The manly beauty of Mr. Max Wylie was of the lantern-jawed order, and in his photograph he conveyed the astonished and pained air of one who has been suddenly seized by an invisible officer of the law from behind. This effect, one presently perceived, was due to the high, stiff collar, the "Torture Brand," Janet called it, when she and her sister were engaged in one of their frequent controversies about life in general: the obvious retort to this remark, which Lise never failed to make, was that Janet could boast of no beaux at all.

It is only fair to add that the photograph scarcely did Mr. Wylie justice. In real life he did not wear the collar, he was free and easy in his manners, sure of his powers of conquest. As Lise observed, he had made a home-run with her at Slattery's Riverside Park. "Sadie Hartmann was sure sore when I tangoed off with him," she would observe reminiscently. . . .

It was Lise's habit to slight her morning toilet, to linger until the last minute in bed, which she left in reluctant haste to stand before the bureau frantically combing out kinks of the brown hair falling over her shoulders before jamming it down across her forehead in the latest mode. Thus occupied, she revealed a certain petulant beauty. Like the majority of shopgirls, she was small, but her figure was good, her skin white; her discontented mouth gave her the touch of piquancy apt to play havoc with the work of the world. In winter breakfast was eaten by the light of a rococo metal lamp set in the centre of the table. This was to save gas. There was usually a rump steak and potatoes, bread and "creamery" butterine, and the inevitable New England doughnuts. At six thirty the whistles screeched again, — a warning note, the signal for Edward's departure; and presently, after a brief respite, the heavy bells once more began their clamour, not to die down until ten minutes of seven, when the last of the stragglers had hurried through the mill gates.

The Bumpus flat included the second floor of a small

wooden house whose owner had once been evilly inspired to paint it a livid clay-yellow — as though insisting that ugliness were an essential attribute of domesticity. A bay ran up the two stories, and at the left were two narrow doorways, one for each flat. On the right the house was separated from its neighbour by a narrow interval, giving but a precarious light to the two middle rooms, the dining-room and kitchen. The very unattractiveness of such a home, however, had certain compensations, for Janet, after the effort of early rising had been surmounted, felt a real relief in leaving it; a relief, too, in leaving Fillmore Street, every feature of which was indelibly fixed in her mind: opposite was the blind brick face of a warehouse, and next to that the converted dwelling house that held the shop of A. Bauer, with the familiar replica of a green ten-cent trading stamp painted above it and the somewhat ironical announcement — when hoar frost whitened the pavement — that ice-cold soda was to be had within, as well as cigars and to-bacco, fruit and candy. Then came a tenement, under which two enterprising Greeks by the name of Pappas — spelled Papas lower down — conducted a business called "The Gentleman," a tailoring, pressing, and dyeing establishment. Janet could see the brilliantined black heads of the two proprietors bending over their boards, and sometimes they would be lifted to smile at her as she passed. The Pappas Brothers were evidently as happy in this drab environment as they had ever been on the sunny mountain slopes of Hellas, and Janet sometimes wondered at this, for she had gathered from her education in the Channing public school that Greece was beautiful.

She was one of the unfortunate who love beauty, who are condemned to dwell in exile, unacquainted with what they love. Desire was incandescent within her breast. Desire for what? It would have been some relief to know.

She could not, like Lise, find joy and forgetfulness at dance halls, at the "movies," at Slattery's Riverside Park in summer, in "joy rides" with the Max Wylies of Hampton. And beside, the Max Wylies were afraid of her.   If at times she wished for wealth, it was because wealth held the magic of emancipation from surroundings against which her soul revolted.   Vividly idealized but unconfided was the memory of a seaside village, the scene of one of the brief sojourns of her childhood, where the air was fragrant with the breath of salt marshes, where she recalled, through the vines of a porch, a shining glimpse of the sea at the end of a little street. . . .

Next to Pappas Brothers was the grey wooden building of Mule Spinners' Hall, that elite organization of skilled labour, and underneath it the store of Johnny Tiernan, its windows piled up with stoves and stovepipes, sheet iron and cooking utensils.   Mr. Tiernan, like the Greeks, was happy, too: unlike the Greeks, he never appeared to be busy, and yet he throve.   He was very proud of the business in which he had invested his savings, but he seemed to have other affairs lying blithely on his mind, affairs of moment to the community, as the frequent presence of the huge policemen, aldermen, and other important looking persons bore witness.   He hailed by name Italians, Greeks, Belgians, Syrians, and "French"; he hailed Janet, too, with respectful cheerfulness, taking off his hat.   He possessed the rare, warm vitality that is irresistible.   A native of Hampton, still in his thirties, his sharp little nose and twinkling blue eyes proclaimed the wisdom that is born and not made; his stiff hair had a twist like the bristles in the cleaning rod of a gun.

He gave Janet the odd impression that he understood her.   And she did not understand herself!

By the time she reached the Common the winter sun,

as though red from exertion, had begun to dispel the smoke
and heavy morning mists.   She disliked winter, the lumpy
brown turf mildewed by the frost, but one day she was moved
by a quality, hitherto unsuspected, in the delicate tracery
against the sky made by the slender branches of the great elms
and maples.   She halted on the pavement, her eyes raised,
heedless of passers-by, feeling within her a throb of the
longing that could be so oddly and unexpectedly aroused.

Her way lay along Faber Street, the main artery of Hampton, a wide strip of asphalt threaded with car tracks, lined
on both sides with incongruous edifices indicative of a rapid,
undiscriminating, and artless prosperity.   There were long
stretches of "ten foot" buildings, so called on account of
the single story, their height deceptively enhanced by the
superimposition of huge and gaudy signs, one on top of
another, announcing the merits of "Stewart's Amberine
Ale," of "Cooley's Oats, the *Digestible* Breakfast Food," of
graphophones and "spring heeled" shoes, tobacco, and
naphtha soaps.   "*No, We don't give Trading Stamps, Our
Products are Worth all You Pay.*"   These "ten foot" stores
were the repositories of pianos, automobiles, hardware, and
millinery, and interspersed amongst them were buildings
of various heights;   *The Bagatelle,* where Lise worked,
the Wilmot Hotel, office buildings, and an occasional relic
of old Hampton, like that housing the *Banner.*   Here,
during those months when the sun made the asphalt soft,
on a scaffolding spanning the window of the store, might
be seen a perspiring young man in his shirt sleeves chalking
up baseball scores for the benefit of a crowd below.   Then
came the funereal, liver-coloured, long-windowed Hinckley
Block (1872), and on the corner a modern, glorified drug-
store thrusting forth plate glass bays — two on Faber
Street and three on Stanley — filled with cameras and candy,
hot water bags, throat sprays, catarrh and kidney cures,

calendars, fountain pens, stationery, and handy alcohol lamps. Flanking the sidewalks, symbolizing and completing the heterogeneous and bewildering effect of the street were long rows of heavy hemlock trunks, unpainted and stripped of bark, with crosstrees bearing webs of wires. Trolley cars rattled along, banging their gongs, trucks rumbled across the tracks, automobiles uttered frenzied screeches behind startled pedestrians. Janet was always galvanized into alertness here, Faber Street being no place to dream. By night an endless procession moved up one sidewalk and down another, staring hypnotically at the flash-in and flash-out electric signs that kept the breakfast foods and ales, the safety razors, soaps, and soups incessantly in the minds of a fickle public.

Two blocks from Faber Street was the North Canal, with a granite-paved roadway between it and the monotonous row of company boarding houses. Even in bright weather Janet felt a sense of oppression here; on dark, misty mornings the stern, huge battlements of the mills lining the farther bank were menacing indeed, bristling with projections, towers, and chimneys, flanked by heavy walls. Had her experience included Europe, her imagination might have seized the medieval parallel, — the arched bridges flung at intervals across the water, lacking only chains to raise them in case of siege. The place was always ominously suggestive of impending strife. Janet's soul was a sensitive instrument, but she suffered from an inability to find parallels, and thus to translate her impressions intellectually. Her feeling about the mills was that they were at once fortress and prison, and she a slave driven thither day after day by an all-compelling power; as much a slave as those who trooped in through the gates in the winter dawn, and wore down, four times a day, the oak treads of the circular tower stairs.

The sound of the looms was like heavy rain hissing on the waters of the canal.

3

The administrative offices of a giant mill such as the Chippering in Hampton are labyrinthine. Janet did not enter by the great gates her father kept, but walked through an open courtyard into a vestibule where, day and night, a watchman stood; she climbed iron-shod stairs, passed the doorway leading to the paymaster's suite, to catch a glimpse, behind the grill, of numerous young men settling down at those mysterious and complicated machines that kept so unerring a record, in dollars and cents, of the human labour of the operatives. There were other suites for the super-intendents, for the purchasing agent; and at the end of the corridor, on the south side of the mill, she entered the outer of the two rooms reserved for Mr. Claude Ditmar, the Agent and general-in-chief himself of this vast establishment. In this outer office, behind the rail that ran the length of it, Janet worked; from the window where her typewriter stood was a sheer drop of eighty feet or so to the river, which ran here swiftly through a wide cañon whose sides were formed by miles and miles of mills, built on buttressed stone walls to retain the banks. The prison-like buildings on the farther shore were also of colossal size, casting their shadows far out into the waters; while in the distance, up and down the stream, could be seen the delicate web of the Stanley and Warren Street bridges, with trolley cars like toys gliding over them, with insect pedestrians creeping along the footpaths.

Mr. Ditmar's immediate staff consisted of Mr. Price, an elderly bachelor of tried efficiency whose peculiar genius lay in computation, of a young Mr. Caldwell who, during the four years since he had left Harvard, had been learning

c

the textile industry, of Miss Ottway, and Janet. Miss
Ottway was the agent's private stenographer, a strongly
built, capable woman with immense reserves seemingly in-
exhaustible. She had a deep, masculine voice, not unmusical,
the hint of a masculine moustache, a masculine manner of
taking to any job that came to hand. Nerves were things
unknown to her : she was granite, Janet tempered steel.
Janet was the second stenographer, and performed, besides,
any odd tasks that might be assigned.

There were, in the various offices of the superintendents,
the paymaster and purchasing agent, other young women
stenographers whose companionship Janet, had she been
differently organized, might have found congenial, but something in her refused to dissolve to their proffered friendship.
She had but one friend, — if Eda Rawle, who worked in
a bank, and whom she had met at a lunch counter by accident,
may be called so. As has been admirably said in another
language, one kisses, the other offers a cheek : Janet offered
the cheek. All unconsciously she sought a relationship
rarely to be found in banks and business offices ; would yield
herself to none other. The young women stenographers
in the Chippering Mill, respectable, industrious girls, were
attracted by a certain indefinable quality, but finding they
made no progress in their advances, presently desisted :
they were somewhat afraid of her ; as one of them remarked,
"You always knew she was there." Miss Lottie Meyers,
who worked in the office of Mr. Orcutt, the superintendent
across the hall, experienced a brief infatuation that turned
to hate. She chewed gum incessantly, Janet found her
cheap perfume insupportable ; Miss Meyers, for her part,
declared that Janet was "queer" and "stuck up," thought
herself better than the rest of them. Lottie Meyers was the
leader of a group of four or five which gathered in the hallway at the end of the noon hour to enter animatedly into a

discussion of waists, hats, and lingerie, to ogle and exchange persiflages with the young men of the paymaster's corps, to giggle, to relate, sotto voce, certain stories that ended invariably in hysterical laughter. Janet detested these conversations. And the sex question, subtly suggested if not openly dealt with, to her was a mystery over which she did not dare to ponder, terrible, yet too sacred to be degraded. Her feelings, concealed under an exterior of self-possession, deceptive to the casual observer, sometimes became molten, and she was frightened by a passion that made her tremble — a passion by no means always consciously identified with men, embodying all the fierce unexpressed and unsatisfied desires of her life.

These emotions, often suggested by some hint of beauty, as of the sun glinting on the river on a bright blue day, had a sudden way of possessing her, and the longing they induced was pain. Longing for what? For some unimagined existence where beauty dwelt, and light, where the ecstasy induced by these was neither moiled nor degraded; where shame, as now, might not assail her. Why should she feel her body hot with shame, her cheeks afire? At such moments she would turn to the typewriter, her fingers striking the keys with amazing rapidity, with extraordinary accuracy and force, — force vaguely disturbing to Mr. Claude Ditmar as he entered the office one morning and involuntarily paused to watch her. She was unaware of his gaze, but her colour was like a crimson signal that flashed to him and was gone. Why had he never noticed her before? All these months, — for more than a year, perhaps, — she had been in his office, and he had not so much as looked at her twice. The unguessed answer was that he had never surprised her in a vivid moment. He had a flair for women, though he had never encountered any possessing the higher values, and it was characteristic of the plane of his mental processes that this one should remind him now of a dark, lithe panther, tensely strung, capable of fierceness. The pain of having her scratch him would be delectable.

When he measured her it was to discover that she was not so little, and the shoulder-curve of her uplifted arms, as her fingers played over the keys, seemed to belie that apparent slimness. And had he not been unacquainted with the subtleties of the French mind and language, he might have classed her as a *fausse maigre*. Her head was small, her hair like a dark, blurred shadow clinging round it. He wanted to examine her hair, to see whether it would not betray, at closer range, an imperceptible wave, — but not daring to linger he went into his office, closed the door, and sat down with a sensation akin to weakness, somewhat appalled by his discovery, considerably amazed at his previous stupidity. He had thought of Janet — when she had entered his mind at all — as unobtrusive, demure; now he recognized this demureness as repression. Her qualities needed illumination, and he, Claude Ditmar, had seen them struck with fire. He wondered whether any other man had been as fortunate.

Later in the morning, quite casually, he made inquiries of Miss Ottway, who liked Janet and was willing to do her a good turn.

"Why, she's a clever girl, Mr. Ditmar, a good stenographer, and conscientious in her work. She's very quick, too."

"Yes, I've noticed that," Ditmar replied, who was quite willing to have it thought that his inquiry was concerned with Janet's aptitude for business.

"She keeps to herself and minds her own affairs. You can see she comes of good stock." Miss Ottway herself was proud of her New England blood. "Her father, you know, is the gatekeeper down there. He's been unfortunate."

"You don't say — I didn't connect her with him. Fine looking old man. A friend of mine who recommended him told me he'd seen better days. . . ."

CHAPTER II

1

In spite of the surprising discovery in his office of a young woman of such a disquieting, galvanic quality, it must not be supposed that Mr. Claude Ditmar intended to infringe upon a fixed principle. He had principles. For him, as for the patriarchs and householders of Israel, the seventh commandment was only relative, yet hitherto he had held rigidly to that relativity, laying down the sound doctrine that women and business would not mix: or, as he put it to his intimates, no sensible man would fool with a girl in his office. Hence it may be implied that Mr. Ditmar's experiences with the opposite sex had been on a property basis. He was one of those busy and successful persons who had never appreciated or acquired the art of quasi-platonic amenities, whose idea of a good time was limited to discreet excursions with cronies, likewise busy and successful persons who, by reason of having married early and unwisely, are strangers to the delights of that higher social intercourse chronicled in novels and the public prints. If one may conveniently overlook the joys of a companionship of the soul, it is quite as possible to have a taste in women as in champagne or cigars. Mr. Ditmar preferred blondes, and he liked them rather stout, a predilection that had led him into matrimony with a lady of this description: a somewhat sticky, candy-eating lady with a mania for card parties, who undoubtedly would have dyed her hair if she had lived. He was not inconsolable, but he had had enough of marriage to learn that it demands a somewhat exorbitant price for joys otherwise more reasonably to be obtained.

He was left a widower with two children, a girl of thirteen and a boy of twelve, both somewhat large for their ages. Amy attended the only private institution for the instruction of her sex of which Hampton could boast; George continued at a public school. The late Mrs. Ditmar for some years before her demise had begun to give evidence of certain restless aspirations to which American ladies of her type and situation seem peculiarly liable, and with a view to their ultimate realization she had inaugurated a Jericho-like campaign. Death had released Ditmar from its increasing pressure. For his wife had possessed that admirable substitute for character, persistence, had been expert in the use of importunity, often an efficient weapon in the hands of the female economically dependent. The daughter of a defunct cashier of the Hampton National Bank, when she had married Ditmar, then one of the superintendents of the Chippering and already a marked man, she had deemed herself fortunate among women, looking forward to a life of ease and idleness and candy in great abundance, — a dream temporarily shattered by the unforeseen discomfort of bringing two children into the world, with an interval of scarcely a year between them. Her parents from an excess of native modesty having failed to enlighten her on this subject, her feelings were those of outraged astonishment, and she was quite determined not to repeat the experience a third time. Knowledge thus belatedly acquired, for a while she abandoned herself to the satisfaction afforded by the ability to take a commanding position in Hampton society, gradually to become aware of the need of a more commodious residence. In a certain kind of intuition she was rich. Her husband had meanwhile become Agent of the Chippering Mill, and she strongly suspected that his prudent reticence on the state of his finances was the best indication of an increasing prosperity. He had indeed made money, been given many opportunities for profitable investments; but the argument for social pre-eminence did not appeal to him : tears and reproaches, recriminations, when frequently applied, succeeded better; like many married men, what he most desired was to be let alone; but in some unaccountable way she had come to suspect that his preference for blondes was of a more liberal nature than at first, in her innocence, she had realized. She was jealous, too, of his cronies, in spite of the fact that these gentlemen, when they met her, treated her with an elaborate politeness; and she accused him with entire justice of being more intimate with them than with her, with whom he was united in holy bonds. The inevitable result of these tactics was the modern mansion in the upper part of Warren Street, known as the "residential" district. Built on a wide lot, with a garage on one side to the rear, with a cement driveway divided into squares, and a wall of democratic height separating its lawn from the sidewalk, the house may for the present be better imagined than described.

A pious chronicler of a more orthodox age would doubtless have deemed it a judgment that Cora Ditmar survived but two years to enjoy the glories of the Warren Street house. For a while her husband indulged in a foolish optimism, only to learn that the habit of matrimonial blackmail, once acquired, is not easily shed. Scarcely had he settled down to the belief that by the gratification of her supreme desire he had achieved comparative peace, than he began to suspect her native self-confidence of cherishing visions of a career contemplating nothing less than the eventual abandonment of Hampton itself as a field too limited for her social talents and his business ability and bank account — at which she was pleased to hint. Hampton suited Ditmar, his passion was the Chippering Mill; and he was in process of steeling himself to resist, whatever the costs, this preposterous plan when he was mercifully released by death. Her intention of sending the children away to acquire a culture and finish Hampton did not afford, — George to Silliston Academy, Amy to a fashionable boarding school, — he had not opposed, yet he did not take the idea with sufficient seriousness to carry it out. The children remained at home, more or less — increasingly less — in the charge of an elderly woman who acted as housekeeper.

Ditmar had miraculously regained his freedom. And now, when he made trips to New York and Boston, combining business with pleasure, there were no questions asked, no troublesome fictions to be composed. More frequently he was in Boston, where he belonged to a large and comfortable club, not too exacting in regard to membership, and here he met his cronies and sometimes planned excursions with them, automobile trips in summer to the White Mountains or choice little resorts to spend Sundays and holidays, generally taking with them a case of champagne and several bags of golf sticks. He was fond of shooting, and belonged to a duck club on the Cape, where poker and bridge were not tabooed. To his intimates he was known as "Dit." Nor is it surprising that his attitude toward women had become in general one of resentment; matrimony he now regarded as unmitigated folly. At five and forty he was a vital, dominating, dust-coloured man six feet and half an inch in height, weighing a hundred and ninety pounds, and thus a trifle fleshy. When relaxed, and in congenial company, he looked rather boyish, an aspect characteristic of many American business men of to-day. His head was large, he wore his hair short, his features also proclaimed him as belonging to a modern American type in that they were not clear-cut, but rather indefinable; a bristling, short-cropped moustache gave him a certain efficient, military look which, when introduced to strangers as "Colonel," was apt to deceive them into thinking him an army officer. The title he had once received as a member of the staff of the governor of the state, and was a tribute to a gregariousness and political influence rather than to a genius for the art of war. *Ex officio*, as the agent of the Chippering Mill and a man of substance to boot, he was "in" politics, hail fellow well met with and an individual to be taken into account by politicians from the governor and member of congress down. He was efficient, of course; he had efficient hands and shrewd, efficient eyes, and the military impression was deepened by his manner of dealing with people, his conversation being yea, yea and nay, nay, — save with his cronies and those of the other sex from whom he had something to gain. His clothes always looked new, of pronounced patterns and light colours set aside for him by an obsequious tailor in Boston.

If a human being in such an enviable position as that of agent of the Chippering Mill can be regarded as property, it might be said that Mr. Claude Ditmar belonged to the Chipperings of Boston, a family still owning a controlling interest in the company. His loyalty to them and to the mill he so ably conducted was the great loyalty of his life. For Ditmar, a Chippering could do no wrong. It had been the keen eye of Mr. Stephen Chippering that first had marked him, questioned him, recognized his ability, and from the moment of that encounter his advance had been rapid. When old Stephen had been called to his fathers, Ditmar's allegiance was automatically, as it were, transferred to the two sons, George and Worthington, already members of the board of directors. Sometimes Ditmar called on them at their homes, which stood overlooking the waters of the

Charles River Basin. The attitude toward him of the Chipperings and their wives was one of an interesting adjustment of feudalism to democracy. They were fond of him, grateful to him, treating him with a frank camaraderie that had in it not the slightest touch of condescension, but Ditmar would have been the first to recognize that there were limits to the intimacy. They did not, for instance — no doubt out of consideration — invite him to their dinner parties or take him to their club, which was not the same as that to which he himself belonged. He felt no animus. Nor would he, surprising though it may seem, have changed places with the Chipperings. At an early age, and quite unconsciously, he had accepted property as the ruling power of the universe, and when family was added thereto the combination was nothing less than divine.

2

There were times, especially during the long winters, when life became almost unbearable for Janet, and she was seized by a desire to run away from Fillmore Street, from the mills, from Hampton itself. Only she did not know where to go, or how to get away. She was convinced of the existence in the world of delightful spots where might be found congenial people with whom it would be a joy to talk. Fillmore Street, certainly, did not contain any such. The office was not so bad. It is true that in the mornings, as she entered West Street, the sight of the dark façade of the fortress-like structure, emblematic of the captivity in which she passed her days, rarely failed to arouse in her sensations of oppression and revolt; but here, at least, she discovered an outlet for her energies; she was often too busy to reflect, and at odd moments she could find a certain solace and companionship in the river, so intent, so purposeful, so beautiful, so undisturbed by the inconcinnity, the clatter and confusion of Hampton as it flowed serenely under the bridges and between the mills toward the sea.   Toward the sea!

It was when, at night, she went back to Fillmore Street — when she thought of the monotony, yes, and the sordidness of home, when she let herself in at the door and climbed the dark and narrow stairway, that her feet grew leaden.   In spite of the fact that Hannah was a good housekeeper and prided herself on cleanliness, the tiny flat reeked with the smell of cooking, and Janet, from the upper hall, had a glimpse of a thin, angular woman with a scrawny neck, with scant grey hair tightly drawn into a knot, in a gingham apron covering an old dress bending over the kitchen stove.   And occasionally, despite a resentment that fate should have dealt thus inconsiderately with the family, Janet felt pity welling within her.   After supper, when Lise had departed with her best young man, Hannah would occasionally, though grudgingly, permit Janet to help her with the dishes.

"You work all day, you have a right to rest."

"But I don't want to rest," Janet would declare, and rub the dishes the harder.   With the spirit underlying this protest, Hannah sympathized.   Mother and daughter were alike in that both were inarticulate, but Janet had a secret contempt for Hannah's uncomplaining stoicism.   She loved her mother, in a way, especially at certain times, — though she often wondered why she was unable to realize more fully the filial affection of tradition; but in moments of softening, such as these, she was filled with rage at the thought of any woman endowed with energy permitting herself to be overtaken and overwhelmed by such a fate as Hannah's: divorce, desertion, anything, she thought, would have been better — anything but to be cheated out of life.   Feeling the fires of rebellion burning hotly within her, — rebellion against environment and driving necessity — she would glance at her mother and ask herself whether it were possible that Hannah had ever known longings, had ever been wrung by inexpressible desires, — desires in which the undiscovered spiritual was so alarmingly compounded with the undiscovered physical. She would have died rather than speak to Hannah of these unfulfilled experiences, and the mere thought of confiding them to any person appalled her. Even if there existed some wonderful, understanding being to whom she might be able thus to empty her soul, the thought of the ecstasy of that kenosis was too troubling to be dwelt upon.

She had tried reading, with unfortunate results, — perhaps because no Virgil had as yet appeared to guide her through the mysteries of that realm. Her schooling had failed to instil into her a discriminating taste for literature; and when, on occasions, she had entered the Public Library opposite the Common it had been to stare hopelessly at rows of books whose authors and titles offered no clew to their contents. Her few choices had not been happy, they had failed to interest and thrill. . . .

Of the Bumpus family Lise alone found refuge, distraction, and excitement in the vulgar modern world by which they were surrounded, and of whose heedlessness and remorselessness they were the victims. Lise went out into it, became a part of it, returning only to sleep and eat, — a tendency Hannah found unaccountable, and against which even her stoicism was not wholly proof. Scarce an evening went by without an expression of uneasiness from Hannah.

"She didn't happen to mention where she was going, did she, Janet?" Hannah would query, when she had finished her work and put on her spectacles to read the *Banner*.

"To the movies, I suppose," Janet would reply. Although well aware that her sister indulged in other distractions, she thought it useless to add to Hannah's disquietude. And if she had little patience with Lise, she had less with the help-less attitude of her parents.

"Well," Hannah would add, "I never can get used to her going out nights the way she does, and with young men and women I don't know anything about. I wasn't brought up that way. But as long as she's got to work for a living I guess there's no help for it."

And she would glance at Edward. It was obviously due to his inability adequately to cope with modern con-ditions that his daughters were forced to toil, but this was the nearest she ever came to reproaching him. If he heard, he acquiesced humbly, and in silence: more often than not he was oblivious, buried in the mazes of the Bumpus family history, his papers spread out on the red cloth of the dining-room table, under the lamp. Sometimes in his simplicity and with the enthusiasm that demands listeners he would read aloud to them a letter, recently received from a distant kinsman, an Alpheus Bumpus, let us say, who had migrated to Calfornia in search of wealth and fame, and who had found neither. In spite of age and misfortunes, the liberal attitude of these western members of the family was always a matter of perplexity to Edward.

"He tells me they're going to give women the ballot, — doesn't appear to be much concerned about his own women-folks going to the polls."

"Why shouldn't they, if they want to?" Janet would exclaim, though she had given little thought to the question.

Edward would mildly ignore this challenge.

"He has a house on what they call Russian Hill, and he can watch the vessels as they come in from Japan," he would continue in his precise voice, emphasizing admirably the last syllables of the words "Russian," "vessels," and "Japan." "Wouldn't you like to see the letter?"

To do Hannah justice, although she was quite incapable of

sharing his passion, she frequently feigned an interest, took the letter, presently handing it on to Janet who, in deciphering Alpheus's trembling calligraphy, pondered over his manifold woes. Alpheus's son, who had had a good position in a sporting goods establishment on Market Street, was sick and in danger of losing it, the son's wife expecting an addition to the family, the house on Russian Hill mortgaged. Alpheus, a veteran of the Civil War, had been for many years preparing his reminiscences, but the newspapers nowadays seemed to care nothing for matters of solid worth, and so far had refused to publish them. . . . Janet, as she read, reflected that these letters invariably had to relate tales of failures, of disappointed hopes; she wondered at her father's perennial interest in failures, — provided they were those of his family; and the next evening, as he wrote painfully on his ruled paper, she knew that he in turn was pouring out his soul to Alpheus, recounting, with an emotion by no means unpleasurable, to this sympathetic but remote relative the story of his own failure!

3

If the city of Hampton was emblematic of our modern world in which haphazardness has replaced order, Fillmore Street may be likened to a back eddy of the muddy and troubled waters, in which all sorts of flotsam and jetsam had collected. Or, to find perhaps an even more striking illustration of the process that made Hampton in general and Fillmore Street in particular, one had only to take the trolley to Glendale, the Italian settlement on the road leading to the old New England village of Shrewsbury. Janet sometimes walked there, alone or with her friend Eda Rawle. Disintegration itself — in a paradoxically pathetic attempt at reconstruction — had built Glendale. Human hands, Italian hands. Nor, surprising though it may seem, were these descendants of the people of the Renaissance in the least offended by their handiwork. When the southern European migration had begun and real estate became valuable, one by one the more decorous edifices of the old American order had been torn down and carried piecemeal by sons of Italy to the bare hills of Glendale, there to enter into new combinations representing, to an eye craving harmony, the last word of a chaos, of a mental indigestion, of a colour scheme crying aloud to heaven for retribution. Standing alone and bare amidst its truck gardens, hideous, extreme, though typical of the entire settlement, composed of fragments ripped from once-appropriate settings, is a house with a tiny body painted strawberry-red, with scroll-work shutters a tender green; surmounting the structure and almost equalling it in size is a sky-blue cupola, once the white crown of the Sutter mansion, the pride of old Hampton. The walls of this dwelling were wrested from the sides of Mackey's Tavern, while the shutters for many years adorned the parsonage of the old First Church. Similarly, in Hampton and in Fillmore Street, lived in enforced neighbourliness human fragments once having their places in crystallized communities where existence had been regarded as solved. Here there was but one order, — if such it may be called, — one relationship, direct or indirect, one necessity claiming them all — the mills.

Like the boards forming the walls of the shacks at Glendale, these human planks torn from an earlier social structure were likewise warped, which is to say they were dominated by obsessions. Edward's was the Bumpus family; and Chris Auermann, who lived in the flat below, was convinced that the history of mankind is a deplorable record of havoc caused by women. Perhaps he was right, but the conviction was none the less an obsession. He came from a little village near Wittenburg that has scarcely changed since Luther's time. Like most residents of Hampton who did not work in the mills, he ministered to those who did, or to those who sold merchandise to the workers, cutting their hair in his barber shop on Faber Street.

The Bumpuses, save Lise, clinging to a native individualism and pride, preferred isolation to companionship with the other pieces of driftwood by which they were surrounded, and with which the summer season compelled a certain enforced contact. When the heat in the little dining-room grew unbearable, they were driven to take refuge on the front steps shared in common with the household of the barber. It is true that the barber's wife was a mild hausfrau who had little to say, and that their lodgers, two young Germans who worked in the mills, spent most of their evenings at a bowling club; but Auermann himself, exhaling a strong odour of bay rum, would arrive promptly at quarter past eight, take off his coat, and thus, as it were stripped for action, would turn upon the defenceless Edward.

"Vill you mention one great man — yoost one — who is not greater if the vimmen leave him alone?" he would demand. "Is it Anthony, the conqueror of Egypt and the East? I vill show you Cleopatra. Und Burns, und Napoleon, the greatest man what ever lived — vimmen again. I tell you there is no Elba, no St. Helena if it is not for the vimmen. Und vat vill you say of Goethe?"

Poor Edward could think of nothing to say of Goethe.

"He is great, I grant you," Chris would admit, "but vat is he if the vimmen leave him alone? Divine — yoost that." And he would proceed to cite endless examples of generals and statesmen whose wives or mistresses had been their bane. Futile Edward's attempts to shift the conversation to the subject of his own obsession; the German was by far the more aggressive, he would have none of it. Perhaps if Edward had been willing to concede that the

D

Bumpuses had been brought to their present lowly estate by the sinister agency of the fair sex Chris might conditionally have accepted the theme. Hannah, contemptuously waving a tattered palm leaf fan, was silent; but on one occasion Janet took away the barber's breath by suddenly observing : —

"You never seem to think of the women whose lives are ruined by men, Mr. Auermann."

It was unheard-of, this invasion of a man's argument by a woman, and by a young woman at that. He glared at her through his spectacles, took them off, wiped them, replaced them, and glared at her again. He did not like Janet; she was capable of what may be called a speaking silence, and he had never been wholly unaware of her disapproval and ridicule. Perhaps he recognized in her, instinctively, the potential qualities of that emerging modern woman who to him was anathema.

"It is somethings I don't think about," he said.

He was a wizened little man with faience-blue eyes, and sat habitually hunched up with his hands folded across his shins.

Nam fuit ante Helenam — as Darwin quotes. Toward all the masculine residents of Fillmore Street, save one, the barber's attitude was one of unconcealed scorn for an inability to recognize female perfidy. With Johnny Tiernan alone he refused to enter the lists. When the popular proprietor of the tin shop came sauntering along the sidewalk with nose uptilted, waving genial greetings to the various groups on the steps, Chris Auermann's expression would suddenly change to one of fatuous playfulness.

"What's this I hear about giving the girls the vote, Chris?" Johnny would innocently inquire, winking at Janet, invariably running his hand through the wiry red hair that resumed its corkscrew twist as soon as he released it. And Chris would as invariably reply : —

"You have the dandruffs — yes? You come to my shop, I give you somethings. . . ."

Sometimes the barber, in search of a more aggressive adversary than Edward, would pay visits, when as likely as not another neighbour with profound convictions and a craving for proselytes would swoop down on the defenceless Bumpuses: Joe Shivers, for instance, who lived in one of the tenements above the cleaning and dyeing establishment kept by the Pappas Bros., and known as "The Gentleman." In the daytime Mr. Shivers was a model of acquiescence in a system he would have designated as one of industrial feudalism, his duty being to examine the rolls of cloth as they came from the looms of the Arundel Mill, in case of imperfections handing them over to the women menders: at night, to borrow a vivid expression from Lise, he was "batty in the belfry" on the subject of socialism. Unlike the barber, whom he could not abide, for him the cleavage of the world was between labour and capital instead of man and woman; his philosophy was stern and naturalistic; the universe — the origin of which he did not discuss — just an accidental assemblage of capricious forces over which human intelligence was one day to triumph. Squatting on the lowest step, his face upturned, by the light of the arc sputtering above the street he looked like a yellow frog, his eager eyes directed toward Janet, whom he suspected of intelligence.

"If there was a God, a nice, kind, all-powerful God, would he permit what happened in one of the loom-rooms last week? A Polak girl gets her hair caught in the belt — pfff!" He had a marvellously realistic gift when it came to horrors: Janet felt her hair coming out by the roots. Although she never went to church, she did not like to think that no God existed. Of this Mr. Shivers was very positive. Edward, too, listened uneasily, hemmed and hawed, making ineffectual attempts to combat Mr. Shivers's socialism with a deeply-rooted native individualism that Shivers declared as defunct as Christianity.

"If it is possible for the workingman to rise under a capitalistic system, why do you not rise, then? Why do I not rise? I'm as good as Ditmar, I'm better educated, but we're all slaves. What right has a man to make you and me work for him just because he has capital?"

"Why, the right of capital," Edward would reply.

Mr. Shivers, with the manner of one dealing with an incurable romanticism and sentimentality, would lift his hands in despair. And in spite of the fact that Janet detested him, he sometimes exercised over her a paradoxical fascination, suggesting as he did unexplored intellectual realms. She despised her father for not being able to crush the little man. Edward would make pathetic attempts to capture the rôle Shivers had appropriated, to be the practical party himself, to convict Shivers of idealism. Socialism scandalized him, outraged, even more than atheism, something within him he held sacred, and he was greatly annoyed because he was unable adequately to express this feeling.

"You can't change human nature, Mr. Shivers," Edward would insist in his precise but ineffectual manner. "We all want property, you would accept a fortune if it was offered to you, and so should I. Americans will never become socialists."

"But look at me, wasn't I born in Meriden, Connecticut? Ain't that Yankee enough for you?" Thus Mr. Shivers sought blandly to confound him.

A Yankee! Shades of the Pilgrim fathers, of seven generations of Bumpuses! A Yankee who used his hands in that way, a Yankee with a nose like that, a Yankee with a bald swathe down the middle of his crown and bunches

of black, moth-eaten hair on either side! But Edward,
too polite to descend to personalities, was silent. . . .

In brief, this very politeness of Edward's, which his
ancestors would have scorned, this consideration and lack
of self-assertion made him the favourite prey of the many
"characters" in Fillmore Street whose sanity had been
disturbed by pressure from above, in whose systems had
lodged the germs of those exotic social doctrines floating so
freely in the air of our modern industrial communities. . . .
Chester Glenn remains for a passing mention. A Yankee
of Yankees, this, born on a New Hampshire farm, and to
the ordinary traveller on the Wigmore branch of the railroad just a good-natured, round-faced, tobacco-chewing
brakeman who would take a seat beside ladies of his acquaintance and make himself agreeable until it was time to rise
and bawl out, in the approved manner of his profession,
the name of the next station. Fillmore Street knew that the
flat visored cap which his corporation compelled him to
wear covered a brain into which had penetrated the maggot
of the Single Tax. When he encountered Mr. Shivers or
Auermann the talk became coruscating. . . .

4

Eda Rawle, Janet's solitary friend of these days, must
also be mentioned, though the friendship was merely an
episode in Janet's life. Their first meeting was at Grady's
quick-lunch counter in Faber Street, which they both frequented at one time, and the fact that each had ordered a
ham sandwich, a cup of coffee, and a confection — new to
Grady's — known as a Napoleon had led to conversation.
Eda, of course, was the aggressor; she was irresistibly
drawn, she would not be repulsed. A stenographer in the
Wessex National Bank, she boarded with a Welsh family

in Spruce Street; matter-of-fact, plodding, commonplace,
resembling — as Janet thought — a horse, possessing, indeed
many of the noble qualities of that animal, she might have
been thought the last person in the world to discern and
appreciate in Janet the hidden elements of a mysterious
fire. In appearance Miss Rawle was of a type not infre-
quent in Anglo-Saxon lands, strikingly blonde, with high
malar bones, white eyelashes, and eyes of a metallic blue,
cheeks of an amazing elasticity that worked rather painfully
as she talked or smiled, drawing back inadequate lips, revealing long, white teeth and vivid gums. It was the craving
in her for romance Janet assuaged; Eda's was the love content to pour out, that demands little. She was capable
of immolation. Janet was by no means ungrateful for the
warmth of such affection, though in moments conscious of
a certain perplexity and sadness because she was able to
give such a meagre return for the wealth of its offering.

In other moments, when the world seemed all disorder
and chaos, — as Mr. Shivers described it, — or when she
felt within her, like demons, those inexpressible longings
and desires, leaping and straining, pulling her, almost irresistibly, she knew not whither, Eda shone forth like a light
in the darkness, like the beacon of a refuge and a shelter.
Eda had faith in her, even when Janet had lost faith in
herself: she went to Eda in the same spirit that Marguerite
went to church; though she, Janet, more resembled Faust,
being — save in these hours of lowered vitality — of the
forth-faring kind. . . . Unable to confess the need that drove
her, she arrived in Eda's little bedroom to be taken into
Eda's arms. Janet was immeasurably the stronger of the
two, but Eda possessed the masculine trait of protectiveness,
the universe never bothered her, she was one of those persons — called fortunate — to whom the orthodox Christian
virtues come as naturally as sun or air. Passion, when

sanctified by matrimony, was her ideal, and now it was always in terms of Janet she dreamed of it, having read about it in volumes her friend would not touch, and never having experienced deeply its discomforts. Sanctified or unsanctified, Janet regarded it with terror, and whenever Eda innocently broached the subject she recoiled. Once Eda exclaimed : —

"When you do fall in love, Janet, you must tell me all about it, every word!"

Janet blushed hotly, and was silent. In Eda's mind such an affair was a kind of glorified fireworks ending in a cluster of stars, in Janet's a volcanic eruption to turn the world red. Such was the difference between them.

Their dissipations together consisted of "sundaes" at a drug-store, or sometimes of movie shows at the *Star* or the *Alhambra.* Stereotyped on Eda's face during the legitimately tender passages of these dramas was an expression of rapture, a smile made peculiarly infatuate by that vertical line in her cheeks, that inadequacy of lip and preponderance of white teeth and red gums. It irritated, almost infuriated Janet, to whom it appeared as the logical reflection of what was passing on the screen; she averted her glance from both, staring into her lap, filled with shame that the relation between the sexes should be thus exposed to public gaze, parodied, sentimentalized, degraded. . . . There were, however, marvels to stir her, strange landscapes, cities, seas, and ships, — once a fire in the forest of a western reserve with gigantic tongues of orange flame leaping from tree to tree. The movies brought the world to Hampton, the great world into which she longed to fare, brought the world to *her!* Remote mountain hamlets from Japan, minarets and muezzins from the Orient, pyramids from Egypt, domes from Moscow resembling gilded beets turned upside down; grey houses of parliament by the Thames, the Tower of London, the Palaces of Potsdam, the Taj Mahal. Strange lands indeed, and stranger peoples! booted Russians in blouses, naked Equatorial savages tattooed and amazingly adorned, soldiers and sailors, presidents, princes and emperors brought into such startling proximity one could easily imagine one's self exchanging the time of day! Incredible to Janet how the audiences, how even Eda accepted with American complacency what were to her never-ending miracles; the yearning to see more, to know more, became acute, like a pain, but even as she sought to devour these scenes, to drink in every detail, with tantalizing swiftness they were whisked away. They were peepholes in the walls of her prison; and at night she often charmed herself to sleep with remembered visions of wide, empty, tree-shaded terraces reserved for kings.

But Eda, however complacent her interest in the scenes themselves, was thrilled to the marrow by their effect on Janet, who was her medium. Emerging from the vestibule of the theatre, Janet seemed not to see the slushy street, her eyes shone with a silver light like that of a mountain lake in a stormy sunset. And they walked in silence until Janet would exclaim: —

"Oh Eda, wouldn't you love to travel!"

Thus Eda Rawle was brought in contact with values she herself was powerless to detect, and which did not become values until they had passed through Janet. One "educative" reel they had seen had begun with scenes in a lumber camp high in the mountains of Galicia, where grow forests of the priceless pine that becomes, after years of drying and seasoning, the sounding board of the Stradivarius and the harp. Even then it must respond to a Player. Eda, though failing to apply this poetic parallel, when alone in her little room in the Welsh boarding-house often indulged in an ecstasy of speculation as to that man, hidden in the

mists of the future, whose destiny it would be to awaken
her friend. Hampton did not contain him, — of this she
was sure; and in her efforts to visualize him she had recourse
to the movies, seeking him amongst that brilliant company
of personages who stood so haughtily or walked so indif-
ferently across the ephemeral brightness of the screen.

5

By virtue of these marvels of the movies Hampton —
ugly and sordid Hampton! — actually began for Janet to
take on a romantic tinge. Were not the strange peoples
of the earth flocking to Hampton? She saw them arriving
at the station, straight from Ellis Island, bewildered, ticketed
like dumb animals, the women draped in the soft, exotic
colours many of them were presently to exchange for the
cheap and gaudy apparel of Faber Street. She sought to
summon up in her mind the glimpses she had had of the
wonderful lands from which they had come, to imagine
their lives in that earlier environment. Sometimes she
wandered, alone or with Eda, through the various quarters
of the city. Each quarter had a flavour of its own, a syn-
thetic flavour belonging neither to the old nor to the new,
yet partaking of both: a difference in atmosphere to which
Janet was keenly sensitive. In the German quarter, to the
north, one felt a sort of ornamental bleakness — if the expression may be permitted: the tenements here were clean
and not too crowded, the scroll-work on their superimposed
porches, like that decorating the Turnverein and the stern
Lutheran Church, was eloquent of a Teutonic inheritance.
The Belgians were to the west, beyond the base-ball park
and the car barns, their grey houses scattered among new
streets beside the scarred and frowning face of Torrey's hill.
Almost under the hill itself, which threatened to roll down
on it, and facing a bottomless, muddy street, was the quaint

little building giving the note of foreign thrift, of socialism and shrewdness, of *joie de vivre* to the settlement, the Franco-Belgian co-operative store, with its *salle de réunion* above and a stage for amateur theatricals. Standing in the mud outside, Janet would gaze through the tiny windows in the stucco wall at the baskets prepared for each household laid in neat rows beside the counter; at the old man with the watery blue eyes and lacing of red in his withered cheeks who spoke no English, whose duty it was to distribute the baskets to the women and children as they called.

Turning eastward again, one came to Dey Street, in the heart of Hampton, where Hibernian Hall stood alone and grim, sole testimony of the departed Hibernian glories of a district where the present Irish rulers of the city had once lived and gossiped and fought in the days when the mill bells had roused the boarding-house keepers at half past four of a winter morning. Beside the hall was a corner lot, heaped high with hills of ashes and rubbish like the vomitings of some filthy volcano; the unsightliness of which was half concealed by huge signs announcing the merits of chewing gums, tobaccos, and cereals. But why had the departure of the Irish, the coming of the Syrians made Dey Street dark, narrow, mysterious, oriental? changed the very aspect of its architecture? Was it the coffee-houses? One of these, in front of which Janet liked to linger, was set weirdly into an old New England cottage, and had, apparently, fathomless depths. In summer the whole front of it lay open to the street, and here all day long, beside the table where the charcoal squares were set to dry, could be seen saffron-coloured Armenians absorbed in a Turkish game played on a backgammon board, their gentleness and that of the loiterers looking on in strange contrast with their hawk-like profiles and burning eyes. Behind this group, in the half light of the middle interior, could be discerned an American soda-water fountain of a bygone fashion, on its marble counter oddly shaped bottles containing rose and violet syrups; there was a bottle-shaped stove, and on the walls, in gilt frames, pictures evidently dating from the period in American art that flourished when Franklin Pierce was President; and there was an array of marble-topped tables extending far back into the shadows. Behind the fountain was a sort of cupboard — suggestive of the Arabian Nights, which Janet had never read — from which, occasionally, the fat proprietor emerged bearing Turkish coffee or long Turkish pipes.

When not thus occupied the proprietor carried a baby. The street swarmed with babies, and mothers nursed them on the door-steps. And in this teeming, prolific street one could scarcely move without stepping on a fat, almond-eyed child, though some, indeed, were wheeled; wheeled in all sorts of queer contrivances by one another, by fathers with ragged black moustaches and eagle noses who, to the despair of mill superintendents, had decided in the morning that three days' wages would suffice to support their families for the week. . . . In the midst of the throng might be seen occasionally the stout and comfortable and not too immaculate figure of a shovel bearded Syrian priest, in a frock coat and square-topped "Derby" hat, sailing along serenely, heedless of the children who scattered out of his path.

Nearby was the quarter of the Canadian French, scarcely now to be called foreigners, though still somewhat reminiscent of the cramped little towns in the northern wilderness of water and forest. On one corner stood almost invariably a "Pharmacie Française"; the signs were in French, and the elders spoke the patois. These, despite the mill pallor, retained in their faces, in their eyes, a suggestion of the outdoor look of their ancestors, the *coureurs des bois*, but the children spoke English, and the young men, as they played

base-ball in the street or in the corner lots might be heard
shouting out derisively the cry of the section hands so
familiar in mill cities, "*Doff, you beggars you, doff!*"

Occasionally the two girls strayed into that wide thoroughfare not far from the canal, known by the classic name of
Hawthorne, which the Italians had appropriated to themselves. This street, too, in spite of the telegraph poles
flaunting crude arms in front of its windows, in spite of the
trolley running down its middle, had acquired a character, a
unity all its own, a warmth and picturesqueness that in the
lingering light of summer evenings assumed an indefinable
significance. It was not Italy, but it was *something* —
something proclaimed in the ornate, leaning lines of the
pillared balconies of the yellow tenement on the second
block, in the stone-vaulted entrance of the low house next
door, in fantastically coloured walls, in curtained windows
out of which leaned swarthy, earringed women. Blocking
the end of the street, in stern contrast, was the huge Clarendon Mill with its sinister brick pillars running up the six
stories between the glass. Here likewise the sidewalks over-
flowed with children, large-headed, with great, lustrous eyes,
mute, appealing, the eyes of cattle. Unlike American children, they never seemed to be playing. Among the groups of
elders gathered for gossip were piratical Calabrians in sombre
clothes, descended from Greek ancestors, once the terrors
of the Adriatic Sea. The women, lingering in the doorways,
hemmed in by more children, were for the most part squat
and plump, but once in a while Janet's glance was caught
and held by a strange, sharp beauty worthy of a cameo.

Opposite the Clarendon Mill on the corner of East Street
was a provision store with stands of fruit and vegetables
encroaching on the pavement. Janet's eye was attracted
by a box of olives.

"Oh Eda," she cried, "do you remember, we saw them

being picked — in the movies? All those old trees on the side of a hill?"

"Why, that's so," said Eda. "You never would have thought anything'd grow on those trees."

The young Italian who kept the store gave them a friendly grin.

"You lika the olives?" he asked, putting some of the shining black fruit into their hands. Eda bit one dubiously with her long, white teeth, and giggled.

"Don't they taste funny!" she exclaimed.

"Good — very good," he asserted gravely, and it was to Janet he turned, as though recognizing a discrimination not to be found in her companion. She nodded affirmatively. The strange taste of the fruit enhanced her sense of adventure, she tried to imagine herself among the gatherers in the grove; she glanced at the young man to perceive that he was tall and well formed, with remarkably expressive eyes almost the colour of the olives themselves. It surprised her that she liked him, though he was an Italian and a foreigner: a certain débonnair dignity in him appealed to her — a quality lacking in many of her own countrymen. And she wanted to talk to him about Italy, — only she did not know how to begin, — when a customer appeared, an Italian woman who conversed with him in soft, liquid tones that moved her. . . .

Sometimes on these walks — especially if the day were grey and sombre — Janet's sense of romance and adventure deepened, became more poignant, charged with presage. These feelings, vague and unaccountable, she was utterly unable to confide to Eda, yet the very fear they inspired was fascinating; a fear and a hope that some day, in all this Babel of peoples, something would happen! It was as though the conflicting soul of the city and her own soul were one. . . .

CHAPTER III

1

LISE was the only member of the Bumpus family who did not find uncongenial such distractions and companionships as were offered by the civilization that surrounded them. The *Bagatelle* she despised; that was slavery — but slavery out of which she might any day be snatched, like Leila Hawtrey, by a prince charming who had made a success in life. Success to Lise meant money. Although what some sentimental sociologists might call a victim of our civilization, Lise would not have changed it, since it produced not only Lise herself, but also those fabulous financiers with yachts and motors and town and country houses she read about in the supplements of the Sunday newspapers. It contained her purgatory, which she regarded in good conventional fashion as a mere temporary place of detention, and likewise the heaven toward which she strained, the dwelling-place of light. In short, her philosophy was that of the modern, orthodox American, tinged by a somewhat commercialized Sunday school tradition of an earlier day, and highly approved by the censors of the movies. The peculiar kind of abstinence once euphemistically known as "virtue," particularly if it were combined with beauty, never failed of its reward. Lise, in this sense, was indeed virtuous, and her mirror told her she was beautiful. Almost anything could happen to such a lady: any day she might be carried up into heaven by that modern chariot of fire, the motor car, driven by a celestial chauffeur.

46

One man's meat being another's poison, Lise absorbed from the movies an element by which her sister Janet was repelled. A popular production known as "Leila of Hawtrey's" contained her creed, — Hawtrey's being a glittering metropolitan restaurant where men of the world are wont to gather and discuss the stock market, and Leila a beautiful, blonde and orphaned waitress upon whom several of the fashionable frequenters had exercised seductive powers in vain. They lay in wait for her at the side entrance, followed her, while one dissipated and desperate person, married, and said to move in the most exclusive circles, sent her an offer of a yearly income in five figures, the note being reproduced on the screen, and Leila pictured reading it in her frigid hall-bed-room. There are complications; she is in debt, and the proprietor of Hawtrey's has threatened to discharge her: and in order that the magnitude of the temptation may be most effectively realized the vision appears of Leila herself, wrapped in furs, stepping out of a limousine and into an elevator lifting her to an apartment containing silk curtains, a Canet bed, a French maid, and a Pomeranian. Virtue totters, but triumphs, being reinforced by two more visions: the first of these portrays Leila, prematurely old, dragging herself along pavements under the metallic Broadway lights accosting gentlemen in evening dress; and the second reveals her in the country, kneeling beside a dying mother's bed, giving her promise to remain true to the Christian teachings of her childhood.

And virtue is rewarded, lavishly, as virtue should be, in dollars and cents, in stocks and bonds, in pearls and diamonds. Popular fancy takes kindly to rough but honest westerners who have begun life in flannel shirts, who have struck gold and come to New York with a fortune but despising effeteness; such a one, tanned by the mountain sun, embarrassed in raiment supplied by a Fifth Avenue tailor, takes a table one evening at Hawtrey's and of course falls desperately in love. He means marriage from the first, and his faith in Leila is great enough to survive what appears to be an almost total eclipse of her virtue. Through the machinations of the influential villain, and lured by the false pretence that one of her girl friends is ill, she is enticed into a mysterious house of a sinister elegance, and apparently irretrievably compromised. The westerner follows, forces his way through the portals, engages the villain, and vanquishes him. Leila becomes a Bride. We behold her, at the end, mistress of one of those magnificent stone mansions with grilled vestibules and negro butlers into whose sacred precincts we are occasionally, in the movies, somewhat breathlessly ushered — a long way from Hawtrey's restaurant and a hall-bedroom. A long way, too, from the *Bagatelle* and Fillmore Street — but to Lise a way not impossible, nor even improbable.

This work of art, conveying the moral that virtue is an economic asset, made a great impression on Lise. Good Old Testament doctrine, set forth in the Book of Job itself. And Leila, pictured as holding out for a higher price and getting it, encouraged Lise to hold out also. Mr. Wiley, in whose company she had seen this play, and whose likeness filled the plush and silver-plated frame on her bureau, remained ironically ignorant of the fact that he had paid out his money to make definite an ambition, an ideal hitherto nebulous in the mind of the lady whom he adored. Nor did Lise enlighten him, being gifted with a certain inscrutableness. As a matter of fact it had never been her intention to accept him, but now that she was able concretely to visualize her Lochinvar of the future, Mr. Wiley's lack of qualifications became the more apparent. In the first place, he had been born in Lowell and had never been west of Worcester; in the second, his salary was sixteen dollars a

week: it is true she had once fancied the Scottish terrier
style of hair-cut abruptly ending in the rounded line of the
shaven neck, but Lochinvar had been close-cropped. Mr.
Wiley, close-cropped, would have resembled a convict.

Mr. Wiley was in love, there could be no doubt about
that, and if he had not always meant marriage, he meant it
now, having reached a state where no folly seems preposterous. The manner of their meeting had had just the adven-
turous and romantic touch that Lise liked, one of her
favourite amusements in the intervals between "steadies"
being to walk up and down Faber Street of an evening after
supper, arm in arm with two or three other young ladies,
all chewing gum, wheeling into store windows and wheeling
out again, pretending the utmost indifference to melting
glances cast in their direction. An exciting sport, though
incomprehensible to masculine intelligence. It was a
principle with Lise to pay no attention to any young man
who was not "presented," those venturing to approach her
with the ready formula "Haven't we met before?" being
instantly congealed. She was strict as to etiquette. But
Mr. Wiley, it seemed, could claim acquaintance with Miss
Schuler, one of the ladies to whose arm Lise's was linked,
and he had the further advantage of appearing in a large
and seductive touring car, painted green, with an eagle
poised above the hood and its name, *Wizard*, in a handwriting
rounded and bold, written in nickel across the radiator.
He greeted Miss Schuler effusively, but his eye was on Lise
from the first, and it was she he took with him in the front
seat, indifferent to the giggling behind. Ever since then
Lise had had a motor at her disposal, and on Sundays they
took long "joy rides" beyond the borders of the state. But
it must not be imagined that Mr. Wiley was the proprietor
of the vehicle; nor was he a chauffeur, — her American
pride would not have permitted her to keep company with

E

a chauffeur : he was the demonstrator for the *Wizard*, something of a wizard himself, as Lise had to admit when they
whizzed over the tarvia of the Riverside Boulevard at fifty
or sixty miles an hour with the muffler cut out — a favourite
diversion of Mr. Wiley's, who did not feel he was going
unless he was accompanied by a noise like that of a *mitra-
illeuse* in action.   Lise, experiencing a ravishing terror,
hung on to her hat with one hand and to Mr. Wiley with
the other, her code permitting this; permitting him also,
occasionally, when they found themselves in tenebrous
portions of Slattery's Riverside Park, to put his arm around
her waist and kiss her.   So much did Lise's virtue allow, and
no more, the result being that he existed in a tantalizing
state of hope and excitement most detrimental to the nerves.

He never lost, however, — in public at least, or before
Lise's family, — the fine careless, jaunty air of the demonstrator, of the free-lance for whom seventy miles an hour
has no terrors; the automobile, apparently, like the ship,
sets a stamp upon its votaries.   No Elizabethan buccaneer
swooping down on defenceless coasts ever exceeded in audacity Mr. Wiley's invasion of quiet Fillmore Street.   He
would draw up with an ear-splitting screaming of brakes
in front of the clay-yellow house, and sometimes the muffler,
as though unable to repress its approval of the performance,
would let out a belated pop that never failed to jar the innermost being of Auermann, who had been shot at, or rather
shot *past*, by an Italian, and knew what it was.   He hated
automobiles, he hated Mr. Wiley.

"Vat you do ?" he would demand, glaring.

And Mr. Wiley would laugh insolently.

"You think *I* done it, do you, Dutchie — huh !"

He would saunter past, up the stairs, and into the Bumpus
dining-room, often before the family had finished their
evening meal.   Lise alone made him welcome, albeit de-

murely; but Mr. Wiley, not having sensibilities, was proof against Hannah's coldness and Janet's hostility. With unerring instinct he singled out Edward as his victim.

"How's Mr. Bumpus this evening?" he would genially inquire.

Edward invariably assured Mr. Wiley that he was well, invariably took a drink of coffee to emphasize the fact, as though the act of lifting his cup had in it some magic to ward off the contempt of his wife and elder daughter.

"Well, I've got it pretty straight that the Arundel's going to run nights, starting next week," Lise's suitor would continue.

And to save his soul Edward could not refrain from answering, "You don't say so!" He feigned interest in the information that the Hampton Ball Team, owing to an unsatisfactory season, was to change managers next year. Mr. Wiley possessed the gift of gathering recondite bits of news, he had confidence in his topics and in his manner of dealing with them; and Edward, pretending to be entertained, went so far in his politeness as to ask Mr. Wiley if he had had supper.

"I don't care if I sample one of Mis' Bumpus's doughnuts," Mr. Wiley would reply politely, reaching out a large hand that gave evidence, in spite of Sapolio, of an intimacy with grease cups and splash pans. "I guess there's nobody in this burg can make doughnuts to beat yours, Mis' Bumpus."

If she had only known which doughnut he would take, Hannah sometimes thought she might have been capable of putting arsenic in it. Her icy silence did not detract from the delights of his gustation.

Occasionally, somewhat to Edward's alarm, Hannah demanded: "Where are you taking Lise this evening?"

Mr. Wiley's wisdom led him to be vague.

"Oh, just for a little spin up the boulevard. Maybe we'll pick up Ella Schuler and one or two other young ladies."

Hannah and Janet knew very well he had no intention of doing this, and Hannah did not attempt to conceal her incredulity. As a matter of fact, Lise sometimes did insist on a "party."

"I want you should bring her back by ten o'clock. That's late enough for a girl who works to be out. It's late enough for any girl."

"Sure, Mis' Bumpus," Wiley would respond easily.

Hannah chafed because she had no power to enforce this, because Mr. Wiley and Lise understood she had no power. Lise went to put on her hat; if she skimped her toilet in the morning, she made up for it in the evening when she came home from the store, and was often late for supper. In the meantime, while Lise was in the bedroom adding these last touches, Edward would contemptibly continue the conversation, fingering the *Evening Banner* as it lay in his lap, while Mr. Wiley helped himself boldly to another doughnut, taking — as Janet observed — elaborate precautions to spill none of the crumbs on a brown suit, supposed to be the last creation in male attire. Behind a plate glass window in Faber Street, belonging to a firm of "custom" tailors whose stores had invaded every important city in the country, and who made clothes for "college" men, only the week before Mr. Wiley had seen this same suit artistically folded, combined with a coloured shirt, brown socks, and tie and "torture" collar — lures for the discriminating. Owing to certain expenses connected with Lise, he had been unable to acquire the shirt and the tie, but he had bought the suit in the hope and belief that she would find him irresistible therein. It pleased him, too, to be taken for a "college" man, and on beholding in the mirror his broadened shoulders and diminished waist he was quite convinced his

money had not been spent in vain; that strange young ladies
— to whom, despite his infatuation for the younger Miss
Bumpus, he was not wholly indifferent — would mistake
him for an undergraduate of Harvard, — an imposition
concerning which he had no scruples. But Lise, though
shaken, had not capitulated. . . .

When she returned to the dining-room, arrayed in her
own finery, demure, triumphant, and had carried off Mr.
Wiley there would ensue an interval of silence broken only
by the clattering together of the dishes Hannah snatched up.

"I guess he's the kind of son-in-law would suit you," she
threw over her shoulder once to Edward.

"Why?" he inquired, letting down his newspaper ner-
vously.

"Well, you seem to favour him, to make things as pleasant
for him as you can."

Edward would grow warm with a sense of injustice, the
inference being that he was to blame for Mr. Wiley; if he
had been a different kind of father another sort of suitor
would be courting Lise.

"I have to be civil," he protested. He pronounced that
word "civil" exquisitely, giving equal value to both syllables.

"Civil!" Hannah scoffed, as she left the room; and to
Janet, who had followed her into the kitchen, she added:
"That's the trouble with your father, he's always be'n
a little _too_ civil. Edward Bumpus is just as simple as a
child, he's afraid of offending folks' feelings. . . . Think of
being polite to _that Wiley!_" In those two words Hannah
announced eloquently her utter condemnation of the demonstrator of the _Wizard_. It was characteristic of her,
however, when she went back for another load of dishes
and perceived that Edward was only pretending to read his
Banner, to attempt to ease her husband's feelings. She

thought it queer because she was still fond of Edward Bumpus, after all he had "brought on her."

"It's Lise," she said, as though speaking to Janet, "she attracts 'em. Sometimes I just can't get used to it that she's my daughter. I don't know who she takes after. She's not like any of my kin, nor any of the Bumpuses."

"What can you do?" asked Edward. "You can't order him out of the house. It's better for him to come here. And you can't stop Lise from going with him — she's earning her own money. . . ."

They had talked over the predicament before, and always came to the same *impasse*. In the privacy of the kitchen Hannah paused suddenly in her energetic rubbing of a plate and with supreme courage uttered a question.

"Janet, do you calculate he means anything *wrong?*"

"I don't know what he means," Janet replied, unwilling to give Mr. Wiley credit for anything, "but I know this, that Lise is too smart to let him take advantage of her."

Hannah ruminated. Cleverness as the modern substitute for feminine virtue did not appeal to her, but she let it pass. She was in no mood to quarrel with any quality that would ward off disgrace.

"I don't know what to make of Lise — she don't appear to have any principles. . . ."

If the Wiley affair lasted longer than those preceding it, this was because former suitors had not commanded automobiles. When Mr. Wiley lost his automobile he lost his luck — if it may be called such. One April evening, after a stroll with Eda, Janet reached home about nine o'clock to find Lise already in their room, to remark upon the absence of Mr. Wiley's picture from the frame.

"I'm through with him," Lise declared briefly, tugging at her hair.

"Through with him?" Janet repeated.

Lise paused in her labours and looked at her sister steadily. "I handed him the mit — do you get me?"

"But why?"

"Why? I was sick of him — ain't that enough? And then he got mixed up with a Glendale trolley and smashed his radiator, and the *Wizard* people sacked him. I always told him he was too fly. It's lucky for him I wasn't in the car."

"It's lucky for you," said Janet. Presently she inquired curiously: "Aren't you sorry?"

"Nix." Lise shook her head, which was now bowed, her face hidden by hair. "Didn't I tell you I was sick of him? But he sure was some spender," she added, as though in justice bound to give him his due.

Janet was shocked by the ruthlessness of it, for Lise appeared relieved, almost gay. She handed Janet a box containing five peppermint creams — all that remained of Mr. Wiley's last gift.

2

One morning in the late spring Janet crossed the Warren Street bridge, the upper of the two spider-like structures to be seen from her office window, spanning the river beside the great Hampton dam. The day, dedicated to the memory of heroes fallen in the Civil War, the thirtieth of May, was a legal holiday. Gradually Janet had acquired a dread of holidays as opportunities never realized, as intervals that should have been filled with unmitigated joys, and yet were invariably wasted, usually in walks with Eda Rawle. To-day, feeling an irresistible longing for freedom, for beauty, for adventure, for quest and discovery of she knew not what, she avoided Eda, and after gazing awhile at the sunlight dancing in the white mist below the falls, she walked on, southward, until she had left behind her the last straggling houses of the city and found herself on a wide, tarvia road that led, ultimately, to Boston. So read the sign.

Great maples, heavy with leaves, stood out against the soft blue of the sky, and the sunlight poured over everything, bathing the stone walls, the thatches of the farmhouses, extracting from the copses of stunted pine a pungent, reviving perfume. Sometimes she stopped to rest on the pine needles, and walked on again, aimlessly, following the road because it was the easiest way. There were spring flowers in the farmhouse yards, masses of lilacs whose purple she drank in eagerly; the air, which had just a tang of New England sharpness, was filled with tender sounds, the clucking of hens, snatches of the songs of birds, the rustling of maple leaves in the fitful breeze. A chipmunk ran down an elm and stood staring at her with beady, inquisitive eyes, motionless save for his quivering tail, and she put forth her hand, shyly, beseechingly, as though he held the secret of life she craved. But he darted away.

She looked around her unceasingly, at the sky, at the trees, at the flowers and ferns and fields, at the vireos and thrushes, the robins and tanagers flashing in and out amidst the foliage, and she was filled with a strange yearning to expand and expand until she should become a part of all nature, be absorbed into it, cease to be herself. Never before had she known just that feeling, that degree of ecstasy mingled with divine discontent. . . . Occasionally, intruding faintly upon the countryside peace, she was aware of a distant humming sound that grew louder and louder until there shot roaring past her an automobile filled with noisy folk, leaving behind it a suffocating cloud of dust. Even these intrusions, reminders of the city she had left, were powerless to destroy her mood, and she began to skip, like a schoolgirl, pausing once in a while to look around her fearfully, lest she was observed; and it pleased her to think that she had escaped

forever, that she would never go back: she cried aloud, as
she skipped, "I *won't* go back, I *won't* go back," keeping
time with her feet until she was out of breath and almost
intoxicated, delirious, casting herself down, her heart beating
wildly, on a bank of ferns, burying her face in them. She
had really stopped because a pebble had got into her shoe,
and as she took it out she looked at her bare heel and remarked ruefully: —

"Those twenty-five cent stockings aren't worth buying!"

Economic problems, however, were powerless to worry
her to-day, when the sun shone and the wind blew and the
ferns, washed by the rill running through the culvert under
the road, gave forth a delicious moist odour reminding
her of the flower store where her sister Lise had once been
employed. But at length she arose, and after an hour or
more of sauntering the farming landscape was left behind,
the crumbling stone fences were replaced by a well-kept
retaining wall capped by a privet hedge, through which,
between stone pillars, a driveway entered and mounted the
shaded slope, turning and twisting until lost to view. But
afar, standing on the distant crest, through the tree trunks
and foliage Janet saw one end of the mansion to which it
led, and ventured timidly but eagerly in among the trees
in the hope of satisfying her new-born curiosity. Try as
she would, she never could get any but disappointing and
partial glimpses of a house which, because of the mystery
of its setting, fired her imagination, started her to wondering
why it was that some were permitted to live in the midst
of such beauty while she was condemned to spend her days
in Fillmore Street and the prison of the mill. She was not
even allowed to look at it! The thought was like a cloud
across the sun.

However, when she had regained the tarvia road and
walked a little way the shadow suddenly passed, and she

stood surprised. The sight of a long common with its ancient trees in the fullness of glory, dense maples, sturdy oaks, strong, graceful elms that cast flickering, lacy shadows across the road filled her with satisfaction, with a sense of peace deepened by the awareness, in the background, ranged along the common on either side, of stately, dignified buildings, each in an appropriate frame of foliage. With the essence rather than the detail of all this her consciousness became steeped; she was naturally ignorant of the great good fortune of Silliston Academy of having been spared — with one or two exceptions — donations during those artistically lean years of the nineteenth century when American architecture affected the Gothic, the Mansard, and the subsequent hybrid. She knew this must be Silliston, the seat of that famous academy of which she had heard.

The older school buildings and instructors' houses, most of them white or creamy yellow, were native Colonial, with tall, graceful chimneys and classic pillars and delicate balustrades, eloquent at once of the racial inheritance of the Republic and of a bygone individuality, dignity, and pride. And the modern architect, of whose work there was an abundance, had graciously and intuitively held this earlier note and developed it. He was an American, but an American who had been trained. The result was harmony, life as it should proceed, the new growing out of the old. And no greater tribute can be paid to Janet Bumpus than that it pleased her, struck and set exquisitely vibrating within her responsive chords. For the first time in her adult life she stood in the presence of tradition, of a tradition inherently if unconsciously the innermost reality of her being: a tradition that miraculously was not dead, since after all the years it had begun to put forth these vigorous shoots....

What Janet chiefly realized was the delicious, contented sense of having come, visually at least, to the home for which she had longed. But her humour was that of a child who has strayed, to find its true dwelling place in a region of beauty hitherto unexplored and unexperienced, tinged, therefore, with unreality, with mystery, — an effect enhanced by the chance stillness and emptiness of the place. She wandered up and down the Common, whose vivid green was starred with golden dandelions; and then, spying the arched and shady vista of a lane, entered it, bent on new discoveries. It led past one of the newer buildings, the library — as she read in a carved inscription over the door — plunged into shade again presently to emerge at a square farmhouse, ancient and weathered, with a great square chimney thrust out of the very middle of the ridge-pole, — a landmark left by one of the earliest of Silliston's settlers. Presiding over it, embracing and protecting it, was a splendid tree. The place was evidently in process of reconstruction and repair, the roof had been newly shingled, new frames, with old-fashioned, tiny panes had been put in the windows; a little garden was being laid out under the sheltering branches of the tree, and between the lane and the garden, half finished, was a fence of an original and pleasing design, consisting of pillars placed at intervals with upright pickets between, the pickets sawed in curves, making a line that drooped in the middle. Janet did not perceive the workman engaged in building this fence until the sound of his hammer attracted her attention. His back was bent, he was absorbed in his task.

"Are there any stores near here?" she inquired.

He straightened up. "Why yes," he replied, "come to think of it, I have seen stores, I'm sure I have."

Janet laughed; his expression, his manner of speech were so delightfully whimsical, so in keeping with the spirit of her day, and he seemed to accept her sudden appearance in the precise make-believe humour she could have wished.

And yet she stood a little struck with timidity, puzzled by the contradictions he presented of youth and age, of shrewdness, experience and candour, of gentility and manual toil. He must have been about thirty-five; he was hatless, and his hair, uncombed but not unkempt, was greying at the temples; his eyes — which she noticed particularly — were keen yet kindly, the irises delicately stencilled in a remarkable blue; his speech was colloquial yet cultivated, his workman's clothes belied his bearing.

"Yes, there are stores, in the village," he went on, "but isn't it a holiday, or Sunday — perhaps — or something of the kind?"

"It's Decoration Day," she reminded him, with deepening surprise.

"So it is! And all the storekeepers have gone on picnics in their automobiles, or else they're playing golf. Nobody's working to-day."

"But you — aren't you working?" she inquired.

"Working?" he repeated. "I suppose some people would call it work. I — I hadn't thought of it in that way."

"You mean — you like it," Janet was inspired to say.

"Well, yes," he confessed. "I suppose I do."

Her cheeks dimpled. If her wonder had increased, her embarrassment had flown, and he seemed suddenly an old acquaintance. She had, however, profound doubts now of his being a carpenter.

"Were you thinking of going shopping?" he asked, and at the very ludicrousness of the notion she laughed again. She discovered a keen relish for this kind of humour, but it was new to her experience, and she could not cope with it.

"Only to buy some crackers, or a sandwich," she replied, and blushed.

"Oh," he said. "Down in the village, on the corner where the cars stop, is a restaurant. It's not as good as the Parker House in Boston, I believe, but they do have sandwiches, yes, and coffee. At least they call it coffee."

"Oh, thank you," she said.

"You'd better wait till you try it," he warned her.

"Oh, I don't mind, I don't want much." And she was impelled to add: "It's such a beautiful day."

"It's absurd to get hungry on such a day — absurd," he agreed.

"Yes, it is," she laughed. "I'm not really hungry, but I haven't time to get back to Hampton for dinner." Suddenly she grew hot at the thought that he might suspect her of hinting. "You see, I live in Hampton," she went on hurriedly, "I'm a stenographer there, in the Chippering Mill, and I was just out for a walk, and — I came farther than I intended." She had made it worse.

But he said, "Oh, you came from Hampton!" with an intonation of surprise, of incredulity even, that soothed and even amused while it did not deceive her. Not that the superior intelligence of which she had begun to suspect him had been put to any real test by the discovery of her home, and she was quite sure her modest suit of blue serge and her $2.99 pongee blouse proclaimed her as a working girl of the mill city. "I've been to Hampton," he declared, just as though it were four thousand miles away instead of four.

"But I've never been here before, to Silliston," she responded in the same spirit: and she added wistfully, "it must be nice to live in such a beautiful place as this!"

"Yes, it is nice," he agreed. "We have our troubles, too, — but it's nice."

She ventured a second, appraising glance. His head, which he carried a little flung back, his voice, his easy and confident bearing — all these contradicted the saw and the hammer, the flannel shirt, open at the neck, the khaki trousers still bearing the price tag. And curiosity beginning to get the better of her, she was emboldened to pay a compliment to the fence. If one had to work, it must be a pleasure to work on things pleasing to the eye — such was her inference.

"Why, I'm glad you like it," he said heartily. "I was just hoping some one would come along here and admire it. Now — what colour would you paint it?"

"Are you a painter, too?"

"After a fashion. I'm a sort of man of all work — I thought of painting it white, with the pillars green."

"I think that would be pretty," she answered, judicially, after a moment's thought. "What else can you do?"

He appeared to be pondering his accomplishments.

"Well, I can doctor trees," he said, pointing an efficient finger at the magnificent maple sheltering, like a guardian deity, the old farmhouse. "I put in those patches."

"They're cement," she exclaimed. "I never heard of putting cement in trees."

"They don't seem to mind."

"Are the holes very deep?"

"Pretty deep."

"But I should think the tree would be dead."

"Well, you see the life of a tree is right under the bark. If you can keep the outer covering intact, the tree will live."

"Why did you let the holes get so deep?"

"I've just come here. The house was like the tree — the shingles all rotten, but the beams were sound. Those beams were hewn out of the forest two hundred and fifty years ago."

"Gracious!" said Janet. "And how old is the tree?"

"I should say about a hundred. I suppose it wouldn't care to admit it."

"How do you know?" she inquired.

"Oh, I'm very intimate with trees. I find out their secrets."

"It's your house!" she exclaimed, somewhat appalled by the discovery.

"Yes — yes it is," he answered, looking around at it and then in an indescribably comical manner down at his clothes. His gesture, his expression implied that her mistake was a most natural one.

"Excuse me, I thought —" she began, blushing hotly, yet wanting to laugh again.

"I don't blame you — why shouldn't you?" he interrupted her. "I haven't got used to it yet, and there *is* something amusing about — my owning a house. When the parlour's finished I'll have to wear a stiff collar, I suppose, in order to live up to it."

Her laughter broke forth, and she tried to imagine him in a stiff collar. . . . But she was more perplexed than ever. She stood balancing on one foot, poised for departure.

"I ought to be going," she said, as though she had been paying him a formal visit.

"Don't hurry," he protested cordially. "Why hurry back to Hampton?"

"I never want to go back!" she cried with a vehemence that caused him to contemplate her anew, suddenly revealing the intense, passionate quality which had so disturbed Mr. Ditmar. She stood transformed. "I hate it!" she declared. "It's so ugly, I never want to see it again."

"Yes, it is ugly," he confessed. "Since you admit it, I don't mind saying so. But it's interesting, in a way." Though his humorous moods had delighted her, she felt subtly flattered because he had grown more serious.

"It *is* interesting," she agreed. She was almost impelled to tell him why, in her excursions to the various quarters, she had found Hampton interesting, but a shyness born of respect for the store of knowledge she divined in him restrained her. She was curious to know what this man saw in Hampton. His opinion would be worth something. Unlike her neighbours in Fillmore Street, he was not what her sister Lise would call "nutty"; he had an air of fine sanity, of freedom, of detachment, — though the word did not occur to her; he betrayed no bitter sense of injustice, and his beliefs were uncoloured by the obsession of a single panacea. "Why do you think it's interesting?" she demanded.

"Well, I'm always expecting to hear that it's blown up. It reminds me of nitro-glycerine," he added, smiling.

She repeated the word.

"An explosive, you know — they put it in dynamite. They say a man once made it by accident, and locked up his laboratory and ran home — and never went back."

"I know what you mean!" she cried, her eyes alight with excitement. "All those foreigners! I've felt it — that something would happen, some day, it frightened me, and yet I wished that something would happen. Only, I never would have thought of — nitro-glycerine."

She was unaware of the added interest in his regard. But he answered lightly enough : —

"Oh, not only the foreigners. Human chemicals — you can't play with human chemicals any more than you can play with real ones — you've got to know something about chemistry."

This remark was beyond her depth.

"Who is playing with them?" she asked.

"Everybody — no one in particular. Nobody seems to know much about them, yet," he replied, and seemed disinclined to pursue the subject. A robin with a worm in its bill was hopping across the grass; he whistled softly, the bird stopped, cocking its head and regarding them. Suddenly, in conflict with her desire to remain indefinitely talking with this strange man, Janet felt an intense impulse to leave. She could bear the conversation no longer, she might burst into tears — such was the extraordinary effect he had produced on her.

"I must go, — I'm ever so much obliged to you," she said.

"Drop in again," he said, as he took her trembling hand. . . . When she had walked a little way she looked back over her shoulder to see him leaning idly against the post, gazing after her, and waving his hammer in friendly fashion.

For a while her feet fairly flew, and her heart beat tumultuously, keeping time with her racing thoughts. She walked about the Common, seeing nothing, paying no attention to the passers-by, who glanced at her curiously. But at length as she grew calmer the needs of a youthful and vigorous body became imperative, and realizing suddenly that she was tired and hungry, sought and found the little restaurant in the village below. She journeyed back to Hampton pondering what this man had said to her; speculating, rather breathlessly, whether he had been impelled to conversation by a natural kindness and courtesy, or whether he really had discovered something in her worthy of addressing, as he implied. Resentment burned in her breast, she became suddenly blinded by tears: she might never see him again, and if only she were "educated" she might know him, become his friend. Even in this desire she was not conventional, and in the few moments of their contact he had developed rather than transformed what she meant by "education." She thought of it not as knowledge reeking of books and schools, but as the acquirement of the freemasonry which he so evidently possessed, — existence on terms of understanding, confidence, and freedom with nature; as having the world open up to one like a flower filled with colour and life. She thought of the robin, of the tree whose secrets he had learned, of a mental range including even that medley of human beings amongst whom she

F

lived.   And the fact that something of his meaning had eluded her grasp made her rebel all the more bitterly against the lack of a greater knowledge. . . .

Often during the weeks that followed he dwelt in her mind as she sat at her desk and stared out across the river, and several times that summer she started to walk to Silliston.   But always she turned back.   Perhaps she feared to break the charm of that memory. . . .

CHAPTER IV

1

OUR American climate is notoriously capricious. Even
as Janet trudged homeward on that Memorial Day afternoon
from her Cinderella-like adventure in Silliston the sun grew
hot, the air lost its tonic, becoming moist and tepid, white
clouds with dark edges were piled up in the western sky.
The automobiles of the holiday makers swarmed ceaselessly
over the tarvia. Valiantly as she strove to cling to her
dream, remorseless reality was at work dragging her back,
reclaiming her; excitement and physical exercise drained her
vitality, her feet were sore, sadness invaded her as she came
in view of the ragged outline of the city she had left so joy-
fully in the morning. Summer, that most depressing of
seasons in an environment of drab houses and grey pavements, was at hand, listless householders and their families
were already seeking refuge on front steps she passed on her
way to Fillmore Street.

It was about half past five when she arrived. Lise, her
waist removed, was seated in a rocking chair at the window
overlooking the littered yards and the backs of the tenements
on Rutger Street. And Lise, despite the heaviness of the
air, was dreaming. Of such delicate texture was the fabric
of Janet's dreams that not only sordid reality, but contact
with other dreams of a different nature, such as her sister's,
often sufficed to dissolve them. She resented, for instance,
the presence in the plush oval of Mr. Eustace Arlington, the
movie star whose likeness had replaced Mr. Wiley's, and who

67

had played the part of the western hero in "Leila of Hawtrey's." With his burning eyes and sensual face betraying
the puffiness that comes from over-indulgence, he was not
Janet's ideal of a hero, western or otherwise. And now Lise
was holding a newspaper : not the *Banner*, whose provincial-
ity she scorned, but a popular Boston sheet to be had for a
cent, printed at ten in the morning and labelled "Three
O'clock Edition," with huge red headlines stretched across
the top of the page : —

"JURY FINDS IN MISS NEALY'S FAVOR."

As Janet entered Lise looked up and exclaimed : —
"Say, that Nealy girl's won out!"
"Who is she?" Janet inquired listlessly.
"You are from the country, all right," was her sister's
rejoinder. "I would have bet there wasn't a Reub in the
state that wasn't wise to the Ferris breach of promise case,
and here you blow in after the show's over and want to know
who Nelly Nealy is. If that doesn't beat the band!"
"This woman sued a man named Ferris — is that it?"
"A man named Ferris!" Lise repeated, with the air of
being appalled by her sister's ignorance. "I guess you
never heard of Ferris, either— the biggest copper man in
Boston. He could buy Hampton, and never feel it, and they
say his house in Brighton cost half a million dollars. Nelly
Nealy put her damages at one hundred and fifty thousand
and stung him for seventy five. I wish I'd been in court
when that jury came back! There's her picture."
To Janet, especially in the mood of reaction in which
she found herself that evening, Lise's intense excitement,
passionate partisanship and approval of Miss Nealy were
incomprehensible, repellent. However, she took the sheet,
gazing at the image of the lady who, recently an obscure

stenographer, had suddenly leaped into fame and become a "headliner," the envied of thousands of working girls all over New England. Miss Nealy, in spite of the "glare of publicity" she deplored, had borne up admirably under the strain, and evidently had been able to consume three meals a day and give some thought to her costumes. Her smile under the picture hat was coquettish, if not bold. The special article, signed by a lady reporter whose sympathies were by no means concealed and whose talents were given free rein, related how the white-haired mother had wept tears of joy; how Miss Nealy herself had been awhile too overcome to speak, and then had recovered sufficiently to express her gratitude to the twelve gentlemen who had vindicated the honour of American womanhood. Mr. Ferris, she reiterated, was a brute; never as long as she lived would she be able to forget how she had loved and believed in him, and how, when at length she unwillingly became convinced of his perfidy, she had been "prostrated," unable to support her old mother. She had not, naturally, yet decided how she would invest her fortune; as for going on the stage, that had been suggested, but she had made no plans. "Scores of women sympathizers" had escorted her to a waiting automobile. . . .

Janet, impelled by the fascination akin to disgust, read thus far, and flinging the newspaper on the floor, began to tidy herself for supper. But presently, when she heard Lise sigh, she could contain herself no longer.

"I don't see how you can read such stuff as that," she exclaimed. "It's — it's horrible."

"Horrible?" Lise repeated.

Janet swung round from the washbasin, her hands dripping.

"Instead of getting seventy five thousand dollars she ought to be tarred and feathered. She's nothing but a black-mailer."

Lise, aroused from her visions, demanded vehemently: "Ain't he a millionaire?"

"What difference does that make?" Janet retorted. "And you can't tell me she didn't know what she was up to all along — with that face."

"I'd have sued him, all right," declared Lise, defiantly.

"Then you'd be a blackmailer, too. I'd sooner scrub floors, I'd sooner starve than do such a thing — take money for my affections. In the first place, I'd have more pride, and in the second place, if I really loved a man, seventy five thousand or seventy five million dollars wouldn't help me any. Where do you get such ideas? Decent people don't have them."

Janet turned to the basin again and began rubbing her face vigorously — ceasing for an instance to make sure of the identity of a sound reaching her ears despite the splashing of water. Lise was sobbing. Janet dried her face and hands, arranged her hair, and sat down on the window-sill; the scorn and anger, which had been so intense as completely to possess her, melting into a pity and contempt not unmixed with bewilderment. Ordinarily Lise was hard, impervious to such reproaches, holding her own in the passionate quarrels that occasionally took place between them: yet there were times, such as this, when her resistance broke down unexpectedly, and she lost all self control. She rocked to and fro in the chair, her shoulders bowed, her face hidden in her hands. Janet reached out and touched her.

"Don't be silly," she began, rather sharply, "just because I said it was a disgrace to have such ideas. Well, it is."

"I'm not silly," said Lise. "I'm sick of that job at the *Bagatelle* —" sob — "there's nothing in it — I'm going to quit — I wish to God I was dead! Standing on your feet all day till you're wore out for six dollars a week — what's

there in it?" — sob — "With that guy Walters who walks
the floor never lettin' up on you. He come up to me yesterday and says, 'I didn't know you was near sighted, Miss
Bumpus' — just because there was a customer Annie Hatch
was too lazy to wait on" — sob — "That's his line of dope
— thinks he's sarcastic — and he's sweet on Annie. To-
morrow I'm going to tell him to go to hell. I'm through —
I'm sick of it, I tell you" — sob — "I'd rather be dead than
slave like that for six dollars."

"Where are you going?" asked Janet.

"I don't know — I don't care. What's the difference?
any place'd be better than this." For awhile she continued
to cry on a ridiculously high, though subdued, whining note,
her breath catching at intervals. A feeling of helplessness,
of utter desolation crept over Janet; powerless to comfort
herself, how could she comfort her sister? She glanced
around the familiar, sordid room, at the magazine pages
against the faded wall-paper, at the littered bureau and the
littered bed, over which Lise's clothes were flung. It was
hot and close even now, in summer it would be stifling.
Suddenly a flash of sympathy revealed to her a glimpse of
the truth that Lise, too, after her own nature, sought beauty
and freedom! Never did she come as near comprehending
Lise as in such moments as this, and when, on dark winter
mornings, her sister clung to her, terrified by the siren.
Lise was a child, and the thought that she, Janet, was
powerless to change her was a part of the tragic tenderness.
What would become of Lise? And what would become of
her, Janet? . . . So she clung, desperately, to her sister's
hand until at last Lise roused herself, her hair awry, her face
puckered and wet with tears and perspiration.

"I can't stand it any more — I've just got to go away —
anywhere," she said, and the cry found an echo in Janet's
heart. . . .

But the next morning Lise went back to the *Bagatelle*, and Janet to the mill. . . .

2

The fact that Lise's love affairs had not been prospering undoubtedly had something to do with the fit of depression into which she had fallen that evening. A month or so before she had acquired another beau. It was understood by Lise's friends and Lise's family, though not by the gentleman himself, that his position was only temporary or at most probationary; he had not even succeeded to the rights, title, and privileges of the late Mr. Wiley, though occupying a higher position in the social scale — being the agent of a patent lawn sprinkler with an office in Faber Street.

"Stick to him and you'll wear diamonds — that's what he tries to put across," was Lise's comment on Mr. Frear's method, and thus Janet gained the impression that her sister's feelings were not deeply involved. "If I thought he'd make good with the sprinkler I might talk business. But say, he's one of those ginks that's always tryin' to beat the bank. He's never done a day's work in his life. Last year he was passing around Foley's magazine, and before that he was with the race track that went out of business because the ministers got nutty over it. Well, he may win out," she added reflectively, "those guys sometimes do put the game on the blink. He sure is a good spender when the orders come in, with a line of talk to make you holler for mercy."

Mr. Frear's "line of talk" came wholly, astonishingly, from one side of his mouth — the left side. As a muscular feat it was a triumph. A deaf person on his right side would not have known he was speaking. The effect was secretive, extraordinarily confidential; enabling him to sell sprinklers, it ought to have helped him to make love, so distinctly personal was it, implying as it did that the individual addressed was alone of all the world worthy of consideration. Among his friends it was regarded as an accomplishment, but Lise was critical, especially since he did not look into one's eyes, but gazed off into space, as though he weren't talking at all.

She had once inquired if the right side of his face was paralyzed.

She permitted him to take her, however, to Gruber's Café, to the movies, and one or two select dance halls, and to Slattery's Riverside Park, where one evening she had encountered the rejected Mr. Wiley.

"Say, he was sore!" she told Janet the next morning, relating the incident with relish, "for two cents he would have knocked Charlie over the ropes. I guess he could do it, too, all right."

Janet found it curious that Lise should display such vindictiveness toward Mr. Wiley, who was more sinned against than sinning. She was moved to inquire after his welfare.

"He's got one of them red motorcycles," said Lise. "He was gay with it too — when we was waiting for the boulevard trolley he opened her up and went right between Charlie and me. I had to laugh. He's got a job over in Haverhill — you can't hold that guy under water long."

Apparently Lise had no regrets. But her premonitions concerning Mr. Frear proved to be justified. He did not "make good." One morning the little office on Faber Street where the sprinklers were displayed was closed, Hampton knew him no more, and the police alone were sincerely regretful. It seemed that of late he had been keeping *all* the money for the sprinklers, and spending a good deal of it on Lise. At the time she accepted the affair with stoical pessimism, as one who has learned what to expect of the world, though her moral sense was not profoundly disturbed by the reflection that she had indulged in the delights of Slattery's and Gruber's and a Sunday at "the Beach" at the expense of the Cascade Sprinkler Company of Boston. Mr. Frear inconsiderately neglected to prepare her for his departure, the news of which was conveyed to her in a singular manner, and by none other than Mr. Johnny Tiernan of the tin shop, — their conversation throwing some light, not only on Lise's sophistication, but on the admirable and intricate operation of Hampton's city government. About five o'clock Lise was coming home along Fillmore Street after an uneventful, tedious and manless holiday spent in the company of Miss Schuler and other friends when she perceived Mr. Tiernan seated on his steps, grinning and waving a tattered palm-leaf fan.

"The mercury is sure on the jump," he observed. "You'd think it was July."

And Lise agreed.

"I suppose you'll be going to Tim Slattery's place tonight," he went on. "It's the coolest spot this side of the Atlantic Ocean."

There was, apparently, nothing cryptic in this remark, yet it is worth noting that Lise instantly became suspicious.

"Why would I be going out there?" she inquired innocently, darting at him a dark, coquettish glance.

Mr. Tiernan regarded her guilelessly, but there was admiration in his soul; not because of her unquestioned feminine attractions, — he being somewhat amazingly proof against such things, — but because it was conveyed to him in some unaccountable way that her suspicions *were* aroused. The brain beneath that corkscrew hair was worthy of a Richelieu. Mr. Tiernan's estimate of Miss Lise Bumpus, if he could have been induced to reveal it, would have been worth listening to.

"And why wouldn't you?" he replied heartily. "Don't I see all the pretty young ladies out there, including yourself, and you dancing with the Cascade man. Why is it you'll never give me a dance?"

"Why is it you never ask me?" demanded Lise.

"What chance have I got, against him?"

"He don't own me," said Lise.

Mr. Tiernan threw back his head, and laughed.

"Well, if you're there to-night, tangoin' with him and I come up and says, 'Miss Bumpus, the pleasure is mine,' I'm wondering what would happen."

"I'm not going to Slattery's to-night," she declared — having that instant arrived at this conclusion.

"And where then? I'll come along, if there's a chance for me."

"Quit your kidding," Lise reproved him.

Mr. Tiernan suddenly looked very solemn.

"Kidding, is it? Me kiddin' you? Give me a chance, that's all I'm asking. Where will you be, now?"

"Is Frear wanted?" she demanded.

Mr. Tiernan's expression changed. His nose seemed to become more pointed, his eyes to twinkle more merrily than ever. He didn't take the trouble, now, to conceal his admiration.

"Sure, Miss Bumpus," he said, "if you was a man, we'd have you on the force to-morrow."

"What's he wanted for?"

"Well," said Johnny, "a little matter of sprinklin'. He's been sprinklin' his company's water without a license."

She was silent a moment before she exclaimed : —

"I ought to have been wise that he was a crook!"

"Well," said Johnny consolingly, "there's others that ought

to have been wise, too.   The Cascade people had no business takin' on a man that couldn't use but half of his mouth."

This seemed to Lise a reflection on her judgment. She proceeded to clear herself.

"He was nothing to me.   He never gave me no rest.   He used to come 'round and pester me to go out with him —"

"Sure!" interrupted Mr. Tiernan.   "Don't I know how it is with the likes of him!   A good time's a good time, and no harm in it.   But the point is —" and here he cocked his nose — "the point is, where is he?   Where will he be to-night?"

All at once Lise grew vehement, almost tearful.

"I don't know — honest to God, I don't.   If I did I'd tell you.   Last night he said he might be out of town.   He didn't say where he was going."   She fumbled in her bag, drawing out an imitation lace handkerchief and pressing it to her eyes.

"There now!" exclaimed Mr. Tiernan, soothingly.   "How would you know?   And he deceivin' you like he did the company —"

"He didn't deceive me," cried Lise.

"Listen," said Mr. Tiernan, who had risen and laid his hand on her arm.   "It's not young ladies like you that works and are self-respecting that any one would be troublin', and you the daughter of such a fine man as your father.   Run along, now, I won't be detaining you, Miss Bumpus, and you'll accept my apology.   I guess we'll never see him in Hampton again. . . ."

Some twenty minutes later he sauntered down the street, saluting acquaintances, and threading his way across the Common entered a grimy brick building where a huge policeman with an insignia on his arm was seated behind a desk. Mr. Tiernan leaned on the desk, and reflectively lighted a Thomas-Jefferson-Five-Cent Cigar, Union Label, the excellencies of which were set forth on large signs above the "ten foot" buildings on Faber Street.

"*She* don't know nothing, Mike," he remarked. "I guess he got wise this morning."

The sergeant nodded. . . .

CHAPTER V

1

To feel potential within one's self the capacity to live and yet to have no means of realizing this capacity is doubtless one of the least comfortable and agreeable of human experiences. Such, as summer came on, was Janet's case. The memory of that visit to Silliston lingered in her mind, sometimes to flare up so vividly as to make her existence seem unbearable. How wonderful, she thought, to be able to dwell in such a beautiful place, to have as friends and companions such amusing and intelligent people as the stranger with whom she had talked! Were all the inhabitants of Silliston like him? They must be, since it was a seat of learning. Lise's cry, "I've just got to go away, anywhere," found an echo in Janet's soul. Why shouldn't she go away? She was capable of taking care of herself, she was a good stenographer, her salary had been raised twice in two years, — why should she allow consideration for her family to stand in the way of what she felt would be self realization? Unconsciously she was a true modern in that the virtues known as duty and self sacrifice did not appeal to her, — she got from them neither benefit nor satisfaction, she understood instinctively that they were impeding to growth. Unlike Lise, she was able to see life as it is, she did not expect of it miracles, economic or matrimonial. Nothing would happen unless she *made* it happen. She was twenty-one, earning nine dollars a week, of which she now contributed five to the household, — her father, with characteristic incompetence, having taken out a larger insurance policy than he could reasonably carry. Of the remaining four dollars she spent more than one on lunches, there were dresses and underclothing, shoes and stockings to buy, in spite of darning and mending; little treats with Eda that mounted up; and occasionally the dentist — for Janet would not neglect her teeth as Lise neglected hers. She managed to save something, but it was very little. And she was desperately unhappy when she contemplated the grey and monotonous vista of the years ahead, saw herself growing older and older, driven always by the stern necessity of accumulating a margin against possible disasters; little by little drying up, losing, by withering disuse, those rich faculties of enjoyment with which she was endowed, and which at once fascinated and frightened her. Marriage, in such an environment, offered no solution; marriage meant dependence, from which her very nature revolted: and in her existence, drab and necessitous though it were, was still a remnant of freedom that marriage would compel her to surrender. . . .

One warm evening, oppressed by such reflections, she had started home when she remembered having left her bag in the office, and retraced her steps. As she turned the corner of West Street, she saw, beside the canal and directly in front of the bridge, a new and smart-looking automobile, painted crimson and black, of the type known as a runabout, which she recognized as belonging to Mr. Ditmar. Indeed, at that moment Mr. Ditmar himself was stepping off the end of the bridge and about to start the engine when, dropping the crank, he walked to the dashboard and apparently became absorbed in some mechanisms there. Was it the glance cast in her direction that had caused him to delay his departure? Janet was seized by a sudden and rather absurd desire to retreat, but Canal Street being empty, such an action would appear eccentric, and she came slowly forward, pretending not to see her employer, ridiculing to herself the idea that he had noticed her. Much to her annoyance, however, her embarrassment persisted, and she knew it was due to the memory of certain incidents, each in itself almost negligible, but cumulatively amounting to a suspicion that for some months he had been aware of her : many times when he had passed through the outer office she had felt his eyes upon her, had been impelled to look up from her work to surprise in them a certain glow to make her bow her head again in warm confusion. Now, as she approached him, she was pleasantly but rather guiltily conscious of the more rapid beating of the blood that precedes an adventure, yet sufficiently self-possessed to note the becoming nature of the light flannel suit and rather rakish Panama he had pushed back from his forehead. It was not until she had almost passed him that he straightened up, lifted the Panama, tentatively, and not too far, startling her.

"Good afternoon, Miss Bumpus," he said. "I thought you had gone."

"I left my bag in the office," she replied, with the outward calmness that rarely deserted her — the calmness, indeed, that had piqued him and was leading him on to rashness.

"Oh," he said. "Simmons will get it for you." Simmons was the watchman who stood in the vestibule of the office entrance.

"Thanks. I can get it myself," she told him, and would have gone on had he not addressed her again. "I was just starting out for a spin. What do you think of the car? It's good looking, isn't it?" He stood off and surveyed it, laughing a little, and in his laugh she detected a note apologetic, at variance with the conception she had formed of his character, though not alien, indeed, to the dust-coloured vigour of the man. She scarcely recognized Ditmar as he stood there, yet he excited her, she felt from him an undercurrent of something that caused her inwardly to tremble. "See how the lines are carried through." He indicated this by a wave of his hand, but his eyes were now on her.

"It is pretty," she agreed.

In contrast to the defensive tactics which other ladies of his acquaintance had adopted, tactics of a patently coy and coquettish nature, this self-collected manner was new and spicy, challenging to powers never as yet fully exerted — while beneath her manner he felt throbbing that rare and dangerous thing in women, a temperament, for which men have given their souls. This conviction of her possession of a temperament, — he could not have defined the word, — emotional rather than intellectual, produced the apologetic attitude she was quick to sense. He had never been, at least during his maturity, at a loss with the other sex, and he found the experience delicious.

"You like pretty things, I'm sure of that," he hazarded. But she did not ask him how he knew, she simply assented. He raised the hood, revealing the engine. "Isn't that pretty? See how nicely everything is adjusted in that little space to do the particular work for which it is designed."

Thus appealed to, she came forward and stopped, still standing off a little way, but near enough to see, gazing at the shining copper caps on the cylinders, at the bright rods and gears.

"It looks intricate," said Mr. Ditmar, "but really it's very simple. The gasoline comes in here from the tank behind — this is called the carburetor, it has a jet to vaporize the gasoline, and the vapour is sucked into each of these cylinders in turn when the piston moves — like this." He sought to explain the action of the piston. "That compresses it, and then a tiny electric spark comes just at the right

G

moment to explode it, and the explosion sends the piston down again, and turns the shaft. Well, all four cylinders have an explosion one right after another, and that keeps the shaft going." Whereupon the most important personage in Hampton, the head of the great Chippering Mill proceeded, for the benefit of a humble assistant stenographer, to remove the floor boards behind the dash. "There's the shaft, — come here and look at it." She obeyed, standing beside him, almost touching him, his arm, indeed, brushing her sleeve, and into his voice crept a tremor. "The shaft turns the rear wheels by means of a gear at right angles on the axle, and the rear wheels drive the car. Do you see?"

"Yes," she answered faintly, honesty compelling her to add: "a little."

He was looking, now, not at the machinery, but intently at her, and she could feel the blood flooding into her cheeks and temples. She was even compelled for an instant to return his glance, and from his eyes into hers leaped a flame that ran scorching through her body. Then she knew with conviction that the explanation of the automobile had been an excuse; she had comprehended almost nothing of it, but she had been impressed by the facility with which he described it, by his evident mastery over it. She had noticed his hands, how thick his fingers were and close together; yet how deftly he had used them, without smearing the cuffs of his silk shirt or the sleeves of his coat with the oil that glistened everywhere.

"I like machinery," he told her as he replaced the boards. "I like to take care of it myself."

"It must be interesting," she assented, aware of the inadequacy of the remark, and resenting in herself an inarticulateness seemingly imposed by inhibition connected with his nearness. Fascination and antagonism were struggling within her. Her desire to get away grew desperate.

"Thank you for showing it to me." With an effort of will she moved toward the bridge, but was impelled by a consciousness of the abruptness of her departure to look back at him once — and smile, to experience again the thrill of the current he sped after her. By lifting his hat, a little higher, a little more confidently than in the first instance, he made her leaving seem more gracious, the act somehow conveying an acknowledgment on his part that their relationship had changed.

Once across the bridge and in the mill, she fairly ran up the stairs and into the empty office, to perceive her bag lying on the desk where she had left it, and sat down for a few minutes beside the window, her heart pounding in her breast as though she had barely escaped an accident threatening her with physical annihilation. Something had happened to her at last! But what did it mean? Where would it lead? Her fear, her antagonism, of which she was still conscious, her resentment that Ditmar had thus surreptitiously chosen to approach her in a moment when they were unobserved were mingled with a throbbing exultation in that he *had* noticed her, that there was something in her to attract him in that way, to make his voice thicker and his smile apologetic when he spoke to her. Of that "something-in-her" she had been aware before, but never had it been so unmistakably recognized and beckoned to from without. She was at once terrified, excited — and flattered.

At length, growing calmer, she made her way out of the building. When she reached the vestibule she had a moment of sharp apprehension, of paradoxical hope, that Ditmar might still be there, awaiting her. But he had gone. . . .

2

In spite of her efforts to dismiss the matter from her mind, to persuade herself there had been no significance in the encounter, when she was seated at her typewriter the next morning she experienced a renewal of the palpitation of the evening before, and at the sound of every step in the corridor she started. Of this tendency she was profoundly ashamed. And when at last Ditmar arrived, though the blood rose to her temples, she kept her eyes fixed on the keys. He went quickly into his room: she was convinced he had not so much as glanced at her. . . . As the days went by, however, she was annoyed by the discovery that his continued ignoring of her presence brought more resentment than relief, she detected in it a deliberation implying between them a guilty secret: she hated secrecy, though secrecy contained a thrill. Then, one morning when she was alone in the office with young Caldwell, who was absorbed in some reports, Ditmar entered unexpectedly and looked her full in the eyes, surprising her into answering his glance before she could turn away, hating herself and hating him. Hate, she determined, was her prevailing sentiment in regard to Mr. Ditmar.

The following Monday Miss Ottway overtook her, at noon, on the stairs.

"Janet, I wanted to speak to you, to tell you I'm leaving," she said.

"Leaving!" repeated Janet, who had regarded Miss Ottway as a fixture.

"I'm going to Boston," Miss Ottway explained, in her deep, musical voice. "I've always wanted to go, I have an unmarried sister there of whom I'm very fond, and Mr. Ditmar knows that. He's got me a place with the Treasurer, Mr. Semple."

"Oh, I'm sorry you're going, though of course I'm glad for you," Janet said sincerely, for she liked and respected Miss Ottway, and was conscious in the older woman of a certain kindly interest.

"Janet, I've recommended you to Mr. Ditmar for my place."

"Oh!" cried Janet, faintly.

"It was he who asked about you, he thinks you are reliable and quick and clever, and I was very glad to say a good word for you, my dear, since I could honestly do so." Miss Ottway drew Janet's arm through hers and patted it affectionately. "Of course you'll have to expect some jealousy, there are older women in the other offices who will think they ought to have the place, but if you attend to your own affairs, as you always have done, there won't be any trouble."

"Oh, I won't take the place, I can't!" Janet cried, so passionately that Miss Ottway looked at her in surprise. "I'm awfully grateful to you," she added, flushing crimson, "I — I'm afraid I'm not equal to it."

"Nonsense," said the other with decision. "You'd be very foolish not to try it. You won't get as much as I do, at first, at any rate, but a little more money won't be unwelcome, I guess. Mr. Ditmar will speak to you this afternoon. I leave on Saturday. I'm real glad to do you a good turn, Janet, and I know you'll get along," Miss Ottway added impulsively as they parted at the corner of Faber Street. "I've always thought a good deal of you."

For awhile Janet stood still, staring after the sturdy figure of her friend, heedless of the noonday crowd that bumped her. Then she went to Grady's Quick Lunch Counter and ordered a sandwich and a glass of milk, which she consumed slowly, profoundly sunk in thought. Presently Eda Rawle arrived, and noticing her preoccupation, inquired what was the matter.

"Nothing," said Janet. . . .

At two o'clock, when Ditmar returned to the office, he called Miss Ottway, who presently came out to summon Janet to his presence. Fresh, immaculate, yet virile in his light suit and silk shirt with red stripes, he was seated at his desk engaged in turning over some papers in a drawer. He kept her waiting a moment, and then said, with apparent casualness : —

"Is that you, Miss Bumpus? Would you mind closing the door?"

Janet obeyed, and again stood before him. He looked up. A suggestion of tenseness in her pose betraying an inner attitude of alertness, of defiance, conveyed to him sharply and deliciously once more the panther-like impression he had received when first, as a woman, she had come to his notice. The renewed and heightened perception of this feral quality in her aroused a sense of danger by no means unpleasurable, though warning him that he was about to take an unprecedented step, being drawn beyond the limits of caution he had previously set for himself in divorcing business and sex. Though he was by no means self-convinced of an intention to push the adventure, preferring to leave its possibilities open, he strove in voice and manner to be business-like; and instinct, perhaps, whispered that she might take alarm.

"Sit down, Miss Bumpus," he said pleasantly, as he closed the drawer.

She seated herself on an office chair.

"Do you like your work here?" he inquired.

"No," said Janet.

"Why not?" he demanded, staring at her.

"Why should I?" she retorted.

"Well — what's the trouble with it? It isn't as hard as it would be in some other places, is it?"

"I'm not saying anything against the place."

"What, then?"

"You asked me if I liked my work. I don't."

"Then why do you do it?" he demanded.

"To live," she replied.

He smiled, but his gesture as he stroked his moustache implied a slight annoyance at her composure. He found it difficult with this dark, self-contained young woman to sustain the rôle of benefactor.

"What kind of work would you like to do?" he demanded.

"I don't know. I haven't got the choice, anyway," she said.

He observed that she did her work well, to which she made no answer. She refused to help him, although Miss Ottway must have warned her. She acted as though she were conferring the favour. And yet, clearing his throat, he was impelled to say: —

"Miss Ottway's leaving me, she's going into the Boston office with Mr. Semple, the treasurer of the corporation. I shall miss her, she's an able and reliable woman, and she knows my ways." He paused, fingering his paper knife. "The fact is, Miss Bumpus, she's spoken highly of you, she tells me you're quick and accurate and painstaking — I've noticed that for myself. She seems to think you could do her work, and recommends that I give you a trial. You understand, of course, that the position is in a way confidential, and that you could not expect at first, at any rate, the salary Miss Ottway has had, but I'm willing to offer you fourteen dollars a week to begin with, and afterwards, if we get along together, to give you more. What do you say?"

"I'd like to try it, Mr. Ditmar," Janet said, and added nothing, no word of gratitude or of appreciation to that consent.

"Very well then," he replied, "that's settled. Miss Ottway will explain things to you, and tell you about — my peculiarities. And when she goes you can take her desk, by the window nearest my door."

Ditmar sat idle for some minutes after she had gone, staring through the open doorway into the outer office. . . .

3

To Ditmar she had given no evidence of the storm his offer had created in her breast, and it was characteristic also that she waited until supper was nearly over to inform her family, making the announcement in a matter-of-fact tone, just as though it were not the unique piece of good fortune that had come to the Bumpuses since Edward had been eliminated from the mercantile establishment at Dolton. The news was received with something like consternation. For the moment Hannah was incapable of speech, and her hand trembled as she resumed the cutting of the pie : but hope surged within her despite her effort to keep it down, her determination to remain true to the fatalism from which she had paradoxically derived so much comfort. The effect on Edward, while somewhat less violent, was temporarily to take away his appetite. Hope, to flower in him, needed but little watering. Great was his faith in the Bumpus blood, and secretly he had always regarded his eldest daughter as the chosen vessel for their redemption.

"Well, I swan !" he exclaimed, staring at her in admiration and neglecting his pie, "I've always thought you had it in you to get on, Janet. I guess I've told you you've always put me in mind of Eliza Bumpus — the one that held out against the Indians till her husband came back with the neighbours. I was just reading about her again the other night."

"Yes, you've told us, Edward," said Hannah.

"She had gumption," he went on, undismayed. "And from what I can gather of her looks I calculate you favour her — she was dark and not so very tall — not so tall as you, I guess. So you're goin'" (he pronounced it very slowly) "you're goin' to be Mr. Ditmar's private stenographer! He's a smart man, Mr. Ditmar, he's a good man, too. All you've got to do is to behave right by him. He always speaks to me when he passes by the gate. I was sorry for him when his wife died — a young woman, too. And he's never married again! Well, I swan!"

"You'd better quit swanning," exclaimed Hannah. "And what's Mr. Ditmar's goodness got to do with it? He's found out Janet has sense, she's willing and hard working, he won't" (pronounced want) "he won't be the loser by it, and he's not giving her what he gave Miss Ottway. It's just like you, thinking he's doing her a good turn."

"I'm not saying Janet isn't smart," he protested, "but I know it's hard to get work with so many folks after every job."

"Maybe it ain't so hard when you've got some get-up and go," Hannah retorted rather cruelly. It was thus characteristically and with unintentional sharpness she expressed her maternal pride by a reflection not only upon Edward, but Lise also. Janet had grown warm at the mention of Ditmar's name.

"It was Miss Ottway who recommended me," she said, glancing at her sister, who during this conversation had sat in silence. Lise's expression, normally suggestive of a discontent not unbecoming to her type, had grown almost sullen. Hannah's brisk gathering up of the dishes was suddenly arrested.

"Lise, why don't you say something to your sister? Ain't you glad she's got the place?"

"Sure, I'm glad," said Lise, and began to unscrew the top of the salt shaker. "I don't see why I couldn't get a raise, too. I work just as hard as she does."

Edward, who had never got a "raise" in his life, was smitten with compunction and sympathy.

"Give 'em time, Lise," he said consolingly. "You ain't so old as Janet."

"Time!" she cried, flaring up and suddenly losing her control. "I've got a picture of Walters giving *me* a raise — I know the girls that get raises from him."

"You ought to be ashamed of yourself," Hannah declared. "There — you've spilled the salt!"

But Lise, suddenly bursting into tears, got up and left the room. Edward picked up the *Banner* and pretended to read it, while Janet collected the salt and put it back into the shaker. Hannah, gathering up the rest of the dishes, disappeared into the kitchen, but presently returned, as though she had forgotten something.

"Hadn't you better go after her?" she said to Janet.

"I'm afraid it won't be any use. She's got sort of queer, lately — she thinks they're down on her."

"I'm sorry I spoke so sharp. But then —" Hannah shook her head, and her sentence remained unfinished.

Janet sought her sister, but returned after a brief interval, with the news that Lise had gone out.

4

One of the delights of friendship, as is well known, is the exchange of confidences of joy or sorrow, but there was, in Janet's promotion, something intensely personal to increase her natural reserve. Her feelings toward Ditmar were so mingled as to defy analysis, and several days went by before she could bring herself to inform Eda Rawle of the new business relationship in which she stood to the agent of the Chippering Mill. The sky was still bright as they walked out Warren Street after supper, Eda bewailing the trials of the day just ended: Mr. Frye, the cashier of the bank, had had one of his cantankerous fits, had found fault with her punctuation, nothing she had done had pleased him. But presently, when they had come to what the *Banner* called the "residential district," she was cheered by the sight of the green lawns, the flowerbeds and shrubbery, the mansions of those inhabitants of Hampton unfamiliar with boarding-houses and tenements. Before one of these she paused, retaining Janet by the arm, exclaiming wistfully : —

"Wouldn't you like to live there ? That belongs to your boss."

Janet, who had been dreaming as she gazed at the façade of rough stucco that once had sufficed to fill the ambitions of the late Mrs. Ditmar, recognized it as soon as Eda spoke, and dragged her friend hastily, almost roughly along the side-walk until they had reached the end of the block. Janet was red.

"What's the matter ? " demanded Eda, as soon as she had recovered from her surprise.

"Nothing," said Janet. "Only — I'm in his office."

"But what of it ? You've got a right to look at his house, haven't you ? "

"Why yes, — a right," Janet assented. Knowing Eda's ambitions for her were not those of a business career, she was in terror lest her friend should scent a romance, and for this reason she had never spoken of the symptoms Ditmar had betrayed. She attempted to convey to Eda the doubtful taste of staring point-blank at the house of one's employer, especially when he might be concealed behind a curtain. "You see," she added, "Miss Ottway's recommended me for her place — she's going away."

"Janet ! " cried Eda. "Why didn't you tell me ? "

"Well," said Janet guiltily, "it's only a trial. I don't know whether he'll keep me or not."

"Of course he'll keep you," said Eda, warmly. " If that isn't just like you, not saying a word about it. Gee, if I'd had a raise like that I just couldn't wait to tell you. But then, I'm not smart like you."

"Don't be silly," said Janet, out of humour with herself,

and annoyed because she could not then appreciate Eda's generosity.

"We've just got to celebrate!" declared Eda, who had the gift, which Janet lacked, of taking her joys vicariously; and her romantic and somewhat medieval proclivities would permit no such momentous occasion to pass without an appropriate festal symbol. "We'll have a spree on Saturday — the circus is coming then."

"It'll be my spree," insisted Janet, her heart warming. "I've got the raise. . . ."

On Saturday, accordingly, they met at Grady's for lunch, Eda attired in her best blouse of pale blue, and when they emerged from the restaurant, despite the torrid heat, she beheld Faber Street as in holiday garb as they made their way to the cool recesses of Winterhalter's to complete the feast. That glorified drug-store with the five bays included in its manifold functions a department rivalling Delmonico's, with electric fans and marble-topped tables and white-clad waiters who took one's order and filled it at the soda fountain. It mattered little to Eda that the young man awaiting their commands had pimples and long hair and grinned affectionately as he greeted them.

"Hello, girls!" he said. "What strikes you to-day?"

"Me for a raspberry nut sundae," announced Eda, and Janet, being unable to imagine any more delectable confection, assented. The penetrating odour peculiar to drug-stores, dominated by menthol and some unnamable but ancient remedy for catarrh, was powerless to interfere with their enjoyment.

The circus began at two. Rather than cling to the straps of a crowded car they chose to walk, following the familiar route of the trolley past the car barns and the base-ball park to the bare field under the seared face of Torrey's Hill, where circuses were wont to settle. A sirocco-like breeze

from the southwest whirled into eddies the clouds of germ-
laden dust stirred up by the automobiles, blowing their
skirts against their legs, and sometimes they were forced to
turn, clinging to their hats, confused and giggling, conscious
of male glances. The crowd, increasing as they proceeded,
was in holiday mood; young men with a newly-washed
aspect, in Faber Street suits, chaffed boisterously groups of
girls, who retorted with shrill cries and shrieks of laughter;
amorous couples strolled, arm in arm, oblivious, as though
the place were as empty as Eden; lady-killers with exag-
gerated square shoulders, wearing bright neckties, their
predatory instincts alert, hovered about in eager search of
adventure. There were men-killers, too, usually to be found
in pairs, in startling costumes they had been persuaded were
the latest Paris models, — imitations of French cocottes
in Hampton, proof of the smallness of our modern world.
Eda regarded them superciliously.

"They'd like you to think they'd never been near a loom
or a bobbin!" she exclaimed.

In addition to these more conspicuous elements, the
crowd contained sober operatives of the skilled sort possessed of sufficient means to bring hither their families,
including the baby; there were section-hands and foremen,
slashers, mule spinners, beamers, French-Canadians, Irish,
Scotch, Welsh and English, Germans, with only an occasional
Italian, Lithuanian, or Jew. Peanut and popcorn men,
venders of tamales and chile-con-carne hoarsely shouted their
wares, while from afar could be heard the muffled booming
of a band. Janet's heart beat faster. She regarded with
a tinge of awe the vast expanse of tent that rose before her
eyes, the wind sending ripples along the heavy canvas from
circumference to tent pole. She bought the tickets; they
entered the circular enclosure where the animals were kept;
where the strong beams of the sun, in trying to force their

way through the canvas roof, created an unnatural, jaundiced twilight, the weirdness of which was somehow enhanced by the hoarse, amazingly penetrating growls of beasts. Suddenly a lion near them raised a shaggy head, emitting a series of undulating, soul-shaking roars.

".Ah, what's eatin' *you?*" demanded a thick-necked youth, pretending not to be awestricken by this demonstration.

"Suppose he'd get out!" cried Eda, drawing Janet away.

"I wouldn't let him hurt you, dearie," the young man assured her.

"You!" she retorted contemptuously, but grinned in spite of herself, showing her gums.

The vague feeling of terror inspired by this tent was a part of its fascination, for it seemed pregnant with potential tragedies suggested by the juxtaposition of helpless babies and wild beasts, the babies crying or staring in blank amazement at padding tigers whose phosphorescent eyes never left these morsels beyond the bars. The two girls wandered about, their arms closely locked, but the strange atmosphere, the roars of the beasts, the ineffable, pungent odour of the circus, of sawdust mingled with the effluvia of animals, had aroused an excitement that was slow in subsiding. Some time elapsed before they were capable of taking a normal interest in the various exhibits.

"'Adjutant Bird,'" Janet read presently from a legend on one of the compartments of a cage devoted to birds, and surveying the somewhat dissolute occupant. "Why, he's just like one of those tall mashers who stay at the Wilmot and stand on the sidewalk, — travelling men, you know."

"Say — isn't he?" Eda agreed. "Isn't he pleased with himself, and his feet crossed!"

"And see this one, Eda — he's a 'Harpy Eagle.' There's somebody we know looks just like that. Wait a minute —

I'll tell you — it's the woman who sits in the cashier's cage at Grady's."

"If it sure isn't!" said Eda.

"She has the same fluffy, light hair — hairpins can't keep it down, and she looks at you in that same sort of surprised way with her head on one side when you hand in your check."

"Why, it's true to the life!" cried Eda enthusiastically. "She thinks she's got all the men cinched, — she does — and she's forty if she's a day."

These comparisons brought them to a pitch of risible enjoyment amply sustained by the spectacle in the monkey cage, to which presently they turned. A chimpanzee, with a solicitation more than human, was solemnly searching a friend for fleas in the midst of a pandemonium of chattering and screeching and chasing, of rattling of bars and trapezes carried on by their companions.

"Well, young ladies," said a voice, "come to pay a call on your relations — have ye?"

Eda giggled hysterically. An elderly man was standing beside them. He was shabbily dressed, his own features were wizened, almost simian, and by his friendly and fatuous smile Janet recognized one of the harmless obsessed in which Hampton abounded.

"Relations!" Eda exclaimed.

"You and me, yes, and her," he answered, looking at Janet, though at first he had apparently entertained some doubt as to this inclusion, "we're all descended from them." His gesture triumphantly indicated the denizens of the cage.

"What are you giving us?" said Eda.

"Ain't you never read Darwin?" he demanded. "If you had, you'd know they're our ancestors, you'd know we came from them instead of Adam and Eve. That there's a fable."

" I'll never believe I came from them," cried Eda, vehement in her disgust.

But Janet laughed. "What's the difference? Some of us aren't any better than monkeys, anyway."

"That's so," said the man approvingly. "That's so." He wanted to continue the conversation, but they left him rather ruthlessly. And when, from the entrance to the performance tent, they glanced back over their shoulders, he was still gazing at his cousins behind the bars, seemingly deriving an acute pleasure from his consciousness of the connection. . . .

CHAPTER VI

1

MODERN business, by reason of the mingling of the sexes it involves, for the playwright and the novelist and the sociologist is full of interesting and dramatic situations, and in it may be studied, undoubtedly, one phase of the evolution tending to transform if not disintegrate certain institutions hitherto the corner-stones of society. Our stage is set. A young woman, conscious of ability, owes her promotion primarily to certain dynamic feminine qualities with which she is endowed. And though she may make an elaborate pretense of ignoring the fact, in her heart she knows and resents it, while at the same time, paradoxically, she gets a thrill from it, — a sustaining and inspiring thrill of power! On its face it is a business arrangement; secretly, — attempt to repudiate this as one may, — it is tinged with the colours of high adventure. When Janet entered into the intimate relationship with Mr. Claude Ditmar necessitated by her new duties as his private stenographer her attitude, slightly defiant, was the irreproachable one of a strict attention to duty. All unconsciously she was a true daughter of the twentieth century, and probably a feminist at heart, which is to say that her conduct was determined by no preconceived or handed-down notions of what was proper and lady-like. For feminism, in a sense, is a return to atavism, and sex antagonism and sex attraction are functions of the same thing. There were moments when she believed herself to hate Mr. Ditmar, when she treated him with an aloofness, an impersonality unsurpassed; moments when he paused in his dictation to stare at her in astonishment. He, who flattered himself that he understood women!

She would show him! — such was her dominating determination. Her promotion assumed the guise of a challenge, of a gauntlet flung down at the feet of her sex. In a certain way, an insult, though incredibly stimulating. If he flattered himself that he had done her a favour, if he entertained the notion that he could presently take advantage of the contact with her now achieved to make unbusinesslike advances — well, he would find out. He had proclaimed his desire for an able assistant in Miss Ottway's place — he would get one, and nothing more. She watched narrowly, *à l'affût*, as the French say, for any signs of sentiment, and indeed this awareness of her being on guard may have had some influence on Mr. Ditmar's own attitude, likewise irreproachable. . . . A rather anæmic young woman, a Miss Annie James, was hired for Janet's old place.

In spite of this aloofness and alertness, for the first time in her life Janet felt the exuberance of being in touch with affairs of import. Hitherto the mill had been merely a greedy monster claiming her freedom and draining her energies in tasks routine, such as the copying of meaningless documents and rows of figures; now, supplied with stimulus and a motive, the Corporation began to take on significance, and she flung herself into the work with an ardour hitherto unknown, determined to make herself so valuable to Ditmar that the time would come when he could not do without her. She strove to memorize certain names and addresses, lest time be lost in looking them up, to familiarize herself with the ordinary run of his correspondence, to recall what letters were to be marked "personal," to anticipate matters of routine, in order that he might not have the tedium of repeating instructions; she acquired the faculty of keeping his engagements in her head; she came early to the office, remaining after hours, going through the files, becoming familiar with his system; and she learned to sort out his correspondence, sifting the important from the unimportant, to protect him, more and more, from numerous visitors who called only to waste his time. Her instinct for the detection of book-agents, no matter how brisk and business-like they might appear, was unerring — she remembered faces and the names belonging to them: an individual once observed to be *persona non grata* never succeeded in passing her twice. On one occasion Ditmar came out of his office to see the back of one of these visitors disappearing into the corridor.

"Who was that?" he asked.

"His name is McCalla," she said. "I thought you didn't want to be bothered."

"But how in thunder did you get rid of him?" he demanded.

"Oh, I just wouldn't let him in," she replied demurely.

And Ditmar went away, wondering. . . . Thus she studied him, without permitting him to suspect it, learning his idiosyncrasies, his attitude toward all those with whom daily he came in contact, only to find herself approving. She was forced to admit that he was a judge of men, compelled to admire his adroitness in dealing with them. He could be democratic or autocratic as occasion demanded; he knew when to yield, and when to remain inflexible. One morning, for instance, there arrived from New York a dapper salesman whose jauntily tied bow, whose thin hair — carefully parted to conceal an incipient baldness — whose wary and slightly weary eyes all impressively suggested the metropolitan atmosphere of high pressure and sophistication from which he had emerged. He had a machine to sell; an amazing machine, endowed with human intelligence and more than human infallibility; for when it made a mistake it stopped. It was designed for the express purpose of eliminating from the payroll the skilled and sharp-eyed women who are known as "drawers-in," who sit all day long under a north light patiently threading the ends of the warp through the heddles of the loom harness. Janet's imagination was gradually fired as she listened to the visitor's eloquence; and the textile industry, which hitherto had seemed to her uninteresting and sordid, took on the colours of romance.

"Now I've made up my mind we'll place one with you, Mr. Ditmar," the salesman concluded. "I don't object to telling you we'd rather have one in the Chippering than in any mill in New England."

Janet was surprised, almost shocked to see Ditmar shake his head, yet she felt a certain reluctant admiration because he had not been swayed by blandishments. At such moments, when he was bent on refusing a request, he seemed physically to acquire massiveness, — and he had a dogged way of chewing his cigar.

"I don't want it, yet," he replied, "not until you improve it." And she was impressed by the fact that he seemed to know as much about the machine as the salesman himself. In spite of protests, denials, appeals, he remained firm. "When you get rid of the defects I've mentioned come back, Mr. Hicks — but don't come back until then."

And Mr. Hicks departed, discomfited. . . .

Ditmar knew what he wanted. Of the mill he was the absolute master, familiar with every process, carrying constantly in his mind how many spindles, how many looms were at work; and if anything untoward happened, becoming aware of it by what seemed to Janet a subconscious process, sending for the superintendent of the department: for Mr. Orcutt, perhaps, whose office was across the hall —

a tall, lean, spectacled man of fifty who looked like a school-master.

"Orcutt, what's the matter with the opener in Cooney's room?"

"Why, the blower's out of order."

"Well, whose fault is it?" . . .

He knew every watchman and foreman in the mill, and many of the second hands. The old workers, men and women who had been in the Chippering employ through good and bad times for years, had a place in his affections, but toward the labour force in general his attitude was im-personal. The mill had to be run, and people to be got to run it. With him, first and last and always it was the mill, and little by little what had been for Janet a heterogeneous mass of machinery and human beings became unified and personified in Claude Ditmar. It was odd how the essence and quality of that great building had changed for her; how the very roaring of the looms, as she drew near the canal in the mornings, had ceased to be sinister and depress-ing, but bore now a burden like a great battle song to excite and inspire, to remind her that she had been snatched as by a miracle from the commonplace. And all this was a func-tion of Ditmar.

Life had become portentous. And she was troubled by no qualms of logic, but gloried, womanlike, in her lack of it. She did not ask herself why she had deliberately enlarged upon Miss Ottway's duties, invaded debatable ground in part inevitably personal, flung herself with such abandon into the enterprise of his life's passion, at the same time main-taining a deceptive attitude of detachment, half deceiving herself that it was zeal for the work by which she was ac-tuated. In her soul she knew better. She was really pour-ing fuel on the flames. She read him, up to a certain point — as far as was necessary; and beneath his attempts at

self-control she was conscious of a dynamic desire that
betrayed itself in many acts and signs, — as when he brushed
against her; and occasionally when he gave evidence with his
subordinates of a certain shortness of temper unusual with
him she experienced a vaguely alarming but delicious thrill
of power. And this, of all men, was the great Mr. Ditmar!
Was she in love with him? That question did not trouble
her either. She continued to experience in his presence
waves of antagonism and attraction, revealing to her depths
and possibilities of her nature that frightened while they
fascinated. It never occurred to her to desist. That
craving in her for high adventure was not to be denied.

2

On summer evenings it had been Ditmar's habit when in
Hampton to stroll about his lawn, from time to time changing the position of the sprinkler, smoking a cigar, and reflecting pleasantly upon his existence. His house, as he gazed
at it against the whitening sky, was an eminently satis-
factory abode, his wife was dead, his children gave him no
trouble; he felt a glow of paternal pride in his son as the
boy raced up and down the sidewalk on a bicycle; George
was manly, large and strong for his age, and had a domineer-
ing way with other boys that gave Ditmar secret pleasure.
Of Amy, who was showing a tendency to stoutness, and who
had inherited her mother's liking for candy and romances,
Ditmar thought scarcely at all: he would glance at her as
she lounged, reading, in a chair on the porch, but she did not
come within his range of problems. He had, in short, everything to make a reasonable man content, a life nicely compounded of sustenance, pleasure, and business, — business
naturally being the greatest of these. He was — though
he did not know it — ethically and philosophically right in
squaring his morals with his occupation, and his had been the

good fortune to live in a world whose codes and conventions had been carefully adjusted to the pursuit of that particular brand of happiness he had made his own. Why, then, in the name of that happiness, of the peace and sanity and pleasurable effort it had brought him, had he allowed and even encouraged the advent of a new element that threatened to destroy the equilibrium achieved? an element refusing to be classified under the head of property, since it involved something he desired and could not buy? A woman who was not property, who resisted the attempt to be turned into property, was an anomaly in Ditmar's universe. He had not, of course, existed for more than forty years without having heard and read of and even encountered in an acquaintance or two the species of sex attraction sentimentally called love that sometimes made fools of men and played havoc with more important affairs, but in his experience it had never interfered with his sanity or his appetite or the Chippering Mill: it had never made his cigars taste bitter; it had never caused a deterioration in the appreciation of what he had achieved and held. But now he was experiencing strange symptoms of an intensity out of all proportion to that of former relations with the other sex. What was most unusual for him, he was alarmed and depressed, at moments irritable. He regretted the capricious and apparently accidental impulse that had made him pretend to tinker with his automobile that day by the canal, that had led him to the incomparable idiocy of getting rid of Miss Ottway and installing the disturber of his peace as his private stenographer.

What the devil was it in her that made him so uncomfortable? When in his office he had difficulty in keeping his mind on matters of import; he would watch her furtively as she went about the room with the lithe and noiseless movements that excited him the more because he suspected beneath her outward and restrained demeanour a fierceness he craved yet feared. He thought of her continually as a panther, a panther he had caught and could not tame; he hadn't even caught her, since she might escape at any time. He took precautions not to alarm her. When she brushed against him he trembled. Continually she baffled and puzzled him, and he never could tell of what she was thinking. She represented a whole set of new and undetermined values for which he had no precedents, and unlike every woman he had known — including his wife — she had an integrity of her own, seemingly beyond the reach of all influences economic and social. All the more exasperating, therefore, was a propinquity creating an intimacy without substance, or without the substance he craved — for she had magically become for him a sort of enveloping, protecting atmosphere. In an astonishingly brief time he had fallen into the habit of talking things over with her; naturally not affairs of the first importance, but matters such as the economy of his time: when, for instance, it was most convenient for him to go to Boston; and he would find that she had telephoned, without being told, to the office there when to expect him, to his chauffeur to be on hand. He never had to tell her a thing twice, nor did she interrupt — as Miss Ottway sometimes had done — the processes of his thought. Without realizing it he fell into the habit of listening for the inflections of her voice, and though he had never lacked the power of making decisions, she somehow made these easier for him — especially if a human equation were involved.

He had, at least, the consolation — if it were one — of reflecting that his reputation was safe, that there would be no scandal, since two are necessary to make the kind of scandal he had always feared, and Miss Bumpus, apparently, had no intention of being the second party. Yet she was not virtuous, as he had hitherto defined the word. Of this he was sure. No woman who moved about as she did, who had such an effect on him, who had on occasions, though inadvertently, returned the lightning of his glances, whose rare laughter resembled grace notes, and in whose hair was that almost imperceptible kink, could be virtuous. This instinctive conviction inflamed him. For the first time in his life he began to doubt the universal conquering quality of his own charms, — and when such a thing happens to a man like Ditmar he is in danger of hell-fire. He indulged less and less in the convivial meetings and excursions that hitherto had given him relaxation and enjoyment, and if his cronies inquired as to the reasons for his neglect of them he failed to answer with his usual geniality.

"Everything going all right up at the mills, Colonel?" he was asked one day by Mr. Madden, the treasurer of a large shoe company, when they met on the marble tiles of the hall in their Boston club.

"All right. Why?"

"Well," replied Madden, conciliatingly, "you seem kind of preoccupied, that's all. I didn't know but what the fifty-four hour bill the legislature's just put through might be worrying you."

"We'll handle that situation when the time comes," said Ditmar. He accepted a gin rickey, but declined rather curtly the suggestion of a little spree over Sunday to a resort on the Cape which formerly he would have found enticing. On another occasion he encountered in the lobby of the Parker House a more intimate friend, Chester Sprole, sallow, self-made, somewhat corpulent, one of those lawyers hail fellows well met in business circles and looked upon askance by the Brahmins of their profession; more than half politician, he had been in Congress, and from time to time was retained by large business interests because of his persuasive gifts with committees of the legislature — though these had been powerless to avert the recent calamity of the women and children's fifty-four hour bill. Mr. Sprole's hair was prematurely white, and the crow's-feet at the corners of his eyes were not the result of legal worries.

"Hullo, Dit," he said jovially.

"Hullo, Ches," said Ditmar.

"Now you're the very chap I wanted to see. Where have you been keeping yourself lately? Come out to the farm to-night, — some of the boys'll be there." Mr. Sprole, like many a self-made man, was proud of his farm, though he did not lead a wholly bucolic existence.

"I can't, Ches," answered Ditmar. "I've got to go back to Hampton."

This statement Mr. Sprole unwisely accepted as a fiction. He took hold of Ditmar's arm.

"A lady — eh — what?"

"I've got to go back to Hampton," repeated Ditmar, with a suggestion of truculence that took his friend aback. Not for worlds would Mr. Sprole have offended the agent of the Chippering Mill.

"I was only joking, Claude," he hastened to explain. Ditmar, somewhat mollified but still dejected, sought the dining-room when the lawyer had gone.

"All alone to-night, Colonel?" asked the coloured head waiter, obsequiously.

Ditmar demanded a table in the corner, and consumed a solitary meal.

3

Very naturally Janet was aware of the change in Ditmar, and knew the cause of it. Her feelings were complicated. He, the most important man in Hampton, the self-sufficient, the powerful, the hitherto distant and unattainable head of the vast organization known as the Chippering Mill, of which she was an insignificant unit, at times became for her just a man — a man for whom she had achieved a delicious contempt. And the knowledge that she, if she chose, could sway and dominate him by the mere exercise of that strange feminine force within her was intoxicating and terrifying. She read this in a thousand signs; in his glances; in his movements revealing a desire to touch her; in little things he said, apparently insignificant, yet fraught with meaning; in a constant recurrence of the apologetic attitude — so alien to the Ditmar formerly conceived — of which he had given evidence that day by the canal: and from this attitude emanated, paradoxically, a virile and galvanic current profoundly disturbing. Sometimes when he bent over her she experienced a commingled ecstasy and fear that he would seize her in his arms. Yet the tension was not constant, rising and falling with his moods and struggles, all of which she read — unguessed by him — as easily as a printed page by the gift that dispenses with laborious processes of the intellect. On the other hand, a resentment boiled within her his masculine mind failed to fathom. Stevenson said of John Knox that many women had come to learn from him, but he had never condescended to become a learner in return — a remark more or less applicable to Ditmar. She was, perforce, thrilled that he was virile and wanted her, but because he wanted her clandestinely her pride revolted, divining his fear of scandal and hating him for it like a thoroughbred. To do her justice, marriage never occurred to her. She was not so commonplace.

There were times, however, when the tension between them would relax, when some incident occurred to focus Ditmar's interest on the enterprise that had absorbed and unified his life, the Chippering Mill. One day in September, for instance, after an absence in New York, he returned to the office late in the afternoon, and she was quick to sense his elation, to recognize in him the restored presence of the quality of *élan*, of command, of singleness of purpose that had characterized him before she had become his stenographer. At first, as he read his mail, he seemed scarcely conscious of her presence. She stood by the window, awaiting his pleasure, watching the white mist as it rolled over the floor of the river, catching glimpses in vivid, saffron blurs of the lights of the Arundel Mill on the farther shore. Autumn was at hand. Suddenly she heard Ditmar speaking.

"Would you mind staying a little while longer this evening, Miss Bumpus?"

"Not at all," she replied, turning.

On his face was a smile, almost boyish.

"The fact is, I think I've got hold of the biggest single order that ever came into any mill in New England," he. declared.

"Oh, I'm glad," she said quickly.

"The cotton cards —?" he demanded.

She knew he referred to the schedules, based on the current prices of cotton, made out in the agent's office and sent in duplicate to the selling house in Boston. She got them from the shelf; and as he went over them she heard him repeating the names of various goods now become familiar, pongees, poplins, percales and voiles, garbardines and galateas, lawns, organdies, crepes, and Madras shirtings, while he wrote down figures on a sheet of paper. So complete was his absorption in this task that Janet, although she had resented the insinuating pressure of his former attitude toward her, felt a paradoxical sensation of jealousy. Presently, without looking up, he told her to call up the Boston office and ask for Mr. Fraile, the cotton buyer; and she learned from the talk over the telephone — though it was mostly about "futures" — that Ditmar had lingered for a conference in Boston on his way back from New York. After-

wards, having dictated two telegrams which she wrote out
on her machine, he leaned back in his chair; and though
the business for the day was ended, showed a desire to de-
tain her. His mood became communicative.

"I've been on the trail of that order for a month," he
declared. "Of course it isn't my business to get orders,
but to manage this mill, and that's enough for one man,
God knows. But I heard the Bradlaughs were in the market
for these goods, and I told the selling house to lie low, that
I'd go after it. I knew I could get away with it, if anybody
could. I went to the Bradlaughs and sat down on 'em, I
lived with 'em, ate with 'em, brought 'em home at night.
I didn't let 'em alone a minute until they handed it over.
I wasn't going to give any other mill in New England or
any of those southern concerns a chance to walk off with
it — not on your life! Why, we have the facilities. There
isn't another mill in the country can turn it out in the time
they ask, and even we will have to go some to do it. But
we'll do it, by George, unless I'm struck by lightning."

He leaned forward, hitting the desk with his fist, and
Janet, standing beside him, smiled. She had the tempting
gift of silence. Forgetting her twinge of jealousy, she was
drawn toward him now, and in this mood of boyish exuberance, of self-confidence and pride in his powers and success
she liked him better than ever before. She had, for the
first time, the curious feeling of being years older than he,
yet this did not detract from a new-born admiration.

"I made this mill, and I'm proud of it," he went on.
"When old Stephen Chippering put me in charge he was
losing money, he'd had three agents in four years. The
old man knew I had it in me, and I knew it, if I do say it
myself. All this union labour talk about shorter hours
makes me sick — why, there was a time when I worked ten
and twelve hours a day, and I'm man enough to do it yet, if

I have to. When the last agent — that was Cort — was sacked I went to Boston on my own hook and tackled the old gentleman — that's the only way to get anywhere. I couldn't bear to see the mill going to scrap, and I told him a thing or two, — I had the facts and the figures. Stephen Chippering was a big man, but he had a streak of obstinacy in him, he was conservative, you bet. I had to get it across to him there was a lot of dead wood in this plant, I had to wake him up to the fact that the twentieth century was here. He had to be shown — he was from Boston, you know —" Ditmar laughed — "but he was all wool and a yard wide, and he liked me and trusted me.

"That was in nineteen hundred. I can remember the interview as well as if it had happened last night — we sat up until two o'clock in the morning in that library of his with the marble busts and the leather-bound books and the double windows looking out over the Charles, where the wind was blowing a gale. And at last he said, 'All right, Claude, go ahead. I'll put you in as agent, and stand behind you.' And by thunder, he did stand behind me. He was quiet, the finest looking old man I ever saw in my life, straight as a ramrod, with a little white goatee and a red, weathered face full of creases, and a skin that looked as if it had been pricked all over with needles — the old Boston sort. They don't seem to turn 'em out any more. Why, I have a picture of him here."

He opened a drawer in his desk and drew out a photograph. Janet gazed at it sympathetically.

"It doesn't give you any notion of those eyes of his," Ditmar said, reminiscently. "They looked right through a man's skull, no matter how thick it was. If anything went wrong, I never wasted any time in telling him about it, and I guess it was one reason he liked me. Some of the people up here didn't understand him, kow-towed to him, they were scared of him, and if he thought they had something up their sleeves he looked as if he were going to eat 'em alive. Regular fighting eyes, the kind that get inside of a man and turn the light on. And he sat so still — made you ashamed of yourself. Well, he was a born fighter, went from Harvard into the Rebellion and was left for dead at Seven Oaks, where one of the company found him and saved him. He set that man up for life, and never talked about it, either. See what he wrote on the bottom — '*To my friend, Claude Ditmar, Stephen Chippering.*' And believe me, when he once called a man a friend he never took it back. I know one thing, I'll never get another friend like him."

With a gesture that gave her a new insight into Ditmar, reverently he took the picture from her hand and placed it back in the drawer. She was stirred, almost to tears, and moved away from him a little, as though to lessen by distance the sudden attraction he had begun to exert: yet she lingered, half leaning, half sitting on the corner of the big desk, her head bent toward him, her eyes filled with light. She was wondering whether he could ever love a woman as he loved this man of whom he had spoken, whether he could be as true to a woman. His own attitude seemed never to have been more impersonal, but she had ceased to resent it; something within her whispered that she was the conductor, the inspirer. . . .

"I wish Stephen Chippering could have lived to see this order," he exclaimed, "to see the Chippering Mill to-day! I guess he'd be proud of it, I guess he wouldn't regret having put me in as agent."

Janet did not reply. She could not. She sat regarding him intently, and when he raised his eyes and caught her luminous glance, his expression changed, she knew Stephen Chippering had passed from his mind.

"I hope you like it here," he said. His voice had become

vibrant, ingratiating, he had changed from the master to the suppliant — and yet she was not displeased. Power had suddenly flowed back into her, and with it an exhilarating self-command.

"I do like it," she answered.

"But you said, when I asked you to be my stenographer, that you didn't care for your work."

"Oh, this is different."

"How?"

"I'm interested, the mill means something to me now — you see, I'm not just copying things I don't know anything about."

"I'm glad you're interested," he said, in the same odd, awkward tone. "I've never had any one in the office who did my work as well. Now Miss Ottway was a good stenographer, she was capable, and a fine woman, but she never got the idea, the spirit of the mill in her as you've got it, and she wasn't able to save me trouble, as you do. It's remarkable how you've come to understand, and in such a short time."

Janet coloured. She did not look at him, but had risen and begun to straighten out the papers beside her.

"There are lots of other things I'd like to understand," she said.

"What?" he demanded.

"Well — about the mill. I never thought much about it before, I always hated it," she cried, dropping the papers and suddenly facing him. "It was just drudgery. But now I want to learn everything, all I can, I'd like to see the machinery."

"I'll take you through myself — to-morrow," he declared.

His evident agitation made her pause. They were alone, the outer office deserted, and the Ditmar she saw now, whom she had summoned up with ridiculous ease by virtue of that mysterious power within her, was no longer the agent of the Chippering Mill, a boy filled with enthusiasm by a business achievement, but a man, the incarnation and expression of masculine desire — desire for her. She knew she could compel him, if she chose, to throw caution to the winds.

"Oh no!" she exclaimed. She was afraid of him, she shrank from such a conspicuous sign of his favour.

"Why not?" he asked.

"Because I don't want you to," she said, and realized, as soon as she had spoken, that her words might imply the existence of a something between them never before hinted at by her. "I'll get Mr. Caldwell to take me through." She moved toward the door, and turned; though still on fire within, her manner had become demure, repressed. "Did you wish anything more this evening?" she inquired.

"That's all," he said, and she saw that he was gripping the arms of his chair. . . .

CHAPTER VII

1

Autumn was at hand. All day it had rained, but now, as night fell and Janet went homeward, the white mist from the river was creeping stealthily over the city, disguising the familiar and sordid landmarks. These had become beautiful, mysterious, somehow appealing. The electric arcs, splotches in the veil, revealed on the Common phantom trees; and in the distance, against the blurred lights from the Warren Street stores skirting the park could be seen phantom vehicles, phantom people moving to and fro. Thus, it seemed to Janet, invaded by a pearly mist was her own soul, in which she walked in wonder, — a mist shot through and through with soft, exhilarating lights half disclosing yet transforming and etherealizing certain landmarks there on which, formerly, she had not cared to gaze. She was thinking of Ditmar as she had left him gripping his chair, as he had dismissed her for the day, curtly, almost savagely. She had wounded and repelled him, and lingering in her was that exquisite touch of fear — a fear now not so much inspired by Ditmar as by the semi-acknowledged recognition of certain tendencies and capacities within herself. Yet she rejoiced in them, she was glad she had hurt Ditmar, she would hurt him again. Still palpitating, she reached the house in Fillmore Street, halting a moment with her hand on the door, knowing her face was flushed, anxious lest her mother or Lise might notice something unusual in her manner. But, when she had slowly mounted

114

the stairs and lighted the gas in the bedroom the sight of her sister's clothes cast over the chairs was proof that Lise had already donned her evening finery and departed. The room was filled with the stale smell of clothes, which Janet detested. She flung open the windows. She took off her hat and swiftly tidied herself, yet the relief she felt at Lise's absence was modified by a sudden, vehement protest against sordidness. Why should she not live by herself amidst clean and tidy surroundings? She had begun to earn enough, and somehow a vista had been opened up — a vista whose end she could not see, alluring, enticing. . . . In the dining-room, by the cleared table, her father was reading the *Banner;* her mother appeared in the kitchen door.

"What in the world happened to you, Janet?" she exclaimed.

"Nothing," said Janet. "Mr. Ditmar asked me to stay — that was all. He'd been away."

"I was worried, I was going to make your father go down to the mill. I've saved you some supper."

"I don't want much," Janet told her, "I'm not hungry."

"I guess you have to work too hard in that new place," said Hannah, as she brought in the filled plate from the oven.

"Well, it seems to agree with her, mother," declared Edward, who could always be counted on to say the wrong thing with the best of intentions. "I never saw her looking as well — why, I swan, she's getting real pretty!"

Hannah darted at him a glance, but restrained herself, and Janet reddened as she tried to eat the beans placed before her. The pork had browned and hardened at the edges, the gravy had spread, a crust covered the potatoes. When her father resumed his reading of the *Banner* and her mother went back into the kitchen she began to speculate rather resentfully and yet excitedly why it was that this adventure with a man, with Ditmar, made her look better, feel better,

— more alive. She was too honest to disguise from herself
that it was an adventure, a high one, fraught with all sorts
of possibilities, dangers, and delights. Her promotion had
been merely incidental. Both her mother and father, did
they know the true circumstances, — that Mr. Ditmar desired her, was perhaps in love with her — would be disturbed. Undoubtedly they would have believed that she
could "take care" of herself. She knew that matters could
not go on as they were, that she would either have to leave
Mr. Ditmar or — and here she baulked at being logical.
She had no intention of leaving him: to remain, according
to the notions of her parents, would be wrong. Why was it
that doing wrong agreed with her, energized her, made her
more alert, cleverer, keying up her faculties? turned life
from a dull affair into a momentous one? To abandon Ditmar would be to slump back into the humdrum, into something from which she had magically been emancipated,
symbolized by the home in which she sat; by the red-checked
tablecloth, the ugly metal lamp, the cherry chairs with the
frayed seats, the horsehair sofa from which the stuffing pro-
truded, the tawdry pillow with its colours, once gay, that
Lise had bought at a bargain at the *Bagatelle*. . . . The
wooden clock with the round face and quaint landscape below — the family's most cherished heirloom — though long
familiar, was not so bad; but the two yellowed engravings
on the wall offended her. They had been wedding presents
to Edward's father. One represented a stupid German
peasant woman holding a baby, and standing in front of a
thatched cottage; its companion was a sylvan scene in
which certain wooden rustics were supposed to be enjoying
themselves. Between the two, and dotted with flyspecks,
hung an insurance calendar on which was a huge head of a
lady, florid, fluffy-haired, flirtatious. Lise thought her
beautiful.

The room was ugly. She had long known that, but to-night the realization came to her that what she chiefly resented in it was the note it proclaimed — the note of a mute acquiescence, without protest or struggle, in what life might send. It reflected accurately the attitude of her parents, particularly of her father. With an odd sense of detachment, of critical remoteness and contempt she glanced at him as he sat stupidly absorbed in his newspaper, his face puckered, his lips pursed, and Ditmar rose before her — Ditmar, the embodiment of an indomitableness that refused to be beaten and crushed. She thought of the story he had told her, how by self-assertion and persistence he had become agent of the Chippering Mill, how he had convinced Mr. Stephen Chippering of his ability. She could not think of the mill as belonging to the Chipperings and the other stockholders, but to Ditmar, who had shaped it into an expression of himself, since it was his ideal. And now it seemed that he had made it hers also. She regretted having repulsed him, pushed her plate away from her, and rose.

"You haven't eaten anything," said Hannah, who had come into the room. "Where are you going?"

"Out — to Eda's," Janet answered. . . .

"It's late," Hannah objected. But Janet departed. Instead of going to Eda's she walked alone, seeking the quieter streets that her thoughts might flow undisturbed. At ten o'clock, when she returned, the light was out in the dining-room, her sister had not come in, and she began slowly to undress, pausing every now and then to sit on the bed and dream; once she surprised herself gazing into the glass with a rapt expression that was almost a smile. What was it about her that had attracted Ditmar? No other man had ever noticed it. She had never thought herself good looking, and now — it was astonishing! — she seemed to have changed, and she saw with pride that her arms and neck were shapely, that her dark hair fell down in a cascade over her white shoulders to her waist. She caressed it; it was fine. When she looked again, a radiancy seemed to envelop her. She braided her hair slowly, in two long plaits, looking shyly in the mirror and always seeing that radiancy. . . .

Suddenly it occurred to her with a shock that she was doing exactly what she had despised Lise for doing, and leaving the mirror she hurried her toilet, put out the light, and got into bed. For a long time, however, she remained wakeful, turning first on one side and then on the other, trying to banish from her mind the episode that had excited her. But always it came back again. She saw Ditmar before her, virile, vital, electric with desire. At last she fell asleep.

Gradually she was awakened by something penetrating her consciousness, something insistent, pervasive, unescapable, which in drowsiness she could not define. The gas was burning, Lise had come in, and was moving peculiarly about the room. Janet watched her. She stood in front of the bureau, just as Janet herself had done, her hands at her throat. At last she let them fall, her head turning slowly, as though drawn by some irresistible, hypnotic power, and their eyes met. Lise's were filmed, like those of a dog whose head is being stroked, expressing a luxuriant dreaminess — uncomprehending, passionate.

"Say, did I wake you?" she asked. "I did my best not to make any noise — honest to God."

"It wasn't the noise that woke me up," said Janet.

"It couldn't have been."

"You've been drinking!" said Janet, slowly.

Lise giggled.

"What's it to you, angel face!" she inquired. "Quiet down, now, and go bye-bye."

Janet sprang from the bed, seized her by the shoulders, and shook her. She was limp. She began to whimper.

"Cut it out — leave me go. It ain't nothing to you what I do — I just had a highball."

Janet released her and drew back.

"I just had a highball — honest to God!"

"Don't say that again!" whispered Janet, fiercely.

"Oh, very well. For God's sake, go to bed and leave me alone — I can take care of myself, I guess — I ain't nutty enough to hit the booze. But I ain't like you — I've got to have a little fun to keep alive."

"A little fun!" Janet exclaimed. The phrase struck her sharply. A little fun to keep alive!

With that same peculiar, cautious movement she had observed, Lise approached a chair, and sank into it, — jerking her head in the direction of the room where Hannah and Edward slept.

"D'you want to wake 'em up? Is that your game?" she asked, and began to fumble at her belt. Overcoming with an effort a disgust amounting to nausea, Janet approached her sister again, little by little undressing her, and finally getting her into bed, when she immediately fell into a profound slumber. Janet, too, got into bed, but sleep was impossible: the odour lurked like a foul spirit in the darkness, mingling with the stagnant, damp air that came in at the open window, fairly saturating her with horror: it seemed the very essence of degradation. But as she lay on the edge of the bed, shrinking from contamination, in the throes of excitement inspired by an unnamed fear, she grew hot, she could feel and almost hear the pounding of her heart. She rose, felt around in the clammy darkness for her wrapper and slippers, gained the door, crept through the dark hall to the dining-room, where she stealthily lit the lamp; darkness had become a terror. A cockroach scurried across the linoleum. The room was warm and close, it reeked with the smell of stale food, but at least she found relief from that other odour. She sank down on the sofa.

Her sister was drunk. That in itself was terrible enough, yet it was not the drunkenness alone that had sickened Janet, but the suggestion of something else. Where had Lise been? In whose company had she become drunk? Of late, in contrast to a former communicativeness, Lise had been singuarly secretive as to her companions, and the manner in which her evenings were spent; and she, Janet, had grown too self-absorbed to be curious. Lise, with her shop-girl's cynical knowledge of life and its pitfalls and the high valuation at which she held her charms, had seemed secure from danger; but Janet recalled her discouragement, her threat to leave the *Bagatelle*. Since then there had been something furtive about her. Now, because that odour of alcohol Lise exhaled had destroyed in Janet the sense of exhilaration, of life on a higher plane she had begun to feel, and filled her with degradation, she hated Lise, felt for her sister no strain of pity. A proof, had she recognized it, that immorality is not a matter of laws and decrees, but of individual emotions. A few hours before she had seen nothing wrong in her relationship with Ditmar: now she beheld him selfish, ruthless, pursuing her for one end, his own gratification. As a man, he had become an enemy. Ditmar was like all other men who exploited her sex without compunction, but the thought that she was like Lise, asleep in a drunken stupor, that their cases differed only in degree, was insupportable.

At last she fell asleep from sheer weariness, to dream she was with Ditmar at some place in the country under spreading trees, Silliston, perhaps — Silliston Common, cleverly disguised: nor was she quite sure, always, that the man was Ditmar; he had a way of changing, of resembling the man she had met in Silliston whom she had mistaken for a carpenter. He was pleading with her, in his voice was the peculiar vibrancy that thrilled her, that summoned some answering thing out of the depths of her, and she felt herself yielding with a strange ecstasy in which were mingled joy and terror. The terror was conquering the joy, and suddenly he stood transformed before her eyes, caricatured, become a shrieking monster from whom she sought in agony to escape. . . . In this paralysis of fear she awoke, staring with wide eyes at the flickering flame of the lamp, to a world filled with excruciating sound — the siren of the Chippering Mill! She lay trembling with the horror of the dream-spell upon her, still more than half convinced that the siren was Ditmar's voice, his true expression. He was waiting to devour her. Would the sound never end? . . .

Then, remembering where she was, alarmed lest her mother might come in and find her there, she left the sofa, turned out the sputtering lamp, and ran into the bedroom. Rain was splashing on the bricks of the passage-way outside, the shadows of the night still lurked in the corners; by the grey light she gazed at Lise, who breathed loudly and stirred uneasily, her mouth open, her lips parched. Janet touched her.

"Lise — get up!" she said. "It's time to get up." She shook her.

"Leave me alone — can't you?"

"It's time to get up. The whistle has sounded."

Lise heavily opened her eyes. They were bloodshot.

"I don't want to get up. I won't get up."

"But you must," insisted Janet, tightening her hold. "You've got to — you've got to eat breakfast and go to work."

"I don't want any breakfast, I ain't going to work any more."

A gust of wind blew inward the cheap lace curtains, and

the physical effect of it emphasized the chill that struck Janet's heart. She got up and closed the window, lit the gas, and returning to the bed, shook Lise again.

. "Listen," she said, "if you don't get up I'll tell mother what happened last night."

"Say, you wouldn't — !" exclaimed Lise, angrily.

"Get up!" Janet commanded, and watched her rather anxiously, uncertain as to the after effects of drunkenness. But Lise got up. She sat on the edge of the bed and yawned, putting her hand to her forehead.

"I've sure got a head on me," she remarked.

Janet was silent, angrier than ever, shocked that tragedy, degradation, could be accepted thus circumstantially. Lise proceeded to put up her hair. She seemed to be mistress of herself; only tired, gaping frequently. Once she remarked : —

"I don't see the good of getting nutty over a highball."

Seeing that Janet was not to be led into controversy, she grew morose.

Breakfast in Fillmore Street, never a lively meal, was more dismal than usual that morning, eaten to the accompaniment of slopping water from the roofs on the pavement of the passage. The indisposition of Lise passed unobserved by both Hannah and Edward; and at twenty minutes to eight the two girls, with rubbers and umbrellas, left the house together, though it was Janet's custom to depart earlier, since she had farther to go. Lise, suspicious, maintained an obstinate silence, keeping close to the curb. They reached the corner by the provision shop with the pink and orange chromos of jellies in the window.

"Lise, has anything happened to you?" demanded Janet suddenly. "I want you to tell me."

"Anything happened — what do you mean? Anything happened?"

"You know very well what I mean."

"Well, suppose something has happened?" Lise's reply was pert, defiant. "What's it to you? If anything's happened, it's happened to *me* — hasn't it?"

Janet approached her.

"What are you trying to do?" said Lise. "Push me into the gutter?"

"I guess you're there already," said Janet.

Lise was roused to a sudden pitch of fury. She turned on Janet and thrust her back.

"Well, if I am who's going to blame me?" she cried. "If you had to work all day in that hole, standing on your feet, picked on by yaps for six a week, I guess you wouldn't talk virtuous, either. It's easy for you to shoot off your mouth, you've got a soft snap — with Ditmar."

Janet was outraged. She could not restrain her anger.

"How dare you say that?" she demanded.

Lise was cowed.

"Well, you drove me to it — you make me mad enough to say anything. Just because I went to Gruber's with Neva Lorrie and a couple of gentlemen — they were gentlemen all right, as much gentlemen as Ditmar — you come at me and tell me I'm all to the bad." She began to sob. "I'm as straight as you are. How was I to know the highball was stiff? Maybe I was tired — anyhow, it put me on the queer, and everything in the joint began to tango 'round me — and Neva came home with me."

Janet felt a surge of relief, in which were mingled anxiety and resentment: relief because she was convinced that Lise was telling the truth, anxiety because she feared for Lise's future, resentment because Ditmar had been mentioned. Still, what she had feared most had not come to pass. Lise left her abruptly, darting down a street that led to a back entrance of the *Bagatelle*, and Janet pursued her way. Where, she wondered, would it all end? Lise had escaped so far, but drunkenness was an ominous sign. And "gentlemen"? What kind of gentlemen had taken her sister to Gruber's? Would Ditmar do that sort of thing if he had a chance?

The pavement in front of the company boarding-houses by the canal was plastered with sodden leaves whipped from the maples by the driving rain in the night. The sky above the mills was sepia. White lights were burning in the loom rooms. When she reached the vestibule Simmons, the watchman, informed her that Mr. Ditmar had already been there, and left for Boston.

2

Janet did not like to acknowledge to herself her disappointment on learning that Ditmar had gone to Boston. She knew he had had no such intention the night before; an accumulated mail and many matters demanding decisions were awaiting him; and his sudden departure seemed an act directed personally against her, in the nature of a retaliation, since she had offended and repulsed him. Through Lise's degrading act she had arrived at the conclusion that all adventure and consequent suffering had to do with Man — a conviction peculiarly maddening to such temperaments as Janet's. Therefore she interpreted her suffering in terms of Ditmar, she had looked forward to tormenting him again, and by departing he had deliberately balked and cheated her. The rain fell ceaselessly out of black skies, night seemed ever ready to descend on the river, a darkness — according to young Mr. Caldwell — due not to the clouds alone, but to forest fires many hundreds of miles away, in Canada. As the day wore on, however, her anger gradually gave place to an extreme weariness and depression, and yet she dreaded going home, inventing things for herself to do; arranging and rearranging Ditmar's papers that he might have less trouble in sorting them, putting those uppermost which she thought he would deem the most important. Perhaps he would come in, late ! In a world of impending chaos the brilliantly lighted office was a tiny refuge to which she clung. At last she put on her coat and rubbers, faring forth reluctantly into the wet.

At first when she entered the bedroom she thought it empty, though the gas was burning, and then she saw Lise lying face downward on the bed. For a moment she stood still, then closed the door softly.

"Lise," she said.

"What?"

Janet sat down on the bed, putting out her hand. Unconsciously she began to stroke Lise's hand, and presently it turned and tightened on her own.

"Lise," she said, "I understand why you — "she could not bring herself to pronounce the words "got drunk," — "I understand why you did it. I oughtn't to have talked to you that way. But it was terrible to wake up and see you."

For awhile Lise did not reply. Then she raised herself, feeling her hair with an involuntary gesture, regarding her sister with a bewildered look, her face puckered. Her eyes burned, and under them were black shadows.

"How do you mean — you understand?" she asked slowly. "You never hit the booze."

Even Lise's language, which ordinarily offended her, failed to change her sudden impassioned and repentant mood. She was astonished at herself for this sudden softening, since she did not really love Lise, and all day she had hated her, wished never to see her again.

"No, but I can understand how it would be to *want* to," Janet said. "Lise, I guess we're searching — both of us — for something we'll never find."

Lise stared at her with a contracted, puzzled expression,

as of a person awaking from sleep, all of whose faculties are being strained toward comprehension.

"What do you mean?" she demanded. "You and me? You're all right — you've got no kick coming."

"Life *is* hard, it's hard on girls like us — we want things we can't have." Janet was at a loss to express herself.

"Well, it ain't any pipe dream," Lise agreed. Her glance turned involuntarily toward the picture of the Olympian dinner party pinned on the wall. "Swells have a good time," she added.

"Maybe they pay for it, too," said Janet.

"I wouldn't holler about paying — it's paying and not getting the goods," declared Lise.

"You'll pay, and you won't get it. That kind of life is — hell," Janet cried.

Self-centered as Lise was, absorbed in her own trouble and present physical discomfort, this unaccustomed word from her sister and the vehemence with which it was spoken surprised and frightened her, brought home to her some hint of the terror in Janet's soul.

"Me for the water wagon," she said.

Janet was not convinced. She had hoped to discover the identity of the man who had taken Lise to Gruber's, but she did not attempt to continue the conversation. She rose and took off her hat.

"Why don't you go to bed?" she asked. "I'll tell mother you have a headache and bring in your supper."

"Well, I don't care if I do," replied Lise, gratefully.

3

Perhaps the most disconcerting characteristic of that complex affair, the human organism, is the lack of continuity of its moods. The soul, so called, is as sensitive to physical conditions as a barometer: affected by lack of sleep, by

smells and sounds, by food, by the weather — whether a
day be sapphire or obsidian. And the resolutions arising
from one mood are thwarted by the actions of the next.
Janet had observed this phenomenon, and sometimes, when
it troubled her, she thought herself the most inconsistent
and vacillating of creatures. She had resolved, for instance,
before she fell asleep, to leave the Chippering Mill, to
banish Ditmar from her life, to get a position in Boston,
whence she could send some of her wages home: and in
the morning, as she made her way to the office, the determination gave her a sense of peace and unity. But the
northwest wind was blowing. It had chased away the
mist and the clouds, the smoke from Canada. The sun shone
with a high brilliancy, the elms of the Common cast sharp,
black shadow-patterns on the pavements, and when she
reached the office and looked out of his window she saw the
blue river covered with quicksilver waves chasing one another across the current. Ditmar had not yet returned to
Hampton. About ten o'clock, as she was copying out some
figures for Mr. Price, young Mr. Caldwell approached her.
He had a Boston newspaper in his hand.

"Have you seen this article about Mr. Ditmar?" he asked.

"About Mr. Ditmar? No."

"It's quite a send-off for the Colonel," said Caldwell,
who was wont at times to use the title facetiously. "Listen; 'One of the most notable figures in the Textile industry
of the United States, Claude Ditmar, Agent of the Chippering Mill.'" Caldwell spread out the page and pointed
to a picture. "There he is, as large as life."

A little larger than life, Janet thought. Ditmar was one
of those men who, as the expression goes, "take" well, a
valuable asset in semi-public careers; and as he stood in
the sunlight on the steps of the building where they had
"snap-shotted" him he appeared even more massive, force-

ful, and preponderant than she had known him. Beholding
him thus set forth and praised in a public print, he seemed
suddenly to have been distantly removed from her, to have
reacquired at a bound the dizzy importance he had possessed
for her before she became his stenographer. She found it
impossible to realize that this was the Ditmar who had pursued and desired her; at times supplicating, apologetic,
abject; and again revealed by the light in his eyes and the
trembling of his hand as the sinister and ruthless predatory
male from whom — since the revelation in her sister Lise —
she had determined to flee, and whom she had persuaded herself she despised. He was a bigger man than she had thought,
and as she read rapidly down the column the fascination that
crept over her was mingled with disquieting doubt of her own
powers : it was now difficult to believe she had dominated or
could ever dominate this self-sufficient, successful person,
the list of whose achievements and qualities was so alluringly
set forth by an interviewer who himself had fallen a victim.

The article carried the implication that the modern,
practical, American business man was the highest type as
yet evolved by civilization : and Ditmar, referred to as "a
wizard of the textile industry," was emphatically one who
had earned the gratitude of the grand old Commonwealth.
By the efforts of such sons she continued to maintain her
commanding position among her sister states. Prominent
among the qualities contributing to his success was open-
mindedness, "a willingness to be shown," to scrap machinery
when his competitors still clung to older methods. The
Chippering Mill had never had a serious strike, — indication
of an ability to deal with labour; and Mr. Ditmar's views
on labour followed : if his people had a grievance, let them
come to him, and settle it between them. No unions. He
had consistently refused to recognize them. There was
mention of the Bradlaugh order as being the largest com-

mission ever given to a single mill, a reference to the excitement and speculation it had aroused in trade circles. Claude Ditmar's ability to put it through was unquestioned; one had only to look at him, — tenacity, forcefulness, executiveness were written all over him. . . . In addition, the article contained much material of an autobiographical nature that must — Janet thought — have been supplied by Ditmar himself, whose modesty had evidently shrunk from the cruder self-eulogy of an interview. But she recognized several characteristic phrases.

Caldwell, watching her as she read, was suddenly fascinated. During a trip abroad, while still an undergraduate, he had once seen the face of an actress, a really good Parisian actress, light up in that way; and it had revealed to him, in a flash, the meaning of enthusiasm. Now Janet became vivid for him. There must be something unusual in a person whose feelings could be so intense, whose emotions rang so true. He was not unsophisticated. He had sometimes wondered why Ditmar had promoted her, though acknowledging her ability. He admired Ditmar, but had no illusions about him. Harvard, and birth in a social stratum where emphasis is superfluous, enabled him to smile at the reporter's exuberance; and he was the more drawn toward her to see on Janet's flushed face the hint of a smile as she looked up at him when she had finished.

"The Colonel hypnotized that reporter," he said, as he took the paper; and her laugh, despite its little tremor, betrayed in her an unsuspected, humorous sense of proportion. "Well, I'll take off my hat to him," Caldwell went on. "He is a wonder, he's got the mill right up to capacity in a week. He's agreed to deliver those goods to the Bradlaughs by the first of April, you know, and Holster, of the Clarendon, swears it can't be done, he says Ditmar's crazy. Well, I stand to lose twenty-five dollars on him."

K

This loyalty pleased Janet, it had the strange effect of reviving loyalty in her. She liked this evidence of Dick Caldwell's confidence. He was a self-contained and industrious young man, with crisp curly hair, cordial and friendly yet never intimate with the other employés; liked by them — but it was tacitly understood his footing differed from theirs. He was a cousin of the Chipperings, and destined for rapid promotion. He went away every Saturday, it was known that he spent Sundays and holidays in delightful places, to return reddened and tanned; and though he never spoke about these excursions, and put on no airs of superiority, there was that in his manner and even in the cut of his well-worn suits proclaiming him as belonging to a sphere not theirs, to a category of fortunate beings whose stumbles are not fatal, who are sustained from above. Even Ditmar was not of these.

"I've just been showing a lot of highbrows through the mill," he told Janet. "They asked questions enough to swamp a professor of economics."

And Janet was suddenly impelled to ask : —

"Will you take me through sometime, Mr. Caldwell?"

"You've never been through?" he exclaimed. "Why, we'll go now, if you can spare the time."

Her face had become scarlet.

"Don't tell Mr. Ditmar," she begged. "You see — he wanted to take me himself."

"Not a word," Caldwell promised as they left the office together and went downstairs to the strong iron doors that led to the Cotton Department. The showing through of occasional visitors had grown rather tiresome; but now his curiosity and interest were aroused, he was conscious of a keen stimulation when he glanced at Janet's face. Its illumination perplexed him. The effect was that of a picture obscurely hung and hitherto scarcely noticed on which the

light had suddenly been turned.   It glowed with a strange
and disturbing radiance. . . .

As for Janet, she was as one brought suddenly to the realization of a miracle in whose presence she had lived for many
years and never before suspected; the miracle of machinery,
of the triumph of man over nature.   In the brief space of an
hour she beheld the dirty bales flung off the freight cars on
the sidings transformed into delicate fabrics wound from the
looms; cotton that only last summer, perhaps, while she
sat typewriting at her window, had been growing in the
fields of the South.   She had seen it torn by the bale-
breakers, blown into the openers, loosened, cleansed, and
dried; taken up by the lappers, pressed into batting, and
passed on to the carding machines, to emerge like a wisp
of white smoke in a sliver and coil automatically in a can.
Once more it was flattened into a lap, given to a comber that
felt out its fibres, removing with superhuman precision those
for the finer fabric too short, thrusting it forth again in another filmy sliver ready for the drawing frames.   Six of these
gossamer ropes were taken up, and again six.   Then came the
slubbers and the roving frames, twisting and winding, the
while maintaining the most delicate of tensions lest the rope
break, running the strands together into a thread constantly
growing stronger and finer, until it was ready for spinning.

Caldwell stood close to her, shouting his explanations in
her ear, while she strained to follow them.   But she was
bewildered and entranced by the marvellous swiftness, accuracy and ease with which each of the complex machines,
fed by human hands, performed its function.   These human
hands were swift, too, as when they thrust the bobbins of
roving on the ring-spinning frames to be twisted into yarn.
She saw a woman, in the space of an instant, mend a broken
thread.   Women and boys were here, doffer boys to lift off
the full bobbins of yarn with one hand and set on the empty

bobbins with the other: while skilled workmen, alert for
the first sign of trouble, followed up and down in its travels
the long frame of the mule-spinner. After the spinning,
the heavy spools of yarn were carried to a beam-warper,
standing alone like a huge spider's web, where hundreds of
threads were stretched symmetrically and wound evenly,
side by side, on a large cylinder, forming the warp of the
fabric to be woven on the loom. First, however, this warp
must be stiffened or "slashed" in starch and tallow, dried
over heated drums, and finally wound around one great beam
from which the multitude of threads are taken up, one by
one, and slipped through the eyes of the loom harnesses by
women who sit all day under the north windows overlooking
the canal — the "drawers-in" of whom Ditmar had spoken.
Then the harnesses are put on the loom, the threads attached to the cylinder on which the cloth is to be wound.
The looms absorbed and fascinated Janet above all else.
It seemed as if she would never tire of watching the rhythmic
rise and fall of the harnesses, — each rapid movement making
a V in the warp, within the angle of which the tiny shuttles
darted to and fro, to and fro, carrying the thread that filled
the cloth with a swiftness so great the eye could scarcely follow it; to be caught on the other side when the angle closed,
and flung back, and back again! And in the elaborate patterns not one, but several harnesses were used, each awaiting its turn for the impulse bidding it rise and fall! . . .
Abruptly, as she gazed, one of the machines halted, a weaver
hurried up, searched the warp for the broken thread, tied it,
and started the loom again.

"That's intelligent of it," said Caldwell, in her ear. But
she could only nod in reply.

The noise in the weaving rooms was deafening, the
heat oppressive. She began to wonder how these men and
women, boys and girls bore the strain all day long. She

had never thought much about them before save to compare vaguely their drudgery with that from which now she had been emancipated; but she began to feel a new respect, a new concern, a new curiosity and interest as she watched them passing from place to place with indifference between the whirling belts, up and down the narrow aisles, flanked on either side by that bewildering, clattering machinery whose polished surfaces continually caught and flung back the light of the electric bulbs on the ceiling. How was it possible to live for hours at a time in this bedlam without losing presence of mind and thrusting hand or body in the wrong place, or becoming deaf? She had never before realized what mill work meant, though she had read of the accidents. But these people — even the children — seemed oblivious to the din and the danger, intent on their tasks, unconscious of the presence of a visitor, save occasionally when she caught a swift glance from a woman or girl — a glance, perhaps, of envy or even of hostility. The dark, foreign faces glowed, and instantly grew dull again, and then she was aware of lurking terrors, despite her exaltation, her sense now of belonging to another world, a world somehow associated with Ditmar. Was it not he who had lifted her farther above all this? Was it not by grace of her association with him she was there, a spectator of the toil beneath? Yet the terror persisted. She, presently, would step out of the noise, the oppressive moist heat of the drawing and spinning rooms, the constant, remorseless menace of whirling wheels and cogs and belts. But they? . . . She drew closer to Caldwell's side.

"I never knew —" she said. "It must be hard to work here."

He smiled at her, reassuringly.

"Oh, they don't mind it," he replied. "It's like a health resort compared to the conditions most of them live in at home. Why, there's plenty of ventilation here, and you've got to have a certain amount of heat and moisture, because when cotton is cold and dry it can't be drawn or spun, and when it's hot and dry the electricity is troublesome. If you think this moisture is bad you ought to see a mill with the old vapour-pot system with the steam shooting out into the room. Look here!" He led Janet to the apparatus in which the pure air is forced through wet cloths, removing the dust, explaining how the ventilation and humidity were regulated automatically, how the temperature of the room was controlled by a thermostat.

"There isn't an agent in the country who's more concerned about the welfare of his operatives than Mr. Ditmar. He's made a study of it, he's spent thousands of dollars, and as soon as these machines became practical he put 'em in. The other day when I was going through the room one of these shuttles flew off, as they sometimes do when the looms are running at high speed. A woman was pretty badly hurt. Ditmar came right down."

"He really cares about them," said Janet. She liked Caldwell's praise of Ditmar, yet she spoke a little doubtfully.

"Of course he cares. But it's common sense to make 'em as comfortable and happy as possible — isn't it? He won't stand for being held up, and he'd be stiff enough if it came to a strike. I don't blame him for that. Do you?"

Janet was wondering how ruthless Ditmar could be if his will were crossed. . . . They had left the room with its noise and heat behind them and were descending the worn, oaken treads of the spiral stairway of a neighbouring tower. Janet shivered a little, and her face seemed almost feverish as she turned to Caldwell and thanked him.

"Oh, it was a pleasure, Miss Bumpus," he declared. "And sometime, when you want to see the Print Works or the Worsted Department, let me know — I'm your man. And — I won't mention it."

She did not answer. As they made their way back to the
office he glanced at her covertly, astonished at the emotional
effect in her their their tour had produced. Though not of an
inflammable temperament, he himself was stirred, and it
was she who, unaccountably, had stirred him : suggested, in
these processes he saw every day, and in which he was
indeed interested, something deeper, more significant and
human than he had guessed, and which he was unable to
define. . . .

4

Janet herself did not know why this intimate view of the
mills, of the people who worked in them had so greatly
moved her. All day she thought of them. And the distant
throb of the machinery she felt when her typewriter was
silent meant something to her now — she could not say
what. When she found herself listening for it, her heart
beat faster. She had lived and worked beside it, and it
had not existed for her, it had had no meaning, the mills
might have been empty. She had, indeed, many, many
times seen these men and women, boys and girls trooping
away from work, she had strolled through the quarters in
which they lived, speculated on the lands from which they
had come; but she had never really thought of them as
human beings, individuals, with problems and joys and sor-
rows and hopes and fears like her own. Some such discovery was borne in upon her. And always an essential
function of this revelation, looming larger than ever in her
consciousness, was Ditmar. It was for Ditmar they toiled,
in Ditmar's hands were their very existences, his was the
stupendous responsibility and power.

As the afternoon wore, desire to see these toilers once more
took possession of her. From the white cupola perched
above the huge mass of the Clarendon Mill across the water

sounded the single stroke of a bell, and suddenly the air was
pulsing with sounds flung back and forth by the walls lining
the river.   Seizing her hat and coat, she ran down the stairs
and through the vestibule and along the track by the canal
to the great gates, which her father was in the act of un-
barring.   She took a stand beside him, by the gatehouse.
Edward showed a mild surprise.

"There ain't anything troubling you — is there, Janet?"
he asked.

She shook her head.

"I wanted to see the hands come out," she said.

Sometimes, as at present, he found Janet's whims unaccountable.

"Well, I should have presumed you'd know what they
look like by this time.   You'd better stay right close to me,
they're a rough lot, with no respect or consideration for
decent folks — these foreigners.   I never could see why the
government lets 'em all come over here."   He put on the
word "foreigners" an emphasis of contempt and indignation,
pathetic because of its peculiar note of futility.   Janet paid
no attention to him.   Her ears were strained to catch the
rumble of feet descending the tower stairs, her eyes to
see the vanguard as it came from the doorway — the first
tricklings of a flood that instantly filled the yard and swept
onward and outward, irresistibly, through the narrow gorge
of the gates.   Impossible to realize this as the force which,
when distributed over the great spaces of the mills, performed
an orderly and useful task! for it was now a turbid and lawless torrent unconscious of its swollen powers, menacing,
breathlessly exciting to behold.   It seemed to Janet indeed
a torrent as she clung to the side of the gatehouse as one
might cling to the steep bank of a mountain brook after a
cloud-burst.   And suddenly she had plunged into it.   The
desire was absurd, perhaps, but not to be denied, — the desire

to mix with it, feel it, be submerged and swept away by it, losing all sense of identity. She heard her father call after her, faintly — the thought crossed her mind that his appeals were always faint, — and then she was being carried along the canal, eastward, the pressure relaxing somewhat when the draining of the side streets began.

She remembered, oddly, the Stanley Street bridge where the many streams met and mingled, streams from the Arundel, the Patuxent, the Arlington and the Clarendon; and, eager to prolong and intensify her sensations, hurried thither, reaching it at last and thrusting her way outward until she had gained the middle, where she stood grasping the rail. The great structure was a-tremble from the assault, its footpaths and its roadway overrun with workers, dodging between trolleys and trucks, — some darting nimbly, dinner pails in hand, along the steel girders. Doffer boys romped and whistled, young girls in jaunty, Faber Street clothes and flowered hats, linked to one another for protection, chewed gum and joked, but for the most part these workers were silent, the apathy of their faces making a strange contrast with the hurry, hurry of their feet and set intentness of their bodies as they sped homeward to the tenements. And the clothes of these were drab, save when the occasional colour of a hooded peasant's shawl, like the slightly faded tints of an old master, lit up a group of women. Here, going home to their children, were Italian mothers bred through centuries to endurance and patience; sallow Jewesses, gaunt, bearded Jews with shadowy, half-closed eyes and wrinkled brows, broad-faced Lithuanians, flat-headed Russians; swarthy Italian men and pale, blond Germans mingled with muddy Syrians and nondescript Canadians. And suddenly the bridge was empty, the army vanished as swiftly as it came!

Janet turned. Through the haze of smoke she saw the sun

drop like a ball of fire cooled to redness, whose course is spent. The delicate lines of the upper bridge were drawn in sepia against crimson-gilt; for an instant the cupola of the Clarendon became jasper, and far, far above floated in the azure a cloud of pink jeweller's cotton.   Even as she strove to fix these colours in her mind they vanished, the western sky faded to magenta, to purple-mauve; the corridor of the river darkened, on either side pale lights sparkled from the windows of the mills, while down the deepened blue of the waters came floating iridescent suds from the washing of the wools.   It was given to her to know that which an artist of living memory has called the incommunicable thrill of things. . . .

CHAPTER VIII

1

THE after-effects of this experience of Janet's were not what ordinarily are called "spiritual," though we may some day arrive at a saner meaning of the term, include within it the impulses and needs of the entire organism. It left her with a renewed sense of energy and restlessness, brought her nearer to high discoveries of mysterious joys which a voice out of the past called upon her to forego, — a voice somehow identified with her father! It was faint, ineffectual. In obeying it, would she not lose all life had to give? When she came in to supper her father was concerned about her because, instead of walking home with him she had left him without explanation to plunge into the crowd of workers. Her evident state of excitement had worried him, her caprice was beyond his comprehension. And how could she explain the motives that led to it? She was sure he had never felt like that; and as she evaded his questions the something within her demanding life and expression grew stronger and more rebellious, more contemptuous of the fear-precepts congenial to a nature timorous and less vitalized.

After supper, unable to sit still, she went out, and, filled with the spirit of adventure, hurried toward Faber Street, which was already thronging with people. It was bright here and gay, the shops glittered, and she wandered from window to window until she found herself staring at a suit of blue cloth hung on a form, beneath which was a card that read, "Marked down to $20." And suddenly the suggestion flashed into her mind, why shouldn't she buy it? She had the money, she needed a new suit for the winter, the one she possessed was getting shabby . . . but behind the excuse of necessity was the real reason triumphantly proclaiming itself — she would look pretty in it, she would be transformed, she would be buying a new character to which she would have to live up. The old Janet would be cast off with the old raiment; the new suit would announce to herself and to the world a Janet in whom were released all those longings hitherto disguised and suppressed, and now become insupportable! This was what the purchase meant, a change of existence as complete as that between the moth and the butterfly; and the realization of this fact, of the audacity she was resolved to commit made her hot as she gazed at the suit. It was modest enough, yet it had a certain distinction of cut, it *looked* expensive: twenty dollars was not cheap, to be sure, but as the placard announced, it had the air of being much more costly — even more costly than thirty dollars, which seemed fabulous. Though she strove to remain outwardly calm, her heart beat rapidly as she entered the store and asked for the costume, and was somewhat reassured by the comportment of the saleswoman, who did not appear to think the request preposterous, to regard her as a spendthrift and a profligate. She took down the suit from the form and led Janet to a cabinet in the back of the shop, where it was tried on.

"It's worth every bit of thirty dollars," she heard the woman say, "but we've had it here for some time, and it's no use for our trade. You can't sell anything like that in Hampton, there's no taste here, it's too good, it ain't showy enough. My, it fits you like it was made for you, and it's just your style — and you can see it wants a *lady* to wear

it. Your old suit is too tight — I guess you've filled out
some since you bought it."

She turned Janet around and around, patting the skirt
here and there, and then stood off a little way, with clasped
hands, her expression almost rapturous. Janet's breath
came fast as she gazed into the mirror and buttoned up the
coat. Was the woman's admiration cleverly feigned? this
image she beheld an illusion? or did she really look different,
distinguished? and if not beautiful — alluring? She had had
a momentary apprehension, almost sickening, that she would
be too conspicuous, but the saleswoman had anticipated
that objection with the magical word "lady."

"I'll take it," she announced.

"Well, you couldn't have done better if you'd gone to
Boston," declared the woman. "It's one chance in a
thousand. Will you wear it?"

"Yes," said Janet faintly. . . . "Just put my old suit in
a box, and I'll call for it in an hour."

The woman's sympathetic smile followed her as she left
the shop. She had an instant of hesitation, of an almost
panicky desire to go back and repair her folly, ere it was
too late. Why had she taken her money with her that
evening, if not with some deliberate though undefined purpose? But she was ashamed to face the saleswoman again,
and her elation was not to be repressed — an elation opti-
cally presented by a huge electric sign on the farther side of
the street that flashed through all the colours of the spectrum, surrounded by running fire like the running fire in
her soul. Deliciously self-conscious, her gaze fixed ahead,
she pressed through the Wednesday night crowds, young
mill men and women in their best clothes, housewives and
fathers of families with children and bundles. In front of
the *Banner* office a group blocked the pavement staring up
at the news bulletin, which she paused to read. "*Five Mil-*

lionaire Directors Indicted in New York," "State Treasurer Accused of Graft," "Murdock Fortune Contested by Heirs." The phrases seemed meaningless, and she hurried on again. . . . She *was* being noticed! A man looked at her, twice, the first glance accidental, the second arresting, appealing, subtly flattering, agitating — she was sure he had turned and was following her. She hastened her steps. It was wicked, what she was doing, but she gloried in it; and even the sight, in burning red letters, of Gruber's Café failed to bring on a revulsion by its association with her sister Lise. The fact that Lise had got drunk there meant nothing to her now. She gazed curiously at the illuminated, orange-coloured panes separated by curving leads, at the design of a harp in green, at the sign "Ladies' Entrance"; listened eagerly to the sounds of voices and laughter that came from within. She looked cautiously over her shoulder, a shadow appeared, she heard a voice, low, insinuating. . . .

Four blocks farther down she stopped. The man was no longer following her. She had been almost self-convinced of an intention to go to Eda's — not quite. Of late her conscience had reproached her about Eda, Janet had neglected her. She told herself she was afraid of Eda's uncanny and somewhat nauseating flair for romance; and to show Eda the new suit, though she would relish her friend's praise, would be the equivalent of announcing an affair of the heart which she, Janet, would have indignantly to deny. She was not going to Eda's. She knew now where she was going. A prepared but hitherto undisclosed decree of fate had bade her put money in her bag that evening, directed her to the shop to buy the dress, and would presently impel her to go to West Street — nay, was even now so impelling her. Ahead of her were the lights of the Chippering Mill, in her ears was the rhythmic sound of the looms working of nights on the Bradlaugh order. She reached the canal. The white arc above the end of the bridge cast sharp, black shadows of the branches of the trees on the granite, the thousand windows of the mill shone yellow, reflected in the black water. Twice she started to go, twice she paused, held by the presage of a coming event, — a presage that robbed her of complete surprise when she heard footsteps on the bridge, saw the figure of a man halting at the crown of the arch to look back at the building he had left, his shoulders squared, his hand firmly clasping the rail. Her heart was throbbing with the looms, and yet she stood motionless, until he turned and came rapidly down the slope of the arch and stopped in front of her. Under the arc lamp it was almost as bright as day.

"Miss Bumpus!" he exclaimed.

"Mr. Ditmar!" she said.

"Were you — were you coming to the office?"

"I was just out walking," she told him. "I thought you were in Boston."

"I came home," he informed her, somewhat superfluously, his eyes never leaving her, wandering hungrily from her face to her new suit, and back again to her face. "I got here on the seven o'clock train, I wanted to see about those new slubbers."

"They finished setting them up this afternoon," she said.

"How did you know?"

"I asked Mr. Orcutt about it — I thought you might telephone."

"You're a wonder," was his comment. "Well, we've got a running start on that order," and he threw a glance over his shoulder at the mill. "Everything going full speed ahead. When we put it through I guess I'll have to give you some of the credit."

"Oh, I haven't done anything," she protested.

"More than you think. You've taken so much off my

shoulders I couldn't get along without you." His voice vibrated, reminding her of the voices of those who made sentimental recitations for the graphophone. It sounded absurd, yet it did not repel her: something within her responded to it. "Which way were you going?" he inquired.

"Home," she said.

"Where do you live?"

"In Fillmore Street." And she added with a touch of defiance: "It's a little street, three blocks above Hawthorne, off East Street."

"Oh yes," he said vaguely, as though he had not understood. "I'll come with you as far as the bridge — along the canal. I've got so much to say to you."

"Can't you say it to-morrow?"

"No, I can't, there are so many people in the office — so many interruptions, I mean. And then, you never give me a chance."

She stood hesitating, a struggle going on within her. He had proposed the route along the canal because nobody would be likely to recognize them, and her pride resented this. On the other hand, there was the sweet allurement of the adventure she craved, which indeed she had come out to seek and by a strange fatality found — since he had appeared on the bridge almost as soon as she reached it. The sense of fate was strong upon her. Curiosity urged her, and, thanks to the eulogy she had read of him that day, to the added impression of his power conveyed by the trip through the mills, Ditmar loomed larger than ever in her consciousness.

"What do you want to say?" she asked.

"Oh, lots of things."

She felt his hand slipping under her arm, his fingers pressing gently but firmly into her flesh, and the experience of being impelled by a power stronger than herself, a masculine power, was delicious. Her arm seemed to burn where he touched her.

"Have I done something to offend you?" she heard him say. "Or is it because you don't like me?"

"I'm not sure whether I like you or not," she told him. "I don't like seeing you — this way. And why should you want to know me and see me outside of the office? I'm only your stenographer."

"Because you're you — because you're different from any woman I ever met. You don't understand what you are — you don't see yourself."

"I made up my mind last night I wouldn't stay in your office any longer," she informed him.

"For God's sake, why?" he exclaimed. "I've been afraid of that. Don't go — I don't know what I'd do. I'll be careful — I won't get you talked about."

"Talked about!" She tore herself away from him. "Why should you get me talked about?" she cried.

He was frightened. "No, no," he stammered, "I didn't mean — "

"What did you mean?"

"Well — as you say, you're my stenographer, but that's no reason why we shouldn't be friends. I only meant — I wouldn't do anything to make our friendship the subject of gossip."

Suddenly she began to find a certain amusement in his confusion and penitence, she achieved a pleasurable sense of advantage, of power over him.

"Why should you want me? I don't know anything, I've never had any advantages — and you have so much. I read an article in the newspaper about you today — Mr. Caldwell gave it to me —"

"Did you like it?" he interrupted, naïvely.

L

"Well, in some places it was rather funny."

"Funny? How?"

"Oh, I don't know." She had been quick to grasp in it the journalistic lack of restraint hinted at by Caldwell. "I liked it, but I thought it praised you too much, it didn't criticize you enough."

He laughed. In spite of his discomfort, he found her candour refreshing. From the women to whom he had hitherto made love he had never got anything but flattery.

"I want you to criticize me," he said.

But she went on relentlessly : —

"When I read in that article how successful you were, and how you'd got everything you'd started out to get, and how some day you might be treasurer and president of the Chippering Mill, well —" Despairing of giving adequate expression to her meaning, she added, "I didn't see how we could be friends."

"You wanted me for a friend?" he interrupted eagerly.

"I couldn't help knowing you wanted me — you've shown it so plainly. But I didn't see how it could be. You asked me where I lived — in a little flat that's no better than a tenement. I suppose you would call it a tenement. It's dark and ugly, it only has four rooms, and it smells of cooking. You couldn't come there — don't you see how impossible it is? And you wouldn't care to be talked about yourself, either," she added vehemently.

This defiant sincerity took him aback. He groped for words.

"Listen!" he urged. "I don't want to do anything you wouldn't like, and honestly I don't know what I'd do if you left me. I've come to depend on you. And you may not believe it, but when I got that Bradlaugh order I thought of you, I said to myself 'She'll be pleased, she'll help me to put it over.'"

She thrilled at this, she even suffered him, for some reason unknown to herself, to take her arm again.

"How could I help you?"

"Oh, in a thousand ways — you ought to know, you do a good deal of thinking for me, and you can help me by just being there. I can't explain it, but I feel somehow that things will go right. I've come to depend on you."

He was a little surprised to find himself saying these things he had not intended to say, and the lighter touch he had always possessed in dealing with the other sex, making him the envied of his friends, had apparently abandoned him. He was appalled at the possibility of losing her.

"I've never met a woman like you," he went on, as she remained silent. "You're different — I don't know what it is about you, but you are." His voice was low, caressing, his head was bent down to her, his shoulder pressed against her shoulder. "I've never had a woman friend before, I've never wanted one until now."

She wondered about his wife.

"You've got brains — I've never met a woman with brains."

"Oh, is that why?" she exclaimed.

"You're beautiful," he whispered. "It's queer, but I didn't know it at first. You're more beautiful to-night than I've ever seen you."

They had come almost to Warren Street. Suddenly realizing that they were standing in the light, that people were passing to and fro over the end of the bridge, she drew away from him once more, this time more gently.

"Let's walk back a little way," he proposed.

"I must go home — it's late."

"It's only nine o'clock."

"I have an errand to do, and they'll expect me. Good night."

"Just one more turn!" he pleaded.

But she shook her head, backing away from him.

"You'll see me to-morrow," she told him. She didn't know why she said that. She hurried along Warren Street without once looking over her shoulder; her feet seemed scarcely to touch the ground, the sound of music was in her ears, the lights sparkled. She had had an adventure, at last, an adventure that magically had transformed her life! She was beautiful! No one had ever told her that before. And he had said that he needed her. She smiled as, with an access of tenderness, in spite of his experience and power she suddenly felt years older than Ditmar. She could help him! . . .

She was breathless when she reached the shop in Faber Street.

"I hope I haven't kept you waiting," she said.

"Oh no, we don't close until ten," answered the saleswoman. She was seated quietly sewing under the lamp.

"I wonder whether you'd mind if I put on my old suit again, and carried this?" Janet asked.

The expression of sympathy and understanding in the woman's eyes, as she rose, brought the blood swiftly to Janet's face. She felt that her secret had been guessed. The change effected, Janet went homeward swiftly, to encounter, on the corner of Faber Street, her sister Lise, whose attention was immediately attracted by the bundle.

"What have you got there, angel face?" she demanded.

"A new suit," said Janet.

"You don't tell me — where'd you get it? at the *Paris*?"

"No, at Dowling's."

"Say, I'll bet it was that plain blue thing marked down to twenty!"

"Well, what if it was?"

Lise, when surprised or scornful, had a peculiarly irritating way of whistling through her teeth.

"Twenty bucks! Gee, you'll be getting your clothes in Boston next. Well, as sure as I live when I went by that window the other day when they first knocked it down I said to Sadie, 'those are the rags Janet would buy if she had the ready.' Have you got another raise out of Ditmar?"

"If I have, it isn't any business of yours," Janet retorted. "I've got a right to do as I please with my own money."

"Oh sure," said Lise, and added darkly: "I guess Ditmar likes to see you look well."

After this Janet refused obstinately to speak to Lise, to answer, when they reached home, her pleadings and complaints to their mother that Janet had bought a new suit and refused to exhibit it. And finally, when they had got to bed, Janet lay long awake in passionate revolt against this new expression of the sordidness and lack of privacy in which she was forced to live, made the more intolerable by the close, sultry darkness of the room and the snoring of Lise.

2

In the morning, however, after a groping period of semi-consciousness during the ringing of the bells, the siren startled her into awareness and alertness. It had not wholly lost its note of terror, but the note had somehow become exhilarating, an invitation to adventure and to life; and Lise's sarcastic comments as to the probable reasons why she did not put on the new suit had lost their power of exasperation. Janet compromised, wearing a blouse of china silk hitherto reserved for "best." The day was bright, and she went rapidly toward the mill, glorying in the sunshine and the autumn sharpness of the air; and her thoughts were not so much of Ditmar as of something beyond him, of which he was the medium. She was going, not to meet him, but to meet *that*. When she reached the office she felt weak, her fingers trembled as she took off her hat and jacket and began to sort out the mail. And she had to calm herself with the assurance that her relationship with Ditmar had undergone no change. She had merely met him by the canal, and he had talked to her. That was all. He had, of course, taken her arm : it tingled when she remembered it. But when he suddenly entered the room her heart gave a bound. He closed the door, he took off his hat, and stood gazing at her — while she continued arranging letters. Presently she was forced to glance at him. His bearing, his look, his confident smile all proclaimed that he, at least, believed things to be changed. He glowed with health and vigour, with an aggressiveness from which she shrank, yet found delicious.

"How are you this morning?" he said at last — *this* morning as distinguished from all other mornings.

"I'm well, as usual," she answered. She herself was sometimes surprised by her ability to remain outwardly calm.

"Why did you run away from me last night?"

"I didn't run away, I had to go home," she said, still arranging the letters.

"We could have had a little walk. I don't believe you had to go home at all. You just wanted an excuse to get away from me."

"I didn't need an excuse," she told him. He moved toward her, but she took a paper from the desk and carried it to a file across the room.

"I thought we were going to be friends," he said.

"Being friends doesn't mean being foolish," she retorted. "And Mr. Orcutt's waiting to see you."

"Let him wait."

He sat down at his desk, but his blood was warm, and he read the typewritten words of the topmost letter of the pile without so much as grasping the meaning of them.   From time to time he glanced up at Janet as she flitted about the room.   By George, she was more desirable than he had ever dared to imagine!   He felt temporarily balked, but hopeful.   On his way to the mill he had dwelt with Epicurean indulgence on this sight of her, and he had not been disappointed.   He had also thought that he might venture upon more than the mere feasting of his eyes, yet found an inspiring alleviation in the fact that she by no means absolutely repulsed him.   Her attitude toward him had undergone a subtle transformation.   There could be no doubt of that.   She was almost coquettish.   His eyes lingered.   The china silk blouse was slightly open at the neck, suggesting the fullness of her throat; it clung to the outline of her shoulders.   Overcome by an impulse he could not control, he got up and went toward her, but she avoided him.

"I'll tell Mr. Orcutt you've come," she said, rather breathlessly, as she reached the door and opened it.   Ditmar halted in his steps at the sight of the tall, spectacled figure of the superintendent on the threshold.

Orcutt hesitated, looking from one to the other.

"I've been waiting for you," he said, after a moment, "the rest of that lot didn't come in this morning.   I've telephoned to the freight agent."

Ditmar stared at him uncomprehendingly.   Orcutt repeated the information.

"Oh well, keep after him, get him to trace them."

"I'm doing that," replied the conscientious Orcutt.

"How's everything else going?" Ditmar demanded, with unlooked-for geniality.   "You mustn't take things too hard, Orcutt, don't wear yourself out."

Mr. Orcutt was relieved.   He had expected an outburst of the exasperation that lately had characterized his superior. They began to chat.   Janet had escaped.

"Miss Bumpus told me you wanted to see me. I was just going to ring you up," Ditmar informed him.

"She's a clever young woman, seems to take such an interest in things," Orcutt observed. "And she's always on the job. Only yesterday I saw her going through the mill with young Caldwell."

Ditmar dropped the paper-weight he held.

"Oh, she went through, did she?"

After Orcutt departed he sat for awhile whistling a tune from a popular musical play, keeping time by drumming with his fingers on the desk.

3

That Mr. Semple, the mill treasurer, came down from Boston that morning to confer with Ditmar was for Janet in the nature of a reprieve. She sat by her window, and as her fingers flew over the typewriter keys she was swept by surges of heat in which ecstasy and shame and terror were strangely commingled. A voice within her said, "This can't go on, this can't go on! It's too terrible! Everyone in the office will notice it — there will be a scandal. I ought to go away while there is yet time — to-day." Though the instinct of flight was strong within her, she was filled with rebellion at the thought of leaving when Adventure was flooding her drab world with light, even as the mill across the waters was transfigured by the heavy golden wash of the autumn sun. She had made at length the discovery that Adventure had to do with Man, was inconceivable without him.

Racked by these conflicting impulses of self-preservation on the one hand and what seemed self-realization on the other, she started when, toward the middle of the afternoon, she heard Ditmar's voice summoning her to take his letters;

and went palpitating, leaving the door open behind her, seating herself on the far side of the desk, her head bent over her book. Her neck, where her hair grew in wisps behind her ear, seemed to burn : Ditmar's glance was focussed there. Her hands were cold as she wrote. . . . Then, like a deliverer, she saw young Caldwell coming in from the outer office, holding a card in his hand which he gave to Ditmar, who sat staring at it.

"Siddons?" he said. "Who's Siddons?"

Janet, who had risen, spoke up.

"Why, he's been making the Hampton 'survey.' You wrote him you'd see him — don't you remember, Mr. Ditmar?"

"Don't go!" exclaimed Ditmar. "You can't tell what those confounded reformers will accuse you of if you don't have a witness."

Janet sat down again. The sharpness of Ditmar's tone was an exhilarating reminder of the fact that, in dealing with strangers, he had come more or less to rely on her instinctive judgment; while the implied appeal of his manner on such occasions emphasized the pleasurable sense of his dependence, of her own usefulness. Besides, she had been curious about the 'survey' at the time it was first mentioned, she wished to hear Ditmar's views concerning it. Mr. Siddons proved to be a small and sallow young man with a pointed nose and bright, bulbous brown eyes like a chipmunk's. Indeed, he reminded one of a chipmunk. As he whisked himself in and seized Ditmar's hand he gave a confused impression of polite self-effacement as well as of dignity and self-assertion; he had the air of one who expects opposition, and though by no means desiring it, is prepared to deal with it. Janet smiled. She had a sudden impulse to drop the heavy book that lay on the corner of the desk to see if he would jump.

"How do you do, Mr. Ditmar?" he said. "I've been hoping to have this pleasure."

"My secretary, Miss Bumpus," said Ditmar.

Mr. Siddons quivered and bowed. Ditmar, sinking ponderously into his chair, seemed suddenly, ironically amused, grinning at Janet as he opened a drawer of his desk and offered the visitor a cigar.

"Thanks, I don't smoke," said Mr. Siddons.

Ditmar lit one for himself.

"Now, what can I do for you?" he asked.

"Well, as I wrote you in my letter, I was engaged to make as thorough an examination as possible of the living conditions and housing of the operatives in the city of Hampton. I'm sure you'd be interested in hearing something of the situation we found."

"I suppose you've been through our mills," said Ditmar.

"No, the fact is —"

"You ought to go through. I think it might interest you," Ditmar put a slight emphasis on the pronoun. "We rather pride ourselves on making things comfortable and healthy for our people."

"I've no doubt of it — in fact, I've been so informed. It's because of your concern for the welfare of your workers in the mills that I ventured to come and talk to you of how most of them live when they're at home," replied Siddons, as Janet thought, rather neatly. "Perhaps, though living in Hampton, you don't quite realize what the conditions are. I know a man who has lived in Boston ten years and who hasn't ever seen the Bunker Hill monument."

"The Bunker Hill monument's a public affair," retorted Ditmar, "anybody can go there who has enough curiosity and interest. But I don't see how you can expect me to follow these people home and make them clean up their garbage and wash their babies. I shouldn't want anybody to interfere with my private affairs."

"But when you get to a point where private affairs become a public menace?" Siddons objected. "Mr. Ditmar, I've seen block after block of tenements ready to crumble. There are no provisions for foundations, thickness of walls, size of timbers and columns, and if these houses had been deliberately erected to make a bonfire they couldn't have answered the purpose better. If it were not for the danger to life and the pity of making thousands of families homeless, a conflagration would be a blessing, although I believe the entire north or south side of the city would go under certain conditions. The best thing you could do would be to burn whole rows of these tenements, they are ideal breeding grounds for disease. In the older sections of the city you've got hundreds of rear houses here, houses moved back on the lots, in some extreme cases with only four-foot courts littered with refuse, — houses without light, without ventilation, and many of the rooms where these people are cooking and eating and sleeping are so damp and foul they're not fit to put dogs in. You've got some blocks with a density of over five hundred to the acre, and your average density is considerably over a hundred."

"Are things any worse than in any other manufacturing city?" asked Ditmar.

"That isn't the point," said Siddons. "The point is that they're bad, they're dangerous, they're inhuman. If you could go into these tenements as I have done and see the way some of these people live, it would make you sick — the Poles and Lithuanians and Italians especially. You wouldn't treat cattle that way. In some households of five rooms, including the kitchen, I found as many as fourteen, fifteen, and once seventeen people living. You've got an alarming infant death-rate."

"Isn't it because these people want to live that way?"
Ditmar inquired. "They actually like it, they wouldn't be
happy in anything but a pig-sty — they had 'em in Europe.
And what do you expect us to do? Buy land and build
flats for them? Inside of a month they'd have all the wood-
work stripped off for kindling, the drainage stopped up, the
bathtubs filled with ashes. I know, because it's been tried."

Tilted back in his chair, he blew a cloud of smoke toward
the ceiling, and his eyes sought Janet's. She avoided them,
resenting a little the assumption of approval she read in
them. Her mind, sensitive to new ideas, had been keenly
stimulated as she listened to Siddons, who began patiently
to dwell once more on the ill effect of the conditions he had
discovered on the welfare of the entire community. She
had never thought of this. She was surprised that Ditmar
should seem to belittle it. Siddons was a new type in her
experience. She could understand and to a certain extent
maliciously enjoy Ditmar's growing exasperation with him;
he had a formal, precise manner of talking, as though he
spent most of his time presenting cases in committees: and
in warding off Ditmar's objections he was forever indulging
in such maddening phrases as, "Before we come to that,
let me say a word just here." Ditmar hated words. His
outbursts, his efforts to stop the flow of them were not unlike
the futile charges of a large and powerful animal harassed
by a smaller and more agile one. With nimble politeness,
with an exasperating air of deference to Ditmar's opinions,
Mr. Siddons gave ground, only to return to the charge;
yet, despite a manner and method which, when contrasted
to Ditmar's, verged on the ludicrous, Mr. Siddons had a
force and fire of his own, nervous, almost fanatical: when
he dwelt on the misery he had seen, and his voice trembled
from the intensity of his feeling, Janet began to be moved.
It was odd, considering the struggle for existence of her

own family, that these foreigners had remained outside the range of her sympathy.

"I guess you'll find," Ditmar had interrupted peremptorily, "I guess you'll find, if you look up the savings banks statistics, these people have got millions tucked away. And they send a lot of it to the other side, they go back themselves, and though they live like cattle, they manage to buy land. Ask the real estate men. Why, I could show you a dozen who worked in the mills a few years ago and are capitalists to-day."

"I don't doubt it, Mr. Ditmar," Siddons gracefully conceded. "But what does it prove? Merely the cruelty of an economic system based on ruthless competition. The great majority who are unable to survive the test pay the price. And the community also pays the price, the state and nation pay it. And we have this misery on our consciences. I've no doubt you could show me some who have grown rich, but if you would let me I could take you to families in desperate want, living in rooms too dark to read in at midday in clear weather, where the husband doesn't get more than seven dollars a week when the mills are running full time, where the woman has to look out for the children and work for the lodgers, and even with lodgers they get into debt, and the woman has to go into the mills to earn money for winter clothing. I've seen enough instances of this kind to offset the savings bank argument. And even then, when you have a family where the wife and older children work, where the babies are put out to board, where there are three and four lodgers in a room, why do you suppose they live that way? Isn't it in the hope of freeing themselves ultimately from these very conditions? And aren't these conditions a disgrace to Hampton and America?"

"Well, what am I to do about it?" Ditmar demanded.

"I see that these operatives have comfortable and health-ful surroundings in the mill, I've spent money to put in the latest appliances. That's more than a good many mills I could mention attempt."

"You are a person of influence, Mr. Ditmar, you have more influence than any man in Hampton. You can bring pressure to bear on the city council to enforce and improve the building ordinances, you can organize a campaign of public opinion against certain property owners."

"Yes," retorted Ditmar, "and what then? You raise the rents, and you won't get anybody to live in the houses. They'll move out to settlements like Glendale full of dirt and vermin and disease and live as they're accustomed to. What you reformers are actually driving at is that we should raise wages — isn't it? If we raised wages they'd live like rats anyway. I give you credit for sincerity, Mr. Siddons, but I don't want you to think I'm not as much interested in the welfare of these people as you and the men behind you. The trouble is, you only see one side of this question. When you're in my position, you're up against hard facts. We can't pay a slubber or a drawing tender any more than he's worth, whether he has a wife or children in the mills or whether he hasn't. We're in competition with other mills, we're in competition with the South. We can't regulate the cost of living. We do our best to make things right in the mills, and that's all we can do. We can't afford to be sentimental about life. Competition's got to be the rule, the world's made that way. Some are efficient and some aren't. Good God, any man who's had anything to do with hiring labour and running a plant has that drummed into him hard. You talk about ordinances, laws — there are enough laws and ordinances in this city and in this state right now. If we have any more the mills will have to shut down, and these people will starve — all of 'em." Ditmar's chair came down on its four legs, and he flung his cigar away. "Send me a copy of your survey when it's published. I'll look it over."

"Well, what do you think of the nerve of a man like that?" Ditmar exploded, when Mr. Siddons had bowed himself out. "Comes in here to advise me that it's my business to look out for the whole city of Hampton. I'd like to see him up against this low-class European labour — trying to run a mill with them. They're here one day and there the next, they don't know what loyalty is. You've got to drive 'em — if you give 'em an inch they'll jump at your throat, dynamite your property. Why, there's nothing I wouldn't do for them if I could depend on them, I'd *build* 'em houses, I'd have automobiles to take 'em home. As it is, I do my best, though they don't deserve it, — in slack seasons I run half time when I oughtn't to be running at all."

His tone betrayed an effort of self-justification, and his irritation had been increased by the suspicion in Janet of a certain lack of the sympathy on which he had counted. She sat silent, gazing searchingly at his face.

"What's the matter?" he demanded. "You don't mean to say you agree with that kind of talk?"

"I was wondering —" she began.

"What?"

"If you were — if you could really understand those who are driven to work in order to keep alive?"

"Understand them! Why not?" he asked.

"Because — because you're on top, you've always been successful, you're pretty much your own master — and that makes it different. I'm not blaming you — in your place I'd be the same, I'm sure. But this man, Siddons, made me think. I've lived like that, you see, I know what it is, in a way."

"Not like these foreigners!" he protested.

"Oh, almost as bad," she cried with vehemence, and Ditmar, stopped suddenly in his pacing as by a physical force, looked at her with the startled air of the male who has inadvertently touched off one of the many hidden springs in the feminine emotional mechanism. "How do you know what it is to live in a squalid, ugly street, in dark little rooms that smell of cooking, and not be able to have any of the finer, beautiful things in life? Unless you'd wanted these things as I've wanted them, you couldn't know. Oh, I can understand what it would feel like to strike, to wish to dynamite men like you!"

"You can!" he exclaimed in amazement. "You!"

"Yes, me. You don't understand these people, you couldn't feel sorry for them any more than you could feel sorry for me. You want them to run your mills for you, you don't want to know how they feel or how they live, and you just want me — for your pleasure."

He was indeed momentarily taken aback by this taunt, which no woman in his experience had had the wit and spirit to fling at him, but he was not the type of man to be shocked by it. On the contrary, it swept away his irritation, and as a revelation of her inner moltenness stirred him to a fever heat as he approached and stood over her.

"You little — panther!" he whispered. "You want beautiful things, do you? Well, I'll give 'em to you. I'll take care of you."

"Do you think I want them from you?" she retorted, almost in tears. "Do you think I want anybody to take care of me? That shows how little you know me. I want to be independent, to do my work and pay for what I get."

Janet herself was far from comprehending the complexity of her feelings. Ditmar had not apologized or feigned an altruism for which she would indeed have despised him. The ruthlessness of his laugh — the laugh of the red-blooded man who makes laws that he himself may be lawless — shook her with a wild appeal. "What do I care about any others — I want you!" such was its message. And against this paradoxical wish to be conquered, intensified by the magnetic field of his passion, battled her self-assertion, her pride, her innate desire to be free, to escape now from a domination the thought of which filled her with terror. She felt his cheek brushing against her hair, his fingers straying along her arm; for the moment she was hideously yet deliciously powerless. Then the emotion of terror conquered — terror of the unknown — and she sprang away, dropping her note-book and running to the window, where she stood swaying.

"Janet, you're killing me," she heard him say. "For God's sake, why can't you trust me?"

She did not answer, but gazed out at the primrose lights beginning to twinkle fantastically in the distant mills. Presently she turned. Ditmar was in his chair. She crossed the room to the electric switch, turning on the flood of light, picked up her note-book and sat down again.

"Don't you intend to answer your letters?" she asked.

He reached out gropingly toward the pile of his correspondence, seized the topmost letter, and began to dictate, savagely. She experienced a certain exultation, a renewed and pleasurable sense of power as she took down his words.

M

CHAPTER IX

1

AT certain moments during the days that followed the degree of tension her relationship with Ditmar had achieved tested the limits of Janet's ingenuity and powers of resistance. Yet the sense of mastery at being able to hold such a man in leash was by no means unpleasurable to a young woman of her vitality and spirit. There was always the excitement that the leash might break — and then what? Here was a situation, she knew instinctively, that could not last, one fraught with all sorts of possibilities, intoxicating or abhorrent to contemplate; and for that very reason fascinating. When she was away from Ditmar and tried to think about it she fell into an abject perplexity, so full was it of anomalies and contradictions, of conflicting impulses; so far beyond her knowledge and experience. For Janet had been born in an age which is rapidly discarding blanket morality and taboos, which has as yet to achieve the morality of scientific knowledge, of the individual instance. Tradition, convention, the awful examples portrayed for gain in the movies, even her mother's pessimistic attitude in regard to the freedom with which the sexes mingle to-day were powerless to influence her. The thought, however, that she might fundamentally resemble her sister Lise, despite a fancied superiority, did occasionally shake her and bring about a revulsion against Ditmar. Janet's problem was in truth, though she failed so to specialize it, the supreme problem of our time: what is the path to self-realization? how achieve emancipation from the common-place?

Was she in love with Ditmar? The question was dis-tasteful, she avoided it, for enough of the tatters of orthodox Christianity clung to her to cause her to feel shame when she contemplated the feelings he aroused in her. It was when she asked herself what his intentions were that her resentment burned, pride and a sense of her own value convinced her that he had deeply insulted her in not offer-ing marriage. Plainly, he did not intend to offer marriage; on the other hand, if he had done so, a profound, self-respect-ing and moral instinct in her would, in her present mood, have led her to refuse. She felt a fine scorn for the woman who, under the circumstances, would insist upon a bond and all a man's worldly goods in return for that which it was her privilege to give freely; while the notion of servility, of economic dependence — though she did not so phrase it — repelled her far more than the possibility of social ruin. This she did not contemplate at all; her impulse to leave Hampton and Ditmar had nothing to do with that. . . .

Away from Ditmar, this war of inclinations possessed her waking mind, invaded her dreams. When she likened herself to the other exploited beings he drove to run his mills and fill his orders, — of whom Mr. Siddons had spoken — her resolution to leave Hampton gained such definite ascendancy that her departure seemed only a matter of hours. In this perspective Ditmar appeared so ruthless, his purpose to use her and fling her away so palpable, that she despised herself for having hesitated. A longing for retaliation consumed her; she wished to hurt him before she left. At such times, however, unforeseen events invariably intruded to complicate her feelings and alter her plans. One evening at supper, for instance, when she seemed at last to have achieved the comparative peace of mind that follows a decision after struggle, she gradually became aware of an outburst from Hannah concerning the stove, the condition of which for many months had been a menace to the welfare of the family. Edward, it appeared, had remarked mildly on the absence of beans.

"Beans!" Hannah cried. "You're lucky to have any supper at all. I just wish I could get you to take a look at that oven — there's a hole you can put your hand through, if you've a mind to. I've done my best, I've made out to patch it from time to time, and to-day I had Mr. Tiernan in. He says it's a miracle I've been able to bake anything. A new one'll cost thirty dollars, and I don't know where the money's coming from to buy it. And the fire-box is most worn through."

"Well, mother, we'll see what we can do," said Edward.

"You're always seeing what you can do, but I notice you never do anything," retorted Hannah; and Edward had the wisdom not to reply. Beside his place lay a lengthy, close-written letter, and from time to time, as he ate his canned pears, his hand turned over one of its many sheets.

"It's from Eben Wheeler, says he's been considerably troubled with asthma," he observed presently. "His mother was a Bumpus, a daughter of Caleb — descended from Robert, who went from Dolton to Tewksbury in 1816, and fought in the war of 1812. I've told you about him. This Caleb was born in '53, and he's living now with his daughter's family in Detroit. . . . Son-in-law's named Nott, doing well with a construction company. Now I never could find out before what became of Robert's descendants. He married Sarah Styles" (reading painfully) "'and they had issue, John, Robert, Anne, Susan, Eliphalet. John went to Middlebury, Vermont, and married —'"

Hannah, gathering up the plates, clattered them together noisily.

"A lot of good it does us to have all that information about Eben Wheeler's asthma!" she complained. "It'll buy us a new stove, I guess. Him and his old Bumpus papers! If the house burned down over our heads that's all he'd think of."

As she passed to and fro from the dining-room to the kitchen Hannah's lamentations continued, grew more and more querulous. Accustomed as Janet was to these frequent arraignments of her father's inefficiency, it was gradually borne in upon her now — despite a preoccupation with her own fate — that the affair thus plaintively voiced by her mother was in effect a family crisis of the first magnitude. She was stirred anew to anger and revolt against a life so precarious and sordid as to be threatened in its continuity by the absurd failure of a stove, when, glancing at her sister, she felt a sharp pang of self-conviction, of self-disgust. Was she, also, like that, indifferent and self-absorbed? Lise, in her evening finery, looking occasionally at the clock, was awaiting the hour set for a rendezvous, whiling away the time with the Boston evening sheet whose glaring red headlines stretched across the page. When the newspaper fell to her lap a dreamy expression clouded Lise's eyes. She was thinking of some *man!* Quickly Janet looked away, at her father, only to be repelled anew by the expression, almost of fatuity, she discovered on his face as he bent over the letter once more. Suddenly she experienced an overwhelming realization of the desperation of Hannah's plight, — the destiny of spending one's days, without sympathy, toiling in the confinement of these rooms to supply their bodily needs. Never had a destiny seemed so appalling. And yet Janet resented that pity. The effect of it was to fetter and inhibit; from the moment of its intrusion she was no longer a free agent, to leave Hampton and Ditmar when she chose. Without her, this family was helpless. She rose, and picked up some of the dishes. Hannah snatched them from her hands.

"Leave 'em alone, Janet!" she said with unaccustomed sharpness. "I guess I ain't too feeble to handle 'em yet."

And a flash of new understanding came to Janet. The dishes were vicarious, a substitute for that greater destiny out of which Hannah had been cheated by fate. A substitute, yes, and perhaps become something of a mania, like her father's Bumpus papers. . . . Janet left the room swiftly, entered the bedroom, put on her coat and hat, and went out. Across the street the light in Mr. Tiernan's shop was still burning, and through the window she perceived Mr. Tiernan himself tilted back in his chair, his feet on the table, the tip of his nose pointed straight at the ceiling. When the bell betrayed the opening of the door he let down his chair on the floor with a bang.

"Why, it's Miss Janet!" he exclaimed. "How are you this evening, now? I was just hoping some one would pay me a call."

Twinkling at her, he managed, somewhat magically, to dispel her temper of pessimism, and she was moved to reply: —

"You know you were having a beautiful time, all by yourself."

"A beautiful time, is it? Maybe it's because I was dreaming of some young lady a-coming to pay me a visit."

"Well, dreams never come up to expectations, do they?"

"Then it's dreaming I am, still," retorted Mr. Tiernan, quickly.

Janet laughed. His tone, though bantering, was respectful. One of the secrets of Mr. Tiernan's very human success was due to his ability to estimate his fellow creatures. His manner of treating Janet, for instance, was quite different from that he employed in dealing with Lise. In the course of one interview he had conveyed to Lise, without arousing her antagonism, the conviction that it was wiser to trust him than to attempt to pull wool over his eyes. Janet had the intelligence to trust him; and to-night, as she faced him, the fact was brought home to her with peculiar force that this wiry-haired little man was the person above all others of her immediate acquaintance to seek in time of trouble. It was his great quality. Moreover, Mr. Tiernan, even in his morning greetings as she passed, always contrived to convey to her, in some unaccountable fashion, the admiration and regard in which he held her, and the effect of her contact with him was invariably to give her a certain objective image of herself, an increased self-confidence and self-respect. For instance, by the light dancing in Mr. Tiernan's eyes as he regarded her, she saw herself now as the mainstay of the helpless family in the clay-yellow flat across the street. And there was nothing, she was convinced, Mr. Tiernan did not know about that family. So she said : —

"I've come to see about the stove."

"Sure," he replied, as much as to say that the visit was not unexpected. "Well, I've been thinking about it, Miss Janet. I've got a stove here I know'll suit your mother. It's a *Reading*, it's almost new. Ye'd better be having a look at it yourself."

He led her into a chaos of stoves, grates, and pipes at the back of the store.

"It's in need of a little polish," he added, as he turned on a light, "but it's sound, and a good baker, and economical with coal." He opened the oven and took off the lids.

"I'm afraid I don't know much about stoves," she told him. "But I'll trust your judgment. How much is it?" she inquired hesitatingly.

He ran his hand through his corkscrewed hair, his familiar gesture.

"Well, I'm willing to let ye have it for twenty-five dollars. If that's too much — mebbe we can find another."

"Can you put it in to-morrow morning?" she asked.

"I can that," he said. She drew out her purse. "Ye needn't be paying for it all at once," he protested, laying a hand on her arm. "You won't be running away."

"Oh, I'd rather — I have the money," she declared hurriedly; and she turned her back that he might not perceive, when she had extracted the bills, how little was left in her purse.

"I'll wager ye won't be wanting another soon," he said, as he escorted her to the door. And he held it open, politely, looking after her, until she had crossed the street, calling out a cheerful "Good-night" that had in it something of a benediction. She avoided the dining-room and went straight to bed, in a strange medley of feelings. The self-sacrifice had brought a certain self-satisfaction not wholly unpleasant. She had been equal to the situation, and a part of her being approved of this, — a part which had been suppressed in another mood wherein she had become convinced that self-realization lay elsewhere. Life was indeed a bewildering thing. . . .

2

The next morning, at breakfast, though her mother's complaints continued, Janet was silent as to her purchase, and she lingered on her return home in the evening because she now felt a reluctance to appear in the rôle of protector and preserver of the family. She would have preferred, if possible, to give the stove anonymously. Not that the expression of Hannah's gratitude was maudlin; she glared at Janet when she entered the dining-room and exclaimed : —

"You hadn't ought to have gone and done it !"

And Janet retorted, with almost equal vehemence : —

"Somebody had to do it — didn't they? Who else was there?"

"It's a shame for you to spend your money on such things. You'd ought to save it — you'll need it," Hannah continued illogically.

"It's lucky I had the money," said Janet.

Both Janet and Hannah knew that these recriminations, from the other, were the explosive expressions of deep feeling. Janet knew that her mother was profoundly moved by her sacrifice. She herself was moved by Hannah's plight, but tenderness and pity were complicated by a renewed sense of rebellion against an existence that exacted such a situation.

"I hope the stove's all right, mother," she said. "Mr. Tiernan seemed to think it was a good one."

"It's a different thing," declared Hannah. "I was just wondering this evening, before you came in, how I ever made out to cook anything on the other. Come and see how nice it looks."

Janet followed her into the kitchen. As they stood close together gazing at the new purchase Janet was uncomfortably aware of drops that ran a little way in the furrows of Hannah's cheeks, stopped, and ran on again. She seized her apron and clapped it to her face.

"You hadn't ought to be made to do it!" she sobbed.

And Janet was suddenly impelled to commit an act rare in their intercourse. She kissed her, swiftly, on the cheek, and fled from the room. . . .

Supper was an ordeal. Janet did not relish her enthronement as a heroine, she deplored and even resented her mother's attitude toward her father, which puzzled her; for the studied cruelty of it seemed to belie her affection for him. Every act and gesture and speech of Hannah's took on the complexion of an invidious reference to her reliability as compared with Edward's worthlessness as a provider; and she contrived in some sort to make the meal a sacrament in commemoration of her elder daughter's act.

"I guess you notice the difference in that pork," she would exclaim, and when he praised it and attributed its excellence to Janet's gift Hannah observed: "As long as you ain't got a son, you're lucky to have a daughter like her!"

Janet squirmed. Her father's acceptance of his comparative worthlessness was so abject that her pity was transferred to him, though she scorned him, as on former occasions, for the self-depreciation that made him powerless before her mother's reproaches. After the meal was over he sat listlessly on the sofa, like a visitor whose presence is endured, pathetically refraining from that occupation in which his soul found refreshment and peace, the compilation of the Bumpus genealogy. That evening the papers remained under the lid of the desk in the corner, untouched.

What troubled Janet above all, however, was the attitude of Lise, who also came in for her share of implied reproach. Of late Lise had become an increased source of anxiety to Hannah, who was unwisely resolved to make this occasion an object lesson. And though parental tenderness had often moved her to excuse and defend Lise for an increasing remissness in failing to contribute to the household expenses, she was now quite relentless in her efforts to wring from Lise an acknowledgment of the nobility of her sister's act, of qualities in Janet that she, Lise, might do well to cultivate. Lise was equally determined to withhold any such acknowledgment; in her face grew that familiar mutinous look that Hannah invariably failed to recognize as a danger signal; and with it another — the sophisticated expression of one who knows life and ridicules the lack of such knowledge in others. Its implication was made certain when the two girls were alone in their bedroom after supper. Lise, feverishly occupied with her toilet, on her departure broke the silence there by inquiring: —

"Say, if I had your easy money, I might buy a stove, too. How much does Ditmar give you, sweetheart?"

Janet, infuriated, flew at her sister. Lise struggled to escape.

"Leave me go!" she whimpered in genuine alarm, and when at length she was released she went to the mirror and began straightening her hat, which had flopped to one side of her head. "I didn't mean nothin', I was only kiddin' you — what's the use of gettin' nutty over a jest?"

"I'm not like you," said Janet.

"I was only kiddin', I tell you," insisted Lise, with a hat pin in her mouth. "Forget it."

When Lise had gone out Janet sat down in the rocking-chair and began to rock agitatedly. What had really made her angry, she began to perceive, was the realization of a certain amount of truth in her sister's intimation concerning Ditmar. Why should she have, in Lise, continually before her eyes a degraded caricature of her own aspirations and ideals? or was Lise a mirror — somewhat tarnished, indeed — in which she read the truth about herself? For some time Janet had more than suspected that her sister possessed a new lover — a lover whom she refrained from discussing; an ominous sign, since it had been her habit to dangle her conquests before Janet's eyes, to discuss their merits and demerits with an engaging though cynical freedom. Although the existence of this gentleman was based on evidence purely circumstantial, Janet was inclined to believe him of a type wholly different from his predecessors; and the fact that his attentions were curiously intermittent and irregular inclined her to the theory that he was not a resident of Hampton. What was he like? It revolted her to reflect that he might in some ways possibly

resemble Ditmar. Thus he became the object of a morbid
speculation, especially at such times as this, when Lise
attired herself in her new winter finery and went forth to
meet him. Janet, also, had recently been self-convicted
of sharing with Lise the same questionable tendency toward
self-adornment to please the eye of man. The very next
Saturday night after she had indulged in that mad extravagance of the blue suit, Lise had brought home from the
window of *The Paris* in Faber Street a hat that had
excited the cupidity and admiration of Miss Schuler and
herself, and in front of which they had stood languishing
on three successive evenings. In its acquisition Lise had
expended almost the whole of a week's salary. Its colour
was purple, on three sides were massed drooping lilac
feathers, but over the left ear the wide brim was caught up
and held by a crescent of brilliant paste stones. Shortly
after this purchase — the next week, in fact, — *The
Paris* had alluringly and craftily displayed, for the tempting sum of $6.29, the very cloak ordained by providence
to "go" with the hat. Miss Schuler declared it would be
a crime to fail to take advantage of such an opportunity —
but the trouble was that Lise had had to wait for two more
pay-days and endure the suspense arising from the possibility that some young lady of taste and means might meanwhile become its happy proprietor. Had not the saleslady
been obdurate, Lise would have had it on credit; but she
did succeed, by an initial payment the ensuing Saturday, in
having it withdrawn from public gaze. The second Saturday Lise triumphantly brought the cloak home; a velvet
cloak, — if the eyes could be believed, — velvet bordering
on plush, with a dark purple ground delicately and artistically spotted with a lilac to match the hat feathers, and
edged with a material which — if not too impudently examined and no questions asked — might be mistaken, by

the uninitiated male, for the fur of a white fox. Both investments had been made, needless to say, on the strength of Janet's increased salary; and Lise, when Janet had surprised her before the bureau rapturously surveying the combination, justified herself with a defiant apology.

"I just had to have something — what with winter coming on," she declared, seizing the hand mirror in order to view the back. "You might as well get your clothes chick, while you're about it — and I didn't have to dig up twenty bones, neither — nor anything like it —" a reflection on Janet's modest blue suit and her abnormal extravagance. For it was Lise's habit to carry the war into the enemy's country. "Sadie's dippy about it — says it puts her in mind of one of the swells snapshotted in last Sunday's supplement. Well, dearie, how does the effect get you?" and she wheeled around for her sister's inspection.

"If you take my advice, you'll be careful not to be caught out in the rain."

"What's chewin' you now?" demanded Lise. She was not lacking in imagination of a certain sort, and Janet's remark did not fail in its purpose of summoning up a somewhat abject image of herself in wet velvet and bedraggled feathers — an image suggestive of a certain hunted type of woman Lise and her kind held in peculiar horror. And she was the more resentful because she felt, instinctively, that the memory of this suggestion would never be completely eradicated : it would persist, like a canker, to mar the completeness of her enjoyment of these clothes. She swung on Janet furiously.

"I get you, all right!" she cried. "I guess I know what's eatin' you! You've got money to burn and you're sore because I spend mine to buy what I need. You don't know how to dress yourself any more than one of them Polak girls in the mills, and you don't want anybody else to look nice."

And Janet was impelled to make a retort of almost equal crudity : —

"If I were a man and saw you in those clothes I wouldn't wait for an introduction. You asked me what I thought. I don't care about the money!" she exclaimed passionately. "I've often told you you were pretty enough without having to wear that kind of thing — to make men stare at you."

"I want to know if I don't always look like a lady! And there's no man living would try to pick me up more than once." The nasal note in Lise's voice had grown higher and shriller, she was almost weeping with anger. "You want me to go 'round lookin' like a floorwasher."

"I'd rather look like a floorwasher than — than another kind of woman," Janet declared.

"Well, you've got your wish, sweetheart," said Lise. "You needn't be scared anybody will pick you up."

"I'm not," said Janet. . . .

This quarrel had taken place a week or so before Janet's purchase of the stove. Hannah, too, was outraged by Lise's costume, and had also been moved to protest; futile protest. Its only effect on Lise was to convince her of the existence of a prearranged plan of persecution, to make her more secretive and sullen than ever before.

"Sometimes I just can't believe she's my daughter," Hannah said dejectedly to Janet when they were alone together in the kitchen after Lise had gone out. "I'm fond of her because she's my own flesh and blood — I'm ashamed of it, but I can't help it. I guess it's what the minister in Dolton used to call a visitation. I suppose I deserve it, but sometimes I think maybe if your father had b'en different he might have b'en able to put a stop to the way she's going on. She ain't like any of the Wenches, nor any of the Bumpuses, so far's I'm able to find out. She just don't seem to have any notion about right and wrong. Well, the world has got all jumbled up — it beats me."

Hannah wrung out the mop viciously and hung it over the sink.

"I used to hope some respectable man would come along, but I've quit hopin'. I don't know as any respectable man would want Lise, or that I could honestly wish him to have her."

"Mother!" protested Janet. Sometimes, in those conversations, she was somewhat paradoxically impelled to defend her sister.

"Well, I don't," insisted Hannah, "that's a fact. I'll tell you what she looks like in that hat and cloak — a bad woman. I don't say she is — I don't know what I'd do if I thought she was, but I never expected my daughter to look like one."

"Oh, Lise can take care of herself," Janet said, in spite of certain recent misgivings.

"This town's Sodom and Gomorrah rolled into one," declared Hannah who, from early habit, was occasionally prone to use scriptural parallels. And after a moment's silence she inquired: "Who's this man that's payin' her attention now?"

"I don't know," replied Janet, "I don't know that there's anybody."

"I guess there is," said Hannah. "I used to think that *that* Wiley was low enough, but I could *see* him. It was *some* satisfaction. I could know the worst, anyhow. . . . I guess it's about time for another flood."

This talk had left Janet in one of these introspective states so frequent in her recent experience. Her mother had used the words "right" and "wrong." But what was "right," or "wrong?" There was no use asking Hannah, who — she perceived — was as confused and bewildered as

herself. Did she refuse to encourage Mr. Ditmar because
it was wrong? because, if she acceded to his desires, and
what were often her own, she would be punished in an after
life? She was not at all sure whether she believed in an
after life, — a lack of faith that had, of late, sorely troubled
her friend Eda Rawle, who had "got religion" from an itinerant evangelist and was now working off, in a "live" church,
some of the emotional idealism which is the result of a
balked sex instinct in young unmarried women of a certain
mentality and unendowed with good looks. This was not,
of course, Janet's explanation of the change in her friend, of
whom she now saw less and less. They had had arguments,
in which neither gained any ground. For the first time in
their intercourse, ideas had come between them, Eda
having developed a surprising self-assertion when her new
convictions were attacked, a dogged loyalty to a scheme of
salvation that Janet found neither inspiring nor convincing.
She resented being prayed for, and an Eda fervent in good
works bored her more than ever. Eda was deeply pained
by Janet's increasing avoidance of her company, yet her
heroine-worship persisted. Her continued regard for her
friend might possibly be compared to the attitude of an
orthodox Baptist who has developed a hobby, let us say,
for Napoleon Bonaparte.

Janet was not wholly without remorse. She valued Eda's
devotion, she sincerely regretted the fact, on Eda's account
as well as her own, that it was a devotion of no use to her
in the present crisis — nor indeed in any crisis likely to
confront her in life : she had felt instinctively from the first
that the friendship was not founded on mental harmony,
and now it was brought home to her that Eda's solution
could never be hers. Eda would have been thrilled on learning of Ditmar's attentions, would have advocated the adop-
tion of a campaign leading up to matrimony. In matrimony,

for Eda, the soul was safe. Eda would have been horrified
that Janet should have dallied with any other relationship;
God would punish her. Janet, in her conflict between
alternate longing and repugnance, was not concerned with
the laws and retributions of God. She felt, indeed, the need
of counsel, and knew not where to turn for it, — the modern
need for other than supernatural sanctions. She did not
resist her desire for Ditmar because she believed, in the
orthodox sense, that it was wrong, but because it involved
a loss of self-respect, a surrender of the personality from the
very contemplation of which she shrank. She was a true
daughter of her time.

3

On Friday afternoon, shortly after Ditmar had begun to
dictate his correspondence, Mr. Holster, the agent of the
Clarendon Mill, arrived and interrupted him. Janet had
taken advantage of the opportunity to file away some answered letters when her attention was distracted from her
work by the conversation, which had gradually grown louder.
The two men were standing by the window, facing one
another, in an attitude that struck her as dramatic. Both
were vital figures, dominant types which had survived and
prevailed in that upper world of unrelenting struggle for
supremacy into which, through her relation to Ditmar, she
had been projected, and the significance of which she had
now begun to realize. She surveyed Holster critically. He
was short, heavily built, with an almost grotesque width
of shoulder, a muddy complexion, thick lips, and kinky,
greasy black hair that glistened in the sun. His nasal
voice was complaining, yet distinctly aggressive, and he
emphasized his words by gestures. The veins stood out on
his forehead. She wondered what his history had been.
She compared him to Ditmar, on whose dust-grey face she
was quick to detect a look she had seen before — a con-

N

traction of the eyes, a tightening of the muscles of the jaw. That look, and the peculiarly set attitude of the body accompanying it, aroused in her a responsive sense of championship.

"All right, Ditmar," she heard the other exclaim. "I tell you again you'll never be able to pull it off."

Ditmar's laugh was short, defiant.

"Why not?" he asked.

"Why not! Because the fifty-four hour law goes into effect in January."

"What's that got to do with it?" Ditmar demanded.

"You'll see — you'll remember what I told you fellows at the conference after that bill went through and that damned demagogue of a governor insisted on signing it. I said, if we tried to cut wages down to a fifty-four hour basis we'd have a strike on our hands in every mill in Hampton, — didn't I? I said it would cost us millions of dollars, and make all the other strikes we've had here look like fifty cents. Didn't I say that? Hammond, our president, backed me up, and Rogers of the wool people. You remember? You were the man who stood out against it, and they listened to you, they voted to cut down the pay and say nothing about it. Wait until those first pay envelopes are opened after that law goes into effect. You'll see what'll happen! You'll never be able to fill that Bradlaugh order in God's world."

"Oh hell," retorted Ditmar, contemptuously. "You're always for lying down, Holster. Why don't you hand over your mill to the unions and go to work on a farm? You might as well, if you're going to let the unions run the state. Why not have socialism right now, and cut out the agony? When they got the politicians to make the last cut from fifty-six to fifty-four and we kept on payin' 'em for fifty-six, against my advice, what happened? Did they thank us? I guess not. Were they contented? Not on your life. They went right on agitating, throwing scares into the party conventions and into the House and Senate Committees, — and now it's fifty-four hours. It'll be fifty in a couple of years, and then we'll have to scrap our machinery and turn over the trade to the South and donate our mills to the state for insane asylums."

"No, if we handle this thing right, we'll have the public on our side. They're getting sick of the unions now."

Ditmar went to the desk for a cigar, bit it off, and lighted it.

"The public!" he exclaimed contemptuously. "A whole lot of good they'll do us."

Holster approached him, menacingly, until the two men stood almost touching, and for a moment it seemed to Janet as if the agent of the Clarendon were ready to strike Ditmar. She held her breath, her blood ran faster, — the conflict between these two made an elemental appeal.

"All right — remember what I say — wait and see where you come out with that order." Holster's voice trembled with anger. He hesitated, and left the office abruptly. Ditmar stood gazing after him for a moment and then, taking his cigar from his mouth, turned and smiled at Janet and seated himself in his chair. His eyes, still narrowed, had in them a gleam of triumph that thrilled her. Combat seemed to stimulate and energize him.

"He thought he could bluff me into splitting that Bradlaugh order with the Clarendon," Ditmar exclaimed. "Well, he'll have to guess again. I've got his number." He began to turn over his letters. "Let's see, where were we? Tell Caldwell not to let in any more idiots, and shut the door."

Janet obeyed, and when she returned Ditmar was making notes with a pencil on a pad. The conversation with Hol-

ster had given her a new idea of Ditmar's daring in attempting to fill the Bradlaugh order with the Chippering Mills
alone, had aroused in her more strongly than ever that hot
loyalty to the mills with which he had inspired her; and
that strange surge of sympathy, of fellow-feeling for the
operatives she had experienced after the interview with Mr.
Siddons, of rebellion against him, the conviction that she
also was one of the slaves he exploited, had wholly disappeared.   Ditmar *was* the Chippering Mills, and she, somehow, enlisted once again on his side.

"By the way," he said abruptly, "you won't mention
this — I know."

"Won't mention what?" she asked.

"This matter about the pay envelopes — that we don't
intend to continue giving the operatives fifty-six hours'
pay for fifty-four when this law goes into effect. They're
like animals, most of 'em, they don't reason, and it might
make trouble if it got out now. You understand. They'd
have time to brood over it, to get the agitators started.
When the time comes they may kick a little, but they'll
quiet down. And it'll teach 'em a lesson."

"I never mention anything I hear in this office," she told
him.

"I know you don't," he assured her, apologetically. "I
oughtn't to have said that — it was only to put you on your
guard, in case you heard it spoken of. You see how important it is, how much trouble an agitator might make
by getting them stirred up? You can see what it means to
me, with this order on my hands. I've staked everything
on it."

"But — when the law goes into effect? when the operatives find out that they are not receiving their full wages
— as Mr. Holster said?" Janet inquired.

"Why, they may grumble a little — but I'll be on the

lookout for any move. I'll see to that. I'll teach 'em a lesson as to how far they can push this business of shorter hours and equal pay. It's the unskilled workers who are mostly affected, you understand, and they're not organized. If we can keep out the agitators, we're all right. Even then, I'll show 'em they can't come in here and exploit my operatives."

In the mood in which she found herself his self-confidence, his aggressiveness continued to inspire and even to agitate her, to compel her to accept his point of view.

"Why," he continued, "I trust you as I never trusted anybody else. I've told you that before. Ever since you've been here you've made life a different thing for me — just by your being here. I don't know what I'd do without you. You've got so much sense about things — about people, — and I sometimes think you've got almost the same feeling about these mills that I have. You didn't tell me you went through the mills with Caldwell the other day," he added, accusingly.

"I — I forgot," said Janet. "Why should I tell you?" She knew that all thought of Holster had already slipped from his mind. She did not look up. "If you're not going to finish your letters," she said, a little faintly, "I've got some copying to do."

"You're a deep one," he said. And as he turned to the pile of correspondence she heard him sigh. He began to dictate. She took down his sentences automatically, scarcely knowing what she was writing; he was making love to her as intensely as though his words had been the absolute expression of his desire instead of the commonplace mediums of commercial intercourse. Presently he stopped and began fumbling in one of the drawers of his desk.

"Where is the memorandum I made last week for Percy and Company?"

"Isn't it there?" she asked.

But he continued to fumble, running through the papers and disarranging them until she could stand it no longer.

"You never know where to find anything," she declared, rising and darting around the desk and bending over the drawer, her deft fingers rapidly separating the papers. She drew forth the memorandum triumphantly.

"There!" she exclaimed. "It was right before your eyes."

As she thrust it at him his hand closed over hers. She felt him drawing her, irresistibly.

"Janet!" he said. "For God's sake — you're killing me — don't you know it? I can't stand it any longer!"

"Don't!" she whispered, terror-stricken, straining away from him. "Mr. Ditmar — let me go!"

A silent struggle ensued, she resisting him with all the aroused strength and fierceness of her nature. He kissed her hair, her neck, — she had never imagined such a force as this, she felt herself weakening, welcoming the annihilation of his embrace.

"Mr. Ditmar!" she cried. "Somebody will come in."

Her fingers sank into his neck, she tried to hurt him — and by a final effort flung herself free and fled to the other side of the room.

"You little — wildcat!" she heard him exclaim, saw him put his handkerchief to his neck where her fingers had been, saw a red stain on it. "I'll have you yet!"

But even then, as she stood leaning against the wall, motionless save for the surging of her breast, there was about her the same strange, feral inscrutableness. He was baffled, he could not tell what she was thinking. She seemed, unconquered, to triumph over her disarray and the agitation of her body. Then, with an involuntary gesture she raised her hands to her hair, smoothing it, and without seeming haste left the room, not so much as glancing at him, closing the door behind her.

She reached her table in the outer office and sat down, gazing out of the window. The face of the world — the river, the mills, and the bridge — was changed, tinged with a new and unreal quality. She, too, must be changed. She wasn't, couldn't be the same person who had entered that room of Ditmar's earlier in the afternoon! Mr. Caldwell made a commonplace remark, she heard herself answer him. Her mind was numb, only her body seemed swept by fire, by emotions — emotions of fear, of anger, of desire — so intense as to make her helpless. And when at length she reached out for a sheet of carbon paper her hand trembled so she could scarcely hold it. Only by degrees was she able to get sufficient control of herself to begin her copying, when she found a certain relief in action — her hands flying over the keys, tearing off the finished sheets, and replacing them with others. She did not want to think, to decide, and yet she knew — something was trying to tell her — that the moment for decision had come. She must leave, *now*. If she stayed on, this tremendous adventure she longed for and dreaded was inevitable. Fear and fascination battled within her. To run away was to deny life; to remain, to taste and savour it. She had tasted it — was it sweet? — that sense of being swept away, engulfed by an elemental power beyond them both, yet in them both? She felt him drawing her to him, and she struggling yet inwardly longing to yield. And the scarlet stain on his handkerchief — when she thought of that her blood throbbed, her face burned.

At last the door of the inner office opened, and Ditmar came out and stood by the rail. His voice was queer, — scarcely recognizable.

"Miss Bumpus — would you mind coming into my room a moment, before you leave?" he said.

She rose instantly and followed him, closing the door behind her, but standing at bay against it, her hand on the knob.

"I'm not going to touch you — you needn't be afraid," he said. Reassured by the unsteadiness of his voice she raised her eyes to perceive that his face was ashy, his manner nervous, apprehensive, conciliatory, — a Ditmar she had difficulty in recognizing. "I didn't mean to frighten, to offend you," he went on. "Something got hold of me. I was crazy, I couldn't help it — I won't do it again, if you'll stay. I give you my word."

She did not reply. After a pause he began again, repeating himself.

"I didn't mean to do it. I was carried away — it all happened before I knew. I — I wouldn't frighten you that way for anything in the world."

Still she was silent.

"For God's sake, speak to me!" he cried. "Say you forgive me — give me another chance!"

But she continued to gaze at him with widened, enigmatic eyes — whether of reproach or contempt or anger he could not say. The situation transcended his experience. He took an uncertain step toward her, as though half expecting her to flee, and stopped.

"Listen!" he pleaded. "I can't talk to you here. Won't you give me a chance to explain — to put myself right? You know what I think of you, how I respect and — admire you. If you'll only let me see you somewhere — anywhere, outside of the office, for a little while, I can't tell you how much I'd appreciate it. I'm sure you don't understand how I feel — I couldn't bear to lose you. I'll be down by the canal — near the bridge — at eight o'clock to-night. I'll wait for you. You'll come? Say you'll come, and give me another chance!"

"Aren't you going to finish your letters?" she asked.

He stared at her in sheer perplexity. "Letters!" he exclaimed. "Damn the letters! Do you think I could write any letters now?"

As a faint ray in dark waters, a gleam seemed to dance in the shadows of her eyes, yet was gone so swiftly that he could not be sure of having seen it. Had she smiled?

"I'll be there," he cried. "I'll wait for you!"

She turned from him, opened the door, and went out.

4

That evening, as Janet was wiping the dishes handed her by her mother, she was repeating to herself "Shall I go — or shan't I?" —just as if the matter were in doubt. But in her heart she was convinced of its predetermination by some power other than her own volition. With this feeling, that she really had no choice, that she was being guided and impelled, she went to her bedroom after finishing her task. The hands of the old dining-room clock pointed to quarter of eight, and Lise had already made her toilet and departed. Janet opened the wardrobe, looked at the new blue suit hanging so neatly on its wire holder, hesitated, and closed the door again. Here, at any rate, seemed a choice. She would not wear that, to-night. She tidied her hair, put on her hat and coat, and went out; but once in the street she did not hurry, though she knew the calmness she apparently experienced to be false: the calmness of fatality, because she was obeying a complicated impulse stronger than herself — an impulse that at times seemed mere curiosity. Somewhere, removed from her immediate consciousness, a storm was raging; she was aware of a disturbance that reached her faintly, like the distant throbbing of the looms she heard when she turned from Faber into West Street. She had not been able to eat any supper. That throbbing of the looms in the night! As it grew louder and louder the tension within her increased, broke its bounds, set her heart to throbbing too — throbbing wildly. She halted, and went on again, precipitately, but once more slowed her steps as she came to West Street and the glare of light at the end of the bridge; at a little distance, under the chequered shadows of the bare branches, she saw something move — a man, Ditmar. She stood motionless as he hurried toward her.

"You've come! You've forgiven me?" he asked.

"Why were you — down there?" she asked.

"Why? Because I thought — I thought you wouldn't want anybody to know —"

It was quite natural that he should not wish to be seen; although she had no feeling of guilt, she herself did not wish their meeting known. She resented the subterfuge *in him*, but she made no comment because his perplexity, his embarrassment were gratifying to her resentment, were restoring her self-possession, giving her a sense of power.

"We can't stay here," he went on, after a moment. "Let's take a little walk — I've got a lot to say to you. I want to put myself right." He tried to take her arm, but she avoided him. They started along the canal in the direction of the Stanley Street bridge. "Don't you care for me a little?" he demanded.

"Why should I?" she parried.

"Then — why did you come?"

"To hear what you had to say."

"You mean — about this afternoon?"

"Partly," said Janet.

"Well — we'll talk it all over. I wanted to explain about this afternoon, especially. I'm sorry —"

"Sorry!" she exclaimed.

The vehemence of her rebuke — for he recognized it

as such — took him completely aback. Thus she was wont, at the most unexpected moments, to betray the passion within her, the passion that made him sick with desire. How was he to conquer a woman of this type, who never took refuge in the conventional tactics of her sex, as he had known them?

"I didn't mean that," he explained desperately. "My God — to feel you, to have you in my arms —! I was sorry because I frightened you. But when you came near me that way I just couldn't help it. You drove me to it."

"Drove you to it!"

"You don't understand, you don't know how — how wonderful you are. You make me crazy. I love you, I want you as I've never wanted any woman before — in a different way. I can't explain it. I've got so that I can't live without you." He flung his arm toward the lights of the mills. "That — that used to be everything to me, I lived for it. I don't say I've been a saint — but I never really cared anything about any woman until I knew you, until that day I went through the office and saw you — what you were. You don't understand, I tell you. I'm sorry for what I did to-day because it offended you — but you drove me to it. Most of the time you seem cold, you're like an iceberg, you make me think you hate me, and then all of a sudden you'll be kind, as you were the other night, as you seemed this afternoon — you make me think I've got a chance, and then, when you came near me, when you touched my hand — why, I didn't know what I was doing. I just had to have you. A man like me can't stand it."

"Then I'd better go away," she said. "I ought to have gone long ago."

"Why?" he cried. "Why? What's your reason? Why do you want to ruin my life? You've — you've woven yourself into it — you're a part of it. I never knew what it was to care for a woman before, I tell you. There's that mill," he repeated, naïvely. "I've made it the best mill in the country, I've got the biggest order that ever came to any mill — if you went away I wouldn't care a continental about it. If you went away I wouldn't have any ambition left. Because you're a part of it, don't you see? You — you sort of stand for it now, in my mind. I'm not literary, I can't express what I'd like to say, but sometimes I used to think of that mill as a woman — and now you've come along —" Ditmar stopped, for lack of adequate eloquence.

She smiled in the darkness at his boyish fervour, — one of the aspects of the successful Ditmar, the Ditmar of great affairs, that appealed to her most strongly. She was softened, touched; she felt, too, a responsive thrill to such a desire as his. Yet she did not reply. She could not. She was learning that emotion is never simple. And some inhibition, the identity of which was temporarily obscured still persisted, pervading her consciousness. . . .

They were crossing the bridge at Stanley Street, now deserted, and by common consent they paused in the middle of it, leaning on the rail. The hideous chocolate factory on the point was concealed by the night, — only the lights were there, trembling on the surface of the river. Against the flushed sky above the city were silhouetted the high chimneys of the power plant. Ditmar's shoulder touched hers. He was still pleading, but she seemed rather to be listening to the symphony of the unseen waters falling over the dam. His words were like that, suggestive of a torrent into which she longed to fling herself, yet refrained, without knowing why. Her hands tightened on the rail; suddenly she let it go, and led the way toward the unfrequented district of the south side. It was the road to Silliston, but she had forgotten that. Ditmar, regaining her side, continued his pleading. He spoke of his loneliness, which he had never realized. He needed her. And she experienced an answering pang. It still seemed incredible that he, too, who had so much, should feel that gnawing need for human sympathy and understanding that had so often made her unhappy. And because of the response his need aroused in her she did not reflect whether he could fulfil her own need, whether he could ever understand her; whether, at any time, she could unreservedly pour herself out to him.

"I don't see why you want me," she interrupted him at last. "I've never had any advantages, I don't know anything. I've never had a chance to learn. I've told you that before."

"What difference does that make? You've got more sense than any woman I ever saw," he declared.

"It makes a great deal of difference to me," she insisted — and the sound of these words on her own lips was like a summons arousing her from a dream. The sordidness of her life, its cruel lack of opportunity in contrast with the gifts she felt to be hers, and on which he had dwelt, was swept back into her mind. Self-pity, dignity, and inherent self-respect struggled against her woman's desire to give; an inherited racial pride whispered that she was worthy of the best, but because she had lacked the chance, he refrained from offering her what he would have laid at the feet of another woman.

"I'll give you advantages — there's nothing I wouldn't give you. Why won't you come to me? I'll take care of you."

"Do you think I want to be taken care of?" She wheeled on him so swiftly that he started back. "Is that what you think I want?"

"No, no," he protested, when he recovered his speech.

"Do you think I'm after — what you can give me?" she shot at him. "What you can buy for me?"

To tell the truth, he had not thought anything about it,

that was the trouble. And her question, instead of enlightening him, only added to his confusion and bewilderment.

"I'm always getting in wrong with you," he told her, pathetically. "There isn't anything I'd stop at to make you happy, Janet, that's what I'm trying to say. I'd go the limit."

"*Your* limit!" she exclaimed.

"What do you mean?" he demanded. But she had become inarticulate — cryptic, to him. He could get nothing more out of her.

"You don't understand me — you never will!" she cried, and burst into tears — tears of rage she tried in vain to control. The world was black with his ignorance. She hated herself, she hated him. Her sobs shook her convulsively, and she scarcely heard him as he walked beside her along the empty road, pleading and clumsily seeking to comfort her. Once or twice she felt his hand on her shoulders. . . . And then, unlooked for and unbidden, pity began to invade her. Absurd to pity him! She fought against it, but the thought of Ditmar reduced to abjectness gained ground. After all, he had tried to be generous, he had done his best, he loved her, he needed her — the words rang in her heart. After all, he did not realize — how could she expect him to realize? and *her* imagination conjured up the situation in a new perspective. Her sobs gradually ceased, and presently she stopped in the middle of the road and regarded him. He seemed utterly miserable, like a hurt child whom she longed to comfort. But what she said was : —

"I ought to be going home."

"Not yet!" he begged. "It's early. You say I don't understand you, Janet — my God, I wish I did! It breaks me all up to see you cry like that."

"I'm sorry," she said, after a moment. "I — I can't

make you understand. I guess I'm not like anybody else — I'm queer — I can't help it. You must let me go, I only make you unhappy."

"Let you go!" he cried — and then in utter self-forgetfulness she yielded her lips to his. A sound penetrated the night, she drew back from his arms and stood silhouetted against the glare of the approaching headlight of a trolley car, and as it came roaring down on them she hailed it. Ditmar seized her arm.

"You're not going — now?" he said hoarsely.

"I must," she whispered. "I want to be alone — I want to think. You must let me."

"I'll see you to-morrow?"

"I don't know — I want to think. I'm — I'm tired."

The brakes screamed as the car came joltingly to a stop. She flew up the steps, glancing around to see whether Ditmar had followed her, and saw him still standing in the road. The car was empty of passengers, but the conductor must have seen her leaving a man in this lonely spot. She glanced at his face, white and pinched and apathetic — he must have seen hundreds of similar episodes in the course of his nightly duties. He was unmoved as he took her fare. Nevertheless, at the thought that these other episodes might resemble hers, her face flamed — she grew hot all over. What should she do now? She could not think. Confused with her shame was the memory of a delirious joy, yet no sooner would she give herself up, trembling, to this memory when in turn it was penetrated by qualms of resentment, defiling its purity. Was Ditmar ashamed of her? . . . When she reached home and had got into bed she wept a little, but her tears were neither of joy nor sorrow. Her capacity for both was exhausted. In this strange mood she fell asleep — nor did she waken when, at midnight, Lise stealthily crept in beside her.

CHAPTER X

1

DITMAR stood staring after the trolley car that bore
Janet away until it became a tiny speck of light in the
distance. Then he started to walk toward Hampton;
in the unwonted exercise was an outlet for the pent-up
energy her departure had thwarted; and presently his body
was warm with a physical heat that found its counterpart
in a delicious, emotional glow of anticipation, of exultant
satisfaction. After all, he could not expect to travel too
fast with her. Had he not at least gained a signal victory?
When he remembered her lips — which she had indubitably
given him! — he increased his stride, and in what seemed
an incredibly brief time he had recrossed the bridge, covered
the long residential blocks of Warren Street, and gained his
own door.

The house was quiet, the children having gone to bed,
and he groped his way through the dark parlour to his den,
turning on the electric switch, sinking into an armchair,
and lighting a cigar. He liked this room of his, which still
retained something of that flavour of a refuge and sanctuary
it had so eminently possessed in the now forgotten days of
matrimonial conflict. One of the few elements of agreement
he had held in common with the late Mrs. Ditmar was a
similarity of taste in household decoration, and they had
gone together to a great emporium in Boston to choose
the furniture and fittings. The lamp in the centre of the
table was a bronze column supporting a hemisphere of

heavy red and emerald glass, the colours woven into an intricate and bizarre design, after the manner of the *art nouveau* — so the zealous salesman had informed them. Cora Ditmar, when exhibiting this lamp to admiring visitors, had remembered the phrase, though her pronunciation of it, according to the standard of the *Sorbonne*, left something to be desired. The table and chairs, of heavy, shiny oak marvellously and precisely carved by machines, matched the big panels of the wainscot. The windows were high in the wall, thus preventing any intrusion from the clothes-yard on which they looked. The bookcases, protected by leaded panes, held countless volumes of the fiction from which Cora Ditmar had derived her knowledge of the great world outside of Hampton, together with certain sets she had bought, not only as ornaments, but with a praiseworthy view to future culture, — such as Whitmarsh's Library of the Best Literature. These volumes, alas, were still uncut; but some of the pages of the novels — if one cared to open them — were stained with chocolate. The steam radiator was a decoration in itself, the fireplace set in the red and yellow tiles that made the hearth. Above the oak mantel, in a gold frame, was a large coloured print of a Magdalen, doubled up in grief, with a glory of loose, Titian hair, chosen by Ditmar himself as expressing the nearest possible artistic representation of his ideal of the female form. Cora Ditmar's objections on the score of voluptuousness and of insufficient clothing had been vain. She had recognized no immorality of sentimentality in the art itself; what she felt, and with some justice, was that this particular Magdalen was unre-pentant, and that Ditmar knew it. And the picture re-mained an offence to her as long as she lived. Formerly he had enjoyed the contemplation of this figure, reminding him, as it did, of mellowed moments in conquests of the past; suggesting also possibilities of the future. For he had been

o

quick to discount the attitude of bowed despair, the sop
flung by a sensuous artist to Christian orthodoxy. He had
been sceptical about despair — feminine despair, which
could always be cured by gifts and baubles. But to-night,
as he raised his eyes, he felt a queer sensation marring the
ecstatic perfection of his mood. That quality in the picture
which so long had satisfied and entranced him had now
become repellent, an ugly significant reflection of something
— something in himself he was suddenly eager to repudiate
and deny.

It was with a certain amazement that he found himself
on his feet with the picture in his hand, gazing at the empty
space where it had hung. For he had had no apparent
intention of obeying that impulse. What should he do
with it? Light the fire and burn it — frame and all? The
frame was an integral part of it. What would his housekeeper say? But now that he had actually removed it from
the wall he could not replace it, so he opened the closet
door and thrust it into a corner among relics which had
found refuge there. He had put his past in the closet;
yet the relief he felt was mingled with the peculiar qualm
that follows the discovery of symptoms never before remarked. Why should this woman have this extraordinary
effect of making him dissatisfied with himself? He sat
down again and tried to review the affair from that first day
when he had surprised in her eyes the flame dwelling in her.
She had completely upset his life, increasingly distracted
his mind until now he could imagine no peace unless he
possessed her. Hitherto he had recognized in his feeling
for her nothing but that same desire he had had for other
women, intensified to a degree never before experienced.
But this sudden access of morality — he did not actually
define it as such — was disquieting. And in the feverish,
semi-objective survey he was now making of his emotional

tract he was discovering the presence of other disturbing symptoms such as an unwonted tenderness, a consideration almost amounting to pity which at times he had vaguely sensed yet never sought imaginatively to grasp. It bewildered him by hampering a ruthlessness hitherto absolute. The fierceness of her inflamed his passion, yet he recognized dimly behind this fierceness an instinct of self-protection — and he thought of her in this moment as a struggling bird that fluttered out of his hands when they were ready to close over her. So it had been to-night. He might have kept her, prevented her from taking the car. Yet he had let her go! There came again, utterly to blot this out, the memory of her lips.

Even then, there had been something sorrowful in that kiss, a quality he resented as troubling, a flavour that came to him after the wildness was spent. What was she struggling against? What was behind her resistance? She loved him! It had never before occurred to him to enter into the nature of her feelings, having been so preoccupied with and tortured by his own. This realization, that she loved him, as it persisted, began to make him uneasy, though it should, according to all experience, have been a reason for sheer exultation. He began to see that with her it involved complications, responsibilities, disclosures, perhaps all of those things he had formerly avoided and resented in woman. He thought of certain friends of his who had become tangled up — of one in particular whose bank account had been powerless to extricate him. . . . And he was ashamed of himself.

In view of the nature of his sex experience, of his habit of applying his imagination solely to matters of business rather than to affairs of the heart, — if his previous episodes may be so designated, — his failure to surmise that a wish for marriage might be at the back of her resistance is not so

surprising as it may seem; he laid down, half smoked, his
third cigar. The suspicion followed swiftly on his recalling
to mind her vehement repudiation of his proffered gifts —
did he think she wanted what he could buy for her! She
was not purchasable — that way. He ought to have known
it, he hadn't realized what he was saying. But marriage!
Literally it had never occurred to him to image her in a
relation he himself associated with shackles. One of the
unconscious causes of his fascination was just her emancipation from and innocence of that herd-convention to which
most women — even those who lack wedding rings — are
slaves. The force of such an appeal to a man of Ditmar's
type must not be underestimated. And the idea that she,
too, might prefer the sanction of the law, the gilded cage —
as a popular song which once had taken his fancy illuminatingly expressed it — seemed utterly incongruous with the
freedom and daring of her spirit, was a sobering shock.
Was he prepared to marry her, if he could obtain her in
no other way? The question demanded a survey of his
actual position of which he was at the moment incapable.
There were his children! He had never sought to arrive
at even an approximate estimate of the boy and girl as
factors in his life, to consider his feelings toward them;
but now, though he believed himself a man who gave no
weight to social considerations — he had scorned this tendency in his wife — he was to realize the presence of ambitions for them. He was young, he was astonishingly
successful; he had reason to think, with his opportunities
and the investments he already had made, that he might
some day be moderately rich; and he had at times even
imagined himself in later life as the possessor of one of those
elaborate country places to be glimpsed from the high
roads in certain localities, which the sophisticated are able
to recognize as the seats of the socially ineligible, but which

to Ditmar were outward and visible emblems of success. He liked to think of George as the inheritor of such a place, as the son of a millionaire, as a "college graduate," as an influential man of affairs; he liked to imagine Amy as the wife of such another. In short, Ditmar's wife had left him, as an unconscious legacy, her aspirations for their children's social prestige. . . .

The polished oak grandfather's clock in the hall had struck one before he went to bed, mentally wearied by an unwonted problem involving, in addition to self-interest, an element of ethics, of affection not wholly compounded of desire.

2

He slept soundly, however. He was one of those fortunate beings who come into the world with digestive organs and thyroid glands in that condition which — so physiologists tell us — makes for a sanguine temperament. And his course of action, though not decided upon, no longer appeared as a problem; it differed from a business matter in that it could wait. As sufficient proof of his liver having rescued him from doubts and qualms he was able to whistle, as he dressed, and without a tremor of agitation, the forgotten tune suggested to his consciousness during the unpleasant reverie of the night before, — "*Only a Bird in a Gilded Cage!*" It was Saturday. He ate a hearty breakfast, joked with George and Amy, and refreshed, glowing with an expectation mingled with just the right amount of delightful uncertainty that made the great affairs of life a gamble, yet with the confidence of the conqueror, he walked in sunlight to the mill. In view of this firm and hopeful tone of his being he found it all the more surprising, as he reached the canal, to be seized by a trepidation strong enough to bring perspiration to his forehead. What if she had gone! He had never thought of that, and he had to admit it would be just like her. You never could tell what she would do.

Nodding at Simmons, the watchman, he hurried up the iron-shod stairs, gained the outer office, and instantly perceived that her chair beside the window was empty! Caldwell and Mr. Price stood with their heads together bending over a sheet on which Mr. Price was making calculations.

"Hasn't Miss Bumpus come yet?" Ditmar demanded. He tried to speak naturally, casually, but his own voice sounded strange, seemed to strike the exact note of sickening apprehension that suddenly possessed him. Both men turned and looked at him in some surprise.

"Good-morning, Mr. Ditmar," Caldwell said. "Why, yes, she's in your room."

"Oh!" said Ditmar.

"The Boston office has just been calling you — they want to know if you can't take the nine twenty-two," Caldwell went on. "It's about that lawsuit. It comes into court Monday morning, and Mr. Sprole is there, and they say they have to see you. Miss Bumpus has the memorandum."

Ditmar looked at his watch.

"Damn it, why didn't they let me know yesterday?" he exclaimed. "I won't see anybody, Caldwell — not even Orcutt — just now. You understand. I've got to have a little time to do some letters. I won't be disturbed — by any one — for half an hour."

Caldwell nodded.

"All right, Mr. Ditmar."

Ditmar went into his office, closing the door behind him. She was occupied as usual, cutting open the letters and laying them in a pile with the deftness and rapidity that characterized all she did.

"Janet!" he exclaimed.

"There's a message for you from Boston. I've made a note of it," she replied.

"I know — Caldwell told me. But I wanted to see you before I went — I had to see you. I sat up half the night thinking of you, I woke up thinking of you. Aren't you glad to see me?"

She dropped the letter opener and stood silent, motionless, awaiting his approach — a pose so eloquent of the sense of fatality strong in her as to strike him with apprehension, unused though he was to the appraisal of inner values. He read, darkly, something of this mystery in her eyes as they were slowly raised to his, he felt afraid; he was swept again by those unwonted emotions of pity and tenderness — but when she turned away her head and he saw the bright spot of colour growing in her cheek, spreading to her temple, suffusing her throat, when he touched the soft contour of her arm, his passion conquered. . . . Still he was acutely conscious of a resistance within her — not as before, physically directed against him, but repudiating her own desire. She became limp in his arms, though making no attempt to escape, and he knew that the essential self of her he craved still evaded and defied him. And he clung to her the more desperately — as though by crushing her peradventure he might capture it.

"You're hurting me," she said at last, and he let her go, standing by helplessly while she went through the movements of readjustment instinctive to women. Even in these he read the existence of the reservation he was loth to acknowledge.

"Don't you love me?" he said.

"I don't know."

"You do!" he said. "You — you proved it — I know it."

She went a little away from him, picking up the paper cutter, but it lay idle in her hand.

"For God's sake, tell me what's the matter!" he exclaimed. "I can't stand this. Janet, aren't you happy?"

She shook her head.

"Why not? I love you. I — I've never been so happy in my life as I was this morning. Why aren't you happy — when we love each other?"

"Because I'm not."

"Why not? There's nothing I wouldn't do to make you happy — you know that. Tell me!"

"You wouldn't understand. I couldn't make you understand."

"Is it something I've done?"

"You don't love me," she said. "You only *want* me. I'm not made that way, I'm not generous enough, I guess. I've got to have work to do."

"Work to do! But you'll share my work — it's nothing without you."

She shook her head. "I knew you couldn't understand. You don't realize how impossible it is. I don't blame you — I suppose a man can't."

She was not upbraiding him, she spoke quietly, in a tone almost lifeless, yet the emotional effect of it was tremendous.

"But," he began, and stopped, and was swept on again by an impulse that drowned all caution, all reason. "But you can help me — when we are married."

"Married!" she repeated. "You want to marry me?"

"Yes, yes — I need you." He took her hands, he felt them tremble in his, her breath came quickly, but her gaze was so intent as seemingly to penetrate to the depths of him. And despite his man's amazement at her hesitation now that he had offered her his all, he was moved, disturbed, ashamed as he had never been in his life. At length, when he could stand no longer the suspense of this inquisition, he stammered out: "I want you to be my wife."

"You've wanted to marry me all along?" she asked.

"I didn't think, Janet. I was mad about you. I didn't know you."

"Do you know me now?"

"That's just it," he cried, with a flash of clairvoyance, "I never will know you — it's what makes you different from any woman I've ever seen. You'll marry me?"

"I'm afraid," she said. "Oh, I've thought over it, and you haven't. A woman has to think, a man doesn't, — so much. And now you're willing to marry me, if you can't get me any other way." Her hand touched his coat, checking his protest. "It isn't that I want marriage — what you can give me — I'm not like that, I've told you so before. But I couldn't live as your — mistress."

The word on her lips shocked him a little — but her courage and candour thrilled him.

"If I stayed here, it would be found out. I wouldn't let you keep me. I'd have to have work, you see, or I'd lose my self-respect — it's all I've got — I'd kill myself." She spoke as calmly as though she were reviewing the situation objectively. "And then, I've thought that you might come to believe you really wanted to marry me — you wouldn't realize what you were doing, or what might happen if we were married. I've tried to tell you that, too, only you didn't seem to understand what I was saying. My father's only a gatekeeper, we're poor — poorer than some of the operatives in the mill, and the people you know here in Hampton wouldn't understand. Perhaps you think you wouldn't care, but — " she spoke with more effort, "there are your children. When I've thought of them, it all seems impossible. I'd make you unhappy — I couldn't bear it, I wouldn't stay with you. You see, I ought to have gone away long ago."

Believing, as he did, that marriage was the goal of all

women, even of the best, the immediate capitulation he had expected would have made matters far less difficult. But these scruples of hers, so startlingly his own, her disquieting insight into his entire mental process had a momentary checking effect, summoned up the vague presage of a future that might become extremely troublesome and complicated. His very reluctance to discuss with her the problem she had raised warned him that he had been swept into deep waters. On the other hand, her splendid resistance appealed to him, enhanced her value. And accustomed as he had been to a life-long self-gratification, the thought of being balked in this supreme desire was not to be borne. Such were the shades of his feeling as he listened to her.

"That's nonsense!" he exclaimed, when she had finished. "You're a lady — I know all about your family, I remember hearing about it when your father came here — it's as good as any in New England. What do you suppose I care, Janet? We love each other — I've got to have you. We'll be married in the spring, when the rush is over."

He drew her to him once more, and suddenly, in the ardour of that embrace, he felt her tenseness suddenly relax — as though against her will — and her passion, as she gave her lips, vied with his own. Her lithe body trembled convulsively, her cheeks were wet as she clung to him and hid her face in his shoulder. His sensations in the presence of this thing he had summoned up in her were incomprehensible, surpassing any he had ever known. It was no longer a woman he held in his arms, the woman he craved, but something greater, more fearful, the mystery of sorrow and suffering, of creation and life — of the universe itself.

"Janet — aren't you happy?" he said again.

She released herself and smiled at him wistfully through her tears.

"I don't know. What I feel doesn't seem like happiness.
I can't believe in it, somehow."

"You must believe in it," he said.

"I can't, — perhaps I may, later. You'd better go now,"
she begged. "You'll miss your train."

He glanced at the office clock. "Confound it, I have to.
Listen! I'll be back this evening, and I'll get that little
car of mine — "

"No, not to-night — I don't want to go — to-night."

"Why not?"

"Not to-night," she repeated.

"Well then, to-morrow. To-morrow's Sunday. Do you
know where the Boat Club is on the River Boulevard? I'll
be there, to-morrow morning at ten. I'd come for you, to
your house," he added quickly, "but we don't want any one
to know, yet — do we?"

She shook her head.

"We must keep it secret for a while," he said. "Wear
your new dress — the blue one. Good-bye — sweetheart."

He kissed her again and hurried out of the office. . . .
Boarding the train just as it was about to start, he settled
himself in the back seat of the smoker, lit a cigar, inhaling
deep breaths of the smoke and scarcely noticing an acquaintance who greeted him from the aisle. Well, he had
done it! He was amazed. He had not intended to propose
marriage, and when he tried to review the circumstances
that had led to this he became confused. But when he
asked himself whether indeed he were willing to pay such a
price, to face the revolution marriage — and this marriage
in particular — would mean in his life, the tumult in his
blood beat down his incipient anxieties. Besides, he possessed the kind of mind able to throw off the consideration
of possible consequences, and by the time the train had
slowed down in the darkness of the North Station in Boston

all traces of worry had disappeared.   The future would take
care of itself.

3

For the Bumpus family, supper that evening was an
unusually harmonious meal.   Hannah's satisfaction over the
new stove had by no means subsided, and Edward ventured,
without reproof, to praise the restored quality of the pie
crust.   And in contrast to her usual moroseness and self-
absorption, even Lise was gay — largely because her pet
aversion, the dignified and allegedly amorous Mr. Walters,
floor-walker at the *Bagatelle*, had fallen down the length of
the narrow stairway leading from the cashier's cage.   She
became almost hysterical with glee as she pictured him
lying prone beneath the counter dedicated to lingerie, draped
with various garments from the pile that toppled over on
him.   "Ruby Nash picked a brassière off his whiskers!"
Lise shrieked.   "She gave the pile a shove when he landed.
He's got her number all right.   But say, it was worth the
price of admission to see that old mutt when he got up, —
he looked like Santa Claus.   All the girls in the floor were
there — we nearly split trying to keep from giving him the
ha-ha.   And Ruby says, sympathetic, as she brushed him
off, 'I hope you ain't hurt, Mr. Walters.'   He was sore!
He went around all afternoon with a bunch on his coco as
big as a potato."   So vivid was Lise's account of this affair —
which apparently she regarded as compensation for many
days of drudgery — that even Hannah laughed, though
deploring a choice of language symbolic of a world she feared
and detested.

"If I talked like you," said Lise, "they wouldn't understand me."

Janet, too, was momentarily amused, drawn out of that
reverie in which she had dwelt all day, ever since Ditmar

had left for Boston. Now she began to wonder what would
happen if she were suddenly to announce "I'm going to
marry Mr. Ditmar." After the first shock of amazement,
she could imagine her father's complete and complacent
acceptance of the news as a vindication of an inherent
quality in the Bumpus blood. He would begin to talk about
the family. For, despite what might have been deemed a
somewhat disillusionizing experience, in the depths of his
being he still believed in the Providence who had presided
over the perilous voyage of the Mayflower and the birth of
Peregrine White, whose omniscient mind was peculiarly
concerned with the family trees of Puritans. And what
could be a more striking proof of the existence of this Providence, or a more fitting acknowledgment on his part of
the Bumpus virtues, than that Janet should become the
wife of the agent of the Chippering Mills? Janet smiled.
She was amused, too, by the thought that Lise's envy would
be modified by the prospect of a heightened social status;
since Lise, it will be remembered, had her Providence likewise. Hannah's god was not a Providence, but one deeply
skilled in persecution, in ingenious methods of torture;
one who would not hesitate to dangle baubles before the
eyes of his children — only to snatch them away again.
Hannah's pessimism would persist as far as the altar, and
beyond!

On the whole, such was Janet's notion of the Deity,
though deep within her there may have existed a hope that
he might be outwitted; that, by dint of energy and brains,
the fair things of life might be obtained despite a malicious
opposition. And she loved Ditmar. This must be love
she felt, this impatience to see him again, this desire to
be with him, this agitation possessing her so utterly that
all day long she had dwelt in an unwonted state like a som-
nambulism: it must be love, though not resembling in the

least the generally accepted, virginal ideal. She saw him as he was, crude, powerful, relentless in his desire; his very faults appealed. His passion had overcome his prudence, he had not intended to propose, but any shame she felt on this score was put to flight by a fierce exultation over the fact that she had brought him to her feet, that he wanted her enough to marry her. It was wonderful to be wanted like that! But she could not achieve the mental picture of herself as Ditmar's wife — especially when, later in the evening, she walked up Warren Street and stood gazing at his house from the opposite pavement. She simply could not imagine herself living in that house as its mistress. Notwithstanding the testimony of the movies, such a Cinderella-like transition was not within the realm of probable facts; things just didn't happen that way.

She recalled the awed exclamation of Eda when they had walked together along Warren Street on that evening in summer: "How would you like to live there!" — and hot with sudden embarrassment and resentment she had dragged her friend onward, to the corner. In spite of its size, of the spaciousness of existence it suggested, the house had not appealed to her then. Janet did not herself realize or estimate the innate if undeveloped sense of form she possessed, the artist-instinct that made her breathless on first beholding Silliston Common. And then the vision of Silliston had still been bright; but now the light of a slender moon was as a gossamer silver veil through which she beheld the house, as in a stage setting, softening and obscuring its lines, lending it qualities of dignity and glamour that made it seem remote, unreal, unattainable. And she felt a sudden, overwhelming longing, as though her breast would burst. . . .

Through the drawn blinds the lights in the second storey gleamed yellow. A dim lamp burned in the deep vestibule, as in a sanctuary. And then, as though some supernaturally penetrating ray had pierced a square hole in the lower walls, a glimpse of the interior was revealed to her, of the living room at the north end of the house. Two figures chased one another around the centre table — Ditmar's children! Was Ditmar there? Impelled irresistibly by a curiosity overcoming repugnance and fear, she went forward slowly across the street, gained the farther pavement, stepped over the concrete coping, and stood, shivering violently, on the lawn, feeling like an interloper and a thief, yet held by morbid fascination. The children continued to romp. The boy was strong and swift, the girl stout and ungainly in her movements, not mistress of her body; he caught her and twisted her arm, roughly — Janet could hear her cries through the window — when an elderly woman entered, seized him, struggling with him. He put out his tongue at her, but presently released his sister, who stood rubbing her arm, her lips moving in evident recrimination and complaint. The faces of the two were plain now; the boy resembled Ditmar, but the features of the girl, heavy and stamped with self-indulgence, were evidently reminiscent of the woman who had been his wife. Then the shade was pulled down, abruptly; and Janet, overcome by a sense of horror at her position, took to flight. . . .

When, after covering the space of a block she slowed down and tried to imagine herself as established in that house, the stepmother of those children, she found it impossible. Despite the fact that her attention had been focussed so strongly on them, the fringe of her vision had included their surroundings, the costly furniture, the piano against the farther wall, the music rack. Evidently the girl was learning to play. She felt a renewed, intenser bitterness against her own lot: she was aware of something within her better and finer than the girl, than the woman who had been her mother had possessed — that in her, Janet, had lacked the advantages of development. Could it — could it ever be developed now? Had this love which had come to her brought her any nearer to the unknown realm of light she craved? . . .

CHAPTER XI

1

THOUGH December had come, Sunday was like an April day before whose sunlight the night-mists of scruples and morbid fears were scattered and dispersed. And Janet, as she fared forth from the Fillmore Street flat, felt resurging in her the divine recklessness that is the very sap of life. The future, save of the immediate hours to come, lost its power over her. The blue and white beauty of the sky proclaimed all things possible for the strong; and the air was vibrant with the sweet music of bells, calling her to happiness. She was going to meet happiness, to meet love — to meet Ditmar! The trolley which she took in Faber Street, though lagging in its mission, seemed an agent of that happiness as it left the city behind it and wound along the heights beside the tarvia roadway above the river, bright glimpses of which she caught through the openings in the woods. And when she looked out of the window on her right she beheld on a little forested rise a succession of tiny "camps" built by residents of Hampton whose modest incomes could not afford more elaborate summer places; camps of all descriptions and colours, with queer names that made her smile: "The Cranny," "The Nook," "Snug Harbour," "Buena Vista," — of course, — which she thought pretty, though she did not know its meaning; and another, in German, equally perplexing, "Klein aber Mein." Though the windows of these places were now boarded up, though the mosquito netting still clung rather dismally to the porches, they were mutely suggestive of contentment and domestic joy.

Scarcely had she alighted from the car at the rendezvous he had mentioned, beside the now deserted boathouse where in the warm weather the members of the Hampton Rowing Club disported themselves, when she saw an automobile approaching — and recognized it as the gay "roadster" Ditmar had exhibited to her that summer afternoon by the canal; and immediately Ditmar himself, bringing it to a stop and leaping from it, stood before her in the sunlight, radiating, as it seemed, more sunlight still. With his clipped, blond moustache and his straw-coloured hair — as yet but slightly grey at the temples — he looked a veritable conquering berserker in his huge coat of golden fur. Never had he appeared to better advantage.

"I was waiting for you," he said, "I saw you in the car." Turning to the automobile, he stripped the tissue paper from a cluster of dark red roses with the priceless long stems of which Lise used to rave when she worked in the flower store. And he held the flowers against her suit — her new suit she had worn for this meeting.

"Oh," she cried, taking a deep, intoxicating breath of their fragrance. "You brought these — for me?"

"From Boston — my beauty!"

"But I can't wear all of them!"

"Why not?" he demanded. "Haven't you a pin?"

She produced one, attaching them with a gesture that seemed habitual, though the thought of their value — revealing in some degree her own worth in his eyes — unnerved her. She was warmly conscious of his gaze. Then he turned, and opening a compartment at the back of the car drew from it a bright tweed motor coat warmly lined.

"Oh, no!" she protested, drawing back. "I'll — I'll be warm enough." But laughingly, triumphantly, he seized her and thrust her arms in the sleeves, his fingers pressing against her. Overcome by shyness, she drew away from him.

"I made a pretty good guess at the size — didn't I, Janet?" he cried, delightedly surveying her. "I couldn't forget it!" His glance grew more concentrated, warmer, penetrating.

"You mustn't look at me like that!" she pleaded with lowered eyes.

"Why not — you're mine — aren't you? You're mine, now."

"I don't know. There are lots of things I want to talk about," she replied, but her protest sounded feeble, unconvincing, even to herself. He fairly lifted her into the automobile — it was a caress, only tempered by the semi-publicity of the place. He was giving her no time to think — but she did not want to think. Starting the engine, he got in and leaned toward her.

"Not here!" she exclaimed.

"All right — I'll wait," he agreed, tucking the robe about her deftly, solicitously, and she sank back against the seat, surrendering herself to the luxury, the wonder of being cherished, the caressing and sheltering warmth she felt of security and love, the sense of emancipation from discontent and sordidness and struggle. For a moment she closed her eyes, but opened them again to behold the transformed image of herself reflected in the windshield to confirm the illusion — if indeed it were one! The tweed coat seemed startlingly white in the sunlight, and the woman she saw, yet recognized as herself, was one of the fortunately placed of the earth with power and beauty at her command! And she could no longer imagine herself as the same person who the night before had stood in front of the house in Warren Street. The car was speeding over the smooth surface of the boulevard; the swift motion, which seemed

to her like that of flying, the sparkling air, the brightness
of the day, the pressure of Ditmar's shoulder against hers,
thrilled her. She marvelled at his sure command over the
machine, that responded like a live thing to his touch.
On the wide, straight stretches it went at a mad pace that
took her breath, and again, in turning a corner or passing
another car, it slowed down, purring in meek obedience.
Once she gasped : —

"Not so fast ! I can't stand it."

He laughed and obeyed her. They glided between river
and sky across the delicate fabric of a bridge which but a
moment before she had seen in the distance. Running
through the little village on the farther bank, they left the
river.

"Where are you going ? " she asked.

"Oh, for a little spin," he answered indulgently, turning
into a side road that wound through the woods and suddenly
stopping. "Janet, we've got this day — this whole day to
ourselves." He seized and drew her to him, and she yielded
dizzily, repaying the passion of his kiss, forgetful of past
and future while he held her, whispering brokenly endearing
phrases.

"You'll ruin my roses," she protested breathlessly, at
last, when it seemed that she could no longer bear this
embrace, nor the pressure of his lips. "There ! you see
you're crushing them ! " She undid them, and buttoning
the coat, held them to her face. Their odour made her
faint : her eyes were clouded.

"Listen, Claude ! " she said at last, — it was the first
time she had called him so — getting free. "You must be
sensible ! some one might come along."

"I'll never get enough of you ! " he said. "I can't believe it yet." And added irrelevantly : "Pin the roses
outside."

She shook her head. Something in her protested against this too public advertisement of their love.

"I'd rather hold them," she answered. "Let's go on." He started the car again. "Listen, I want to talk to you, seriously. I've been thinking."

"Don't I know you've been thinking!" he told her exuberantly. "If I could only find out what's always going on in that little head of yours! If you keep on thinking you'll dry up, like a New England school-marm. And now do you know what you are? One of those dusky red roses just ready to bloom. Some day I'll buy enough to smother you in 'em."

"Listen!" she repeated, making a great effort to calm herself, to regain something of that frame of mind in which their love had assumed the proportions of folly and madness, to summon up the scruples which, before she had left home that morning, she had resolved to lay before him, which she knew would return when she could be alone again. "I have to think — you won't," she exclaimed, with a fleeting smile.

"Well, what is it?" he assented. "You might as well get it off now."

And it took all her strength to say: "I don't see how I can marry you. I've told you the reasons. You're rich, and you have friends who wouldn't understand — and your children — they wouldn't understand. I — I'm nothing, I know it isn't right, I know you wouldn't be happy. I've never lived — in the kind of house you live in and known the kind of people you know, I shouldn't know what to do."

He took his eyes off the road and glanced down at her curiously. His smile was self-confident, exultant.

"Now do you feel better — you little Puritan?" he said.

And perforce she smiled in return, a pucker appearing between her eyebrows.

"I mean it," she said. "I came out to tell you so. I know — it just isn't possible."

"I'd marry you to-day if I could get a license," he declared. "Why, you're worth any woman in America, I don't care who she is, or how much money she has."

In spite of herself she was absurdly pleased.

"Now that is over, we won't discuss it again, do you understand? I've got you," he said, "and I mean to hold on to you."

She sighed. He was driving slowly now along the sandy road, and with his hand on hers she simply could not think. The spell of his nearness, of his touch, which all nature that morning conspired to deepen, was too powerful to be broken, and something was calling to her, "Take this day, take this day," drowning out the other voice demanding an accounting. She was living — what did it all matter? She yielded herself to the witchery of the hour, the sheer delight of forthfaring into the unknown.

They turned away from the river, crossing the hills of a rolling country now open, now wooded, passing white farmhouses and red barns, and ancient, weather-beaten dwellings with hipped roofs and "lean-tos" which had been there in colonial days when the road was a bridle-path. Cows and horses stood gazing at them from warm paddocks, where the rich, black mud glistened, melted by the sun; chickens scratched and clucked in the barnyards or flew frantically across the road, sometimes within an ace of destruction. Janet flinched, but Ditmar would laugh, gleefully, boyishly.

"We nearly got that one!" he would exclaim. And then he had to assure her that he wouldn't run over them.

"I haven't run over one yet, — have I?" he would demand.

"No, but you will, it's only luck."

"Luck!" he cried derisively. "Skill! I wish I had a dollar for every one I got when I was learning to drive. There was a farmer over here in Chester —" and he proceeded to relate how he had had to pay for two turkeys. "He got my number, the old hayseed, he was laying for me, and the next time I went back that way he held me up for five dollars. I can remember the time when a man in a motor was an easy mark for every reuben in the county. They got rich on us."

She responded to his mood, which was wholly irresponsible, exuberant, and they laughed together like children, every little incident assuming an aspect irresistibly humorous. Once he stopped to ask an old man standing in his dooryard how far it was to Kingsbury.

"Wal, mebbe it's two mile, they mostly call it two," said the patriarch, after due reflection, gathering his beard in his hand. "Mebbe it's more." His upper lip was blue, shaven, prehensile.

"What did you ask him for, when you know?" said Janet, mirthfully, when they had gone on, and Ditmar was imitating him. Ditmar's reply was to wink at her. Presently they saw another figure on the road.

"Let's see what he'll say," Ditmar proposed. This man was young, the colour of mahogany, with glistening black hair and glistening black eyes that regarded the too palpable joyousness of their holiday humour in mute surprise.

"I no know — stranger," he said.

"No speaka Portugueso?" inquired Ditmar, gravely.

"The country is getting filthy with foreigners," he observed, when he had started the car. "I went down to Plymouth last summer to see the old rock, and by George, it seemed as if there wasn't anybody could speak American on the whole cape. All the Portuguese islands are dumped there — cranberry pickers, you know."

"I didn't know that," said Janet.

"Sure thing!" he exclaimed. "And when I got there, what do you think? there was hardly enough of the old stone left to stand on, and that had a fence around it like an exhibit in an exposition. It had all been chipped away by souvenir hunters."

She gazed at him incredulously.

"You don't believe me! I'll take you down there sometime. And another thing, the rock's high and dry — up on the land. I said to Charlie Crane, who was with me, that it must have been a peach of a jump for old Miles Standish and Priscilla what's her name."

"How I'd love to see the ocean again!" Janet exclaimed.

"Why, I'll take you — as often as you like," he promised. "We'll go out on it in summer, up to Maine, or down to the Cape."

Her enchantment was now so great that nothing seemed impossible.

"And we'll go down to Plymouth, too, some Sunday soon, if this weather keeps up. If we start early enough we can get there for lunch, easy. We'll see the rock. I guess some of your ancestors must have come over with that Mayflower outfit — first cabin, eh? You look like it."

Janet laughed. "It's a joke on them, if they did. I wonder what they'd think of Hampton, if they could see it now. I counted up once, just to tease father — he's the seventh generation from Ebenezer Bumpus, who came to Dolton. Well, I proved to him he might have one hundred and twenty-six other ancestors besides Ebenezer and his wife."

"That must have jarred him some," was Ditmar's comment. "Great old man, your father. I've talked to him — he's a regular historical society all by himself. Well, there must be something in it, this family business. Now, you can tell he comes from fine old American stock — he looks it."

Janet flushed. "A lot of good it does!" she exclaimed.

"I don't know," said Ditmar. "It's something to fall back on — a good deal. And he hasn't got any of that nonsense in his head about labour unions — he's a straight American. And you look the part," he added. "You remind me — I never thought of it until now — you remind me of a picture of Priscilla I saw once in a book of poems — Longfellow's, you know. I'm not much on literature, but I remember that, and I remember thinking she could have me. Funny isn't it, that you should have come along? But you've got more ginger than the woman in that picture. I'm the only man that ever guessed it — isn't that so?" he asked jealously.

"You're wonderful!" retorted Janet, daringly.

"You just bet I am, or I couldn't have landed you," he asserted. "You're chock full of ginger, but it's been all corked up. You're so prim — so *Priscilla*." He was immensely pleased with the adjective he had coined, repeating it. "It's a great combination. When I think of it, I want to shake you, to squeeze you until you scream."

"Then please don't think of it," she said.

"That's easy!" he exclaimed, mockingly.

At a quarter to one they entered a sleepy village reminiscent of a New England of other days. The long street, deeply shaded in summer, was bordered by decorous homes, some of which had stood there for a century and a half; others were of the Mansard period. The high school, of strawberry-coloured brick, had been the pride and glory of the Kingsbury of the '70s: there were many churches, some graceful and some hideous. At the end of the street they came upon a common, surrounded by stone posts and

a railing, with a monument in the middle of it, and facing
the common on the north side was a rambling edifice with
many white gables, in front of which, from an iron arm on
a post, swung a quaint sign, "Kingsbury Tavern." In
revolutionary and coaching days the place had been a famous
inn; and now, thanks to the enterprise of a man who had
foreseen the possibilities of an era of automobiles, it had
become even more famous. A score of these modern vehicles were drawn up before it under the bare, ancient elms;
there was a scene of animation on the long porch, where
guests strolled up and down or sat in groups in the rocking-
chairs which the mild weather had brought forth again.
Ditmar drew up in line with the other motors, and stopped.

"Well, here we are!" he exclaimed, as he pulled off his
gauntlets. "I guess I could get along with something to
eat. How about you? They treat you as well here as any
place I know of in New England."

He assumed their lunching together at a public place as
a matter of course to which there could not possibly be an
objection, springing out of the car, removing the laprobe
from her knees, and helping her to alight. She laid the
roses on the seat.

"Aren't you going to bring them along?" he demanded.

"I'd rather not," she said. "Don't you think they'll be
safe here?"

"Oh, I guess so," he replied. She was always surprising
him; but her solicitation concerning them was a balm, and
he found all such instinctive acts refreshing.

"Afraid of putting up too much of a front, are you?"
he asked smilingly.

"I'd rather leave them here," she replied. As she walked
beside Ditmar to the door she was excited, unwontedly
self-conscious, painfully aware of inspection by the groups
on the porch. She had seen such people as these hurrying

in automobiles through the ugliness of Faber Street in
Hampton toward just such delectable spots as this village
of Kingsbury — people of that world of freedom and privilege from which she was excluded; Ditmar's world. He was
at home here. But she? The delusion that she somehow
had been miraculously snatched up into it was marred by
their glances. What were they thinking of her? Her face
was hot as she passed them and entered the hall, where more
people were gathered. But Ditmar's complacency, his ease
and self-confidence, his manner of owning the place, as it
were, somewhat reassured her. He went up to the desk,
behind which stood a burly, red-complexioned man who
greeted him effusively, yet with the air of respect accorded
the powerful.

"Hullo, Eddie," said Ditmar. "You've got a good crowd
here to-day. Any room for me?"

"Sure, Mr. Ditmar, we can always make room for you.
Well, I haven't laid eyes on you for a dog's age. Only
last Sunday Mr. Crane was here, and I was asking him where
you'd been keeping yourself."

"Why, I've been busy, Eddie. I've landed the biggest
order ever heard of in Hampton. Some of us have to work,
you know; all you've got to do is to loaf around this place
and smoke cigars and rake in the money."

The proprietor of the Kingsbury Tavern smiled indulgently at this persiflage.

"Let me present you to Miss Bumpus," said Ditmar.
"This is my friend, Eddie Hale," he added, for Janet's
benefit. "And when you've eaten his dinner you'll believe
me when I say he's got all the other hotel men beaten a mile."

Janet smiled and flushed. She had been aware of Mr.
Hale's discreet glance.

"Pleased to meet you, Miss Bumpus," he said, with a
somewhat elaborate bow.

"Eddie," said Ditmar, "have you got a nice little table for us?"

"It's a pity I didn't know you was coming, but I'll do my best," declared Mr. Hale, opening the door in the counter.

"Oh, I guess you can fix us all right, if you want to, Eddie."

"Mr. Ditmar's a great josher," Mr. Hale told Janet confidentially as he escorted them into the dining-room. And Ditmar, gazing around over the heads of the diners, spied in an alcove by a window a little table with tilted chairs.

"That one'll do," he said.

"I'm sorry, but it's engaged," apologized Mr. Hale.

"Forget it, Eddie — tell 'em they're late," said Ditmar, making his way toward it.

The proprietor pulled out Janet's chair.

"Say," he remarked, "it's no wonder *you* get along in business."

"Well, this is cosy, isn't it?" said Ditmar to Janet when they were alone. He handed her the menu, and snapped his fingers for a waitress.

"Why didn't you tell me you were coming to this place?" she asked.

"I wanted to surprise you. Don't you like it?"

"Yes," she replied. "Only —"

"Only, what?"

"I wish you wouldn't look at me like that — here."

"All right. I'll try to be good until we get into the car again. You watch me! I'll behave as if we'd been married ten years."

He snapped his fingers again, and the waitress hurried up to take their orders.

"Kingsbury's still dry, I guess," he said to the girl, who smiled sympathetically, somewhat ruefully. When she had gone he began to talk to Janet about the folly, in general, of prohibition, the fusel oil distributed on the sly. "I'll bet I could go out and find half a dozen rum shops within a mile of here!" he declared.

Janet did not doubt it. Ditmar's aplomb, his faculty of getting what he wanted, had amused and distracted her. She was growing calmer, able to scrutinize, at first covertly and then more boldly the people at the other tables, only to discover that she and Ditmar were not the objects of the universal curiosity she had feared. Once in a while, indeed, she encountered and then avoided the glance of some man, felt the admiration in it, was thrilled a little, and her sense of exhilaration returned as she regained her poise. She must be nice looking — more than that — in her new suit. On entering the tavern she had taken off the tweed coat, which Ditmar had carried and laid on a chair. This new and amazing adventure began to go to her head like wine. . . .

When luncheon was over they sat in a sunny corner of the porch while Ditmar smoked his cigar. His digestion was good, his spirits high, his love-making — on account of the public nature of the place — surreptitious yet fervent. The glamour to which Janet had yielded herself was on occasions slightly troubled by some new and enigmatic element to be detected in his voice and glances suggestive of intentions vaguely disquieting. At last she said : —

"Oughtn't we to be going home?"

"Home!" he ridiculed the notion. "I'm going to take you to the prettiest road you ever saw — around by French's Lower Falls. I only wish it was summer."

"I must be home before dark," she told him. "You see, the family don't know where I am. I haven't said anything to them about — about this."

"That's right," he said, after a moment's hesitation.

"I didn't think you would. There's plenty of time for that — after things get settled a little — isn't there?"

She thought his look a little odd, but the impression passed as they walked to the motor. He insisted now on her pinning the roses on the tweed coat, and she humoured him. The winter sun had already begun to drop, and with the levelling rays the bare hillsides, yellow and brown in the higher light, were suffused with pink; little by little, as the sun fell lower, imperceptible clouds whitened the blue cambric of the sky, distant copses were stained lilac. And Janet, as she gazed, wondered at a world that held at once so much beauty, so much joy and sorrow, — such strange sorrow as began to invade her now, not personal, but cosmic. At times it seemed almost to suffocate her; she drew in deep breaths of air : it was the essence of all things — of the man by her side, of herself, of the beauty so poignantly revealed to her.

Gradually Ditmar became conscious of this detachment, this new evidence of an extraordinary faculty of escaping him that seemed unimpaired. Constantly he tried by leaning closer to her, by reaching out his hand, to reassure himself that she was at least physically present. And though she did not resent these tokens, submitting passively, he grew perplexed and troubled; his optimistic atheism concerning things unseen was actually shaken by the impression she conveyed of beholding realities hidden from him. Shadows had begun to gather in the forest, filmy mists to creep over the waters. He asked if she were cold, and she shook her head and sighed as one coming out of a trance, smiling at him.

"It's been a wonderful day!" she said.

"The greatest ever!" he agreed. And his ardour, mounting again, swept away the unwonted mood of tenderness and awe she had inspired in him, made him bold to suggest the plan which had been the subject of an ecstatic contemplation.

"I'll tell you what we'll do," he said, "we'll take a little run down to Boston and have dinner together. We'll be there in an hour, and back by ten o'clock."

"To Boston!" she repeated. "Now?"

"Why not?" he said, stopping the car. "Here's the road — it's a boulevard all the way."

It was not so much the proposal as the passion in his voice, in his touch, the passion to which she felt herself responding that filled her with apprehension and dismay, and yet aroused her pride and anger.

"I told you I had to be home," she said.

"I'll have you home by ten o'clock, I promise. We're going to be married, Janet," he whispered.

"Oh, if you meant to marry me you wouldn't ask me to do this!" she cried. "I want to go back to Hampton. If you won't take me, I'll walk."

She had drawn away from him, and her hand was on the door. He seized her arm.

"For God's sake, don't take it that way!" he cried, in genuine alarm. "All I meant was — that we'd have a nice little dinner. I couldn't bear to leave you, it'll be a whole week before we get another day. Do you suppose I'd — I'd do anything to insult you, Janet?"

With her fingers still tightened over the door-catch she turned and looked at him.

"I don't know," she said slowly. "Sometimes I think you would. Why shouldn't you? Why should you marry me? Why shouldn't you try to do with me what you've done with other women? I don't know anything about the world, about life. I'm nobody. Why shouldn't you?"

"Because you're not like the other women — that's why. I love you — won't you believe it?" He was beside himself with anxiety. "Listen — I'll take you home if you want to go. You don't know how it hurts me to have you think such things!"

"Well, then, take me home," she said. It was but gradually that she became pacified. A struggle was going on within her between these doubts of him he had stirred up again and other feelings aroused by his pleadings. Night fell, and when they reached the Silliston road the lights of Hampton shone below them in the darkness.

"You'd better let me out here," she said. "You can't drive me home."

He brought the car to a halt beside one of the small wooden shelters built for the convenience of passengers.

"You forgive me — you understand, Janet?" he asked.

"Sometimes I don't know what to think," she said, and suddenly clung to him. "I — I forgive you. I oughtn't to suspect such things, but I'm like that. I'm horrid — and I can't help it." She began to unbutton the coat he had bought for her.

"Aren't you going to take it?" he said. "It's yours."

"And what do you suppose my family would say if I told them Mr. Ditmar had given it to me?"

"Come on, I'll drive you home, I'll tell them I gave it to you, that we're going to be married," he announced recklessly.

"Oh, no!" she exclaimed in consternation. "You couldn't. You said so yourself — that you didn't want any one to know, now. I'll get on the trolley."

"And the roses?" he asked.

She pressed them to her face, and chose one. "I'll take this," she said, laying the rest on the seat. . . .

He waited until he saw her safely on the trolley car, and then drove slowly homeward in a state of amazement. He had been on the verge of announcing himself to the family in Fillmore Street as her prospective husband! He tried to imagine what that household was like; and again he found himself wondering why she had not consented to his proposal. And the ever-recurring question presented itself — was he prepared to go that length? He didn't know. She was beyond him, he had no clew to her, she was to him as mysterious as a symphony. Certain strains of her moved him intensely — the rest was beyond his grasp. . . . At supper, while his children talked and laughed boisterously, he sat silent, restless, and in spite of their presence the house seemed appallingly empty.

2

When Janet returned home she ran to her bedroom, and taking from the wardrobe the tissue paper that had come with her new dress, and which she had carefully folded, she wrapped the rose in it, and put it away in the back of a drawer. Thus smothered, its fragrance stifled, it seemed emblematic, somehow, of the clandestine nature of her love. . . .

The weeks that immediately followed were strange ones. All the elements of life that previously had been realities, trivial yet fundamental, her work, her home, her intercourse with the family, became fantastic. There was the mill to which she went every day: she recognized it, yet it was not the same mill, nor was Fillmore Street the Fillmore Street of old. Nor did the new and feverish existence over whose borderland she had been transported seem real, save in certain hours she spent in Ditmar's company, when he made her forget — hers being a temperament to feel the weight of an unnatural secrecy. She was aware, for instance, that her mother and even her father thought her conduct odd, were anxious as to her absences on certain nights and on Sundays. She offered no explanation. It was impossible.

Q

She understood that the reason why they refrained from questioning her was due to a faith in her integrity as well as to a respect for her as a breadwinner who had earned a right to independence. And while her suspicion of Hannah's anxiety troubled her, on the occasions when she thought of it, Lise's attitude disturbed her even more. From Lise she had been prepared for suspicion, arraignment, ridicule. What a vindication if it were disclosed that she, Janet, had a lover — and that lover Ditmar! But Lise said nothing. She was remote, self-absorbed. Hannah spoke about it on the evenings Janet stayed at home.

She would not consent to meet Ditmar every evening. Yet, as the days succeeded one another, Janet was often astonished by the fact that their love remained apparently unsuspected by Mr. Price and Caldwell and others in the office. They must have noticed, on some occasions, the manner in which Ditmar looked at her; and in business hours she had continually to caution him, to keep him in check. Again, on the evening excursions to which she consented, though they were careful to meet in unfrequented spots, someone might easily have recognized him; and she did not like to ponder over the number of young women in the other offices who knew her by sight. These reflections weighed upon her, particularly when she seemed conscious of curious glances. But what caused her the most concern was the constantly recurring pressure to which Ditmar himself subjected her, and which, as time went on, she found increasingly difficult to resist. He tried to take her by storm, and when this method failed, resorted to pleadings and supplications even harder to deny because of the innate feminine pity she felt for him. To recount these affairs would be a mere repetition of identical occurrences. On their second Sunday excursion he had actually driven her, despite her opposition, several miles on the Boston road; and her resistance only served to inflame him the more. It seemed, afterwards, as she sat unnerved, a miracle that she had stopped him. Then came reproaches: she would not trust him; they could not be married at once; she must understand that! — an argument so repugnant as to cause her to shake with sobs of inarticulate anger. After this he would grow bewildered, then repentant, then contrite. In contrition — had he known it — he was nearest to victory.

As has been said, she did not intellectualize her reasons, but the core of her resistance was the very essence of an individuality having its roots in a self-respecting and self-controlling inheritance — an element wanting in her sister Lise. It must have been largely the thought of Lise, the spectacle of Lise — often perhaps unconsciously present — that dominated her conduct; yet reinforcing such an ancestral sentiment was another, environmental and more complicated, the result in our modern atmosphere of an undefined feminism apt to reveal itself in many undesirable ways, but which in reality is a logical projection of the American tradition of liberty. To submit was not only to lose her liberty, to become a dependent, but also and inevitably, she thought, to lose Ditmar's love. . . .

No experience, however, is emotionally continuous, nor was their intimacy by any means wholly on this plane of conflict. There were hours when, Ditmar's passion having spent itself, they achieved comradeship, in the office and out of it; revelations for Janet when he talked of himself, relating the little incidents she found most illuminating. And thus by degrees she was able to build up a new and truer estimate of him. For example, she began to perceive that his life outside of his interest in the mills, instead of being the romance of privileged joys she had once imagined, had been almost as empty as her own, without either unity or direction. Her per-

ception was none the less keen ¦because definite terms
were wanting for its expression. The idea of him that first
had captivated her was that of an energized and focussed
character controlling with a sure hand the fortunes of a
great organization; of a power in the city and state, of a
being who, in his leisure moments, dwelt in a delectable
realm from which she was excluded. She was still acutely
conscious of his force, but what she now felt was its lack of
direction — save for the portion that drove the Chippering
Mills. The rest of it, like the river, flowed away on the line
of least resistance to the sea.

As was quite natural, this gradual discovery of what he
was — or of what he wasn't — this truer estimate, this partial disillusionment, merely served to deepen and intensify
the feeling he had aroused in her; to heighten, likewise,
the sense of her own value by confirming a belief in her
possession of certain qualities, of a kind of fibre he needed
in a helpmate. She dwelt with a woman's fascination upon
the prospect of exercising a creative influence — even while
she acknowledged the fearful possibility of his power in
unguarded moments to overwhelm and destroy her. Here
was another incentive to resist the gusts of his passion. She
could guide and develop him by helping and improving herself. Hope and ambition throbbed within her, she felt a
contempt for his wife, for the women who had been her
predecessors. He had not spoken of these, save once or
twice by implication, but with what may seem a surprising
leniency she regarded them as consequences of a life lacking
in content. If only she could keep her head, she might
supply that content, and bring him happiness! The thought
of his children troubled her most, but she was quick to perceive that he got nothing from them; and even though it
were partly his own fault, she was inclined to lay the heavier
blame on the woman who had been their mother. The

triviality, the emptiness of his existence outside of the walls of the mill made her heart beat with pure pity.   For she could understand it.

One of the many, and often humorous, incidents that served to bring about this realization of a former aimlessness happened on their second Sunday excursion.   This time he had not chosen the Kingsbury Tavern, but another automobilists' haunt, an enlightening indication of established habits involving a wide choice of resorts.   While he was paying for luncheon and chatting with the proprietor, Ditmar snatched from the change he had flung down on the counter a five dollar gold coin.

"Now how in thunder did that get into my right-hand pocket?   I always keep it in my vest," he exclaimed; and the matter continued to disturb him after they were in the automobile.   "It's my lucky piece.   I guess I was so excited at the prospect of seeing you when I dressed this morning I put it into my change.   Just see what you do to me!"

"Does it bring you luck?" she inquired smilingly.

"How about you!   I call you the biggest piece of luck I ever had."

"You'd better not be too sure," she warned him.

"Oh, I'm not worrying.   I had that piece in my pocket the day I went down to see old Stephen Chippering, when he made me agent, and I've kept it ever since.   And I'll tell you a funny thing — it's enough to make any man believe in luck.   Do you remember that day last summer I was tinkering with the car by the canal and you came along?"

"The day you pretended to be tinkering," she corrected him.

He laughed.   "So you were on to me?" he said.   "You're a foxy one!"

"Anyone could see you were only pretending.   It made me angry, when I thought of it afterwards."

"I just had to do it — I wanted to talk to you. But listen to what I'm going to tell you! It's a miracle, all right,— happening just at that time — that very morning. I was coming back to Boston from New York on the midnight, and when the train ran into Back Bay and I was putting on my trousers the piece rolled out among the bed clothes. I didn't know I'd lost it until I sat down in the Parker House to eat my breakfast, and I suddenly felt in my pocket. It made me sick to think it was gone. Well, I started to telephone the Pullman office, and then I made up my mind I'd take a taxi and go down to the South Station myself, and just as I got out of the cab there was the nigger porter, all dressed up in his glad rags, coming out of the station! I knew him, I'd been on his car lots of times. 'Say, George,' I said, 'I didn't forget you this morning, did I?'

"'No, suh,' said George, 'you done give me a quarter.'

"'I guess you're mistaken, George,' says I, and I fished out a ten dollar bill. You ought to have seen that nigger's eyes.

"'What's this for, Mister Ditmar?' says he.

"'For that lucky gold piece you found in lower seven,' I told him. 'We'll trade.'

"'Was you in lower seven? — so you was!' says George. Well, he had it all right — you bet he had it. Now wasn't that queer? The very day you and I began to know each other!"

"Wonderful!" Janet agreed. "Why don't you put it on your watch chain?"

"Well, I've thought of that," he replied, with the air of having considered all sides of the matter. "But I've got that charm of the secret order I belong to — that's on my chain. I guess I'll keep it in my vest pocket."

"I didn't know you were so superstitious," she mocked.

"Pretty nearly everybody's superstitious," he declared. And she thought of Lise.

"I'm not. I believe if things are going to happen — well, they're going to happen. Nothing can prevent it."

"By thunder!" he exclaimed, struck by her remark. "You are like that! You're different from any person I ever knew. . . ."

From such anecdotes she pieced together her new Ditmar. He spoke of a large world she had never seen, of New York and Washington and Chicago, where he intended to take her. In the future he would never travel alone. And he told her of his having been a delegate to the last National Republican Convention, explaining what a delegate was. He gloried in her innocence, and it was pleasant to dazzle her with impressions of his cosmopolitanism. In this, perhaps, he was not quite so successful as he imagined, but her eyes shone. She had never even been in a sleeping car! For her delectation he launched into an enthusiastic description of these vehicles, of palatial compartment cars, of limited, transcontinental trains, where one had a stenographer and a barber at one's disposal.

"Neither of them would do me any good," she complained.

"You could go to the manicure," he said.

3

There had been in Ditmar's life certain events which, in his anecdotal moods, were magnified into matters of climacteric importance; high, festal occasions on which it was sweet to reminisce, such as his visit as Delegate at Large to that Chicago Convention. He had travelled on a special train stocked with cigars and White Seal champagne, in the company of senators and congressmen and ex-governors, state treasurers, collectors of the port, mill owners, and bankers to whom he referred, as the French say, in terms of

their "little" names. He dwelt on the magnificence of the
huge hotel set on the borders of a lake like an inland sea,
and related such portions of the festivities incidental to
"the seeing of Chicago" as would bear repetition. No
women belonged to this realm; no women, at least, who
were to be regarded as persons. Ditmar did not mention
them, but no doubt they existed, along with the cigars and
the White Seal champagne, contributing to the amenities.
And the excursion, to Janet, took on the complexion of a
sort of glorified picnic in the course of which, incidentally,
a President of the United States had been chosen. In her
innocence she had believed the voters to perform this function. Ditmar laughed.

"Do you suppose we're going to let the mob run this
country?" he inquired. "Once in a while we can't get
away with it as we'd like, we have to take the best
we can."

Thus was brought home to her more and more clearly
that what men strove and fought for were the joys of
prominence, privilege, and power. Everywhere, in the great
world, they demanded and received consideration. It was
Ditmar's boast that if nobody else could get a room in a
crowded New York hotel, he could always obtain one. And
she was fain to concede — she who had never known privilege
— a certain intoxicating quality to this eminence. If you
could get the power, and refused to take it, the more fool
you! A topsy-turvy world, in which the stupid toiled day
by day, week by week, exhausting their energies and craving joy, while others adroitly carried off the prize; and
virtue had apparently as little to do with the matter as
fair hair or a club foot. If Janet had ever read Darwin,
she would have recognized in her lover a creature rather
wonderfully adapted to his environment; and what puzzled
her, perhaps, was the riddle that presents itself to many

better informed than herself — the utter absence in this environment of the sign of any being who might be called God. Her perplexities — for she did have them — took the form of an instinctive sense of inadequacy, of persistently recurring though inarticulate convictions of the existence of elements not included in Ditmar's categories — of things that money could not buy; of things, too, alas! that poverty was as powerless to grasp. Stored within her, sometimes rising to the level of consciousness, was that experience at Silliston in the May weather when she had had a glimpse — just a glimpse! — of a garden where strange and precious flowers were in bloom. On the other hand, this mysterious perception by her of things unseen and hitherto unguessed, of rays of delight in the spectrum of values to which his senses were unattuned, was for Ditmar the supreme essence of her fascination. At moments he was at once bewildered and inebriated by the rare delicacy of fabric of the woman whom he had somehow stumbled upon and possessed.

Then there were the hours when they worked together in the office. Here she beheld Ditmar at his best. It cannot be said that his infatuation for her was ever absent from his consciousness: he knew she was there beside him, he betrayed it continually. But here she was in the presence of what had been and what remained his ideal, the Chippering Mill; here he acquired unity. All his energies were bent toward the successful execution of the Bradlaugh order, which had to be completed on the first of February. And as day after day went by her realization of the magnitude of the task he had undertaken became keener. Excitement was in the air. Ditmar seemed somehow to have managed to infuse not only Orcutt, the superintendent, but the foremen and second hands and even the workers with a common spirit of pride and loyalty, of interest, of determination to carry off this matter triumphantly. The mill seemed fairly to hum with effort. Janet's increasing knowledge of its organization and processes only served to heighten her admiration for the confidence Ditmar had shown from the beginning. It was superb. And now, as the probability of the successful execution of the task tended more and more toward certainty, he sometimes gave vent to his boyish, exuberant spirits.

"I told Holster, I told all those croakers I'd do it, and by thunder I will do it, with three days' margin, too! I'll get the last shipment off on the twenty-eighth of January. Why, even George Chippering was afraid I couldn't handle it. If the old man was alive *he* wouldn't have had cold feet." Then Ditmar added, half jocularly, half seriously, looking down on her as she sat with her note-book, waiting for him to go on with his dictation: "I guess you've had your share in it, too. You've been a wonder, the way you've caught on and taken things off my shoulders. If Orcutt died I believe you could step right into his shoes."

"I'm sure I could step into his shoes," she replied. "Only I hope he won't die."

"I hope he won't, either," said Ditmar. "And as for you —"

"Never mind me, now," she said.

He bent over her.

"Janet, you're the greatest girl in the world."

Yes, she was happiest when she felt she was helping him, it gave her confidence that she could do more, lead him into paths beyond which they might explore together. She was useful. Sometimes, however, he seemed to her oversanguine; though he had worked hard, his success had come too easily, had been too uniform. His temper was quick, the prospect of opposition often made him overbearing, yet on occasions he listened with surprising patience to his subordinates when they ventured to differ from his opinions. At other times Janet had seen him overrule them ruthlessly, humiliate them. There were days when things went wrong, when there were delays, complications, more matters to attend to than usual. On one such day, after the dinner hour, Mr. Orcutt entered the office. His long, lean face wore a certain expression Janet had come to know, an expression that always irritated Ditmar — the conscientious superintendent having the unfortunate faculty of exaggerating annoyances by his very bearing. Ditmar stopped in the midst of dictating a peculiarly difficult letter, and looked up sharply.

"Well," he asked, "what's the trouble now?"

Orcutt seemed incapable of reading storm signals. When anything happened, he had the air of declaring, "I told you so."

"You may remember I spoke to you once or twice, Mr. Ditmar, of the talk over the fifty-four hour law that goes into effect in January."

"Yes, what of it?" Ditmar cut in. "The notices have been posted, as the law requires."

"The hands have been grumbling, there are trouble makers among them. A delegation came to me this noon and wanted to know whether we intended to cut the pay to correspond to the shorter working hours."

"Of course it's going to be cut," said Ditmar. "What do they suppose? That we're going to pay 'em for work they don't do? The hands not paid by the piece are paid practically by the hour, not by the day. And there's got to be some limit to this thing. If these damned demagogues in the legislature keep on cutting down the hours of women and children every three years or so — and we can't run the mill without the women and children — we might as well shut down right now. Three years ago, when they made it fifty-six hours, we were fools to keep up the pay. I said so then, at the conference, but they wouldn't listen to me. They listened this time. Holster and one or two others croaked, but we shut 'em up. No, they won't get any more pay, not a damned cent."

Orcutt had listened patiently, lugubriously.

"I told them that."

"What did they say?"

"They said they thought there'd be a strike."

"Pooh! Strike!" exclaimed Ditmar with contemptuous violence. "Do you believe that? You're always borrowing trouble, you are. They may have a strike at one mill, the Clarendon. I hope they do, I hope Holster gets it in the neck — he don't know how to run a mill anyway. We won't have any strike, our people understand when they're well off, they've got all the work they can do, they're sending fortunes back to the old country or piling them up in the banks. It's all bluff."

"There was a meeting of the English branch of the I. W. W. last night. A committee was appointed," said Orcutt, who as usual took a gloomy satisfaction in the prospect of disaster.

"The I. W. W.! My God, Orcutt, don't you know enough not to come in here wasting my time talking about the I. W. W.? Those anarchists haven't got any organization. Can't you get that through your head?"

"All right," replied Orcutt, and marched off. Janet felt rather sorry for him, though she had to admit that his manner was exasperating. But Ditmar's anger, instead of cooling, increased: it all seemed directed against the unfortunate superintendent.

"Would you believe that a man who's been in this mill twenty-five years could be such a fool?" he demanded. "The I. W. W.! Why not the Ku Klux? He must think

I haven't anything to do but chin. I don't know why I keep him here, sometimes I think he'll drive me crazy."

His eyes seemed to have grown small and red, as was always the case when his temper got the better of him. Janet did not reply, but sat with her pencil poised over her book.

"Let's see, where was I?" he asked. "I can't finish that letter now. Go out and do the others."

4

Mundane experience, like a badly mixed cake, has a tendency to run in streaks, and on the day following the incident related above Janet's heart was heavy. Ditmar betrayed an increased shortness of temper and preoccupation; and the consciousness that her love had lent her a clairvoyant power to trace the source of his humours — though these were often hidden from or unacknowledged by himself — was in this instance small consolation. She saw clearly enough that the apprehensions expressed by Mr. Orcutt, whom he had since denounced as an idiotic old woman, had made an impression, aroused in him the ever-abiding concern for the mill which was his life's passion and which had been but temporarily displaced by his infatuation with her. That other passion was paramount. What was she beside it? Would he hesitate for a moment to sacrifice her if it came to a choice between them? The tempestuousness of these thoughts, when they took possession of her, hinting as they did of possibilities in her nature hitherto unguessed and unrevealed, astonished and frightened her; she sought to thrust them away, to reassure herself that his concern for the successful delivery of the Bradlaugh order was natural. During the morning, in the intervals between interviews with the superintendents, he was self-absorbed, and she found herself inconsistently resenting the absence of those expressions of endearment — the glances and stolen caresses — for indulgence in which she had hitherto rebuked him : and though pride came to her rescue, fuel was added to her feeling by the fact that he did not seem to notice her coolness. Since he failed to appear after lunch, she knew he must be investigating the suspicions Orcutt had voiced; but at six o'clock, when he had not returned, she closed up her desk and left the office. An odour of cheap perfume pervading the corridor made her aware of the presence of Miss Lottie Myers.

"Oh, it's you!" said that young woman, looking up from the landing of the stairs. "I might have known it — you never make a get-away until after six, do you?"

"Oh, sometimes," said Janet.

"I stayed as a special favour to-night," Miss Myers declared. "But I'm not so stuck on my job that I can't tear myself away from it."

"I don't suppose you are," said Janet.

For a moment Miss Myers looked as if she was about to be still more impudent, but her eye met Janet's, and wavered. They crossed the bridge in silence. "Well, ta-ta," she said. "If you like it, it's up to you. Five o'clock for mine," — and walked away, up the canal, swinging her hips defiantly. And Janet, gazing after her, grew hot with indignation and apprehension. Her relations with Ditmar were suspected, after all, made the subject of the kind of comment indulged in, *sotto voce*, by Lottie Myers and her friends at the luncheon hour. She felt a mad, primitive desire to run after the girl, to spring upon and strangle her and compel her to speak what was in her mind and then retract it; and the motor impulse, inhibited, caused a sensation of sickness, of unhappiness and degradation as she turned her steps slowly homeward. Was it a misinterpretation, after all — what Lottie Myers had implied and feared to say? . . .

In Fillmore Street supper was over, and Lise, her face contorted, her body strained, was standing in front of the bureau "doing" her hair, her glance now seeking the mirror, now falling again to consult a model in one of those periodicals of froth and fashion that cause such numberless heart burnings in every quarter of our democracy, and which are filled with photographs of "prominent" persons at race meetings, horse shows, and resorts, and with actresses, dancers, — and mannequins.   Janet's eyes fell on the open page to perceive that the coiffure her sister so painfully imitated was worn by a young woman with an insolent, vapid face and hard eyes, whose knees were crossed, revealing considerably more than an ankle. The picture was labelled, "A dance at Palm Beach — A flashlight of Mrs. 'Trudy' Gascoigne-Schell," — one of those mysterious, hybrid names which, in connection with the thoughts of New York and the visible rakish image of the lady herself, cause involuntary shudders down the spine of the reflecting American provincial. Some such responsive quiver, akin to disgust, Janet herself experienced.

"It's the very last scream," Lise was saying. "And say, if I owned a ball dress like that I'd be somebody's Lulu all right! Can I have the pleasure of the next maxixe, Miss Bumpus?" With deft and rapid fingers she had parted her hair far on the right side and pulled it down over the left eyebrow, twisted it over her ear and tightly around her head, inserting here and there a hairpin, seizing the hand mirror with the cracked back, and holding it up behind her. Finally, when the operation was finished to her satisfaction she exclaimed, evidently to the paragon in the picture, "I get you!" Whereupon, from the wardrobe, she produced a hat. "You sure had my number when you guessed the feathers on that other would get draggled," she observed in high good humour, generously ignoring their former unpleasantness on the subject. When she had pinned it on she bent mockingly over her sister, who sat on the bed. "How d'you like my new toque? Peekaboo! That's the way the guys rubberneck to see if you're good lookin'."

Lise was exalted, feverish, apparently possessed by some high secret; her eyes shone, and when she crossed the room she whistled bars of ragtime and executed mincing steps of the maxixe. Fumbling in the upper drawer for a pair of white gloves (also new), she knocked off the corner of the bureau her velvet bag; it opened as it struck the floor, and out of it rolled a lilac vanity case and a yellow coin. Casting a suspicious, lightning glance at Janet, she snatched up the vanity case and covered the coin with her foot.

"Lock the doors!" she cried, with an hysteric giggle. Then removing her foot she picked up the coin surreptitiously. To her amazement her sister made no comment, did not seem to have taken in the significance of the episode. Lise had expected a tempest of indignant, searching questions, a "third degree," as she would have put it. She snapped the bag together, drew on her gloves, and, when she was ready to leave, with characteristic audacity crossed the room, taking her sister's face between her hands and kissing her.

"Tell me your troubles, sweetheart!" she said — and did not wait to hear them.

Janet was incapable of speech — nor could she have brought herself to ask Lise whether or not the money had been earned at the *Bagatelle*, and remained miraculously unspent. It was possible, but highly incredible. And then, the vanity case and the new hat were to be accounted for! The sight of the gold piece, indeed, had suddenly revived in Janet the queer feeling of faintness, almost of nausea she had experienced after parting with Lottie Myers. And by some untoward association she was reminded of a conversation she had had with Ditmar on the Saturday afternoon following their first Sunday excursion, when, on opening her pay envelope, she had found twenty dollars.

"Are you sure I'm worth it?" she had demanded — and he had been quite sure. He had added that she was worth more, much more, but that he could not give her as yet, without the risk of comment, a sum commensurate with the value of her services. . . . But now she asked herself again, was she worth it? or was it merely — part of her price? Going to the wardrobe and opening a drawer at the bottom she searched among her clothes until she discovered the piece of tissue paper in which she had wrapped the rose rescued from the cluster he had given her. The petals were dry, yet they gave forth, still, a faint, reminiscent fragrance as she pressed them to her face. Janet wept. . . .

5

The following morning as she was kneeling in a corner of the room by the letter files, one of which she had placed on the floor, she recognized his step in the outer office, heard him pause to joke with young Caldwell, and needed not the visual proof — when after a moment he halted on the threshold — of the fact that his usual, buoyant spirits were restored. He held a cigar in his hand, and in his eyes was the eager look with which she had become familiar, which indeed she had learned to anticipate as they swept the room in search of her. And when they fell on her he closed the door and came forward impetuously. But her exclamation caused him to halt in bewilderment.

"Don't touch me!" she said.

And he stammered out, as he stood over her : —

R

"What's the matter?"

"Everything. You don't love me — I was a fool to believe you did."

"Don't love you!" he repeated. "My God, what's the trouble now? What have I done?"

"Oh, it's nothing you've done, it's what you haven't done, it's what you can't do. You don't really care for me — all you care for is this mill — when anything happens here you don't know I'm alive."

He stared at her, and then an expression of comprehension, of intense desire grew in his eyes; and his laugh, as he flung his cigar out of the open window and bent down to seize her, was almost brutal. She fought him, she tried to hurt him, and suddenly, convulsively pressed herself to him.

"You little tigress!" he said, as he held her. "You were jealous — were you — jealous of the mill?" And he laughed again. "I'd like to see you with something really to be jealous about. So you love me like that, do you?"

She could feel his heart beating against her.

"I won't be neglected," she told him tensely. "I want *all* of you — if I can't have all of you, I don't want any. Do you understand?"

"Do I understand? Well, I guess I do."

"You didn't yesterday," she reproached him, somewhat dazed by the swiftness of her submission, and feeling still the traces of a lingering resentment. She had not intended to surrender. "You forgot all about me, you didn't know I was here, much less that I was hurt. Oh, I was hurt! And you — I can tell at once when anything's wrong with you — I know without your saying it."

He was amazed, he might indeed have been troubled and even alarmed by this passion he had aroused had his own passion not been at the flood. And as he wiped away her tears with his handkerchief he could scarcely believe his senses that this was the woman whose resistance had demanded all his force to overcome. Indeed, although he recognized the symptoms she betrayed as feminine, as having been registered — though feebly compared to this! — by incidents in his past, precisely his difficulty seemed to be in identifying this complex and galvanic being *as* a woman, not as something almost fearful in her significance, outside the bounds of experience. . . .

Presently she ceased to tremble, and he drew her to the window. The day was as mild as autumn, the winter sun like honey in its mellowness; a soft haze blurred the outline of the upper bridge.

"Only two more days until Sunday," he whispered, caressingly, exultantly. . . .

CHAPTER XII

1

IT had been a strange year in Hampton, unfortunate for coal merchants, welcome to the poor. But Sunday lacked the transforming touch of sunshine. The weather was damp and cold as Janet set out from Fillmore Street. Ditmar, she knew, would be waiting for her, he counted on her, and she could not bear to disappoint him, to disappoint herself. And all the doubts and fears that from time to time had assailed her were banished by this impulse to go to him, to be with him. He loved her! The words, as she sat in the trolley car, ran in her head like the lilt of a song. What did the weather matter?

When she alighted at the lonely cross-roads snow had already begun to fall. But she spied the automobile, with its top raised, some distance down the lane, and in a moment she was in it, beside him, wrapped in the coat she had now come to regard as her own. He buttoned down the curtains and took her in his arms.

"What shall we do to-day," she asked, "if it snows?"

"Don't let that worry you, sweetheart," he said. "I have the chains on, I can get through anything in this car."

He was in high, almost turbulent spirits as he turned the car and drove it out of the rutty lane into the state road. The snow grew thicker and thicker still, the world was blotted out by swiftly whirling, feathery flakes that melted on the windshield, and through the wet glass Janet caught distorted glimpses of black pines and cedars beside the highway.

The ground was spread with fleece. Occasionally, and with startling suddenness, other automobiles shot like dark phantoms out of the whiteness, and like phantoms disappeared. Presently, through the veil, she recognized Silliston — a very different Silliston from that she had visited on the fragrant day in springtime, when the green on the common had been embroidered with dandelions, and the great elms — whose bare branches were now fantastically traced against the flowing veil of white — heavy with leaf. Vignettes emerged — only to fade! — of the old-world houses whose quaint beauty had fascinated and moved her. And she found herself wondering what had become of the strange man she had mistaken for a carpenter. All that seemed to have taken place in a past life. She asked Ditmar where he was going.

"Boston," he told her. "There's no other place to go."

"But you'll never get back if it goes on snowing like this."

"Well, the trains are still running," he assured her, with a quizzical smile. "How about it, little girl?" It was a term of endearment derived, undoubtedly, from a theatrical source, in which he sometimes indulged.

She did not answer. Surprisingly, to-day, she did not care. All she could think of, all she wanted was to go on and on beside him with the world shut out — on and on forever. She was his — what did it matter? They were on their way to Boston! She began, dreamily, to think about Boston, to try to restore it in her imagination to the exalted place it had held before she met Ditmar; to reconstruct it from vague memories of childhood when, in two of the family peregrinations, she had crossed it. Traces remained of emotionally-toned impressions acquired when she had walked about the city holding Edward's hand — of a long row of stately houses with forbidding fronts, set on a hillside, of a wide, tree-covered space where children were playing.

And her childish verdict, persisting to-day, was one of inaccessibility, impenetrability, of jealously guarded wealth and beauty. Those houses, and the treasures she was convinced they must contain, were not for her! Some of the panes of glass in their windows were purple — she remembered a little thing like that, and asking her father the reason! He hadn't known. This purple quality had somehow steeped itself into her memory of Boston, and even now the colour stood for the word, impenetrable. That was extraordinary. Even now! Well, they were going to Boston; if Ditmar had said they were going to Bagdad it would have been quite as credible — and incredible. Wherever they were going, it was into the larger, larger life, and walls were to crumble before them, walls through which they would pass, even as they rent the white veil of the storm, into regions of beauty. . . .

And now the world seemed abandoned to them alone, so empty, so still were the white villages flitting by; so empty, so still the great parkway of the Fells stretching away and away like an enchanted forest under the snow, like the domain of some sleeping king. And the flakes melted silently into the black waters. And the wide avenue to which they came led to a sleeping palace! No, it was a city, Somerville, Ditmar told her, as they twisted in and out of streets, past stores, churches and fire-engine houses, breasted the heights, descended steeply on the far side into Cambridge, and crossed the long bridge over the Charles. And here at last was Boston — Beacon Street, the heart or funnel of it, as one chose. Ditmar, removing one of the side curtains that she might see, with just a hint in his voice of a reverence she was too excited to notice, pointed out the stern and respectable façades of the twin Chippering mansions standing side by side. Save for these shrines — for such in some sort they were to him — the Back Bay in his eyes was nothing more than a collection of houses inhabited by people whom money and social position made unassailable.   But to-day he, too, was excited.   Never had he been more keenly aware of her sensitiveness to experience; and he to whom it had not occurred to wonder at Boston wondered at her, who seemed able to summon forth a presiding, brooding spirit of the place from out of the snow.   Deep in her eyes, though they sparkled, was the reflection of some mystic vision; her cheeks were flushed.   And in her delight, vicariously his own, he rejoiced; in his trembling hope of more delight to come, — which this mentorship would enhance, — despite the fast deepening snow he drove her up one side of Commonwealth Avenue and down the other, encircling the Common and the Public Garden; stopping at the top of Park Street that she might gaze up at the State House, whose golden dome, seen through the veil, was tinged with blue.   Boston!   Why not Russia?   Janet was speechless for sheer lack of words to describe what she felt. . . .

At length he brought the car to a halt opposite an imposing doorway in front of which a glass roof extended over the pavement, and Janet demanded where they were.

"Well, we've got to eat, haven't we?" Ditmar replied. She noticed that he was shivering.

"Are you cold?" she inquired with concern.

"I guess I am, a little," he replied.   "I don't know why I should be, in a fur coat.   But I'll be warm soon enough, now."

A man in blue livery hurried toward them across the side-walk, helping them to alight.   And Ditmar, after driving the car a few paces beyond the entrance, led her through the revolving doors into a long corridor, paved with marble and lighted by bulbs glowing from the ceiling, where benches were set against the wall, overspread by the leaves of potted plants set in the intervals between them.

"Sit down a moment," he said to her. "I must telephone to have somebody take that car, or it'll stay there the rest of the winter."

She sat down on one of the benches. The soft light, the warmth, the exotic odour of the plants, the well-dressed people who trod softly the strip of carpet set on the marble with the air of being at home — all contributed to an excitement, intense yet benumbing. She could not think. She didn't want to think — only to feel, to enjoy, to wring the utmost flavour of enchantment from these new surroundings; and her face wore the expression of one in a dream. Presently she saw Ditmar returning followed by a boy in a blue uniform.

"All right," he said. At the end of the corridor was an elevator in which they were shot to one of the upper floors; and the boy, inserting a key in a heavy mahogany door, revealed a sitting-room. Between its windows was a table covered with a long, white cloth reaching to the floor, on which, amidst the silverware and glass, was set a tall vase filled with dusky roses. Janet, drawing in a deep breath of their fragrance, glanced around the room. The hangings, the wall-paper, the carpet, the velvet upholstery of the mahogany chairs, of the wide lounge in the corner were of a deep and restful green; the marble mantelpiece, with its English coal grate, was copied — had she known it — from a mansion of the Georgian period. The hands of a delicate Georgian clock pointed to one. And in the large mirror behind the clock she beheld an image she supposed, dreamily, to be herself. The bell boy was taking off her coat, which he hung, with Ditmar's, on a rack in a corner.

"Shall I light the fire, sir?" he asked.

"Sure," said Ditmar. "And tell them to hurry up with lunch."

The boy withdrew, closing the door silently behind him.

"We're going to have lunch here!" Janet exclaimed.

"Why not? I thought it would be nicer than a public dining-room, and when I got up this morning and saw what the weather was I telephoned." He placed two chairs before the fire, which had begun to blaze. "Isn't it cosy?" he said, taking her hands and pulling her toward him. His own hands trembled, the tips of his fingers were cold.

"You are cold!" she said.

"Not now — not now," he replied. The queer vibrations were in his voice that she had heard before. "Sweetheart! This is the best yet, isn't it? And after that trip in the storm!"

"It's beautiful!" she murmured, gently drawing away from him and looking around her once more. "I never was in a room like this."

"Well, you'll be in plenty more of them," he exulted. "Sit down beside the fire, and get warm yourself."

She obeyed, and he took the chair at her side, his eyes on her face. As usual, she was beyond him; and despite her exclamations of surprise, of appreciation and pleasure she maintained the outward poise, the inscrutability that summed up for him her uniqueness in the world of woman. She sat as easily upright in the delicate Chippendale chair as though she had been born to it. He made wild surmises as to what she might be thinking. Was she, as she seemed, taking all this as a matter of course? She imposed on him an impelling necessity to speak, to say anything — it did not matter what — and he began to dwell on the excellences of the hotel. She did not appear to hear him, her eyes lingering on the room, until presently she asked : —

"What's the name of this hotel?"

He told her.

"I thought they only allowed married people to come, like this, in a private room."

"Oh!" he began — and the sudden perception that she had made this statement impartially added to his perplexity. "Well," he was able to answer, "we're as good as married, aren't we, Janet?" He leaned toward her, he put his hand on hers. "The manager here is an old friend of mine. He knows we're as good as married."

"Another old friend!" she queried. And the touch of humour, in spite of his taut nerves, delighted him.

"Yes, yes," he laughed, rather uproariously. "I've got 'em everywhere, as thick as landmarks."

"You seem to," she said.

"I hope you're hungry," he said.

"Not very," she replied. "It's all so strange — this day, Claude. It's like a fairy story, coming here to Boston in the snow, and this place, and — and being with you."

"You still love me?" he cried, getting up.

"You must know that I do," she answered simply, raising her face to his. And he stood gazing down into it, with an odd expression she had never seen before. . . . "What's the matter?" she asked.

"Nothing — nothing," he assured her, but continued to look at her. "You're so — so wonderful," he whispered, "I just can't believe it."

"And if it's hard for you," she answered, "think what it must be for me!" And she smiled up at him.

Ditmar had known a moment of awe. . . . Suddenly he took her face between his hands and pressed his rough cheek against it, blindly. His hands trembled, his body was shaken, as by a spasm.

"Why, you're still cold, Claude!" she cried anxiously.

And he stammered out: "I'm not — it's you — it's having you!"

Before she could reply to this strange exclamation, to which, nevertheless, some fire in her leaped in response,

there came a knock at the door, and he drew away from
her as he answered it. Two waiters entered obsequiously,
one bearing a serving table, the other holding above his head
a large tray containing covered dishes and glasses.

"I could do with a cocktail!" Ditmar exclaimed, and the
waiter smiled as he served them. "Here's how!" he said,
giving her a glass containing a yellow liquid.

She tasted it, made a grimace, and set it down hastily.

"What's the trouble?" he asked, laughing, as she hurried
to the table and took a drink of water.

"It's horrid!" she cried.

"Oh, you'll get over that idea," he told her. "You'll
be crazy about 'em."

"I never want to taste another," she declared.

He laughed again. He had taken his at a swallow, but
almost nullifying its effect was this confirmation — if
indeed he had needed it — of the extent of her inexperience.
She was, in truth, untouched by the world — the world in
which he had lived. He pulled out her chair for her and she
sat down, confronted by a series of knives, forks, and spoons
on either side of a plate of oysters. Oysters served in this
fashion, needless to say, had never formed part of the menu
in Fillmore Street, or in any Hampton restaurant where she
had lunched. But she saw that Ditmar had chosen a little
fork with three prongs, and she followed his example.

"You mustn't tell me you don't like Cotuits!" he exclaimed.

She touched one, delicately, with her fork.

"They're alive!" she exclaimed, though the custom of
consuming them thus was by no means unknown to her. Lise
had often boasted of a taste for oysters on the shell, though
really preferring them smothered with red catsup in a "cocktail."

"They're alive, but they don't know it. They won't

eat you," Ditmar replied gleefully. "Squeeze a little lemon on one." Another sort of woman, he reflected, would have feigned a familiarity with the dish.

She obeyed him, put one in her mouth, gave a little shiver, and swallowed it quickly.

"Well?" he said. "It isn't bad, is it?"

"It seems so queer to eat anything alive, and enjoy it," she said, as she ate the rest of them.

"If you think they're good here you ought to taste them on the Cape, right out of the water," he declared, and went on to relate how he had once eaten a fabulous number in a contest with a friend of his, and won a bet. He was fond of talking about wagers he had won. Betting had lent a zest to his life. "We'll roll down there together some day next summer, little girl. It's a great place. You can go in swimming three times a day and never feel it. And talk about eating oysters, you can't swallow 'em as fast as a fellow I know down there, Joe Pusey, can open 'em. It's some trick to open 'em."

He described the process, but she scarcely listened. She was striving to adjust herself to the elements of a new and revolutionary experience; to the waiters who came and went, softly, deferentially putting hot plates before her, helping her to strange and delicious things; a creamy soup, a fish with a yellow sauce whose ingredients were artfully disguised, a breast of guinea fowl, a salad, an ice, and a small cup of coffee. Instincts and tastes hitherto unsuspected and ungratified were aroused in her. What would it be like always to be daintily served, to eat one's meals in this leisurely and luxurious manner? As her physical hunger was satisfied by the dainty food, even as her starved senses drank in the caressing warmth and harmony of the room, the gleaming fire, the heavy scent of the flowers, the rose glow of the lights in contrast to the storm without, — so the storm flinging itself against the windows, powerless to reach her, seemed to typify a former existence of cold, black mornings and factory bells and harsh sirens, of toil and limitations. Had her existence been like that? or was it a dream, a nightmare from which she had awakened at last? From time to time, deep within her, she felt persisting a conviction that that was reality, this illusion, but she fought it down. She wanted — oh, how she wanted to believe in the illusion!

Facing her was the agent, the genius, the Man who had snatched her from that existence, who had at his command these delights to bestow. She loved him, she belonged to him, he was to be her husband — yet there were moments when the glamour of this oddly tended to dissolve, when an objective vision intruded and she beheld herself, as though removed from the body, lunching with a strange man in a strange place. And once it crossed her mind — what would she think of another woman who did this? What would she think if it were Lise? She could not then achieve a sense of identity; it was as though she had partaken of some philtre lulling her, inhibiting her power to grasp the fact in its enormity. And little by little grew on her the realization of what all along she had known, that the spell of these surroundings to which she had surrendered was an expression of the man himself. He was the source of it. More and more, as he talked, his eyes troubled and stirred her; the touch of his hand, as he reached across the table and laid it on hers, burned her. When the waiters had left them alone she could stand the strain no longer, and she rose and strayed about the room, examining the furniture, the curtains, the crystal pendants, faintly pink, that softened and diffused the light; and she paused before the grand piano in the corner.

"I'd like to be able to play!" she said.

"You can learn," he told her.

"I'm too old!"

He laughed. And as he sat smoking his eyes followed her ceaselessly.

Above the sofa hung a large print of the Circus Maximus, with crowded tiers mounting toward the sky, and awninged boxes where sat the Vestal Virgins and the Emperor high above a motley, serried group on the sand. At the mouth of a tunnel a lion stood motionless, menacing, regarding them. The picture fascinated Janet.

"It's meant to be Rome, isn't it?" she asked.

"What? That? I guess so." He got up and came over to her. "Sure," he said. "I'm not very strong on history, but I read a book once, a novel, which told how those old fellows used to like to see Christians thrown to the lions — just as we like to see football games. I'll get the book again — we'll read it together."

Janet shivered. . . . "Here's another picture," he said, turning to the other side of the room. It was, apparently, an engraved copy of a modern portrait, of a woman in evening dress with shapely arms and throat and a small, aristocratic head. Around her neck was hung a heavy rope of pearls.

"Isn't she beautiful!" Janet sighed.

"Beautiful!" He led her to the mirror. "Look!" he said. "I'll buy you pearls, Janet, I want to see them gleaming against your skin. She can't compare to you. I'll — I'll drape you with pearls."

"No, no," she cried. "I don't want them, Claude. I don't want them. Please!" She scarcely knew what she was saying. And as she drew away from him her hands went out, were pressed together with an imploring, supplicating gesture. He seized them. His nearness was suffocating her, she flung herself into his arms, and their lips met

in a long, swooning kiss. She began instinctively but
vainly to struggle, not against him — but against a primal
thing stronger than herself, stronger than he, stronger than
codes and conventions and institutions, which yet she craved
fiercely as her being's fulfilment. It was sweeping them
dizzily — whither? The sheer sweetness and terror of it!

"Don't, don't!" she murmured desperately. "You
mustn't!"

"Janet — we're going to be married, sweetheart, — just
as soon as we can. Won't you trust me? For God's sake,
don't be cruel. You're my wife, now —"

His voice seemed to come from a great distance. And
from a great distance, too, her own in reply, drowned as by
falling waters.

"Do you love me? — will you love me always — always?"

And he answered hoarsely, "Yes — always — I swear it,
Janet." He had found her lips again, he was pulling her
toward a door on the far side of the room, and suddenly,
as he opened it, her resistance ceased. . . .

2

The snow made automobiling impossible, and at half past
nine that evening Ditmar had escorted Janet to the station
in a cab, and she had taken the train for Hampton. For a
while she sat as in a trance. She knew that something had
happened, something portentous, cataclysmic, which had
irrevocably changed her from the Janet Bumpus who had
left Hampton that same morning — an age ago. But
she was unable to realize the metamorphosis. In the course
of a single day she had lived a lifetime, exhausted the range
of human experience, until now she was powerless to feel
any more. The car was filled with all sorts and conditions
of people returning to homes scattered through the suburbs

and smaller cities north of Boston — a mixed, Sunday-night crowd; and presently she began, in a detached way, to observe them. Their aspects, their speech and manners had the queer effect of penetrating her consciousness without arousing the emotional judgments of approval or disapproval which normally should have followed. Ordinarily she might have felt a certain sympathy for the fragile young man on the seat beside her who sat moodily staring through his glasses at the floor: and the group across the aisle would surely have moved her to disgust. Two couples were seated *vis-à-vis*, the men apparently making fun of a "pony" coat one of the girls was wearing. In spite of her shrieks, which drew general attention, they pulled it from her back — an operation regarded by the conductor himself with tolerant amusement. Whereupon her companion, a big, blond Teuton with an inane guffaw, boldly thrust an arm about her waist and held her while he presented the tickets. Janet beheld all this as one sees dancers through a glass, without hearing the music.

Behind her two men fell into conversation.

"I guess there's well over a foot of snow. I thought we'd have an open winter, too."

"Look out for them when they start in mild!"

"I was afraid this darned road would be tied up if I waited until morning. I'm in real estate, and there's a deal on in my town I've got to watch every minute. . . ."

Even the talk between two slouch-hatted millhands, foreigners, failed at the time to strike Janet as having any significance. They were discussing with some heat the prospect of having their pay reduced by the fifty-four hour law which was to come into effect on Monday. They denounced the mill owners.

"They speed up the machine and make work harder," said one. "I think we goin' to have a strike sure."

"Bad sisson too to have strike," replied the second pessimistically. "It will be cold winter, now."

Across the black square of the window drifted the stray lights of the countryside, and from time to time, when the train stopped, she gazed out, unheeding, at the figures moving along the dim station platforms. Suddenly, without premeditation or effort, she began to live over again the day, beginning with the wonders, half revealed, half hidden, of that journey through the whiteness to Boston. . . . Awakened, listening, she heard beating louder and louder on the shores of consciousness the waves of the storm which had swept her away — waves like crashing chords of music. She breathed deeply, she turned her face to the window, seeming to behold reflected there, as in a crystal, all her experiences, little and great, great and little. She was seated once more leaning back in the corner of the carriage on her way to the station, she felt Ditmar's hand working in her own, and she heard his voice pleading forgiveness — for her silence alarmed him. And she heard herself saying : —

"It was my fault as much as yours."

And his vehement reply : —

"It wasn't anybody's fault — it was natural, it was wonderful, Janet. I can't bear to see you sad."

To see her sad ! Twice, during the afternoon and evening, he had spoken those words — or was it three times ? Was there a time she had forgotten ? And each time she had answered : "I'm not sad." What she had felt indeed was not sadness, — but how could she describe it to him when she herself was amazed and dwarfed by it ? Could he not feel it, too ? Were men so different ? . . . In the cab his solicitation, his tenderness were only to be compared with his bewilderment, his apparent awe of the feeling he himself had raised up in her, and which awed her, likewise. She had actually *felt* that bewilderment of his when, just before

s

they had reached the station, she had responded passionately to his last embrace. Even as he returned her caresses, it had been conveyed to her amazingly by the quality of his touch. Was it a lack all women felt in men? and were these, even in supreme moments, merely the perplexed transmitters of life? — not life itself? Her thoughts did not gain this clarity, though she divined the secret. And yet she loved him — loved him with a fierceness that frightened her, with a tenderness that unnerved her. . . .

At the Hampton station she took the trolley, alighting at the Common, following the narrow path made by pedestrians in the heavy snow to Fillmore Street. She climbed the dark stairs, opened the dining-room door, and paused on the threshold. Hannah and Edward sat there under the lamp, Hannah scanning through her spectacles the pages of a Sunday newspaper. On perceiving Janet she dropped it hastily in her lap.

"Well, I was concerned about you, in all this storm!" she exclaimed. "Thank goodness you're home, anyway. You haven't seen Lise, have you?"

"Lise?" Janet repeated. "Hasn't she been home?"

"Your father and I have been alone all day long. Not that it is so uncommon for Lise to be gone. I wish it wasn't! But you! When you didn't come home for supper I was considerably worried."

Janet sat down between her mother and father and began to draw off her gloves.

"I'm going to marry Mr. Ditmar," she announced.

For a few moments the silence was broken only by the ticking of the old-fashioned clock.

"Mr. Ditmar!" said Hannah, at length. "You're going to marry Mr. Ditmar!"

Edward was still inarticulate. His face twitched, his eyes watered as he stared at her.

"Not right away," said Janet.

"Well, I must say you take it rather cool," declared Hannah, almost resentfully. "You come in and tell us you're going to marry Mr. Ditmar just like you were talking about the weather."

Hannah's eyes filled with tears. There had been indeed an unconscious lack of consideration in Janet's abrupt announcement, which had fallen like a spark on the dry tinder of Hannah's hope. The result was a suffocating flame. Janet, whom love had quickened, had a swift perception of this. She rose quickly and took Hannah in her arms and kissed her. It was as though the relation between them were reversed, and the daughter had now become the mother and the comforter.

"I always knew something like this would happen!" said Edward. His words incited Hannah to protest.

"You didn't anything of the kind, Edward Bumpus," she exclaimed.

"Just to think of Janet livin' in that big house up in Warren Street!" he went on, unheeding, jubilant. "You'll drop in and see the old people once in a while, Janet, you won't forget us?"

"I wish you wouldn't talk like that, father," said Janet.

"Well, he's a fine man, Claude Ditmar, I always said that. The way he stops and talks to me when he passes the gate —"

"That doesn't make him a good man," Hannah declared, and added: "If he wasn't a good man, Janet wouldn't be marrying him."

"I don't know whether he's good or not," said Janet.

"That's so, too," observed Hannah, approvingly. "We can't any of us tell till we've tried 'em, and then it's too late to change. I'd like to see him, but I guess he wouldn't care to come down here to Fillmore Street." The difference between Ditmar's social and economic standing and their own suggested appalling complications to her mind. "I suppose I won't get a sight of him till after you're married, and not much then."

"There's plenty of time to think about that, mother," answered Janet.

"I'd want to have everything decent and regular," Hannah insisted. "We may be poor, but we come of good stock, as your father says."

"It'll be all right — Mr. Ditmar will behave like a gentleman," Edward assured her.

"I thought I ought to tell you about it," Janet said, "but you mustn't mention it, yet, not even to Lise. Lise will talk. Mr. Ditmar's very busy now, — he hasn't made any plans."

"I wish Lise could get married!" exclaimed Hannah, irrelevantly. "She's been acting so queer lately, she's not been herself at all."

"Now there you go, borrowing trouble, mother," Edward exclaimed. He could not take his eyes from Janet, but continued to regard her with benevolence. "Lise'll get married some day. I don't suppose we can expect another Mr. Ditmar. . . ."

"Well," said Hannah, presently, "there's no use sitting up all night." She rose and kissed Janet again. "I just can't believe it," she declared, "but I guess it's so if you say it is."

"Of course it's so," said Edward.

"I so want you should be happy, Janet," said Hannah. . . .

Was it so? Her mother and father, the dwarfed and ugly surroundings of Fillmore Street made it seem incredible once more. And — what would they say if they knew what had happened to her this day? When she had reached her room, Janet began to wonder why she had told her parents.

Had it not been in order to relieve their anxiety — especially her mother's — on the score of her recent absences from home ? Yes, that was it, and because the news would make them happy. And then the mere assertion to them that she was to marry Ditmar helped to make it more real to herself. But now that reality was fading again, she was unable to bring it within the scope of her imagination, her mind refused to hold one remembered circumstance long enough to coördinate it with another : she realized that she was tired — too tired to think any more. But despite her exhaustion there remained within her, possessing her, as it were overshadowing her, unrelated to future or past, the presence of the man who had awakened her to an intensity of life hitherto unconceived. When her head touched the pillow she fell asleep. . . .

3

When the bells and the undulating scream of the siren awoke her, she lay awhile groping in the darkness. Where was she? Who was she? The discovery of the fact that the nail of the middle finger on her right hand was broken, gave her a clew. She had broken that nail in reaching out to save something — a vase of roses — that was it ! — a vase of roses on a table with a white cloth. Ditmar had tipped it over. The sudden flaring up of this trivial incident served to re-establish her identity, to light a fuse along which her mind began to run like fire, illuminating redly all the events of the day before. It was sweet to lie thus, to possess, as her very own, these precious, passionate memories of life lived at last to fulness, to feel that she had irrevocably given herself and taken — all. A longing to see Ditmar again invaded her : he would take an early train, he would be at the office by nine. How could she wait until then?

With a movement that had become habitual, subconscious, she reached out her hand to arouse her sister. The coldness of the sheets on the right side of the bed sent a shiver through her — a shiver of fear.

"Lise!" she called. But there was no answer from the darkness. And Janet, trembling, her heart beating wildly, sprang from the bed, searched for the matches, and lit the gas. There was no sign of Lise; her clothes, which she had the habit of flinging across the chairs, were nowhere to be seen. Janet's eyes fell on the bureau, marked the absence of several knick-knacks, including a comb and brush, and with a sudden sickness of apprehension she darted to the wardrobe and flung open the doors. In the bottom were a few odd garments, above was the hat with the purple feather, now shabby and discarded, on the hooks a skirt and jacket Lise wore to work at the *Bagatelle* in bad weather. That was all. . . . Janet sank down in the rocking-chair, her hands clasped together, overwhelmed by the sudden apprehension of the tragedy that had lurked, all unsuspected, in the darkness: a tragedy, not of Lise alone, but in which she herself was somehow involved. Just why this was so, she could not for the moment declare. The room was cold, she was clad only in a nightdress, but surges of heat ran through her body. What should she do? She must think. But thought was impossible. She got up and closed the window and began to dress with feverish rapidity, pausing now and again to stand motionless. In one such moment there entered her mind an incident that oddly had made little impression at the time of its occurrence because she, Janet, had been blinded by the prospect of her own happiness — that happiness which, a few minutes ago, had seemed so real and vital a thing! And it was the memory of this incident that suddenly threw a glaring, evil light on all of Lise's conduct during the past months — her accidental dropping of the vanity case and the gold coin! Now she knew for a certainty what had happened to her sister.

Having dressed herself, she entered the kitchen, which was warm, filled with the smell of frying meat. Streaks of grease smoke floated fantastically beneath the low ceiling, and Hannah, with the frying-pan in one hand and a fork in the other, was bending over the stove. Wisps of her scant, whitening hair escaped from the ridiculous, tightly drawn knot at the back of her head; in the light of the flickering gas-jet she looked so old and worn that a sudden pity smote Janet and made her dumb — pity for her mother, pity for herself, pity for Lise; pity that lent a staggering insight into life itself. Hannah had once been young, desirable, perhaps, swayed by those forces which had swayed her. Janet wondered why she had never guessed this before, and why she had guessed it now. But it was Hannah who, looking up and catching sight of Janet's face, was quick to divine the presage in it and gave voice to the foreboding that had weighed on her for many weeks.

"Where's Lise?"

And Janet could not answer. She shook her head. Hannah dropped the fork, the handle of the frying pan and crossed the room swiftly, seizing Janet by the shoulders.

"Is she gone? I knew it, I felt it all along. I thought she'd done something she was afraid to tell about — I tried to ask her, but I couldn't — I couldn't! And now she's gone. Oh, my God, I'll never forgive myself!"

The unaccustomed sight of her mother's grief was terrible. For an instant only she clung to Janet, then becoming mute, she sat down in the kitchen chair and stared with dry, unseeing eyes at the wall. Her face twitched. Janet could not bear to look at it, to see the torture in her mother's eyes. She, Janet, seemed suddenly to have grown old herself, to have lived through ages of misery and tragedy. . . . She was aware of a pungent odour, went to the stove, picked up the fork, and turned the steak. Now and then she glanced at Hannah. Grief seemed to have frozen her. Then, from the dining-room she heard footsteps, and Edward stood in the doorway.

"Well, what's the matter with breakfast?" he asked. From where he stood he could not see Hannah's face, but gradually his eyes were drawn to her figure. His intuition was not quick, and some moments passed before the rigidity of the pose impressed itself upon him.

"Is mother sick?" he asked falteringly.

Janet went to him. But it was Hannah who spoke.

"Lise has gone," she said.

"Lise — gone," Edward repeated. "Gone where?"

"She's run away — she's disgraced us," Hannah replied, in a monotonous, dulled voice.

Edward did not seem to understand, and presently Janet felt impelled to break the silence.

"She didn't come home last night, father."

"Didn't come home? Mebbe she spent the night with a friend," he said.

It seemed incredible, at such a moment, that he could still be hopeful.

"No, she's gone, I tell you, she's lost, we'll never lay eyes on her again. My God, I never thought she'd come to this, but I might have guessed it. Lise! Lise! To think it's my Lise!"

Hannah's voice echoed pitifully through the silence of the flat. So appealing, so heartbroken was the cry one might have thought that Lise, wherever she was, would have heard it. Edward was dazed by the shock, his lower lip quivered and fell. He walked over to Hannah's chair and put his hand on her shoulder.

"There, there, mother," he pleaded. "If she's gone, we'll find her, we'll bring her back to you."

Hannah shook her head. She pushed back her chair abruptly and going over to the stove took the fork from Janet's hand and put the steak on the dish.

"Go in there and set down, Edward," she said. "I guess we've got to have breakfast just the same, whether she's gone or not."

It was terrible to see Hannah, with that look on her face, going about her tasks automatically. And Edward, too, seemed suddenly to have become aged and broken; his trust in the world, so amazingly preserved through many vicissitudes, shattered at last. He spilled his coffee when he tried to drink, and presently he got up and wandered about the room, searching for his overcoat. It was Janet who found it and helped him on with it. He tried to say something, but failing, departed heavily for the mill. Janet began to remove the dishes from the table.

"You've got to eat something, too, before you go to work," said Hannah.

"I've had all I want," Janet replied.

Hannah followed her into the kitchen. The scarcely touched food was laid aside, the coffee-pot emptied, Hannah put the cups in the basin in the sink and let the water run. She turned to Janet and seized her hands convulsively.

"Let me do this, mother," said Janet. She knew her mother was thinking of the newly-found joy that Lise's disgrace had marred, but she released her hands, gently, and took the mop from the nail on which it hung.

"You sit down, mother," she said.

Hannah would not. They finished the dishes together in silence while the light of the new day stole in through the windows. Janet went into her room, set it in order,

made up the bed, put on her coat and hat and rubbers.
Then she returned to Hannah, who seized her.

"It ain't going to spoil your happiness?"

But Janet could not answer. She kissed her mother, and
went out, down the stairs into the street. The day was
sharp and cold and bracing, and out of an azure sky the sun
shone with dazzling brightness on the snow, which the west
wind was whirling into little eddies of white smoke, leaving
on the drifts delicate scalloped designs like those printed by
waves on the sands of the sea. They seemed to Janet that
morning hatefully beautiful. In front of his tin shop, whistling cheerfully and labouring energetically with a shovel to
clean his sidewalk, was Johnny Tiernan, the tip of his pointed
nose made very red by the wind.

"Good morning, Miss Bumpus," he said. "Now, if you'd
only waited awhile, I'd have had it as clean as a parlour. It's
fine weather for coal bills."

She halted.

"Can I see you a moment, Mr. Tiernan?"

Johnny looked at her.

"Why sure," he said. Leaning his shovel against the
wall, he gallantly opened the door that she might pass
in before him and then led the way to the back of
the shop where the stove was glowing hospitably. He
placed a chair for her. "Now what can I be doing to serve
you?" he asked.

"It's about my sister," said Janet.

"Miss Lise?"

"I thought you might know what man she's been going
with lately," said Janet.

Mr. Tiernan had often wondered how much Janet knew
about her sister. In spite of a momentary embarrassment most unusual in him, the courage of her question
made a strong appeal, and his quick sympathies suspected

the tragedy behind her apparent calmness. He met her magnificently.

"Why," he said, "I have seen Miss Lise with a fellow named Duval — Howard Duval — when he's been in town. He travels for a Boston shoe house, Humphrey and Gillmount."

"I'm afraid Lise has gone away with him," said Janet. "I thought you might be able to find out something about him, and — whether any one had seen them. She left home yesterday morning."

For an instant Mr. Tiernan stood silent before her, his legs apart, his fingers running through his bristly hair.

"Well, ye did right to come straight to me, Miss Janet. It's me that can find out, if anybody can, and it's glad I am to help you. Just you stay here — make yourself at home while I run down and see some of the boys. I'll not be long — and don't be afraid I'll let on about it."

He seized his overcoat and departed. Presently the sun, glinting on the sheets of tin, started Janet's glance straying around the shop, noting its disorderly details, the heaped-up stovepipes, the littered work-bench with the shears lying across the vise. Once she thought of Ditmar arriving at the office and wondering what had happened to her. . . . The sound of a bell made her jump. Mr. Tiernan had returned.

"She's gone with him," said Janet, not as a question, but as one stating a fact.

Mr. Tiernan nodded.

"They took the nine-thirty-six for Boston yesterday morning. Eddy Colahan was at the depot."

Janet rose. "Thank you," she said simply.

"What are you going to do?" he asked.

"I'm going to Boston," she answered. "I'm going to find out where she is."

"Then it's me that's going with you," he announced.

"Oh no, Mr. Tiernan!" she protested. "I couldn't let you do that."

"And why not?" he demanded. "I've got a little business there myself. I'm proud to go with you. It's your sister you want, isn't it?"

"Yes."

"Well, what would you be doing by yourself — a young lady? How will you find your sister?"

"Do you think you can find her?"

"Sure I can find her," he proclaimed, confidently. He had evidently made up his mind that casual treatment was what the affair demanded. "Haven't I good friends in Boston?" By friendship he swayed his world: nor was he completely unknown — though he did not say so — to certain influential members of his race of the Boston police department. Pulling out a large nickel watch and observing that they had just time to catch the train, he locked up his shop, and they set out together for the station. Mr. Tiernan led the way, for the path was narrow. The dry snow squeaked under his feet.

After escorting her to a seat on the train, he tactfully retired to the smoking car, not to rejoin her until they were on the trestle spanning the Charles River by the North Station. All the way to Boston she had sat gazing out of the window at the blinding whiteness of the fields, incapable of rousing herself to the necessity of thought, to a degree of feeling commensurate with the situation. She did not know what she would say to Lise if she should find her; and in spite of Mr. Tiernan's expressed confidence, the chances of success seemed remote. When the train began to thread the crowded suburbs, the city, spreading out over its hills, instead of thrilling her, as yesterday, with a sense of dignity and power, of opportunity and emancipation, seemed a labyrinth with many warrens where vice and crime and sorrow could hide. In front of the station the traffic was already crushing the snow into filth. They passed the spot where, the night before, the carriage had stopped, where Ditmar had bidden her good-bye. Something stirred within her, became a shooting pain. . . . She asked Mr. Tiernan what he intended to do.

"I'm going right after the man, if he's here in the city," he told her. And they boarded a street car, which almost immediately shot into the darkness of the subway. Emerging at Scollay Square, and walking a few blocks, they came to a window where guns, revolvers, and fishing tackle were displayed, and on which was painted the name, "Timothy Mulally." Mr. Tiernan entered.

"Is Tim in?" he inquired of one of the clerks, who nodded his head towards the rear of the store, where a middle-aged, grey-haired Irishman was seated at a desk under a drop light.

"Is it you, Johnny?" he exclaimed, looking up.

"It's meself," said Mr. Tiernan. "And this is Miss Bumpus, a young lady friend of mine from Hampton."

Mr. Mulally rose and bowed.

"How do ye do, ma'am," he said.

"I've got a little business to do for her," Mr. Tiernan continued. "I thought you might offer her a chair and let her stay here, quiet, while I was gone."

"With pleasure, ma'am," Mr. Mulally replied, pulling forward a chair with alacrity. "Just sit there comfortable —no one will disturb ye."

When, in the course of half an hour, Mr. Tiernan returned, there was a grim yet triumphant look in his little blue eyes, but it was not until Janet had thanked Mr. Mulally for his hospitality and they had reached the sidewalk that he announced the result of his quest.

"Well, I caught him. It's lucky we came when we did —

he was just going out on the road again, up to Maine. I know where Miss Lise is."

"He told you!" exclaimed Janet.

"He told me indeed, but it wasn't any joy to him. He was all for bluffing at first. It's easy to scare the likes of him. He was as white as his collar before I was done with him. He knows who I am, all right — he's heard of me in Hampton," Mr. Tiernan added, with a pardonable touch of pride.

"What did you say?" inquired Janet, curiously.

"Say?" repeated Mr. Tiernan. "It's not much I had to say, Miss Janet. I was all ready to go to Mr. Gillmount, his boss. I'm guessing he won't take much pleasure on this trip."

She asked for no more details.

CHAPTER XIII

1

Once more Janet and Mr. Tiernan descended into the subway, taking a car going to the south and west, which finally came out of the tunnel into a broad avenue lined with shabby shops, hotels and saloons, and long rows of boarding- and rooming-houses. They alighted at a certain corner, walked a little way along a street unkempt and dreary, Mr. Tiernan scrutinizing the numbers until he paused in front of a house with a basement kitchen and snow-covered, sandstone steps. Climbing these, he pulled the bell, and they stood waiting in the twilight of a half-closed vestibule until presently shuffling steps were heard within; the door was cautiously opened, not more than a foot, but enough to reveal a woman in a loose wrapper, with an untidy mass of bleached hair and a puffy face like a fungus grown in darkness.

"I want to see Miss Lise Bumpus," Mr. Tiernan demanded.

"You've got the wrong place. There ain't no one of that name here," said the woman.

"There ain't! All right," he insisted aggressively, pushing open the door in spite of her. "If you don't let this young lady see her quick, there's trouble coming to you."

"Who are you?" asked the woman, impudently, yet showing signs of fear.

"Never mind who I am," Mr. Tiernan declared. "I know all about you, and I know all about Duval. If you don't want any trouble you won't make any, and you'll take this young lady to her sister. I'll wait here for you, Miss Janet," he added.

"I don't know nothing about her — she rented my room — that's all I know," the woman replied sullenly. "If you mean that couple that came here yesterday —"

She turned and led the way upstairs, mounting slowly, and Janet followed, nauseated and almost overcome by the foul odours of dead cigarette smoke which, mingling with the smell of cooking cabbage rising from below, seemed the very essence and reek of hitherto unimagined evil. A terror seized her such as she had never known before, an almost overwhelming impulse to turn and regain the air and sunlight of the day. In the dark hallway of the second story the woman knocked at the door of a front room.

"She's in there, unless she's gone out." And indeed a voice was heard petulantly demanding what was wanted — Lise's voice! Janet hesitated, her hand on the knob, her body fallen against the panels. Then, as she pushed open the door, the smell of cigarette smoke grew stronger, and she found herself in a large bedroom, the details of which were instantly photographed on her mind — the dingy claret-red walls, the crayon over the mantel of a buxom lady in a décolleté costume of the '90's, the outspread fan concealing the fireplace, the soiled lace curtains. The bed was unmade, and on the table beside two empty beer bottles and glasses and the remains of a box of candy — suggestive of a Sunday purchase at a drug store — she recognized Lise's vanity case. The effect of all this, integrated at a glance, was a paralyzing horror. Janet could not speak. She remained gazing at Lise, who paid no attention to her entrance, but stood with her back turned before an old-fashioned bureau with a marble top and raised sides. She was dressed, and engaged in adjusting her hat. It was not until Janet pronounced her name that she turned swiftly.

"You!" she exclaimed. "What the — what brought you here?"

"Oh, Lise!" Janet repeated.

"How did you get here?" Lise demanded, coming toward her. "Who told you where I was? What business have you got sleuthing 'round after me like this?"

For a moment Janet was speechless once more, astounded that Lise could preserve her effrontery in such an atmosphere, could be insensible to the evils lurking in this house — evils so real to Janet that she seemed actually to feel them brushing against her.

"Lise, come away from here," she pleaded, "come home with me!"

"Home!" said Lise, defiantly, and laughed. "What do you take me for? Why would I be going home when I've been trying to break away for two years? I ain't so dippy as that — not me! Go home like a good little girl and march back to the *Bagatelle* and ask 'em to give me another show standing behind a counter all day. Nix! No home sweet home for me! I'm all for easy street when it comes to a home like that."

Heartless, terrific as the repudiation was, it struck a self-convicting, almost sympathetic note in Janet. She herself had revolted against the monotony and sordidness of that existence! She herself —! She dared not complete the thought, now.

"But this!" she exclaimed.

"What's the matter with it?" Lise demanded. "It ain't Commonwealth Avenue, but it's got Fillmore Street beat a mile. There ain't no whistles here to get you out of bed at six A.M., for one thing. There ain't no geezers, like Walters, to nag you 'round all day long. What's the matter with it?"

Something in Lise's voice roused Janet's spirit to battle.

T

"What's the matter with it?" she cried. "It's hell — that's the matter with it. Can't you see it? Can't you feel it? You don't know what it means, or you'd come home with me."

"I guess I know what it means as well as you do," said Lise, sullenly. "We've all got to croak sometime, and I'd rather croak this way than be smothered up in Hampton. I'll get a run for my money, anyway."

"No, you don't know what it means," Janet repeated, "or you wouldn't talk like that. Do you think this man will support you, stick to you? He won't, he'll desert you, and you'll have to go on the streets."

A dangerous light grew in Lise's eyes.

"He's as good as any other man, he's as good as Ditmar," she said. "They're all the same, to girls like us."

Janet's heart caught, it seemed to stop beating. Was this a hazard on Lise's part, or did she speak from knowledge? And yet what did it matter whether Lise knew or only suspected, if her words were true, if men were all alike? Had she been a dupe as well as Lise? and was the only difference between them now the fact that Lise was able, without illusion, to see things as they were, to accept the consequences, while she, Janet, had beheld visions and dreamed dreams? was there any real choice between the luxurious hotel to which Ditmar had taken her and this detestable house? Suddenly, seemingly by chance, her eyes fell on the box of drug-store candy from which the cheap red ribbon had been torn, and by some odd association of ideas it suggested and epitomized Lise's Sunday excursion with a man— a hideous travesty on the journey of wonders she herself had taken. Had that been heaven, and this of Lise's, hell? . . . And was Lise's ambition to be supported in idleness and luxury to be condemned because she had believed her own to be higher? Did not both lead to destruction? The weight that had lain on her breast since the siren had awakened her that morning and she had reached out and touched the chilled, empty sheets now grew almost unsupportable.

"It's true," said Janet, "all men are the same."

Lise was staring at her.

"My God!" she exclaimed. "You?"

"Yes—me," cried Janet. "And what are you going to do about it? Stay here with him in this filthy place until he gets tired of you and throws you out on the street? Before I'd let any man do that to me I'd kill him."

Lise began to whimper, and suddenly buried her face in the pillow. But a new emotion had begun to take possession of Janet — an emotion so strong as to give her an unlooked-for sense of detachment. And the words Lise had spoken between her sobs at first conveyed no meaning.

"I'm going to have a baby. . . ."

Lise was going to have a child! Why hadn't she guessed it? A child! Perhaps she, Janet, would have a child! This enlightenment as to Lise's condition and the possibility it suggested in regard to herself brought with it an over-whelming sympathy which at first she fiercely resented — then yielded to. The bond between them, instead of snapping, had inexplicably strengthened. And Lise, despite her degradation, was more than ever her sister! Forgetting her repugnance to the bed, Janet sat down beside Lise and put an arm around her.

"He said he'd marry me, he swore he was rich — and he was a spender all right. And then some guy came up to me one night at Gruber's and told me he was married already."

"What?" Janet exclaimed.

"Sure! He's got a wife and two kids here in Boston. That was a twenty-one round knockout! Maybe I didn't have something to tell him when he blew into Hampton last

Friday! But he said he couldn't help it — he loved me."
Lise sat up, seemingly finding relief in the relation of her
wrongs, dabbing her eyes with a cheap lace handkerchief.
"Well, while he'd been away — this thing came. I didn't
know what was the matter at first, and when I found out
I was scared to death, I was ready to kill myself. When I
told him he was scared too, and then he said he'd fix it. Say,
I was a goat to think he'd marry me!" Lise laughed hysterically.

"And then —" Janet spoke with difficulty, "and then
you came down here?"

"I told him he'd have to see me through, I'd start something if he didn't. Say, he almost got down on his knees,
right there in Gruber's! But he came back inside of ten
seconds — he's a jollier, for sure, he was right there with the
goods, it was because he loved me, he couldn't help himself,
I was his cutie, and all that kind of baby talk."

Lise's objective manner of speaking about her seducer
amazed Janet.

"Do you love him?" she asked.

"Say, what is love?" Lise demanded. "Do you ever run
into it outside of the movies? Do I love him? Well, he's
a good looker and a fancy dresser, he ain't a tight wad,
and he can start a laugh every minute. If he hadn't put
it over on me I wouldn't have been so sore. I don't know —
he ain't so bad. He's weak, that's the trouble with him."

This was the climax! Lise's mental processes, her
tendency to pass from wild despair to impersonal comment,
her inability, her courtesan's temperament that prevented
her from realizing tragedy for more than a moment at a
time — even though the tragedy were her own — were incomprehensible to Janet.

"Get on to this," Lise adjured her. "When I first was
acquainted with him he handed me a fairy tale that he was

taking five thousand a year from Humphrey and Gillmount, he was going into the firm. He had me razzle-dazzled. He's some hypnotizer as a salesman, too, they say. Nothing was too good for me; I saw myself with a house on the avenue shopping in a limousine. Well, he blew up, but I can't help liking him."

"Liking him!" cried Janet passionately. "I'd kill him — that's what I'd do."

Lise regarded her with unwilling admiration.

"That's where you and me is different," she declared. "I wish I was like that, but I ain't. And where would I come in? Now you're wise why I can't go back to Hampton. Even if I was stuck on the burg and cryin' my eyes out for the *Bagatelle* I couldn't go back."

"What are you going to do?" Janet demanded.

"Well," said Lise, "he's come across — I'll say that for him. Maybe it's because he's scared, but he's stuck on me, too. When you dropped in I was just going down town to get a pair of patent leathers, these are all wore out," she explained, twisting her foot, "they ain't fit for Boston. And I thought of lookin' at blouses — there's a sale on I was reading about in the paper. Say, it's great to be on easy street, to be able to stay in bed until you're good and ready to get up and go shopping, to gaze at the girls behind the counter and ask the price of things. I'm going to Walling's and give the salesladies the ha-ha — that's what I'm going to do."

"But —?" Janet found words inadequate.

Lise understood her.

"Oh, I'm due at the doctor's this afternoon."

"Where?"

"The doctor's. Don't you get me? — it's a private hospital." Lise gave a slight shudder at the word, but instantly recovered her sang-froid. "Howard fixed it up yesterday — and they say it ain't very bad if you take it early."

For a space Janet was too profoundly shocked to reply.

"Lise! That's a crime!" she cried.

"Crime, nothing!" retorted Lise, and immediately became indignant. "Say, I sometimes wonder how you could have lived all these years without catching on to a few things! What do you take me for! What'd I do with a baby?"

What indeed! The thought came like an avalanche, stripping away the veneer of beauty from the face of the world, revealing the scarred rock and crushed soil beneath. This was reality! What right had society to compel a child to be born to degradation and prostitution? to beget, perhaps, other children of suffering? Were not she and Lise of the exploited, of those duped and tempted by the fair things the more fortunate enjoyed unscathed? And now, for their natural cravings, their family must be disgraced, they must pay the penalty of outcasts! Neither Lise nor she had had a chance. She saw that, now. The scorching revelation of life's injustice lighted within her the fires of anarchy and revenge. Lise, other women might submit tamely to be crushed, might be lulled and drugged by bribes: she would not. A wild desire seized her to get back to Hampton.

"Give me the address of the hospital," she said.

"Come off!" cried Lise, in angry bravado. "Do you think I'm going to let you butt into this? I guess you've got enough to do to look out for your own business."

Janet produced a pencil from her bag, and going to the table tore off a piece of the paper in which had been wrapped the candy box.

"Give me the address," she insisted.

"Say, what are you going to do?"

"I want to know where you are, in case anything happens to you."

"Anything happens! What do you mean?" Janet's words had frightened Lise, the withdrawal of Janet's opposition bewildered her. But above all, she was cowed by the sudden change in Janet herself, by the attitude of steely determination eloquent of an animus persons of Lise's type are incapable of feeling, and which to them is therefore incomprehensible. "Nothing's going to happen to me," she whined. "The place is all right — *he'd* be scared to send me there if it wasn't. It costs something, too. Say, you ain't going to tell 'em at home?" she cried with a fresh access of alarm.

"If you do as I say, I won't tell anybody," Janet replied, in that odd, impersonal tone her voice had acquired. "You must write me as soon — as soon as it is over. Do you understand?"

"Honest to God I will," Lise assured her.

"And you mustn't come back to a house like this."

"Where'll I go?" Lise asked.

"I don't know. We'll find out when the time comes," said Janet, significantly.

"You've seen *him!*" Lise exclaimed.

"No," said Janet, "and I don't want to see him unless I have to. Mr. Tiernan has seen him. Mr. Tiernan is downstairs now, waiting for me."

"Johnny Tiernan! Is Johnny Tiernan downstairs?"

Janet wrote the address, and thrust the slip of paper in her bag.

"Good-bye, Lise," she said. "I'll come down again — I'll come down whenever you want me." Lise suddenly seized her and clung to her, sobbing. For a while Janet submitted, and then, kissing her, gently detached herself. She felt, indeed, pity for Lise, but something within her seemed to have hardened — something that pity could not melt, possessing her and thrusting her on to action. She knew not what action. So strong was this thing that it overcame and drove off the evil spirits of that darkened house as she descended the stairs to join Mr. Tiernan, who opened the door for her to pass out. Once in the street, she breathed deeply of the sunlit air. Nor did she observe Mr. Tiernan's glance of comprehension. . . . When they arrived at the North Station he said : —

"You'll be wanting a bite of dinner, Miss Janet," and as she shook her head he did not press her to eat. He told her that a train for Hampton left in ten minutes. "I think I'll stay in Boston the rest of the day, as long as I'm here," he added.

She remembered that she had not thanked him, she took his hand, but he cut her short.

"It's glad I was to help you," he assured her. "And if there's anything more I can do, Miss Janet, you'll be letting me know — you'll call on Johnny Tiernan, won't you?"

He left her at the gate. He had intruded with no advice, he had offered no comment that she had come downstairs alone, without Lise. His confidence in her seemed never to have wavered. He had respected, perhaps partly imagined her feelings, and in spite of these now a sense of gratitude to him stole over her, mitigating the intensity of their bitterness. Mr. Tiernan alone seemed stable in a chaotic world. He was a man.

2

No sooner was she in the train, however, than she forgot Mr. Tiernan utterly. Up to the present the mental process of dwelling upon her own experience of the last three months had been unbearable, but now she was able to take a fearful satisfaction in the evolving of parallels between her case

and Lise's. Despite the fact that the memories she had
cherished were now become hideous things, she sought to
drag them forth and compare them, ruthlessly, with what
must have been the treasures of Lise. Were her own any
less tawdry? Only she, Janet, had been the greater fool of
the two, the greater dupe because she had allowed herself to
dream, to believe that what she had done had been for love,
for light! because she had not listened to the warning
voice within her! It had always been on the little, unpremeditated acts of Ditmar that she had loved to linger, and
now, in the light of Lise's testimony, of Lise's experience,
she saw them all as false. It seemed incredible, now, that
she had ever deceived herself into thinking that Ditmar
meant to marry her, that he loved her enough to make her
his wife. Nor was it necessary to summon and marshal
incidents to support this view, they came of themselves,
crowding one another, a cumulative and appalling array of
evidence, before which she stood bitterly amazed at her
former stupidity. And in the events of yesterday, which
she pitilessly reviewed, she beheld a deliberate and prearranged plan for her betrayal. Had he not telephoned to
Boston for the rooms, rehearsed in his own mind every detail
of what had subsequently happened? Was there any essential difference between the methods of Ditmar and Duval?
Both were skilled in the same art, and Ditmar was the cleverer
of the two. It had only needed her meeting with Lise, in
that house, to reveal how he had betrayed her faith and her
love, sullied and besmirched them. And then came the
odd reflection, — how strange that that same Sunday had
been so fateful for herself and Lise!

The agony of these thoughts was mitigated by the scorching hatred that had replaced her love, the desire for retaliation, revenge. Occasionally, however, that stream of consciousness was broken by the recollection of what she had

permitted and even advised her sister to do; and though the idea of the place to which Lise was going sickened her, though she achieved a certain objective amazement at the transformation in herself enabling her to endorse such a course, she was glad of having endorsed it, she rejoiced that Lise's child would not be born into a world that had seemed — so falsely — fair and sweet, and in reality was black and detestable. Her acceptance of the act — for Lise — was a function of the hatred consuming her, a hatred which, growing in bigness, had made Ditmar merely the personification of that world. From time to time her hands clenched, her brow furrowed, powerful waves of heat ran through her, the craving for action became so intense she could scarcely refrain from rising in her seat.

By some odd whim of the weather the wind had backed around into the east, gathering the clouds once more. The brilliancy of the morning had given place to greyness, the high slits of windows seemed dirtier than ever as the train pulled into the station at Hampton, shrouded in Gothic gloom. As she left the car Janet was aware of the presence on the platform of an unusual number of people; she wondered vaguely, as she pushed her way through them, why they were there, what they were talking about? One determination possessed her, to go to the Chippering Mill, to Ditmar. Emerging from the street, she began to walk rapidly, the change from inaction to exercise bringing a certain relief, starting the working of her mind, arousing in her a realization of the necessity of being prepared for the meeting. Therefore, instead of turning at Faber Street, she crossed it. But at the corner of the Common she halted, her glance drawn by a dark mass of people filling the end of Hawthorne Street, where it was blocked by the brick-coloured façade of the Clarendon Mill. In the middle distance men and boys were running to join this crowd. A girl, evidently an Irish-American mill hand of the higher paid sort, hurried toward her from the direction of the mill itself. Janet accosted her.

"It's the strike," she explained excitedly, evidently surprised at the question. "The Polaks and the Dagoes and a lot of other foreigners quit when they got their envelopes — stopped their looms and started through the mill, and when they came into our room I left. I didn't want no trouble with 'em. It's the fifty-four hour law — their pay's cut two hours. You've heard about it, I guess."

Janet nodded.

"They had a big mass meeting last night in Maxwell Hall," the girl continued, "the foreigners — not the skilled workers. And they voted to strike. They tell me they're walking out over at the Patuxent, too."

"And the Chippering?" asked Janet, eagerly.

"I don't know — I guess it'll spread to all of 'em, the way these foreigners are going on — they're crazy. But say," the girl added, "it ain't right to cut our pay, either, is it? They never done it two years ago when the law came down to fifty-six."

Janet did not wait to reply. While listening to this explanation, excitement had been growing in her again, and some fearful, overpowering force of attraction emanating from that swarm in the distance drew her until she yielded, fairly running past the rows of Italian tenements in their strange setting of snow, not to pause until she reached the fruit shop where she and Eda had eaten the olives. Now she was on the outskirts of the crowd that packed itself against the gates of the Clarendon. It spread over the width of East Street, growing larger every minute, until presently she was hemmed in. Here and there hoarse shouts of approval and cheers arose in response to invisible orators haranguing their audiences in weird, foreign tongues;

tiny American flags were waved; and suddenly, in one of those unforeseen and incomprehensible movements to which mobs are subject, a trolley car standing at the end of the Hawthorne Street track was surrounded, the desperate clanging of its bell keeping pace with the beating of Janet's heart. A dark Sicilian, holding aloft the green, red, and white flag of Italy, leaped on the rear platform and began to speak, the Slav conductor regarding him stupidly, pulling the bellcord the while. Three or four policemen fought their way to the spot, striving to clear the tracks, bewildered and impotent in the face of the alien horde momentarily growing more and more conscious of power.

Janet pushed her way deeper and deeper into the crowd. She wanted to savour to the full its wrath and danger, to surrender herself to be played upon by these sallow, stubby-bearded exhorters, whose menacing tones and passionate gestures made a grateful appeal, whose wild, musical words, just because they were uncomprehended, aroused in her dim suggestions of a race-experience not her own, but in which she was now somehow summoned to share. That these were the intruders whom she, as a native American, had once resented and despised did not occur to her. The racial sense so strong in her was drowned in a sense of fellowship. Their anger seemed to embody and express, as nothing else could have done, the revolt that had been rising, rising within her soul; and the babel to which she listened was not a confusion of tongues, but one voice lifted up to proclaim the wrongs of all the duped, of all the exploited and oppressed. She was fused with them, their cause was her cause, their betrayers her betrayers.

Suddenly was heard the cry for which she had been tensely but unconsciously awaiting. Another cry like that had rung out in another mob across the seas more than a century before. "A la Bastille!" became "To the Chippering!" Some man shouted it out in shrill English, hundreds repeated it; the Sicilian leaped from the trolley car, and his path could be followed by the agitated progress of the alien banner he bore. "To the Chippering!" It rang in Janet's ears like a call to battle. Was she shouting it, too? A galvanic thrill ran through the crowd, an impulse that turned their faces and started their steps down East Street toward the canal, and Janet was irresistibly carried along. Nay, it seemed as if the force that second by second gained momentum was in her, that she herself had released and was guiding it! Her feet were wet as she ploughed through the trampled snow, but she gave no thought to that. The odour of humanity was in her nostrils. On the left a gaunt Jew pressed against her, on the right a solid Ruthenian woman, one hand clasping her shawl, the other holding aloft a miniature emblem of New World liberty. Her eyes were fixed on the grey skies, and from time to time her lips were parted in some strange, ancestral chant that could be heard above the shouting. All about Janet were dark, awakening faces. . . .

It chanced that an American, a college graduate, stood gazing down from a point of vantage upon this scene. He was ignorant of anthropology, psychology, and the phenomena of environment; but bits of "knowledge" — which he embodied in a newspaper article composed that evening — stuck wax-like in his brain. Not thus, he deplored, was the Anglo-Saxon wont to conduct his rebellions. These Czechs and Slavs, Hebrews and Latins and Huns might have appropriately been clad in the skins worn by the hordes of Attila. Had they not been drawn hither by the renown of the Republic's wealth? And how essentially did they differ from those other barbarians before whose bewildered, lustful gaze had risen the glittering palaces on the hills of the Tiber? The spoils of Rome! The spoils of America! They appeared to him ferocious, atavistic beasts as they broke into the lumberyard beneath his window to tear the cord-wood from the piles and rush out again, armed with billets. . . .

Janet, in the main stream sweeping irresistibly down the middle of the street, was carried beyond the lumberyard into the narrow roadway beside the canal — presently to find herself packed in the congested mass in front of the bridge that led to the gates of the Chippering Mill. Across the water, above the angry hum of human voices could be heard the whirring of the looms, rousing the mob to a higher pitch of fury. The halt was for a moment only. The bridge rocked beneath the weight of their charge, they battered at the great gates, they ran along the snow-filled tracks by the wall of the mill. Some, in a frenzy of passion, hurled their logs against the windows; others paused, seemingly to measure the distance and force of the stroke, thus lending to their act a more terrible and deliberate significance. A shout of triumph announced that the gates, like a broken dam, had given way, and the torrent poured in between the posts, flooding the yard, pressing up the towered stairways and spreading through the compartments of the mill. More ominous than the tumult seemed the comparative silence that followed this absorption of the angry spirits of the mob. Little by little, as the power was shut off, the antiphonal throbbing of the looms was stilled. Pinioned against the parapet above the canal — almost on that very spot where, the first evening, she had met Ditmar — Janet awaited her chance to cross. Every crashing window, every resounding blow on the panels gave her a fierce throb of joy. She had not expected the gates to yield — her father must have insecurely fastened them. Gaining the farther side of the canal, she perceived him flattened against the wall of the gatehouse shaking his fist in the faces of the intruders, who rushed past him unheeding. His look arrested her. His face was livid, his eyes were red with anger, he stood transformed by a passion she had not believed him to possess. She had indeed heard him give vent to a mitigated indignation against foreigners in general, but now the old-school Americanism in which he had been bred, the Americanism of individual rights, of respect for the convention of property, had suddenly sprung into flame. He was ready to fight for it, to die for it. The curses he hurled at these people sounded blasphemous in Janet's ears.

"Father!" she cried. "Father!"

He looked at her uncomprehendingly, seemingly failing to recognize her.

"What are you doing here?" he demanded, seizing her and attempting to draw her to the wall beside him. But she resisted. There sprang from her lips an unpremeditated question: "Where is Mr. Ditmar?" She was, indeed, amazed at having spoken it.

"I don't know," Edward replied distractedly. "We've been looking for him everywhere. My God, to think that this should happen with me at the gates!" he lamented. "Go home, Janet. You can't tell what'll happen, what these fiends will do, you may get hurt. You've got no business here." Catching sight of a belated and breathless policeman, he turned from her in desperation. "Get 'em out! For God's sake, can't you get 'em out before they ruin the machines?"

But Janet waited no longer. Pushing her way frantically through the people filling the yard she climbed the tower stairs and made her way into one of the spinning rooms. The frames were stilled, the overseer and second hands, thrust aside, looked on helplessly while the intruders harangued, cajoled or threatened the operatives, some of whom were cowed and already departing; others, sullen and resentful, remained standing in the aisles; and still others seemed to have caught the contagion of the strike. Suddenly, with reverberating strokes, the mill bells rang out, the electric gongs chattered, the siren screeched, drowning the voices. Janet did not pause, but hurried from room to room until, in passing through an open doorway in the weaving department she ran into Mr. Caldwell. He halted a moment, in surprise at finding her there, calling her by name. She clung to his sleeve, and again she asked the question : —

"Where's Mr. Ditmar?"

Caldwell shook his head. His answer was the same as Edward's. "I don't know," he shouted excitedly above the noise. "We've got to get this mob out before they do any damage."

He tore himself away, she saw him expostulating with the overseer, and then she went on. These tower stairs, she remembered, led to a yard communicating by a little gate with the office entrance. The door of the vestibule was closed, but the watchman, Simmons, recognizing her, permitted her to enter. The offices were deserted, silent, for the bells and the siren had ceased their clamour; the stenographers and clerks had gone. The short day was drawing to a close, shadows were gathering in the corners of Ditmar's room as she reached the threshold and gazed about her at the objects there so poignantly familiar. She took off her coat. His desk was littered with books and papers, and she started, mechanically, to set it in order, replacing the schedule books on the shelves, sorting out the letters and putting them in the basket. She could not herself have told why she should take up again these trivial tasks as though no cataclysmic events had intervened to divide forever the world of yesterday from that of to-morrow. With a movement suggestive of tenderness she was picking up Ditmar's pen to set it in the glass rack when her ear caught the sound of voices, and she stood transfixed, listening intently. There were footsteps in the corridor, the voices came nearer; one, loud and angered, she detected above the others. It was Ditmar's! Nothing had happened to him! Dropping the pen, she went over to the window, staring out over the grey waters, trembling so violently that she could scarcely stand.

She did not look around when they entered the room — Ditmar, Caldwell, Orcutt, and evidently a few watchmen and overseers. Some one turned on the electric switch, darkening the scene without. Ditmar continued to speak in vehement tones of uncontrolled rage.

"Why in hell weren't those gates bolted tight?" he demanded. "That's what I want to know! There was plenty of time after they turned the corner of East Street. You might have guessed what they would do. But instead of that you let 'em into the mill to shut off the power and intimidate our own people." He called the strikers an unprintable name, and though Janet stood, with her back turned, directly before him, he gave no sign of being aware of her presence.

"It wasn't the gatekeeper's fault," she heard Orcutt reply in a tone quivering with excitement and apprehension. "They really didn't give us a chance — that's the truth. They were down Canal Street and over the bridge before we knew it."

"It's just as I've said a hundred times," Ditmar retorted. "I can't afford to leave this mill a minute, I can't trust anybody —" and he broke out in another tirade against the intruders. "By God, I'll fix 'em for this — I'll crush 'em. And if any operatives try to walk out here I'll see that they starve before they get back — after all I've done for 'em, kept the mill going in slack times just to give 'em work. If they desert me now, when I've got this Bradlaugh order on my hands —" Speech became an inadequate expression of his feelings, and suddenly his eye fell on Janet. She had

ʊ

turned, but her look made no impression on him.   "Call up the Chief of Police," he said.

Automatically she obeyed, getting the connection and handing him the receiver, standing by while he denounced the incompetence of the department for permitting the mob to gather in East Street and demanded deputies.   The veins of his forehead were swollen as he cut short the explanations of the official and asked for the City Hall.   In making an appointment with the Mayor he reflected on the management of the city government.   And when Janet by his command obtained the Boston office, he gave the mill treasurer a heated account of the afternoon's occurrences, explaining circumstantially how, in his absence at a conference in the Patuxent Mill, the mob had gathered in East Street and attacked the Chippering; and he urged the treasurer to waste no time in obtaining a force of detectives, in securing in Boston and New York all the operatives that could be hired, in order to break the impending strike.   Save for this untimely and unreasonable revolt he was bent on stamping out, for Ditmar the world to-day was precisely the same world it had been the day before.   It seemed incredible to Janet that he could so regard it, could still be blind to the fact that these workers whom he was determined to starve and crush if they dared to upset his plans and oppose his will were human beings with wills and passions and grievances of their own.   Until to-day her eyes had been sealed.   In agony they had been opened to the panorama of sorrow and suffering, of passion and evil; and what she beheld now as life was a vast and terrible cruelty.   She had needed only this final proof to be convinced that in his eyes she also was but one of those brought into the world to minister to his pleasure and profit.   He had taken from her, as his meed, the most precious thing a woman has to give, and now that she was here again at his side, by some impulse incomprehensible to herself — in spite of the wrong he had done her ! — had sought him out in danger, he had no thought of her, no word for her, no use save a menial one : he cared nothing for any help she might be able to give, he had no perception of the new light which had broken within her soul. . . . The telephoning seemed interminable, yet she waited with a strange patience while he talked with Mr. George Chippering and two of the most influential directors. These conversations had covered the space of an hour or more. And perhaps as a result of self-suggestion, of his repeated assurances to Mr. Semple, to Mr. Chippering, and the directors of his ability to control the situation, Ditmar's habitual self-confidence was gradually restored. And when at last he hung up the instrument and turned to her, though still furious against the strikers, his voice betrayed the joy of battle, the assurance of victory.

"They can't bluff me, they'll have to guess again. It's that damned Holster — he hasn't any guts — he'd give in to 'em right now if I'd let him. It's the limit the way he turned the Clarendon over to them. I'll show him how to put a crimp in 'em if they don't turn up here to-morrow morning."

He was so magnificently sure of her sympathy ! She did not reply, but picked up her coat from the chair where she had laid it.

"Where are you going?" he demanded. And she replied laconically, "Home."

"Wait a minute," he said, rising and taking a step toward her.

"You have an appointment with the Mayor," she reminded him.

"I know," he said, glancing at the clock over the door. "Where have you been? — where were you this morning? I was worried about you, I — I was afraid you might be sick."

"Were you?" she said. "I'm all right. I had business in Boston."

"Why didn't you telephone me? In Boston?" he repeated.

She nodded. He started forward again, but she avoided him.

"What's the matter?" he cried. "I've been worried about you all day — until this damned strike broke loose. I was afraid something had happened."

"You might have asked my father," she said.

"For God's sake, tell me what's the matter!"

His desire for her mounted as his conviction grew more acute that something had happened to disturb a relationship which, he had congratulated himself, after many vicissitudes and anxieties had at last been established. He was conscious, however, of irritation because this whimsical and unanticipated grievance of hers should have developed at the moment when the caprice of his operatives threatened to interfere with his cherished plans — for Ditmar measured the inconsistencies of humanity by the yardstick of his desires. Her question as to why he had not made inquiries of her father added a new element to his disquietude. As he stood thus, worried, exasperated, and perplexed, the fact that there was in her attitude something ominous, dangerous, was slow to dawn on him. His faculties were wholly unprepared for the blow she struck him.

"I hate you!" she said. She did not raise her voice, but the deliberate, concentrated conviction she put into the sentence gave it the dynamic quality of a bullet. And save for the impact of it — before which he physically recoiled — its import was momentarily without meaning.

"What?" he exclaimed, stupidly.

"I might have known you never meant to marry me," she went on. Her hands were busy with the buttons of her coat.

"All you want is to use me, to enjoy me and turn me out when you get tired of me — the way you've done with other women. It's just the same with these mill hands, they're not human beings to you, they're — they're cattle. If they don't do as you like, you turn them out; you say they can starve for all you care."

"For God's sake, what do you mean?" he demanded. "What have I done to you, Janet? I love you, I need you!"

"Love me!" she repeated. "I know how men of your sort love — I've seen it — I know. As long as I give you what you want and don't bother you, you love me. And I know how these workers feel," she cried, with sudden, passionate vehemence. "I never knew before, but I know now. I've been with them, I marched up here with them from the Clarendon when they battered in the gates and smashed your windows — and I wanted to smash your windows, too, to blow up your mill."

"What are you saying? You came here with the strikers? you were with that mob?" asked Ditmar, astoundedly.

"Yes, I was in that mob. I belong there, with them, I tell you — I don't belong here, with you. But I was a fool even then, I was afraid they'd hurt you, I came into the mill to find you, and you — and you — you acted as if you'd never seen me before. I was a fool, but I'm glad I came — I'm glad I had a chance to tell you this."

"My God — won't you trust me?" he begged, with a tremendous effort to collect himself. "You trusted me yesterday. What's happened to change you? Won't you tell me? It's nothing I've done — I swear. And what do you mean when you say you were in that mob? I was almost crazy when I came back and found they'd been here in this mill — can't you understand? It wasn't that I didn't think of you. I'd been worrying about you all day. Look at this thing sensibly. I love you, I can't get along with-

out you — I'll marry you. I said I would, I meant it —
I'll marry you just as soon as I can clean up this mess of a
strike. It won't take long."

"Don't touch me!" she commanded, and he recoiled again.
"I'll tell you where I've been, if you want to know, — I've
been to see my sister in — in a house, in Boston. I guess
you know what kind of a house I mean, you've been in them,
you've brought women to them, — just like the man that
brought her there. Would you marry me now — with my
sister there? And am I any different from her? You —
you've made me just like her." Her voice had broken,
now, into furious, uncontrolled weeping to which she paid
no heed.

Ditmar was stunned; he could only stare at her.

"If I have a child," she said, "I'll — I'll kill you — I'll
kill myself."

And before he could reply — if indeed he had been able
to reply — she had left the office and was running down the
stairs. . . .

CHAPTER XIV

1

WHAT was happening to Hampton? Some hundreds of ignorant foreigners, dissatisfied with the money in their pay envelopes, had marched out of the Clarendon Mill and attacked the Chippering — and behold, the revered structure of American Government had quivered and tumbled down like a pack of cards! Despite the feverish assurances in the *Banner* "extra" that the disturbance was merely local and temporary, solid citizens became panicky, vaguely apprehending the release of elemental forces hitherto unrecognized and unknown. Who was to tell these solid, educated business men that the crazy industrial Babel they had helped to rear, and in which they unconsciously dwelt, was no longer the simple edifice they thought it? that Authority, spelled with a capital, was a thing of the past? that human instincts suppressed become explosives to displace the strata of civilization and change the face of the world? that conventions and institutions, laws and decrees crumble before the whirlwind of human passions? that their city was not of special, but of universal significance? And how were these, who still believed themselves to be dwelling under the old dispensation, to comprehend that environments change, and changing demand new and terrible Philosophies? When night fell on that fateful Tuesday the voice of Syndicalism had been raised in a temple dedicated to ordered, Anglo-Saxon liberty — the Hampton City Hall.

Only for a night and a day did the rebellion lack both

a leader and a philosophy. Meanwhile, in obedience to the unerring instinct for drama peculiar to great metropolitan dailies, newspaper correspondents were alighting from every train, interviewing officials and members of labour unions and mill agents : interviewing Claude Ditmar, the strongest man in Hampton that day. He at least knew what ought to be done, and even before his siren broke the silence of the morning hours in vigorous and emphatic terms he had informed the Mayor and Council of their obvious duty. These strikers were helots, unorganized scum ; the regular unions — by comparison respectable — held aloof from them. Here, in effect, was his argument : a strong show of force was imperative ; if the police and deputies were inadequate, request the Governor to call out the local militia ; but above all, waste no time, arrest the ringleaders, the plotters, break up all gatherings, keep the streets clear. He demanded from the law protection of his property, protection for those whose right to continue at work was inalienable. He was listened to with sympathy and respect — but nothing was done! The world had turned upside down indeed if the City Government of Hampton refused to take the advice of the agent of the Chippering Mill! American institutions were a failure! But such was the fact. Some unnamed fear, outweighing their dread of the retributions of Capital, possessed these men, made them supine, derelict in the face of their obvious duty.

By the faint grey light of that bitter January morning Ditmar made his way to the mill. In Faber Street dark figures flitted silently across the ghostly whiteness of the snow, and gathered in groups on the corners ; seeking to avoid these, other figures hurried along the sidewalks close to the buildings, to be halted, accosted, pleaded with — threatened, perhaps. Picketing had already begun! The effect of this pantomime of the eternal struggle for survival.

which he at first beheld from a distance, was to exaggerate appallingly the emptiness of the wide street, to emphasize the absence of shoppers and vehicles; and a bluish darkness lurked in the stores, whose plate glass windows were frosted in quaint designs. Where were the police? It was not fear that Ditmar felt, he was galvanized and dominated by anger, by an overwhelming desire for action; physical combat would have brought him relief, and as he quickened his steps he itched to seize with his own hands these foreigners who had dared to interfere with his cherished plans, who had had the audacity to challenge the principles of his government which welcomed them to its shores. He would have liked to wring their necks. *His* philosophy, too, was environmental. And beneath this wrath, stimulating and energizing it the more, was the ache in his soul from the loss for which he held these enemies responsible. Two days ago happiness and achievement had both been within his grasp. The only woman — so now it seemed — he had ever really wanted! What had become of her? What obscure and passionate impulse had led her suddenly to defy and desert him, to cast in her lot with these insensate aliens? A hundred times during the restless, inactive hours of a sleepless night this question had intruded itself in the midst of his scheming to break the strike, as he reviewed, word by word, act by act, that almost incomprehensible revolt of hers which had followed so swiftly — a final, vindictive blow of fate — on that other revolt of the workers. At moments he became confused, unable to separate the two. He saw her fire in that other. . . . Her sister, she had said, had been disgraced; she had defied him to marry her in the face of that degradation — and this suddenly *had* sickened him. He had let her go. What a fool he had been to let her go! Had she herself been —! He did not finish this thought. Throughout the long night he had known, for a certainty, that this woman was a vital part of him, flame of his flame. Had he never seen her he would have fought these strikers to their knees, but now the force of this incentive was doubled. He would never yield until he had crushed them, until he had reconquered her.

He was approaching one of the groups of strikers, and unconsciously he slowed his steps. The whites of his eyes reddened. The great coat of golden fur he wore gave to his aspect an added quality of formidableness. There were some who scattered as he drew near, and of the less timorous spirits that remained only a few raised dark, sullen glances to encounter his, which was unflinching, passionately contemptuous. Throughout the countless generations that lay behind them the instinct of submission had played its dominant, phylogenetic rôle. He was the Master. The journey across the seas had not changed that. A few shivered — not alone because they were thinly clad. He walked on, slowly, past other groups, turned the corner of West Street, where the groups were more numerous, while the number of those running the gantlet had increased. And he heard, twice or thrice, the word "Scab!" cried out menacingly. His eyes grew redder still as he spied a policeman standing idly in a doorway.

"Why in hell don't you do your duty?" he demanded. "What do you mean by letting them interfere with these workers?"

The man flinched. He was apologetic. "So long as they're peaceable, Mr. Ditmar — those are my orders. I do try to keep 'em movin'."

"Your orders? You're a lot of damned cowards," Ditmar replied, and went on. There were mutterings here; herded together, these slaves were bolder; and hunger and cold, discouragement at not being able to stop the flow toward the mills were having their effect. By the frozen canal, the scene of the onslaught of yesterday, the crowd had grown comparatively thick, and at the corner of the lodging-house row Ditmar halted a moment, unnoticed save by a few who nudged one another and murmured. He gave them no attention, he was trying to form an estimate of the effect of the picketing on his own operatives. Some came with timid steps; others, mostly women, fairly ran; still others were self-possessed, almost defiant — and such he marked. There were those who, when the picketers held them by the sleeve, broke precipitately from their annoyers, and those who hesitated, listening with troubled faces, with feelings torn between dread of hunger for themselves and their children and sympathy with the revolt. A small number joined the ranks of the picketers. Ditmar towered above these foreigners, who were mostly undersized: a student of human nature and civilization, free from industrial complexes, would from that point of vantage have had much to gather from the expressions coming within his view, but to Ditmar humanity was a means to an end. Suddenly, from the cupolas above the battlement of the mill, the bells shattered the early morning air, the remnant of the workers hastened across the canal and through the guarded gates, which were instantly closed. Ditmar was left alone among the strikers. As he moved toward the bridge they made a lane for him to pass; one or two he thrust out of his way. But there were mutterings, and from the sidewalk he heard a man curse him.

2

Perhaps we shall understand some day that the social body, also, is subject to the operation of cause and effect. It was not what an ingenuous orthodoxy, keeping alive the fate of the ancient city from which Lot fled, would call the wrath of heaven that visited Hampton, although a sermon on these lines was delivered from more than one of her pulpits on the following Sunday. Let us surmise, rather, that a decrepit social system in a moment of lowered vitality becomes an easy prey to certain diseases which respectable communities are not supposed to have. The germ of a philosophy evolved in decadent Europe flies across the sea to prey upon a youthful and vigorous America, lodging as host wherever industrial strife has made congenial soil. In four and twenty hours Hampton had "caught" Syndicalism. All day Tuesday, before the true nature of the affection was developed, prominent citizens were outraged and appalled by the supineness of their municipal phagocytes. Property, that sacred fabric of government, had been attacked and destroyed, law had been defied, and yet the City Hall, the sanctuary of American tradition, was turned over to the alien mob for a continuous series of mass meetings. All day long that edifice, hitherto chastely familiar with American doctrine alone, with patriotic oratory, with perorations that dwelt upon the wrongs and woes of Ireland — part of our national propaganda — all day long that edifice rang with strange, exotic speech, sometimes guttural, often musical, but always impassioned, weirdly cadenced and intoned. From the raised platform, in place of the shrewd, matter-of-fact New England politician alive to the vote-getting powers of Fourth of July patriotism, in place of the vehement but fun-loving son of Erin, men with wild, dark faces, with burning black eyes and unkempt hair, unshaven, flannel shirted — made more alien, paradoxically, by their conventional, ready-made American clothes — gave tongue to the inarticulate aspirations of the peasant drudge of Europe. From lands long steeped in blood they came, from low countries by misty northern seas, from fair and ancient plains of Lombardy, from Guelph and Ghibelline hamlets in the Apennines, from vine-covered slopes in Sicily and

Greece; from the Balkans, from Caucasus and Carpathia, from the mountains of Lebanon, whose cedars lined the palaces of kings; and from villages beside swollen rivers that cross the dreary steppes. Each peasant listened to a recital in his own tongue — the tongue in which the folklore, the cradle sayings of his race had been preserved — of the common wrongs of all, of misery still present, of happiness still unachieved in this land of liberty and opportunity they had found a mockery; to appeals to endure and suffer for a common cause. But who was to weld together this medley of races and traditions, to give them the creed for which their passions were prepared, to lead into battle these ignorant and unskilled from whom organized labour held aloof? Even as dusk was falling, even as the Mayor, the Hon. Michael McGrath, was making from the platform an eloquent plea for order and peace, promising a Committee of Arbitration and thinking about soldiers, the leader and the philosophy were landing in Hampton.

The "five o'clock" edition of the *Banner* announced him, Antonio Antonelli, of the *Industrial Workers of the World!* An ominous name, an ominous title, — compared by a well-known publicist to the sound of a fire-bell in the night. *The Industrial Workers*, not of America, but *of the World!* No wonder it sent shivers down the spine of Hampton! The writer of the article in the *Banner* was unfamiliar with the words "syndicalism" and "sabotage," or the phrase "direct action," he was too young to know the history of the Knights, he had never heard of a philosophy of labour, or of Sorel or Pouget, but the West he had heard of, — the home of lawlessness, of bloodshed, rape, and murder. For obvious reasons he did not betray this opinion, but for him the I.W.W. was born in the West, where it had ravaged and wrecked communities. His article was guardedly respectful, but he ventured to remind his readers that Mr.

Antonelli had been a leader in some of these titanic struggles between crude labour and capital — catastrophes that hitherto had seemed to the citizens of Hampton as remote as Kansas cyclones. . . .

Some of the less timorous of the older inhabitants, curious to learn what doctrine this interloper had to proclaim, thrust their way that evening into the City Hall, which was crowded, as the papers said, "to suffocation." Not prepossessing, this modern Robespierre; younger than he looked, for life had put its mark on him; once, in the days of severe work in the mines, his body had been hard, and now had grown stout. In the eyes of a complacent, armchair historian he must have appeared one of the strange and terrifying creatures which, in times of upheaval, are thrust from the depths of democracies to the surface, with gifts to voice the longings and passions of those below. He did not blink in the light; he was sure of himself, he had a creed and believed in it; he gazed around him with the leonine stare of the conqueror, and a hush came over the hall as he arose. His speech was taken down verbatim, to be submitted to the sharpest of legal eyes, when was discovered the possession of a power — rare among agitators — to pour forth in torrents apparently unpremeditated appeals, to skirt the border of sedition and never transgress it, to weigh his phrases before he gave them birth, and to remember them. If he said an incendiary thing one moment he qualified it the next; he justified violence only to deprecate it; and months later, when on trial for his life and certain remarks were quoted against him, he confounded his prosecutors by demanding the contexts. Skilfully, always within the limits of their intelligence, he outlined to his hearers his philosophy and proclaimed it as that of the world's oppressed. Their cause was his — the cause of human progress; he universalized it. The world belonged to the "producer," if

only he had the courage to take possession of his own. . . .
Suddenly the inspirer was transformed into the man of
affairs who calmly proposed the organization of a strike committee, three members of which were to be chosen by each
nationality. And the resolution, translated into many
tongues, was adopted amidst an uproar of enthusiasm.
Until that moment the revolt had been personal, local,
founded on a particular grievance which had to do with wages
and the material struggle for existence. Now all was
changed; now they were convinced that the deprivation
and suffering to which they had pledged themselves were
not for selfish ends alone, but also vicarious, dedicated to
the liberation of all the downtrodden of the earth. Antonelli became a saviour; they reached out to touch him as
he passed; they trooped into the snowy street, young men
and old, and girls, and women holding children in their arms,
their faces alight with something never known or felt before.

Such was Antonelli to the strikers. But to those staid
residents of Hampton who had thought themselves still to
be living in the old New England tradition, he was the genius
of an evil dream. Hard on his heels came a nightmare
troop, whose coming brought to the remembrance of the
imaginative the old nursery rhyme: —

> "Hark! Hark! The dogs do bark,
> The beggars are come to town."

It has, indeed, a knell-like ring. Do philosophies tend also
to cast those who adopt them into a mould? These were of
the self-same breed, indubitably the followers of Antonelli.
The men wore their hair long, affected, like their leader,
soft felt hats and loose black ties that fell over the lapels
of their coats. Loose morals and loose ties! The projection of these against a Puritan background! Ties symboli-
cal of everything the Anglo-Saxon shudders at and abhors;

of anarchy and mob rule, of bohemia and vagabondia, of sedition and murder, of Latin revolutions and reigns of terror; of sex irregularity — not of the clandestine sort to be found in decent communities — but of free love that flaunts itself in the face of an outraged public. For there were women in the band. All this, and more, the invaders suggested — atheism, unfamiliarity with soap and water, and, more vaguely, an exotic poetry and art that to the virile of American descent is saturated with something indefinable yet abhorrent. Such things are felt. Few of the older citizens of Hampton were able to explain why something rose in their gorges, why they experienced a new and clammy quality of fear and repulsion when, on the day following Antonelli's advent, these strangers arrived from nowhere to install themselves — with no baggage to speak of — in Hampton's more modest but hitherto respectable hostelries. And no sooner had the city been rudely awakened to the perilous presence, in overwhelming numbers, of ignorant and inflammable foreigners than *these* turned up and presumed to lead the revolt, to make capital out of it, to interpret it in terms of an exotic and degenerate creed. Hampton would take care of itself — or else the sovereign state within whose borders it was would take care of it. And his Honour the Mayor, who had proclaimed his faith in the reasonableness of the strikers, who had scorned the suggestions of indignant inhabitants that the Governor be asked for soldiers, twenty-four hours too late arranged for the assembly of three companies of local militia in the armory, and swore in a hundred extra police.

3

The hideous stillness of Fillmore Street was driving Janet mad. What she burned to do was to go to Boston and take a train for somewhere in the West, to lose herself, never to see Hampton again. But — there was her mother. She could not leave Hannah in these empty rooms, alone; and Edward was to remain at the mill, to eat and sleep there, until the danger of the strike had passed. A messenger had come to fetch his clothes. After leaving Ditmar in the office of the mill, Janet crept up the dark stairs to the flat and halted in the hallway. Through the open doorway of the dining-room she saw Hannah seated on the horsehair sofa — for the first time within memory idle at this hour of the day. Nothing else could have brought home to her like this the sheer tragedy of their plight. Until then Janet had been sustained by anger and excitement, by physical action. She thought Hannah was staring at her; after a moment it seemed that the widened pupils were fixed in fascination on something beyond, on the Thing that had come to dwell here with them forever.

Janet entered the room. She sat down on the sofa and took her mother's hand in hers. And Hannah submitted passively. Janet could not speak. A minute might have passed, and the silence, which neither had broken, acquired an intensity that to Janet became unbearable. Never had the room been so still! Her glance, raised instinctively to the face of the picture-clock, saw the hands pointing to ten. Every Monday morning, as far back as she could recall, her father had wound it before going to work — and to-day he had forgotten. Getting up, she opened the glass door, and stood trying to estimate the hour: it must be, she thought, about six. She set the hands, took the key from the nail above the shelf, wound up the weight, and started the pendulum. And the sound of familiar ticking was a relief, releasing at last her inhibited powers of speech.

"Mother," she said, "I'll get some supper for you."

On Hannah, these simple words had a seemingly magical

x

effect. Habit reasserted itself. She started, and rose almost briskly.

"No you won't," she said, "I'll get it. I'd ought to have thought of it before. You must be tired and hungry."

Her voice was odd and thin. Janet hesitated a moment, and ceded.

"Well, I'll set the dishes on the table, anyway."

Janet had sought refuge, wistfully, in the commonplace. And when the meal was ready she strove to eat, though food had become repulsive.

"You must take something, mother," she said.

"I don't feel as if I ever wanted to eat anything again," she replied.

"I know," said Janet, "but you've got to." And she put some of the cold meat, left over from Sunday's dinner, on Hannah's plate. Hannah took up a fork, and laid it down again. Suddenly she said : —

"You saw Lise?"

"Yes," said Janet.

"Where is she?"

"In a house — in Boston."

"One of — those houses?"

"I — I don't know," said Janet. "I think so."

"You went there?"

"Mr. Tiernan went with me."

"She wouldn't come home?"

"Not — not just now, mother."

"You left her there, in that place? You didn't make her come home?"

The sudden vehemence of this question, the shrill note of reproach in Hannah's voice that revealed, even more than the terrible inertia from which she had emerged, the extent of her suffering, for the instant left Janet utterly dismayed. "Oh mother!" she exclaimed. "I tried — I — I couldn't."

Hannah pushed back her chair.

"I'll go to her, I'll make her come. She's disgraced us, but I'll make her. Where is she? Where is the house?"

Janet, terrified, seized her mother's arm. Then she said:—

"Lise isn't there any more — she's gone away."

"Away! and you let her go away? You let your sister go away and be a — a woman of the town? You never loved her — you never had any pity for her."

Tears sprang into Janet's eyes — tears of pity mingled with anger. The situation had grown intolerable! Yet how could she tell Hannah where Lise was!

"You haven't any right to say that, mother!" she cried. "I did my best. She wouldn't come. I — I can't tell you where she's gone, but she promised to write, to send me her address."

"Lise!" Hannah's cry seemed like the uncomprehending whimper of a stricken child, and then a hidden cadence made itself felt, a cadence revealing to Janet with an eloquence never before achieved the mystery of mother love, and by some magic of tone was evoked a new image of Lise — of Lise as she must be to Hannah. No waywardness, no degradation or disgrace could efface it. The infant whom Hannah had clutched to her breast, the woman, her sister, whom Janet had seen that day were one — immutably one. This, then, was what it meant to be a mother! All the years of deadening hope had not availed to kill the craving — even in this withered body it was still alive and quick. The agony of that revelation was scarcely to be borne. And it seemed that Lise, even in the place where she was, must have heard that cry and heeded it. And yet — the revelation of Lise's whereabouts, of Lise's contemplated act Janet had nearly been goaded into making, died on her lips. She could not tell Hannah! And Lise's child must not come into a world like this. Even now the conviction remained, fierce, exultant, final. But if Janet had spoken now Hannah would not have heard her. Under the storm she had begun to rock, weeping convulsively. . . . But gradually her weeping ceased. And to Janet, helplessly watching, this process of congealment was more terrible even than the release that only an unmitigated violence of grief had been able to produce. In silence Hannah resumed her shrunken duties, and when these were finished sat awhile, before going to bed, her hands lying listless in her lap. She seemed to have lived for centuries, to have exhausted the gamut of suffering which, save for that one wild outburst, had been the fruit of commonplace, passive, sordid tragedy that knows no touch of fire. . . .

The next morning Janet was awakened by the siren. Never, even in the days when life had been routine and commonplace, had that sound failed to arouse in her a certain tremor of fear; with its first penetrating shriek, terror invaded her : then, by degrees, overcoming her numbness, came an agonizing realization of tragedy to be faced. The siren blew and blew insistently, as though it never meant to stop ; and now for the first time she seemed to detect in it a note of futility. There were those who would dare to defy it. She, for one, would defy it. In that reflection she found a certain fierce joy. And she might lie in bed if she wished — how often had she longed to ! But she could not. The room was cold, appallingly empty and silent as she hurried into her clothes. The dining-room lamp was lighted, the table set, her mother was bending over the stove when she reached the kitchen. After the pretence of breakfast was gone through Janet sought relief in housework, making her bed, tidying her room. It was odd, this morning, how her notice of little, familiar things had the power to add to her pain, brought to mind memories become excruciating :

as she filled the water pitcher from the kitchen tap she found herself staring at the nick broken out of it when Lise had upset it. She recalled Lise's characteristically flippant remark. And there was the streak in the wall-paper caused one night by the rain leaking through the roof. After the bed was made and the room swept she stood a moment, motionless, and then, opening the drawer in the wardrobe took from it the rose which she had wrapped in tissue paper and hidden there, and with a perverse desire as it were to increase the bitterness consuming her, to steep herself in pain, she undid the parcel and held the withered flower to her face. Even now a fragrance, faint yet poignant, clung to it. . . . She wrapped it up again, walked to the window, hesitated, and then with a sudden determination to destroy this sole relic of her happiness went to the kitchen and flung it into the stove. Hannah, lingering over her morning task of cleaning, did not seem to notice the act. Janet turned to her.

"I think I'll go out for a while, mother," she said.

"You'd ought to," Hannah replied. "There's no use settin' around here."

The silence of the flat was no longer to be endured. And Janet, putting on her coat and hat, descended the stairs. Not once that morning had her mother mentioned Lise; nor had she asked about her own plans — about Ditmar. This at least was a relief; it was the question she had feared most. In the street she met the postman.

"I have a letter for you, Miss Janet," he said. And on the pink envelope he handed her, in purple ink, she recognized the unformed, childish handwriting of Lise. "There's great doings down at the City Hall," the postman added: "the foreigners are holding mass meetings there."

Janet scarcely heard him as she tore open the envelope. "Dear Janet," the letter ran. "The doctor told me I had a false alarm, there was nothing to it. Wouldn't that jar you? Boston's a slow burg, and there's no use of my staying here now. I'm going to New York, and maybe I'll come back when I've had a look at the great white way. I've got the coin, and I gave *him* the mit to-night. If you haven't anything better to do, drop in at the *Bagatelle* and give Walters my love, and tell them not to worry at home. There's no use trying to trail me. Your affectionate sister Lise."

Janet thrust the letter in her pocket. Then she walked rapidly westward until she came to the liver-coloured façade of the City Hall, opposite the Common. Pushing through the crowd of operatives lingering on the pavement in front of it, she entered the building. . . .

CHAPTER XV

1

OCCASIONALLY the art of narrative may be improved by borrowing the method of the movies. Another night has passed, and we are called upon to imagine the watery sunlight of a mild winter afternoon filtering through bare trees on the heads of a multitude. A large portion of Hampton Common is black with the people of sixteen nationalities who have gathered there, trampling down the snow, to listen wistfully and eagerly to a new doctrine of salvation. In the centre of this throng on the bandstand — reminiscent of concerts on sultry, summer nights — are the itinerant apostles of the cult called Syndicalism, exhorting by turns in divers tongues. Antonelli had spoken, and many others, when Janet, impelled by a craving not to be denied, had managed to push her way little by little from the outskirts of the crowd until now she stood almost beneath the orator who poured forth passionate words in a language she recognized as Italian. Her curiosity was aroused, she was unable to classify this tall man whose long and narrow face was accentuated by a pointed brown beard, whose lips gleamed red as he spoke, whose slim hands were eloquent. The artist as propagandist — the unsuccessful artist with more facility than will. The nose was classic, and wanted strength; the restless eyes that at times seemed fixed on her were smouldering windows of a burning house : the fire that stirred her was also consuming him. Though he could have been little more than five and thirty, his hair was thinned and

311

greying at the temples. And somehow emblematic of this physiognomy and physique, summing it up and expressing it in terms of apparel, were the soft collar and black scarf tied in a flowing bow. Janet longed to know what he was saying. His phrases, like music, played on her emotions, and at last, when his voice rose in crescendo at the climax of his speech, she felt like weeping.

"Un poeta!" a woman beside her exclaimed.

"Who is he?" Janet asked.

"Rolfe," said the woman.

"But he's an Italian?"

The woman shrugged her shoulders. "It is his name — that is all I know." He had begun to speak again, and now in English, with an enunciation, a distinctive manner of turning his phrases new to such gatherings in America, where labour intellectuals are little known; surprising to Janet, diverting her attention, at first, from the meaning of his words. "Labour," she heard, "labour is the creator of all wealth, and wealth belongs to the creator. The wage system must be abolished. You, the creators, must do battle against these self-imposed masters until you shall come into your own. You who toil miserably for nine hours and produce, let us say, nine dollars of wealth — do you receive it? No, what is given you is barely enough to keep the slave and the slave's family alive! The master, the capitalist, seizes the rightful reward of your labour and spends it on luxuries, on automobiles and fine houses and women, on food he can't eat, while you are hungry. Yes, you are slaves," he cried, "because you submit like slaves."

He waited, motionless and scornful, for the noise to die down. "Since I have come here to Hampton, I have heard some speak of the state, others of the unions. Yet the state is your enemy, it will not help you to gain your freedom. The legislature has shortened your hours, — but why?

Because the politicians are afraid of you, and because they
think you will be content with a little. And now that the
masters have cut your wages, the state sends its soldiers to
crush you. Only fifty cents, they say — only fifty cents most
of you miss from your envelopes. What is fifty cents to
them? But I who speak to you have been hungry, I know
that fifty cents will buy ten loaves of bread, or three pounds
of the neck of pork, or six quarts of milk for the babies.
Fifty cents will help pay the rent of the rat-holes where you
live." Once more he was interrupted by angry shouts of
approval. "And the labour unions, have they aided you?
Why not? I will tell you why — because they are the ser-
vile instruments of the masters. The unions say that capital
has rights, bargain with it, but for us there can be only one
bargain, complete surrender of the tools to the workers. For
the capitalists are parasites who suck your blood and your
children's blood. From now on there can be no compromise,
no truce, no peace until they are exterminated. It is war."

War! In Janet's soul the word resounded like a tocsin.
And again, as when swept along East Street with the mob,
that sense of identity with these people and their wrongs, of
submergence with them in their cause possessed her. Despite her ancestry, her lot was cast with them. She, too,
had been precariously close to poverty, had known the sordidness of life; she, too, and Lise and Hannah had been
duped and cheated of the fairer things. Eagerly she had
drunk in the vocabulary of that new and terrible philosophy.
The master class must be exterminated! Was it not true,
if she had been of that class, that Ditmar would not have
dared to use and deceive her? Why had she never thought
of these things before? . . . The light was beginning to
fade, the great meeting was breaking up, and yet she lingered. At the foot of the bandstand steps, conversing with
a small group of operatives that surrounded him, she per-

ceived the man who had just spoken. And as she stood
hesitating, gazing at him, a desire to hear more, to hear all
of this creed he preached, that fed the fires in her soul, urged
her forward. Her need, had she known it, was even greater
than that of these toilers whom she now called comrades.
Despite some qualifying reserve she felt, and which had had
to do with the redness of his lips, he attracted her. He had
a mind, an intellect, he must possess stores of the knowledge
for which she thirsted; he appeared to her as one who had
studied and travelled, who had ascended heights and gained
the wider view denied her. A cynical cosmopolitanism would
have left her cold, but here, apparently, was a cultivated
man burning with a sense of the world's wrongs. Ditmar,
who was to have led her out of captivity, had only thrust
her the deeper into bondage. . . . She joined the group,
halting on the edge of it, listening. Rolfe was arguing with
a man about the labour unions, but almost at once she knew
she had fixed his attention. From time to time, as he talked,
his eyes sought hers boldly, and in their dark pupils were
tiny points of light that stirred and confused her, made her
wonder what was behind them, in his soul. When he had
finished his argument, he singled her out.

"You do not work in the mills?" he asked.

"No, I'm a stenographer — or I was one."

"And now?"

"I've given up my place."

"You want to join us?"

"I was interested in what you said. I never heard anything like it before."

He looked at her intently.

"Come, let us walk a little way," he said. And she
went along by his side, through the Common, feeling a
neophyte's excitement in the freemasonry, the contempt
for petty conventions of this newly achieved doctrine of

brotherhood. "I will give you things to read, you shall be one of us."

"I'm afraid I shouldn't understand them," Janet replied. "I've read so little."

"Oh, you will understand," he assured her, easily. "There is too much learning, too much reason and intelligence in the world, too little impulse and feeling, intuition. Where do reason and intelligence lead us? To selfishness, to thirst for power — straight into the master class. They separate us from the mass of humanity. No, our fight is against those who claim more enlightenment than their fellow-men, who control the public schools and impose reason on our children, because reason leads to submission, makes us content with our station in life. The true syndicalist is an artist, a revolutionist!" he cried.

Janet found this bewildering and yet through it seemed to shine for her a gleam of light. Her excitement grew. Never before had she been in the presence of one who talked like this, with such assurance and ease. And the fact that he despised knowledge, yet possessed it, lent him glamour.

"But you have studied!" she exclaimed.

"Oh yes, I have studied," he replied, with a touch of weariness, "only to learn that life is simple, after all, and that what is needed for the social order is simple. We have only to take what belongs to us, we who work, to follow our feelings, our inclinations."

"You would take possession of the mills?" she asked.

"Yes," he said quickly, "of all wealth, and of the government. There would be no government — we should not need it. A little courage is all that is necessary, and we come into our own. You are a stenographer, you say. But you — you are not content, I can see it in your face, in your eyes. You have cause to hate them, too, these masters, or you would not have been here in this place, to-day. Is it not so?"

She shivered, but was silent.

"Is it not so?" he repeated. "They have wronged you, too, perhaps, — they have wronged us all, but some are too stupid, too cowardly to fight and crush them. Christians and slaves submit. The old religion teaches that the world is cruel for most of us, but if we are obedient and humble we shall be rewarded in heaven." Rolfe laughed. "The masters approve of that teaching. They would not have it changed. But for us it is war. We'll strike and keep on striking, we'll break their machinery, spoil their mills and factories, and drive them out. And even if we do not win at once, it is better to suffer and die fighting than to have the life ground out of us — is it not?"

"Yes, it is better!" she agreed. The passion in her voice did not escape him.

"Some day, perhaps sooner than we think, we shall have the true Armageddon, the general strike, when the last sleeping toiler shall have aroused himself from his lethargy to rise up and come into his inheritance." He seemed to detach himself from her, his eyes became more luminous.

"'Like unseen music in the night,' — so Sorel writes about it. They may scoff at it, the wise ones, but it will come. 'Like music in the night!' You respond to that!"

Again she was silent. They had walked on, through familiar streets that now seemed strange.

"You respond — I can tell," he said. "And yet, you are not like these others, like me, even. You are an American. And yet you are not like most of your countrywomen."

"Why do you say that?"

"I will tell you. Because they are cold, most of them, and trivial, they do not feel. But you — you can feel, you can love and hate. You look calm and cold, but you are not — I knew it when I looked at you, when you came up to me."

She did not know whether to resent or welcome his clair-voyance, his assumption of intimacy, his air of appropria-tion. But her curiosity was tingling.

"And you?" she asked. "Your name is Rolfe, isn't it?" He assented. "And yours?"

She told him.

"You have been in America long — your family?"

"Very long," she said. "But you speak Italian, and Rolfe isn't an Italian name."

"My father was an Englishman, an artist, who lived in Italy — my mother a peasant woman from Lombardy, such as these who come to work in the mills. When she was young she was beautiful — like a Madonna by an old master."

"An old master?"

"The old masters are the great painters who lived in Italy four hundred years ago. I was named after one of them — the greatest. I am called Leonard. He was Leonardo da Vinci."

The name, as Rolfe pronounced it, stirred her. And art, painting! It was a realm unknown to her, and yet the very suggestion of it evoked yearnings. And she recalled a pic-ture in the window of Hartmann's book-store, a coloured print before which she used to stop on her way to and from the office, the copy of a landscape by a California artist. The steep hillside in the foreground was spread with the misty green of olive trees, and beyond — far beyond — a snow-covered peak, like some high altar, flamed red in the sunset. She had not been able to express her feeling for this picture, it had filled her with joy and sadness. Once she had ventured to enter and ask its price — ten dollars. And then came a morning when she had looked for it, and it was gone.

"And your father — did he paint beautiful pictures, too?"

"Ah, he was too much of a socialist. He was always away when I was a child, and after my mother's death he

used to take me with him.   When I was seventeen we went
to Milan to take part in the great strike, and there I saw the
soldiers shooting down the workers by the hundreds, putting
them in prison by the thousands.   Then I went to live in
England, among the socialists there, and I learned the printer's
trade.   When I first came to this country I was on a labour
paper in New York, I set up type, I wrote articles, and once
in a while I addressed meetings on the East Side.   But even
before I left London I had read a book on Syndicalism by one
of the great Frenchmen, and after a while I began to realize
that the proletariat would never get anywhere through
socialism."

"The proletariat?"   The word was new to Janet's ear.

"The great mass of the workers, the oppressed, the people
you saw here to-day.   Socialism is not for them.   Socialism
— political socialism — betrays them into the hands of the
master class.   Direct action is the thing, the general strike,
war, — the new creed, the new religion that will bring salvation.   I joined the Industrial Workers of the World —
that is the American organization of Syndicalism.   I went
west, to Colorado and California and Oregon, I preached to
the workers wherever there was an uprising, I met the leaders,
Ritter and Borkum and Antonelli and Jastro and Nellie
Bond, I was useful to them, I understand Syndicalism as
they do not.   And now we are here, to sow the seed in the
East.   Come," he said, slipping his arm through hers, "I
will take you to Headquarters, I will enlist you, you shall
be my recruit.   I will give you the cause, the religion you
need."

She longed to go, and yet she drew back, puzzled.   The
man fired and fascinated her, but there were reservations,
apprehensions concerning him, felt rather than reasoned.   Because of her state of rebellion, of her intense desire to satisfy
in action the emotion aroused by a sense of wrong, his creed

had made a violent appeal, but in his voice, in his eyes, in his manner she had been quick to detect a personal, sexual note that disturbed and alarmed her, that implied in him a lack of unity.

"I can't, to-night," she said. "I must go home —my mother is all alone. But I want to help, I want to do something."

They were standing on a corner, under a street lamp. And she averted her eyes from his glance.

"Then come to-morrow," he said eagerly. "You know where Headquarters is, in the Franco-Belgian Hall?"

"What could I do?" she asked.

"You? You could help in many ways — among the women. Do you know what picketing is?"

"You mean keeping the operatives out of the mills?"

"Yes, in the morning, when they go to work. And out of the Chippering Mill, especially. Ditmar, the agent of that mill, is the ablest of the lot, I'm told. He's the man we want to cripple."

"Cripple!" exclaimed Janet.

"Oh, I don't mean to harm him personally." Rolfe did not seem to notice her tone. "But he intends to crush the strike, and I understand he's importing scabs here to finish out an order — a big order. If it weren't for him, we'd have an easier fight; he stiffens up the others. There's always one man like that, in every place. And what we want to do is to make him shut down, especially."

"I see," said Janet.

"You'll come to Headquarters?" Rolfe repeated.

"Yes, I'll come, to-morrow," she promised.

After she had left him she walked rapidly through several streets, not heeding her direction — such was the driving power of the new ideas he had given her. Certain words and phrases he had spoken rang in her head, and like martial

music kept pace with her steps. She strove to remember
all that he had said, to grasp its purport; and because it
seemed recondite, cosmic, it appealed to her and excited her
the more. And he, the man himself, had exerted a kind of
hypnotic force that partially had paralyzed her faculties
and aroused her fears while still in his presence: her first
feeling in escaping had been one of relief — and then she
began to regret not having gone to Headquarters. Hadn't
she been foolish? In the retrospect, the elements in him
that had disturbed her were less disquieting, his intellectual
fascination was enhanced: and in that very emancipation
from cant and convention, characteristic of the Order to
which he belonged, had lain much of his charm. She *had*
attracted him as a woman, there was no denying that. He,
who had studied and travelled and known life in many lands,
had discerned in her, Janet Bumpus, some quality to make
him desire her, acknowledge her as a comrade! Tremblingly
she exulted in the possession of that quality — whatever it
might be. Ditmar, too, had perceived it! He had not
known how to value it. With this thought came a flaming
suggestion — Ditmar should see her with this man Rolfe,
she would make him scorch with the fires of jealousy. Ditmar should know that she had joined his enemies, the Industrial Workers of the World. Of the world! Her shackles
had been cast off at last! . . . And then, suddenly, she felt
tired. The prospect of returning to Fillmore Street, to the
silent flat — made the more silent by her mother's tragic
presence — overwhelmed her. The ache in her heart began
to throb again. How could she wait until the dawn of another day? . . .

2

In the black hours of the morning, with the siren dinning
in her ears a hoarse call to war, Janet leaped from her bed

and began to dress. There is a degree of cold so sharp that
it seems actually to smell, and as she stole down the stairs
and out of the door she shivered, assailed by a sense of loneliness and fear. Yet an insistent voice urged her on, whispering that to remain at home, inactive, was to go mad;
salvation and relief lay in plunging into the struggle, in
contributing her share toward retribution and victory.
Victory! In Faber Street the light of the electric arcs
tinged the snow with blue, and the flamboyant advertise-
ments of breakfast foods, cigarettes and ales seemed but
the mockery of an activity now unrealizable. The groups
and figures scattered here and there farther down the street
served only to exaggerate its wide emptiness. What could
these do, what could she accomplish against the mighty
power of the mills? Gradually, as she stood gazing, she
became aware of a beating of feet upon the snow; over her
shoulder she caught the gleam of steel. A squad of soldiers
muffled in heavy capes and woolen caps was marching along
the car-tracks. She followed them. At the corner of
West Street, in obedience to a sharp command she saw them
halt, turn, and advance toward a small crowd gathered
there. It scattered, only to collect again when the soldiers
had passed on. Janet joined them. She heard men cursing
the soldiers. The women stood a little aside; some were
stamping to keep warm, and one, with a bundle in her
arms which Janet presently perceived to be a child, sank
down on a stone step and remained there, crouching, resigned.

"We gotta right to stay here, in the street. We gotta
right to live, I guess." The girl's teeth were chattering, but
she spoke with such vehemence and spirit as to attract
Janet's attention. "You worked in the Chippering, like
me — yes?" she asked.

Janet nodded. The faded, lemon-coloured shawl the girl

Y

had wrapped about her head emphasized the dark beauty of her oval face. She smiled, and her white teeth were fairly dazzling. Impulsively she thrust her arm through Janet's.

"You American — you comrade, you come to help?" she asked.

"I've never done any picketing."

"I showa you."

The dawn had begun to break, revealing little by little the outlines of cruel, ugly buildings, the great mill looming darkly at the end of the street, and Janet found it scarcely believable that only a little while ago she had hurried thither in the mornings with anticipation and joy in her heart, eager to see Ditmar, to be near him! The sight of two policemen hurrying toward them from the direction of the canal aroused her. With sullen murmurs the group started to disperse, but the woman with the baby, numb with cold, was slow in rising, and one of the policemen thrust out his club threateningly.

"Move on, you can't sit here," he said.

With a lithe movement like the spring of a cat the Italian girl flung herself between them — a remarkable exhibition of spontaneous inflammability; her eyes glittered like the points of daggers, and, as though they had been dagger points, the policeman recoiled a little. The act, which was absolutely natural, superb, electrified Janet, restored in an instant her own fierceness of spirit. The girl said something swiftly, in Italian, and helped the woman to rise, paying no more attention to the policeman. Janet walked on, but she had not covered half the block before she was overtaken by the girl; her anger had come and gone in a flash, her vivacity had returned, her vitality again found expression in an abundant good nature and good will. She asked Janet's name, volunteering the information that her own was Gemma, that she was a "fine speeder" in the Chippering Mill, where she had received nearly seven dollars a week. She had been among the first to walk out.

"Why did you walk out?" asked Janet curiously.

"Why? I get mad when I know that my wages is cut. I want the money — I get married."

"Is that why you are striking?" asked Janet curiously.

"That is why — of course."

"Then you haven't heard any of the speakers? They say it is for a cause — the workers are striking for freedom, some day they will own the mills. I heard a man named Rolfe yesterday —"

The girl gave her a radiant smile.

"Rolfe! It is beautiful, what Rolfe said. You think so? I think so. I am for the cause, I hate the capitalist. We will win, and get more money, until we have all the money. We will be rich. And you, why do you strike?"

"I was mad, too," Janet replied simply.

"Revenge!" exclaimed the girl, glittering again. "I understan'. Here come the scabs! Now I show you."

The light had grown, but the stores were still closed and barred. Along Faber Street, singly or in little groups, anxiously glancing around them, behind them, came the workers who still clung desperately to their jobs. Gemma fairly darted at two girls who sought the edge of the sidewalk, seizing them by the sleeves, and with piteous expressions they listened while she poured forth on them a stream of Italian. After a moment one tore herself away, but the other remained and began to ask questions. Presently she turned and walked slowly away in the direction from which she had come.

"I get her," exclaimed Gemma, triumphantly.

"What did you say?" asked Janet.

"Listen — that she take the bread from our mouths, she is traditore — scab. We strike for them, too, is it not so?

It is no use for them to work for wages that starve. We win the strike, we get good wages for all. Here comes another — she iṣ a Jewess — you try, you spik."

Janet failed with the Jewess, who obstinately refused to listen or reply as the two walked along with her, one on either side. Near West Street they spied a policeman, and desisted. Up and down Faber Street, everywhere, the game went on: but the police were watchful, and once a detachment of militia passed. The picketing had to be done quickly, in the few minutes that were to elapse before the gates should close. Janet's blood ran faster, she grew excited, absorbed, bolder as she perceived the apologetic attitude of the "scabs" and she began to despise them with Gemma's heartiness; and soon she had lost all sense of surprise at finding herself arguing, pleading, appealing to several women in turn, fluently, in the language of the industrial revolution. Some — because she was an American — examined her with furtive curiosity; others pretended not to understand, accelerating their pace. She gained no converts that morning, but one girl, pale, anemic with high cheek bones — evidently a Slav — listened to her intently.

"I gotta raït to work," she said.

"Not if others will starve because you work," objected Janet.

"If I don't work I starve," said the girl.

"No, the Committee will take care of you — there will be food for all. How much do you get now?"

"Four dollar and a half."

"You starve now," Janet declared contemptuously. "The quicker you join us, the sooner you'll get a living wage."

The girl was not quite convinced. She stood for a while undecided, and then ran abruptly off in the direction of West Street. Janet sought for others, but they had ceased coming; only the scattered, prowling picketers remained.

Over the black rim of the Clarendon Mill to the eastward
the sky had caught fire. The sun had risen, the bells were
ringing riotously, resonantly in the clear, cold air. Another
working day had begun.

3

Janet, benumbed with cold, yet agitated and trembling
because of her unwonted experience of the morning, made
her way back to Fillmore Street. She was prepared to answer
any questions her mother might ask; as they ate their dismal
breakfast, and Hannah asked no questions, she longed to
blurt out where she had been, to announce that she had
cast her lot with the strikers, the foreigners, to defend
them and declare that these were not to blame for the misfortunes of the family, but men like Ditmar and the owners
of the mills, the capitalists. Her mother, she reflected
bitterly, had never once betrayed any concern as to her
shattered happiness. But gradually, as from time to time
she glanced covertly at Hannah's face, her resentment gave
way to apprehension. Hannah did not seem now even
to be aware of her presence; this persistent apathy filled
her with a dread she did not dare to acknowledge.

"Mother!" she cried at last.

Hannah started. "Have you finished?" she asked.

"Yes."

"You've b'en out in the cold, and you haven't eaten much."

Janet fought back her tears. "Oh yes, I have," she managed to reply, convinced of the futility of speech, of all attempts to arouse her mother to a realization of the situation.
Perhaps — though her heart contracted at the thought —
perhaps it was a merciful thing! But to live, day after
day, in the presence of that comfortless apathy! . . . Later
in the morning she went out, to walk the streets, and again
in the afternoon; and twice she turned her face eastward,

in the direction of the Franco-Belgian Hall. Her courage
failed her. How would these foreigners and the strange
leaders who had come to organize them receive her, Ditmar's stenographer? She would have to tell them she was
Ditmar's stenographer; they would find it out. And now
she was filled with doubts about Rolfe. Had he really
thought she could be of use to them! Around the Common,
in front of the City Hall men went about their affairs alertly,
or stopped one another to talk about the strike. In Faber
Street, indeed, an air of suppressed excitement prevailed,
newsboys were shouting out extras; but business went on
as though nothing had happened to disturb it. There was,
however, the spectacle, unusual at this time of day, of operatives mingling with the crowd, while policemen stood watch-
fully at the corners; a company of soldiers marched by,
drawing the people in silence to the curb. Janet scanned the
faces of these idle operatives; they seemed for the most
part either calm or sullen, wanting the fire and passion of
the enthusiasts who had come out to picket in the early hours
of the day; she sought vainly for the Italian girl with whom
she had made friends. Despondency grew in her, a sense of
isolation, of lacking any one, now, to whom she might turn,
and these feelings were intensified by the air of confidence
prevailing here. The strike was crushed, injustice and wrong
had triumphed — would always triumph. In front of the
Banner office she heard a man say to an acquaintance who
had evidently just arrived in town : —

"The Chippering? Sure, that's running. By to-morrow
Ditmar'll have a full force there. Now that the militia
has come, I guess we've got this thing scotched. . . ."

Just how and when that order and confidence of Faber
Street began to be permeated by disquietude and alarm,
Janet could not have said. Something was happening,
somewhere — or about to happen. An obscure, apparently

telepathic process was at work. People began to hurry westward, a few had abandoned the sidewalk and were running; while other pedestrians, more timid, were equally concerned to turn and hasten in the opposite direction. At the corner of West Street was gathering a crowd that each moment grew larger and larger, despite the efforts of the police to disperse it. These were strikers, angry strikers. They blocked the traffic, halted the clanging trolleys, surged into the mouth of West Street, booing and cursing at the soldiers whose threatening line of bayonets stretched across that thoroughfare half-way down toward the canal, guarding the detested Chippering Mill. Bordering West Street, behind the company's lodging-houses on the canal, were certain low buildings, warehouses, and on their roofs tense figures could be seen standing out against the sky. The vanguard of the mob, thrust on by increasing pressure from behind, tumbled backward the thin cordon of police, drew nearer and nearer the bayonets, while the soldiers grimly held their ground. A voice was heard on the roof, a woman in the front rank of the mob gave a warning shriek, and two swift streams of icy water burst forth from the warehouse parapet, tearing the snow from the cobbles, flying in heavy, stinging spray as it advanced and mowed the strikers down and drove them like flies toward Faber Street. Screams of fright, curses of defiance and hate mingled with the hissing of the water and the noise of its impact with the ground — like the tearing of heavy sail-cloth. Then, from somewhere near the edge of the mob, came a single, sharp detonation, quickly followed by another — below the watchmen on the roof a window crashed. The nozzles on the roof were raised, their streams, sweeping around in a great semi-circle, bowled down the rioters below the tell-tale wisps of smoke, and no sooner had the avalanche of water passed than the policemen who, forewarned, had sought refuge along the walls, rushed forward and seized a man who lay gasping on the snow. Dazed, half drowned, he had dropped his pistol. They handcuffed him and dragged him away through the ranks of the soldiers, which opened for him to pass. The mob, including those who had been flung down, bruised and drenched, and who had painfully got to their feet again, had backed beyond the reach of the water, and for a while held that ground, until above its hoarse, defiant curses was heard, from behind, the throbbing of drums.

"Cossacks!   More Cossacks!"

The cry was taken up by Canadians, Italians, Belgians, Poles, Slovaks, Jews, and Syrians. The drums grew louder, the pressure from the rear was relaxed, the throng in Faber Street began a retreat in the direction of the power plant. Down that street, now in double time, came three companies of Boston militia, newly arrived in Hampton, blue-caped, gaitered, slouch-hatted. From columns of fours they wheeled into line, and with bayonets at charge slowly advanced. Then the boldest of the mob, who still lingered, sullenly gave way, West Street was cleared, and on the wider thoroughfare the long line of traffic, the imprisoned trolleys began to move again. . . .

Janet had wedged herself into the press far enough to gain a view down West Street of the warehouse roofs, to see the water turned on, to hear the screams and the curses and then the shots. Once more she caught the contagious rage of the mob; the spectacle had aroused her to fury; it seemed ignominious, revolting that human beings, already sufficiently miserable, should be used thus. As she retreated reluctantly across the car tracks her attention was drawn to a man at her side, a Slovak. His face was white and pinched, his clothes were wet. Suddenly he stopped, turned and shook his fist at the line of soldiers.

"The Cossack, the politzman belong to the boss, the

capitalist!" he cried. "We ain't got no raït to live. I say, kill the capitalist — kill Ditmar!"

A man with a deputy's shield ran toward them.

"Move on!" he said brutally. "Move on, or I'll run you in." And Janet, once clear of the people, fled westward, the words the foreigner had spoken ringing in her ears. She found herself repeating them aloud, "Kill Ditmar!" as she hurried through the gathering dusk past the power house with its bottle-shaped chimneys, and crossed the little bridge over the stream beside the chocolate factory. She gained the avenue she had trod with Eda on that summer day of the circus. Here was the ragpicker's shop, the fence covered with bedraggled posters, the deserted grand-stand of the base-ball park spread with a milky-blue mantle of snow; and beyond, the monotonous frame cottages all built from one model. Now she descried looming above her the outline of Torrey's Hill blurred and melting into a darkening sky, and turned into the bleak lane where stood the Franco-Belgian Hall — Hampton Headquarters of the Industrial Workers of the World. She halted a moment at sight of the crowd of strikers loitering in front of it, then went on again, mingling with them excitedly beside the little building. Its lines were simple and unpretentious, and yet it had an exotic character all its own, differing strongly from the surrounding houses: it might have been transported from a foreign country and set down here. As the home of that odd, co-operative society of thrifty and gregarious Belgians it had stimulated her imagination, and once before she had gazed, as now, through the yellowed, lantern-like windows of the little store at the women and children waiting to fill their baskets with the day's provisions. In the middle of the building was an entrance leading up to the second floor. Presently she gathered the courage to enter. Her heart was pounding as she climbed the dark stairs and thrust open the door, and she stood a moment on the threshold almost choked by the fumes of tobacco, bewildered by the scene within, confused by the noise. Through a haze of smoke she beheld groups of swarthy foreigners fiercely disputing among themselves — apparently on the verge of actual combat, while a sprinkling of silent spectators of both sexes stood at the back of the hall. At the far end was a stage, still set with painted, sylvan scenery, and seated there, alone, above the confusion and the strife, with a calmness, a detachment almost disconcerting, was a stout man with long hair and a loose black tie. He was smoking a cigar and reading a newspaper which he presently flung down, taking up another from a pile on the table beside him. Suddenly one of the groups, shouting and gesticulating, surged toward him and made an appeal through their interpreter. He did not appear to be listening; without so much as lowering his newspaper he spoke a few words in reply, and the group retired, satisfied. By some incomprehensible power he dominated. Panting, fascinated, loath to leave yet fearful, Janet watched him, breathing now deeply this atmosphere of smoke, of strife, and turmoil. She found it grateful, for the strike, the battle was in her own soul as well. Momentarily she had forgotten Rolfe, who had been in her mind as she had come hither, and then she caught sight of him in a group in the centre of the hall. He saw her, he was making his way toward her, he was holding her hands, looking down into her face with that air of appropriation, of possession she remembered. But she felt no resentment now, only a fierce exultation at having dared.

"You've come to join us!" he exclaimed. "I thought I'd lost you."

He bent closer to her that she might hear.

"We are having a meeting of the Committee," he said, and she smiled. Despite her agitation, this struck her as humorous. And Rolfe smiled back at her. "You wouldn't think so, but Antonelli knows how to manage them. He is a general. Come, I will enlist you, you shall be my recruit."

"But what can I do?" she asked.

"I have been thinking. You said you were a stenographer — we need stenographers, clerks. You will not be wasted. Come in here."

Behind her two box-like rooms occupying the width of the building had been turned into offices, and into one of these Rolfe led her. Men and women were passing in and out, while in a corner a man behind a desk sat opening envelopes, deftly extracting bills and post-office orders and laying them in a drawer. On the wall of this same room was a bookcase half filled with nondescript volumes.

"The Bibliothèque — that's French for the library of the Franco-Belgian Coöperative Association," explained Rolfe. "And this is Comrade Sanders. Sanders is easier to say than Czernowitz. Here is the young lady I told you about, who wishes to help us — Miss Bumpus."

Mr. Sanders stopped counting his money long enough to grin at her.

"You will be welcome," he said, in good English. "Stenographers are scarce here. When can you come?"

"To-morrow morning," answered Janet.

"Good," he said. "I'll have a machine for you. What kind do you use?"

She told him. Instinctively she took a fancy to this little man, whose flannel shirt and faded purple necktie, whose blue, unshaven face and tousled black hair seemed incongruous with an alert, business-like, and efficient manner. His nose, though not markedly Jewish, betrayed in him the blood of that vital race which has triumphantly survived so many centuries of bondage and oppression.

"He was a find, Czernowitz — he calls himself Sanders,"

Rolfe explained, as they entered the hall once more. "An operative in the Patuxent, educated himself, went to night school—might have been a capitalist like so many of his tribe if he hadn't loved humanity. You'll get along with him."

"I'm sure I shall," she replied.

Rolfe took from his pocket a little red button with the letters I.W.W. printed across it. He pinned it, caressingly, on her coat.

"Now you are one of us!" he exclaimed. "You'll come to-morrow?"

"I'll come to-morrow," she repeated, drawing away from him a little.

"And — we shall be friends?"

She nodded. "I must go now, I think."

"Addio!" he said. "I shall look for you. For the present I must remain here, with the Committee."

4

When Janet reached Faber Street she halted on the corner of Stanley to stare into the window of the glorified drugstore. But she gave no heed to the stationery, the cameras and candy displayed there, being in the emotional state that reduces to unreality objects of the commonplace, everyday world. Presently, however, she became aware of a man standing beside her.

"Haven't we met before?" he asked. "Or — can I be mistaken?"

Some oddly familiar quizzical note in his voice stirred, as she turned to him, a lapsed memory. The hawklike yet benevolent and illuminating look he gave her recalled the man at Silliston whom she had thought a carpenter — though he was dressed now in a warm suit of gray wool, and wore a white, low collar.

"In Silliston!" she exclaimed. "Why — what are you doing here?"

"Well — this instant I was just looking at those note-papers, wondering which I should choose if I really had good taste. But it's very puzzling — isn't it? — when one comes from the country. Now that saffron with the rough edges is very — artistic. Don't you think so?"

She looked at him and smiled, though his face was serious.

"You don't really like it, yourself," she informed him.

"Now you're reflecting on my taste," he declared.

"Oh no — it's because I saw the fence you were making. Is it finished yet?"

"I put the last pineapple in place the day before Christmas. Do you remember the pineapples?"

She nodded. "And the house? and the garden?"

"Oh, those will never be finished. I shouldn't have anything more to do."

"Is that — all you do?" she asked.

"It's more important than anything else. But you — have you been back to Silliston since I saw you? I've been waiting for another call."

"You haven't even thought of me since," she was moved to reply in the same spirit.

"Haven't I?" he exclaimed. "I wondered, when I came up here to Hampton, whether I mightn't meet you — and here you are! Doesn't that prove it?"

She laughed, somewhat surprised at the ease with which he had diverted her, drawn her out of the tense, emotional mood in which he had discovered her. As before, he puzzled her, but the absence of any flirtatious suggestion in his talk gave her confidence. He was just friendly.

"Sometimes I hoped I might see you in Hampton," she ventured.

"Well, here I am. I heard the explosion, and came."

"The explosion! The strike!" she exclaimed, suddenly enlightened. "Now I remember! You said something about Hampton being nitro-glycerine — human nitro-glycerine. You predicted this strike."

"Did I? perhaps I did," he assented. "Maybe you suggested the idea."

"I suggested it! Oh no, I didn't — it was new to me, it frightened me at the time, but it started me thinking about a lot of things that had never occurred to me."

"You might have suggested the idea without intending to, you know. There are certain people who inspire prophecies — perhaps you are one."

His tone was playful, but she was quick to grasp at an inference — since his glance was fixed on the red button she wore.

"You meant that I would explode, too!"

"Oh no — nothing so terrible as that," he disclaimed. "And yet most of us have explosives stored away inside of us — instincts, impulses and all that sort of thing that won't stand too much bottling-up."

"Yes, I've joined the strike." She spoke somewhat challengingly, though she had an uneasy feeling that defiance was somewhat out of place with him. "I suppose you think it strange, since I'm not a foreigner and haven't worked in the mills. But I don't see why that should make any difference if you believe that the workers haven't had a chance."

"No difference," he agreed, pleasantly, "no difference at all."

"Don't you sympathize with the strikers?" she insisted. "Or — are you on the other side, the side of the capitalists?"

"I? I'm a spectator — an innocent bystander."

"You don't sympathize with the workers?" she cried.

"Indeed I do. I sympathize with everybody."

"With the capitalists?"

"Why not?"

"Why not? Because they've had everything their own way, they've exploited the workers, deceived and oppressed them, taken all the profits." She was using glibly her newly acquired labour terminology.

"Isn't that a pretty good reason for sympathizing with them?" he inquired.

"What do you mean?"

"Well, I should think it might be difficult to be happy and have done all that. At any rate, it isn't my notion of happiness. Is it yours?"

For a moment she considered this.

"No — not exactly," she admitted. "But they seem happy," she insisted vehemently, "they have everything they want and they do exactly as they please without considering anybody except themselves. What do they care how many they starve and make miserable? You — you don't know, you can't know what it is to be driven and used and flung away!"

Almost in tears, she did not notice his puzzled yet sympathetic glance.

"The operatives, the workers create all the wealth, and the capitalists take it from them, from their wives and children."

"Now I know what you've been doing," he said accusingly. "You've been studying economics."

Her brow puckered.

"Studying what?"

"Economics — the distribution of wealth. It's enough to upset anybody."

"But I'm not upset," she insisted, smiling in spite of herself at his comical concern.

"It's very exciting. I remember reading a book once on

economics and such things, and I couldn't sleep for a week. It was called 'The Organization of Happiness,' I believe, and it described just how the world ought to be arranged — and isn't. I thought seriously of going to Washington and telling the President and Congress about it."

"It wouldn't have done any good," said Janet.

"No, I realized that."

"The only thing that will do any good is to strike and keep on striking until the workers own the mills — take everything away from the capitalists."

"It's very simple," he agreed, "much simpler than the book I read. That's what they call syndicalism, isn't it?"

"Yes." She was conscious of his friendliness, of the fact that his skepticism was not cynical, yet she felt a strong desire to convince him, to vindicate her new creed. "There's a man named Rolfe, an educated man who's lived in Italy and England, who explains it wonderfully. He's one of the I.W.W. leaders — you ought to hear him."

"Rolfe converted you? I'll go to hear him."

"Yes — but you have to feel it, you have to know what it is to be kept down and crushed. If you'd only stay here awhile —"

"Oh, I intend to," he replied.

She could not have said why, but she felt a certain relief on hearing this.

"Then you'll see for yourself!" she cried. "I guess that's what you've come for, isn't it?"

"Well, partly. To tell the truth, I've come to open a restaurant."

"To open a restaurant!" Somehow she was unable to imagine him as the proprietor of a restaurant. "But — isn't it rather a bad time?" she gasped.

"I don't look as if I had an eye for business — do I? But I have. No, it's a good time — so many people will be hungry, especially children. I'm going to open a restaurant for children. Oh, it will be very modest, of course — I suppose I ought to call it a soup kitchen."

"Oh!" she exclaimed, staring at him. "Then you really — " the sentence remained unfinished. "I'm sorry," she said simply. "You made me think —"

"Oh, you mustn't pay any attention to what I say. Come 'round and see my establishment, Number 77 Dey Street, one flight up, no elevator. Will you?"

She laughed tremulously as he took her hand.

"Yes indeed, I will," she promised. And she stood awhile staring after him. She was glad he had come to Hampton, and yet she did not even know his name.

z

CHAPTER XVI

1

SHE had got another place — such was the explanation of her new activities Janet gave to Hannah, who received it passively. And the question dreaded about Ditmar was never asked. Hannah had become as a child, performing her tasks by the momentum of habituation, occasionally talking simply of trivial, every-day affairs, as though the old life were going on continuously. At times, indeed, she betrayed concern about Edward, wondering whether he were comfortable at the mill, and she washed and darned the clothes he sent home by messenger. She hoped he would not catch cold. Her suffering seemed to have relaxed. It was as though the tortured portion of her brain had at length been seared. To Janet, her mother's condition — when she had time to think of it — was at once a relief and a new and terrible source of anxiety.

Mercifully, however, she had little leisure to reflect on that tragedy, else her own sanity might have been endangered. As soon as breakfast was over she hurried across the city to the Franco-Belgian Hall, and often did not return until nine o'clock at night, usually so tired that she sank into bed and fell asleep. For she threw herself into her new labours with the desperate energy that seeks forgetfulness, not daring to pause to think about herself, to reflect upon what the future might hold for her when the strike should be over. Nor did she confine herself to typewriting, but, as with Ditmar, constantly assumed a greater burden of duty, helping Czernowitz — who had the work of five men — with his accounts, with the distribution of the funds to the ever-increasing number of the needy who were facing starvation. The money was paid out to them in proportion to the size of their families; as the strike became more and more effective their number increased until many mills had closed; other mills, including the Chippering, were still making a desperate attempt to operate their looms, and sixteen thousand operatives were idle. She grew to know these operatives who poured all day long in a steady stream through Headquarters; she heard their stories, she entered into their lives, she made decisions. Some, even in those early days of the strike, were frauds, were hiding their savings; but for the most part investigation revealed an appalling destitution, a resolution to suffer for the worker's cause. A few complained, the majority were resigned; some indeed showed exaltation and fire, were undaunted by the task of picketing in the cold mornings, by the presence of the soldiery. In this work of dealing with the operatives Janet had the advice and help of Anna Mower, a young woman who herself had been a skilled operative in the Clarendon Mill, and who was giving evidence of unusual qualities of organization and leadership. Anna, with no previous practise in oratory, had suddenly developed the gift of making speeches, the more effective with her fellow workers because unstudied, because they flowed directly out of an experience she was learning to interpret and universalize. Janet, who heard her once or twice, admired and envied her. They became friends.

The atmosphere of excitement in which Janet now found herself was cumulative. Day by day one strange event followed another, and at times it seemed as if this extraordinary existence into which she had been plunged were all a feverish dream. Hither, to the absurd little *salle de*

réunion of the Franco-Belgian Hall came notables from the
great world, emissaries from an uneasy Governor, delega-
tions from the Legislature, Members of the Congress of the
United States and even Senators; students, investigators,
men and women of prominence in the universities, magazine
writers to consult with uncouth leaders of a rebellion that
defied and upset the powers which hitherto had so serenely
ruled, unchallenged. Rolfe identified these visitors, and
one morning called her attention to one who he said was
the nation's foremost authority on social science. Janet
possessed all unconsciously the New England reverence
for learning, she was stirred by the sight of this distinguished-
looking person who sat on the painted stage, fingering his
glasses and talking to Antonelli. The two men made a
curious contrast. But her days were full of contrasts of
which her mood exultingly approved. The politicians
were received cavalierly. Toward these, who sought to act
as go-betweens in the conflict, Antonelli was contemptuous;
he behaved like the general of a conquering army, and his
audacity was reflected in the other leaders, in Rolfe, in the
Committee itself.

That Committee, a never-ending source of wonder to
Janet, with its nine or ten nationalities and interpreters,
was indeed a triumph over the obstacles of race and language, a Babel made successful; in a community of Anglo-
Saxon traditions, an amazing anomaly. The habiliments of
the west, the sack coats and sweaters, the slouch hats and
caps, the so-called Derbies pulled down over dark brows
and flashing eyes lent to these peasant types an incongruity
that had the air of ferocity. The faces of most of them
were covered with a blue-black stubble of beard. Some
slouched in their chairs, others stood and talked in groups,
gesticulating with cigars and pipes; yet a keen spectator,
after watching them awhile through the smoke, might have

been able to pick out striking personalities among them. He would surely have noticed Froment, the stout, limping man under whose white eyebrows flashed a pair of livid blue and peculiarly Gallic eyes; he held the Belgians in his hand: Lindtzki, the Pole, with his zealot's face; Radeau, the big Canadian in the checked Mackinaw; and Findley, the young American — less by any arresting quality of feature than by an expression suggestive of practical wisdom.

Imagine then, on an afternoon in the middle phase of the strike, some half dozen of the law-makers of a sovereign state, top-hatted and conventionally garbed in black, accustomed to authority, to conferring favours instead of requesting them, climbing the steep stairs and pausing on the threshold of that hall, fingering their watch chains, awaiting recognition by the representatives of the new and bewildering force that had arisen in an historic commonwealth. A "debate" was in progress. Some of the debaters, indeed, looked over their shoulders, but the leader, who sat above them framed in the sylvan setting of the stage, never so much as deigned to glance up from his newspaper. A half-burned cigar rolled between his mobile lips, he sat on the back of his neck, and yet he had an air Napoleonic; Nietzschean, it might better be said — although it is safe to assert that these moulders of American institutions knew little about that terrible philosopher who had raised his voice against the "slave morals of Christianity." It was their first experience with the superman. . . . It remained for the Canadian, Radeau, when a lull arrived in the turmoil, to suggest that the gentlemen be given chairs.

"Sure, give them chairs," assented Antonelli in a voice hoarse from speech-making. Breath-taking audacity to certain spectators who had followed the delegation hither, some of whom could not refrain from speculating whether it heralded the final scrapping of the machinery of the state;

amusing to cynical metropolitan reporters, who grinned at
one another as they prepared to take down the proceedings;
evoking a fierce approval in the breasts of all rebels —
among whom was Janet. The Legislative Chairman, a
stout and suave gentleman of Irish birth, proceeded to explain how greatly concerned was the Legislature that the
deplorable warfare within the state should cease; they had
come, he declared, to aid in bringing about justice between
labour and capital.

"We'll get justice without the help of the state," remarked
Antonelli curtly, while a murmur of approval ran through
the back of the hall.

That was scarcely the attitude, said the Chairman, he
had expected. He knew that such a strike as this had
engendered bitterness, there had been much suffering, sacrifice undoubtedly on both sides, but he was sure, if Mr.
Antonelli and the Committee would accept their services —
here he was interrupted.

Had the mill owners accepted their services?

The Chairman cleared his throat.

The fact was that the mill owners were more difficult to
get together in a body. A meeting would be arranged —

"When you arrange a meeting, let me know," said Antonelli.

A laugh went around the room. It was undoubtedly
very difficult to keep one's temper under such treatment.
The Chairman looked it.

"A meeting would be arranged," he declared, with a long-
suffering expression. He even smiled a little. "In the
meantime —"

"What can your committee do?" demanded one of the
strike leaders, passionately — it was Findley. "If you
find one party wrong, can your state force it to do right?
Can you legislators be impartial when you have not lived

the bitter life of the workers? Would you arbitrate a
question of life and death? And are the worst wages paid
in these mills anything short of death? Do you investigate
because conditions are bad? or because the workers broke
loose and struck? Why did you not come before the strike?"

This drew more approval from the rear. Why, indeed?
The Chairman was adroit, he had pulled himself out of many
tight places in the Assembly Chamber, but now he began
to perspire, to fumble in his coat tails for a handkerchief.
The Legislature, he maintained, could not undertake to investigate such matters until called to its attention. . . .

Later on a tall gentleman, whom heaven had not blessed
with tact, saw fit to deplore the violence that had occurred;
he had no doubt the leaders of the strike regretted it as
much as he, he was confident it would be stopped, when
public opinion would be wholly and unreservedly on the
side of the strikers.

"Public opinion!" savagely cried Lindtzki, who spoke
English with only a slight accent. "If your little boy, if
your little girl come to you and ask for shoes, for bread, and
you say, 'I have no shoes, I have no bread, but public opinion
is with us,' would that satisfy you?"

This drew so much applause that the tall law-maker sat
down again with a look of disgust on his face. . . . The Committee withdrew, and for many weeks thereafter the state
they represented continued to pay some four thousand
dollars daily to keep its soldiers on the streets of Hampton. . . .

2

In the meanwhile Janet saw much of Rolfe. Owing to
his facile command of language he was peculiarly fitted to
draft those proclamations, bombastically worded in the
French style, issued and circulated by the Strike Committee

— appeals to the polyglot army to withstand the pangs of hunger, to hold out for the terms laid down, assurances that victory was at hand. Walking up and down the *bibliothèque*, his hands behind his back, his red lips gleaming as he spoke, he dictated these documents to Janet. In the ecstasy of this composition he had a way of shaking his head slowly from side to side, and when she looked up she saw his eyes burning down at her. A dozen times a day, while she was at her other work, he would come in and talk to her. He excited her, she was divided between attraction and fear of him, and often she resented his easy assumption that a tie existed between them — the more so because this seemed to be taken for granted among certain of his associates. In their eyes, apparently, she was Rolfe's recruit in more senses than one. It was indeed a strange society in which she found herself, and Rolfe typified it. He lived on the plane of the impulses and intellect, discarded as inhibiting factors what are called moral standards, decried individual discipline and restraint. And while she had never considered these things, the spectacle of a philosophy — embodied in him — that frankly and cynically threw them overboard was disconcerting. He regarded her as his proselyte, he called her a Puritan, and he seemed more concerned that she should shed these relics of an ancestral code than acquire the doctrines of Sorel and Pouget. And yet association with him presented the allurement of a dangerous adventure. Intellectually he fascinated her; and still another motive — which she partially disguised from herself — prevented her from repelling him. That motive had to do with Ditmar. She tried to put Ditmar from her mind; she sought in desperation, not only to keep busy, but to steep and lose herself in this fierce creed as an antidote to the insistent, throbbing pain that lay ambushed against her moments of idleness. The second evening of her installation at Headquarters she had worked beyond the supper hour, helping Sanders with his accounts. She was loath to go home. And when at last she put on her hat and coat and entered the hall Rolfe, who had been talking to Jastro, immediately approached her. His liquid eyes regarded her solicitously.

"You must be hungry," he said. "Come out with me and have some supper."

But she was not hungry; what she needed was air. Then he would walk a little way with her — he wanted to talk to her. She hesitated, and then consented. A fierce hope had again taken possession of her, and when they came to Warren Street she turned into it.

"Where are you going?" Rolfe demanded.

"For a walk," she said. "Aren't you coming?"

"Will you have supper afterwards?"

"Perhaps."

He followed her, puzzled, yet piqued and excited by her manner, as with rapid steps she hurried along the pavement. He tried to tell her what her friendship meant to him; they were, he declared, kindred spirits — from the first time he had seen her, on the Common, he had known this. She scarcely heard him, she was thinking of Ditmar; and this was why she had led Rolfe into Warren Street — they might meet Ditmar! It was possible that he would be going to the mill at this time, after his dinner! She scrutinized every distant figure, and when they reached the block in which he lived she walked more slowly. From within the house came to her, faintly, the notes of a piano — his daughter Amy was practising. It was the music, a hackneyed theme of Schubert's played heavily, that seemed to arouse the composite emotion of anger and hatred, yet of sustained attraction and wild regret she had felt before, but never so poignantly as now. And she lingered, perversely resolved to steep herself in the agony.

"Who lives here?" Rolfe asked.

"Mr. Ditmar," she answered.

"The agent of the Chippering Mill?"

She nodded.

"He's the worst of the lot," Rolfe said angrily. "If it weren't for him, we'd have this strike won to-day. He owns this town, he's run it to suit himself. He stiffens up the owners and holds the other mills in line. He's a type, a driver, the kind of man we must get rid of. Look at him — he lives in luxury while his people are starving."

"Get rid of!" repeated Janet, in an odd voice.

"Oh, I don't mean to shoot him," Rolfe declared. "But he may get shot, for all I know, by some of these slaves he's made desperate."

"They wouldn't dare shoot him," Janet said. "And whatever he is, he isn't a coward. He's stronger than the others, he's more of a man."

Rolfe looked at her curiously.

"What do you know about him?" he asked.

"I — I know all about him. I was his stenographer."

"You! His stenographer! Then why are you here with us?"

"Because I hate him!" she cried vehemently. "Because I've learned that it's true — what you say about the masters — they only think of themselves and their kind, and not of us. They use us."

"He tried to use you! You loved him!"

"How dare you say that!"

He fell back before her anger.

"I didn't mean to offend you," he exclaimed. "I was jealous — I'm jealous of every man you've known. I want you. I've never met a woman like you."

They were the very words Ditmar had used! She did not answer, and for a while they walked along in silence, leaving

Warren Street and cutting across the city until they came in sight of the Common. Rolfe drew nearer to her.

"Forgive me!" he pleaded. "You know I would not offend you. Come, we'll have supper together, and I will teach you more of what you have to know."

"Where?" she asked.

"At the Hampton — it is a little café where we all go. Perhaps you've been there."

"No," said Janet.

"It doesn't compare with the cafés of Europe — or of New York. Perhaps we shall go to them sometime, together. But it is cosy, and warm, and all the leaders will be there. You'll come — yes?"

"Yes, I'll come," she said. . . .

3

The Hampton was one of the city's second-class hotels, but sufficiently pretentious to have, in its basement, a "café" furnished in the "mission" style of brass tacks and dull red leather. In the warm, food-scented air fantastic wisps of smoke hung over the groups; among them Janet made out several of the itinerant leaders of Syndicalism, loose-tied, débonnair, giving a tremendous impression of freedom as they laughed and chatted with the women. For there were women, ranging from the redoubtable Nellie Bond herself down to those who may be designated as camp-followers. Rolfe, as he led Janet to a table in a corner of the room, greeted his associates with easy camaraderie. From Miss Bond he received an illuminating smile. Janet wondered at her striking good looks, at the boldness and abandon with which she talked to Jastro or exchanged sallies across the room. The atmosphere of this tawdry resort, formerly frequented by shop girls and travelling salesmen, was magically transformed by the presence of this company, made bohemian, cosmopolitan, exhilarating. And Janet, her face flushed, sat gazing at the scene, while Rolfe consulted the bill of fare and chose a beefsteak and French fried potatoes. The apathetic waiter in the soiled linen jacket he addressed as "comrade." Janet protested when he ordered cocktails.

"You must learn to live, to relax, to enjoy yourself," he declared.

But a horror of liquor held her firm in her refusal. Rolfe drank his, and while they awaited the beefsteak she was silent, the prey of certain misgivings that suddenly assailed her. Lise, she remembered, had sometimes mentioned this place, though preferring Gruber's: and she was struck by the contrast between this spectacle and the grimness of the strike these people had come to encourage and sustain, the conflict in the streets, the suffering in the tenements. She glanced at Rolfe, noting the manner in which he smoked cigarettes, sensually, as though seeking to wring out of each all there was to be got before flinging it down and lighting another. Again she was struck by the anomaly of a religion that had indeed enthusiasms, sacrifices perhaps, but no disciplines. He threw it out in snatches, this religion, while relating the histories of certain persons in the room: of Jastro, for instance, letting fall a hint to the effect that this evangelist and Miss Bond were dwelling together in more than amity.

"Then you don't believe in marriage?" she demanded, suddenly.

Rolfe laughed.

"What is it," he exclaimed, "but the survival of the system of property? It's slavery, taboo, a device upheld by the master class to keep women in bondage, in superstition, by inducing them to accept it as a decree of God.

Did the masters themselves ever respect it, or any other decrees of God they preached to the slaves? Read history, and you will see. They had their loves, their mistresses. Read the newspapers, and you will find out whether they respect it to-day. But they are very anxious to have you and me respect it and all the other Christian commandments, because they will prevent us from being discontented. They say that we must be satisfied with the situation in this world in which God has placed us, and we shall have our reward in the next."

She shivered slightly, not only at the ideas thus abruptly enunciated, but because it occurred to her that those others must be taking for granted a certain relationship between herself and Rolfe. . . . But presently, when the supper arrived, these feelings changed. She was very hungry, and the effect of the food, of the hot coffee was to dispel her doubt and repugnance, to throw a glamour over the adventure, to restore to Rolfe's arguments an exciting and alluring appeal. And with renewed physical energy she began to experience once more a sense of fellowship with these free and daring spirits who sought to avenge her wrongs and theirs.

"For us who create there are no rules of conduct, no conventions," Rolfe was saying, "we do not care for the opinions of the middle class, of the bourgeois. With us men and women are on an equality. It is fear that has kept the workers down, and now we have cast that off — we know our strength. As they say in Italy, *il mondo è a chi se lo piglia*, the world belongs to him who is bold."

"Italian is a beautiful language," she exclaimed.

"I will teach you Italian," he said.

"I want to learn — so much!" she sighed.

"Your soul is parched," he said, in a commiserating tone. "I will water it, I will teach you everything." His

words aroused a faint, derisive echo: Ditmar had wished
to teach her, too! But now she was strongly under the
spell of the new ideas hovering like shining, gossamer
spirits just beyond her reach, that she sought to grasp and
correlate. Unlike the code which Rolfe condemned, they
seemed not to be separate from life, opposed to it, but entered
even into that most important of its elements, sex. In
deference to that other code Ditmar had made her his
mistress, and because he was concerned for his position
and the security of the ruling class had sought to hide the
fact. . . . Rolfe, with a cigarette between his red lips, sat
back in his chair, regarding with sensuous enjoyment the
evident effect of his arguments.

"But love?" she interrupted, when presently he had
begun to talk again. She strove inarticulately to express
an innate feminine objection to relationships that were made
and broken at pleasure.

"Love is nothing but attraction between the sexes, the
life-force working in us. And when that attraction ceases,
what is left? Bondage. The hideous bondage of Christian
marriage, in which women promise to love and obey forever."

"But women — women are not like men. When once
they give themselves they do not so easily cease to love.
They — they suffer."

He did not seem to observe the bitterness in her voice.

"Ah, that is sentiment," he declared, "something that
will not trouble women when they have work to do, inspiring
work. It takes time to change our ideas, to learn to see
things as they are." He leaned forward eagerly. "But
you will learn, you are like some of those rare women in
history who have had the courage to cast off traditions.
You were not made to be a drudge. . . ."

But now her own words, not his, were ringing in her head
— women do not so easily cease to love, they suffer. In

spite of the new creed she had so eagerly and fiercely embraced, in which she had sought deliverance and retribution, did she still love Ditmar, and suffer because of him? She repudiated the suggestion, yet it persisted as she glanced at Rolfe's red lips and compared him with Ditmar.   Love! Rolfe might call it what he would — the life-force, attraction between the sexes, but it was proving stronger than causes and beliefs.   He too was making love to her; like Ditmar, he wanted her to use and fling away when he should grow weary.   Was he not pleading for himself rather than for the human cause he professed? taking advantage of her ignorance and desperation, of her craving for new experience and knowledge?   The suspicion sickened her. Were all men like that?   Suddenly, without apparent premeditation or connection, the thought of the stranger from Silliston entered her mind.   Was he like that?... Rolfe was bending toward her across the table, solicitously.

"What's the matter?" he asked.

Her reply was listless.

"Nothing — except that I'm tired.   I want to go home."

"Not now," he begged.   "It's early yet."

But she insisted. . . .

CHAPTER XVII

1

THE next day at the noon hour Janet entered Dey Street. Cheek by jowl there with the tall tenements whose spindled-pillared porches overhung the darkened pavements were smaller houses of all ages and descriptions, their lower floors altered to accommodate shops; while in the very midst of the block stood a queer wooden building with two rows of dormer windows let into its high-pitched roof. It bore a curious resemblance to a town hall in the low countries. In front of it the street was filled with children gazing up at the doorway where a man stood surveying them — the stranger from Silliston. There was a rush toward him, a rush that drove Janet against the wall almost at his side, and he held up his hands in mock despair, gently impeding the little bodies that strove to enter. He bent over them to examine the numerals, printed on pasteboard, they wore on their breasts. His voice was cheerful, yet compassionate.

"It's hard to wait, I know. I'm hungry myself," he said. "But we can't all go up at once. The building would fall down! One to one hundred now, and the second hundred will be first for supper. That's fair, isn't it?"

Dozens of hands were raised.

"I'm twenty-nine!"

"I'm three, mister!"

"I'm forty-one!"

He let them in, one by one, and they clattered up the

stairs, as he seized a tiny girl bundled in a dark red muffler and set her on the steps above him. He smiled at Janet.

"This is my restaurant," he said.

But she could not answer. She watched him as he continued to bend over the children, and when the smaller ones wept because they had to wait, he whispered in their ears, astonishing one or two into laughter. Some ceased crying and clung to him with dumb faith. And after the chosen hundred had been admitted he turned to her again.

"You allow visitors?"

"Oh dear, yes. They'd come anyway. There's one up there now, a very swell lady from New York — so swell I don't know what to say to her. Talk to her for me."

"But I shouldn't know what to say, either," replied Janet. She smiled, but she had an odd desire to cry. "What is she doing here?"

"Oh, thrashing 'round, trying to connect with life — she's one of the unfortunate unemployed."

"Unemployed?"

"The idle rich," he explained. "Perhaps you can give her a job — enlist her in the I.W.W."

"We don't want that kind," Janet declared.

"Have pity on her," he begged. "Nobody wants them — that's why they're so pathetic."

She accompanied him up the narrow stairway to a great loft, the bareness of which had been tempered by draped American flags. From the trusses of the roof hung improvised electric lights, and the children were already seated at the four long tables, where half a dozen ladies were supplying them with enamelled bowls filled with steaming soup. They attacked it ravenously, and the absence of the talk and laughter that ordinarily accompany children's feasts touched her, impressed upon her, as nothing else had done, the destitution of the homes from which these little ones

2 A

had come. The supplies that came to Hampton, the money that poured into Headquarters were not enough to allay the suffering even now. And what if the strike should last for months! Would they be able to hold out, to win? In this mood of pity, of anxiety mingled with appreciation and gratitude for what this man was doing, she turned to speak to him, to perceive on the platform at the end of the room a lady seated. So complete was the curve of her back that her pose resembled a letter u set sidewise, the gap from her crossed knee to her face being closed by a slender fore-arm and hand that held a lorgnette, through which she was gazing at the children with an apparently absorbed interest. This impression of willowy flexibility was somehow height-ened by large, pear-shaped pendants hanging from her ears, by a certain filminess in her black costume and hat. Flung across the table beside her was a long coat of grey fur. She struck an odd note here, presented a strange contrast to Janet's friend from Silliston, with his rough suit and fine but rugged features.

"I'm sorry I haven't a table for you just at present," he was saying. "But perhaps you'll let me take your order," — and he imitated the obsequious attitude of a waiter. "A little fresh caviar and a clear soup, and then a fish — ?"

The lady took down her lorgnette and raised an appealing face.

"You're always joking, Brooks," she chided him, "even when you're doing things like this! I can't get you to talk seriously even when I come all the way from New York to find out what's going on here."

"How hungry children eat, for instance?" he queried.

"Dear little things, it's heartrending!" she exclaimed. "Especially when I think of my own children, who have to be made to eat. Tell me the nationality of that adorable tot at the end."

"Perhaps Miss Bumpus can tell you," he ventured. And Janet, though distinctly uncomfortable and hostile to the lady, was surprised and pleased that he should have remembered her name. "Brooks," she had called him. That was his first name. This strange and sumptuous person seemed intimate with him. Could it be possible that he belonged to her class? "Mrs. Brocklehurst, Miss Bumpus."

Mrs. Brocklehurst focussed her attention on Janet, through the lorgnette, but let it fall immediately, smiling on her brightly, persuasively.

"How d'ye do?" she said, stretching forth a slender arm and taking the girl's somewhat reluctant hand. "Do come and sit down beside me and tell me about everything here. I'm sure you know — you look so intelligent."

Her friend from Silliston shot at Janet an amused but fortifying glance and left them, going down to the tables. Somehow that look of his helped to restore in her a sense of humour and proportion, and her feeling became one of curiosity concerning this exquisitely soignéed being of an order she had read about, but never encountered — an order which her newly acquired views declared to be usurpers and parasites. But despite her palpable effort to be gracious — perhaps because of it — Mrs. Brocklehurst had an air about her that was disconcerting! Janet, however, seemed composed as she sat down.

"I'm afraid I don't know very much. Maybe you will tell me something, first."

"Why, certainly," said Mrs. Brocklehurst, sweetly — when she had got her breath.

"Who is that man?" Janet asked.

"Whom do you mean — Mr. Insall?"

"Is that his name? I didn't know. I've seen him twice, but he never told me."

"Why, my dear, do you mean to say you haven't heard of Brooks Insall?"

"Brooks Insall." Janet repeated the name, as her eyes sought his figure between the tables. "No."

"I'm sure I don't know why I should have expected you to hear of him," declared the lady, repentantly. "He's a writer — an author." And at this Janet gave a slight exclamation of pleasure and surprise. "You admire writers? He's done some delightful things."

"What does he write about?" Janet asked.

"Oh, wild flowers and trees and mountains and streams, and birds and humans — he has a wonderful insight into people."

Janet was silent. She was experiencing a swift twinge of jealousy, of that familiar rebellion against her limitations.

"You must read them, my dear," Mrs. Brocklehurst continued softly, in musical tones. "They are wonderful, they have such distinction. He's walked, I'm told, over every foot of New England, talking to the farmers and their wives and — all sorts of people." She, too, paused to let her gaze linger upon Insall laughing and chatting with the children as they ate. "He has such a splendid, 'out-door' look — don't you think? And he's clever with his hands — he bought an old abandoned farmhouse in Silliston and made it all over himself until it looks as if one of our great-great-grandfathers had just stepped out of it to shoot an Indian — only much prettier. And his garden is a dream. It's the most unique place I've ever known."

Janet blushed deeply as she recalled how she had mistaken him for a carpenter: she was confused, overwhelmed, she had a sudden longing to leave the place, to be alone, to think about this discovery. Yet she wished to know more.

"But how did he happen to come here to Hampton — to be doing this?" she asked.

"Well, that's just what makes him interesting, one never can tell what he'll do. He took it into his head to collect the money to feed these children; I suppose he gave much of it himself. He has an income of his own, though he likes to live so simply."

"This place—it's not connected with any organization?" Janet ejaculated.

"That's the trouble, he doesn't like organizations, and he doesn't seem to take any interest in the questions or movements of the day," Mrs. Brocklehurst complained. "Or at least he refuses to talk about them, though I've known him for many years, and his people and mine were friends. Now there are lots of things I want to learn, that I came up from New York to find out. I thought of course he'd introduce me to the strike leaders, and he tells me he doesn't know one of them. Perhaps you know them," she added, with sudden inspiration.

"I'm only an employee at Strike Headquarters," Janet replied, stiffening a little despite the lady's importuning look — which evidently was usually effective.

"You mean the I.W.W.?"

"Yes."

Meanwhile Insall had come up and seated himself below them on the edge of the platform.

"Oh, Brooks, your friend Miss Bumpus is employed in the Strike Headquarters!" Mrs. Brocklehurst cried, and turning to Janet she went on. "I didn't realize you were a factory girl, I must say you don't look it."

Once more a gleam of amusement from Insall saved Janet, had the effect of compelling her to meet the affair somewhat after his own manner. He seemed to be putting the words into her mouth, and she even smiled a little, as she spoke.

"You never can tell what factory girls do look like in these days," she observed mischievously.

"That's so," Mrs. Brocklehurst agreed, "we are living in such extraordinary times, everything topsy turvy. I ought to have realized — it was stupid of me — I know several factory girls in New York, I've been to their meetings, I've had them at my house — shirtwaist strikers."

She assumed again the willowy, *u* position, her fingers clasped across her knee, her eyes supplicatingly raised to Janet. Then she reached out her hand and touched the I.W.W. button. "Do tell me all about the Industrial Workers, and what they believe," she pleaded.

"Well," said Janet, after a slight pause, "I'm afraid you won't like it much. Why do you want to know?"

"Because I'm so interested — especially in the women of the movement. I feel for them so, I want to help — to do something, too. Of course you're a suffragist."

"You mean, do I believe in votes for women? Yes, I suppose I do."

"But you *must*," declared Mrs. Brocklehurst, still sweetly, but with emphasis. "You wouldn't be working, you wouldn't be striking unless you did."

"I've never thought about it," said Janet.

"But how are you working girls ever going to raise wages unless you get the vote? It's the only way men ever get anywhere — the politicians listen to them." She produced from her bag a gold pencil and a tablet. "Mrs. Ned Carfax is here from Boston — I saw her for a moment at the hotel — she's been here investigating for nearly three days, she tells me. I'll have her send you suffrage literature at once, if you'll give me your address."

"You want a vote?" asked Janet, curiously, gazing at the pearl earrings.

"Certainly I want one."

"Why?"

"Why?" repeated Mrs. Brocklehurst.

"Yes. You must have everything you want."

Even then the lady's sweet reasonableness did not desert her. She smiled winningly, displaying two small and even rows of teeth.

"On principle, my dear. For one reason, because I have such sympathy with women who toil, and for another, I believe the time has come when women must no longer be slaves, they must assert themselves, become individuals, independent."

"But you?" exclaimed Janet.

Mrs. Brocklehurst continued to smile encouragingly, and murmured "Yes?"

"You are not a slave."

A delicate pink, like the inside of a conch shell, spread over Mrs. Brocklehurst's cheeks.

"We're all slaves," she declared with a touch of passion. "It's hard for you to realize, I know, about those of us who seem more fortunate than our sisters. But it's true. The men give us jewels and automobiles and clothes, but they refuse to give us what every real woman craves — liberty."

Janet had become genuinely interested.

"But what kind of liberty?"

"Liberty to have a voice, to take part in the government of our country, to help make the laws, especially those concerning working women and children, what they ought to be."

Here was altruism, truly! Here were words that should have inspired Janet, yet she was silent. Mrs. Brocklehurst gazed at her solicitously.

"What are you thinking?" she urged — and it was Janet's turn to flush.

"I was just thinking that you seemed to have everything life has to give, and yet — and yet you're not happy."

"Oh, I'm not unhappy," protested the lady. "Why do you say that?"

"I don't know.   You, too, seem to be wanting something."

"I want to be of use, to count," said Mrs. Brocklehurst, — and Janet was startled to hear from this woman's lips the very echo of her own desires.

Mrs. Brocklehurst's feelings had become slightly complicated. It is perhaps too much to say that her complacency was shaken. She was, withal, a person of resolution — of resolution taking the form of unswerving faith in herself, a faith persisting even when she was being carried beyond her depth. She had the kind of pertinacity that never admits being out of depth, the happy buoyancy that does not require to feel the bottom under one's feet. She floated in swift currents. When life became uncomfortable, she evaded it easily; and she evaded it now, as she gazed at the calm but intent face of the girl in front of her, by a characteristic inner refusal to admit that she had accidentally come in contact with something baffling. Therefore she broke the silence.

"Isn't that what you want — you who are striking?" she asked.

"I think we want the things that you've got," said Janet. A phrase one of the orators had used came into her mind, "Enough money to live up to American standards" — but she did not repeat it. "Enough money to be free, to enjoy life, to have some leisure and amusement and luxury." The last three she took from the orator's mouth.

"But surely," exclaimed Mrs. Brocklehurst, "surely you want more than that!"

Janet shook her head.

"You asked me what we believed, the I.W.W., the syndicalists, and I told you you wouldn't like it. Well, we believe in doing away with you, the rich, and taking all you have for ourselves, the workers, the producers. We believe you haven't any right to what you've got, that you've fooled and cheated us out of it. That's why we women don't care much about the vote, I suppose, though I never thought of it. We mean to go on striking until we've got all that you've got."

"But what will become of us?" said Mrs. Brocklehurst. "You wouldn't do away with all of us! I admit there are many who don't — but some do sympathize with you, will help you get what you want, help you, perhaps, to see things more clearly, to go about it less — ruthlessly."

"I've told you what we believe," repeated Janet.

"I'm so glad I came," cried Mrs. Brocklehurst. "It's most interesting! I never knew what the syndicalists believed. Why, it's like the French Revolution — only worse. How are you going to get rid of us? cut our heads off?"

Janet could not refrain from smiling.

"Let you starve, I suppose."

"Really!" said Mrs. Brocklehurst, and appeared to be trying to visualize the process. She was a true Athenian, she had discovered some new thing, she valued discoveries more than all else in life, she collected them, though she never used them save to discuss them with intellectuals at her dinner parties. "Now you must let me come to Headquarters and get a glimpse of some of the leaders — of Antonelli, and I'm told there's a fascinating man named Rowe."

"Rolfe," Janet corrected.

"Rolfe — that's it." She glanced down at the diminutive watch, set with diamonds, on her wrist, rose and addressed Insall. "Oh dear, I must be going, I'm to lunch with Nina Carfax at one, and she's promised to tell me a lot of things. She's writing an article for *Craven's Weekly* all about the strike and the suffering and injustice — she says it's been horribly misrepresented to the public, the mill owners have had it all their own way. I think what you're doing is splendid, Brooks, only —" here she gave him an appealing, rather commiserating look — "only I do wish you would take more interest in — in underlying principles."

Insall smiled.

"It's a question of brains. You have to have brains to be a sociologist," he answered, as he held up for her the fur coat. With a gesture of gentle reproof she slipped into it, and turned to Janet.

"You must let me see more of you, my dear," she said. "I'm at the best hotel, I can't remember the name, they're all so horrible — but I'll be here until to-morrow afternoon. I want to find out everything. Come and call on me. You're quite the most interesting person I've met for a long time — I don't think you realize how interesting you are. Au revoir!" She did not seem to expect any reply, taking acquiescence for granted. Glancing once more at the rows of children, who had devoured their meal in an almost uncanny silence, she exclaimed, "The dears! I'm going to send you a cheque, Brooks, even if you have been horrid to me — you always are."

"Horrid!" repeated Insall, "put it down to ignorance."

He accompanied her down the stairs. From her willowy walk a sophisticated observer would have hazarded the guess that her search for an occupation had included a course of lessons in fancy dancing.

2

Somewhat dazed by this interview which had been so suddenly forced upon her, Janet remained seated on the platform. She had the perception to recognize that in Mrs. Brocklehurst and Insall she had come in contact with a social stratum hitherto beyond the bounds of her experience; those who belonged to that stratum were not characterized by the possession of independent incomes alone, but by an attitude toward life, a manner of not appearing to take its issues desperately. Ditmar was not like that. She felt convicted of enthusiasms, she was puzzled, rather annoyed and ashamed. Insall and Mrs. Brocklehurst, different though they were, had this attitude in common. . . . Insall, when he returned, regarded her amusedly.

"So you'd like to exterminate Mrs. Brocklehurst?" he asked.

And Janet flushed. "Well, she forced me to say it."

"Oh, it didn't hurt her," he said.

"And it didn't help her," Janet responded quickly.

"No, it didn't help her," Insall agreed, and laughed.

"But I'm not sure it isn't true," she went on, "that we want what she's got." The remark, on her own lips, surprised Janet a little. She had not really meant to make it. Insall seemed to have the quality of forcing one to think out loud.

"And what she wants, *you've* got," he told her.

"What have I got?"

"Perhaps you'll find out, some day."

"It may be too late," she exclaimed. "If you'd only tell me, it might help."

"I think it's something you'll have to discover for yourself," he replied, more gravely than was his wont.

She was silent a moment, and then she demanded : "Why didn't you tell me who you were? You let me think, when I met you in Silliston that day, that you were a carpenter. I didn't know you'd written books."

"You can't expect writers to wear uniforms, like policemen — though perhaps we ought to, it might be a little fairer to the public," he said. "Besides, I am a carpenter, a better carpenter than a writer."

"I'd give anything to be an author!" she cried.

"It's a hard life," he assured her. "We have to go about seeking inspiration from others."

"Is that why you came to Hampton?"

"Well, not exactly. It's a queer thing about inspiration, you only find it when you're not looking for it."

She missed the point of this remark, though his eyes were on her. They were not like Rolfe's eyes, insinuating, possessive; they had the anomalistic quality of being at once personel and impersonal, friendly, alight, evoking curiosity yet compelling trust.

"And you didn't tell me," he reproached her, "that you were at I.W.W. Headquarters."

A desire for self-justification impelled her to exclaim: "You don't believe in Syndicalism — and yet you've come here to feed these children!"

"Oh, I think I understand the strike," he said.

"How? Have you seen it? Have you heard the arguments?"

"No. I've seen you. You've explained it."

"To Mrs. Brocklehurst?"

"It wasn't necessary," he replied — and immediately added, in semi-serious apology: "I thought it was admirable, what you said. If she'd talked to a dozen syndicalist leaders, she couldn't have had it put more clearly. Only — I'm afraid she doesn't know the truth when she hears it."

"Now you're making fun of me!"

"Indeed I'm not," he protested.

"But I didn't give any of the arguments, any of the — philosophy," she pronounced the word hesitatingly. "I don't understand it yet as well as I should."

"You *are* it," he said. "It's not always easy to understand what we are — it's generally after we've become something else that we comprehend what we have been."

And while she was pondering over this one of the ladies who had been waiting on the table came toward Insall.

"The children have finished, Brooks," she informed him. "It's time to let in the others."

Insall turned to Janet. "This is Miss Bumpus — and this is Mrs. Maturin," he said. "Mrs. Maturin lives in Silliston."

The greeting of this lady differed from that of Mrs. Brocklehurst. She, too, took Janet's hand.

"Have you come to help us?" she asked.

And Janet said: "Oh, I'd like to, but I have other work."

"Come in and see us again," said Insall, and Janet, promising, took her leave. . . .

"Who is she, Brooks?" Mrs. Maturin asked, when Janet had gone.

"Well," he answered, "I don't know. What does it matter?"

Mrs. Maturin smiled.

"I should say that it did matter," she replied. "But there's something unusual about her—where did you find her?"

"She found me." And Insall explained. "She was a stenographer, it seems, but now she's enlisted heart and soul with the syndicalists," he added.

"A history?" Mrs. Maturin queried. "Well, I needn't ask — it's written on her face."

"That's all I know," said Insall.

"I'd like to know," said Mrs. Maturin. "You say she's in the strike?"

"I should rather put it that the strike is in her."

"What do you mean, Brooks?"

But Insall did not reply.

3

Janet came away from Dey Street in a state of mental and emotional confusion. The encounter with Mrs. Brockle-hurst had been upsetting; she had an uneasy feeling of having made a fool of herself in Insall's eyes; she desired his approval; even on that occasion when she had first met him and mistaken him for a workman she had been conscious of a compelling faculty in him, of a pressure he exerted demanding justification of herself; and to-day, because she was now pledged to Syndicalism, because she had made the startling discovery that he was a writer of some renown, she had been more than ever anxious to vindicate her cause. She found herself, indeed, wondering uneasily whether there were a higher truth of which he was in possession. And the fact that his attitude toward her had been one of sympathy and friendliness rather than of disapproval, that his insight seemed to have fathomed her case, apprehended it in all but the details, was even more disturbing — yet vaguely consoling. The consolatory ele-ment in the situation was somehow connected with the lady, his friend from Silliston, to whom he had introduced her and whose image now came before her — the more vividly, perhaps, in contrast with that of Mrs. Brocklehurst. Mrs. Maturin — could Janet have so expressed her thought ! — had appeared as an extension of Insall's own personality. She was a strong, tall, vital woman with a sweet irregu-larity of feature, with a heavy crown of chestnut hair turn-ing slightly grey, quaintly braided, becomingly framing her face. Her colour was high. The impression she con-veyed of having suffered was emphasized by the simple mourning gown she wore, but the dominant note she had struck was one of dependability. It was, after all, Insall's dominant, too. Insall had asked her to call again; and the reflection that she might do so was curiously comforting. The soup kitchen in the loft, with these two presiding over it, took on something of the aspect of a sanctuary. . . .

4

Insall, in some odd manner, and through the medium of that frivolous lady, had managed to reënforce certain doubts that had been stirring in Janet — doubts of Rolfe, of the verity of the doctrine which with such abandon she had embraced. It was Insall who, though remaining silent, just by being there seemed to have suggested her manner of dealing with Mrs. Brocklehurst. It had, indeed, been *his* manner of dealing with Mrs. Brocklehurst. Janet had somehow been using his words, his method, and thus for the first time had been compelled to look objectively on what she had deemed a part of herself. We never know what we are, he had said, until we become something else! He had forced her to use an argument that failed to harmonize, somehow, with Rolfe's poetical apologetics. Stripped of the glamour of these, was not Rolfe's doctrine just one of taking, taking? And when the workers were in possession of all, would not they be as badly off as Mrs. Brocklehurst or Ditmar? Rolfe, despite the inspiring intellectual creed he professed, lacked the poise and unity that go with happiness. He wanted things, for himself: whereas she beheld in Insall one who seemed emancipated from possessions, whose life was so organized as to make them secondary affairs. And she began to wonder what Insall would think of Ditmar.

These sudden flashes of tenderness for Ditmar startled and angered her. She had experienced them before, and always had failed to account for their intrusion into a hatred she cherished. Often, at her desk in the *bibliothèque*,

she had surprised herself speculating upon what Ditmar
might be doing at that moment; and it seemed curious,
living in the same city with him, that she had not caught
a glimpse of him during the strike. More than once, moved
by a perverse impulse, she had ventured of an evening down
West Street toward the guard of soldiers in the hope of
catching sight of him. He had possessed her, and the
memory of the wild joy of that possession, of that surrender
to great strength, refused to perish. Why, at such moments,
should she glory in a strength that had destroyed her?
and why, when she heard him cursed as the man who stood,
more than any other, in the way of the strikers' victory,
should she paradoxically and fiercely rejoice? why should
she feel pride when she was told of the fearlessness with
which he went about the streets, and her heart stop beating
when she thought of the possibility of his being shot? For
these unwelcome phenomena within herself Janet could
not account. When they disturbed and frightened her,
she plunged into her work with the greater zeal. . . .

As the weeks went by, the strain of the strike began
to tell on the weak, the unprepared, on those who had many
mouths to feed. Shivering with the cold of that hardest
of winters, these unfortunates flocked to the Franco-Belgian
Hall, where a little food or money in proportion to the size
of their families was doled out to them. In spite of the
contributions received by mail, of the soup kitchens and
relief stations set up by various organizations in various
parts of the city, the supply little more than sufficed to keep
alive the more needy portion of the five and twenty thousand who now lacked all other means of support. Janet's
heart was wrung as she gazed at the gaunt, bewildered
faces growing daily more tragic, more bewildered and gaunt;
she marvelled at the animal-like patience of these Euro-
peans, at the dumb submission of most of them to priva-

tions that struck her as appalling. Some indeed complained, but the majority recited in monotonous, unimpassioned tones their stories of suffering, or of ill treatment by the "Cossacks" or the police. The stipends were doled out by Czernowitz, but all through the week there were special appeals. Once it was a Polish woman, wan and white, who carried her baby wrapped in a frayed shawl.

"Wahna littel money for milk," she said, when at length their attention was drawn to her.

"But you get your money, every Saturday," the secretary informed her kindly.

She shook her head.

"Baby die, 'less I have littel milk — I show you."

Janet drew back before the sight of the child with its sunken cheeks and ghastly blue lips. . . . And she herself went out with the woman to buy the milk, and afterwards to the dive in Kendall Street which she called home — in one of those "rear" tenements separated from the front buildings by a narrow court reeking with refuse. The place was dank and cold, malodorous. The man of the family, the lodgers who lived in the other room of the kennel, were out on the streets. But when her eyes grew used to the darkness she perceived three silent children huddled in the bed in the corner. . . .

On another occasion a man came running up the stairs of the Hall and thrust his way into a meeting of the Committee — one of those normally happy, irresponsible Syrians who, because of a love for holidays, are the despair of mill overseers. Now he was dazed, breathless, his great eyes grief-stricken like a wounded animal's.

"She is killidd, my wife — de polees, dey killidd her!"

It was Anna Mower who investigated the case. "The girl wasn't doing nothing but walk along Hudson Street when one of those hirelings set on her and beat her. She

2 B

put out her hand because she thought he'd hit her — and he gave her three or four with his billy and left her in the gutter. If you'd see her you'd know she wouldn't hurt a fly, she's that gentle looking, like all the Syrian women. She had a '*Don't be a scab*' ribbon on — that's all she done! Somebody'll shoot that guy, and I wouldn't blame 'em." Anna stood beside Janet's typewriter, her face red with anger as she told the story.

"And how is the woman now?" asked Janet.

"In bed, with two ribs broken and a bruise on her back and a cut on her head. I got a doctor. He could hardly see her in that black place they live." . . .

Such were the incidents that fanned the hatred into hotter and hotter flame. Daily reports were brought in of arrests, of fines and imprisonments for picketing, or sometimes merely for booing at the remnant of those who still clung to their employment. One magistrate in particular, a Judge Hennessy, was hated above all others for giving the extreme penalty of the law, and even stretching it. "Minions, slaves of the capitalists, of the masters," the courts were called, and Janet subscribed to these epithets, beheld the judges as willing agents of a tyranny from which she, too, had suffered. There arrived at Headquarters frenzied bearers of rumours such as that of the reported intention of landlords to remove the windows from the tenements if the rents were not paid. Antonelli himself calmed these. "Let the landlords try it!" he said phlegmatically. . . .

After a while, as the deadlock showed no signs of breaking, the siege of privation began to tell, ominous signs of discontent became apparent. Chief among the waverers were those who had come to America with visions of a fortune, who had practised a repulsive thrift in order to acquire real estate, who carried in their pockets dog-eared

bank books recording payments already made. These
had consented to the strike reluctantly, through fear, or
had been carried away by the eloquence and enthusiasm of
the leaders, by the expectation that the mill owners would
yield at once. Some went back to work, only to be "seen"
by the militant, watchful pickets — generally in their rooms,
at night. One evening, as Janet was walking home, she
chanced to overhear a conversation taking place in the dark
vestibule of a tenement.

"Working to-day?"

"Yah."

"Work to-morrow?"

Hesitation. "I d'no."

"You work, I cut your throat." A significant noise.

"Naw, I no work."

"Shake!"

She hurried on trembling, not with fear, but exultingly.
Nor did she reflect that only a month ago such an occurrence
would have shocked and terrified her. This was war. . . .
On her way to Fillmore Street she passed, at every street
corner in this district, a pacing sentry, muffled in great-
coat and woollen cap, alert and watchful, the ugly knife on
the end of his gun gleaming in the blue light of the arc.
It did not occur to her, despite the uniform, that the souls
of many of these men were divided also, that their voices
and actions, when she saw them threatening with their bayonets, were often inspired by that inner desperation characteristic of men who find themselves unexpectedly in false
situations. Once she heard a woman shriek as the sharp
knife grazed her skirt: at another time a man whose steps
had been considerably hurried turned, at a safe distance,
and shouted defiantly : —

"Say, who are you working for? Me or the Wool
Trust?"

"Aw, get along," retorted the soldier, "or I'll give you yours."

The man caught sight of Janet's button as she overtook him. He was walking backward.

"That feller has a job in a machine shop over in Barrington, I seen him there when I was in the mills. And here he is tryin' to put us out — ain't that the limit?"

The thud of horses' feet in the snow prevented her reply. The silhouettes of the approaching squad of cavalry were seen down the street, and the man fled precipitately into an alleyway. . . .

There were ludicrous incidents, too, though never lacking in a certain pathos. The wife of a Russian striker had her husband arrested because he had burned her clothes in order to prevent her returning to the mill. From the police station he sent a compatriot with a message to Headquarters. "Oye, he fix her! She no get her jawb now — she gotta stay in bed!" this one cried triumphantly.

"She was like to tear me in pieces when I brought her the clothes," said Anna Mower, who related her experience with mingled feelings. "I couldn't blame her. You see, it was the kids crying with cold and starvation, and she got so she just couldn't stand it. I couldn't stand it, neither."

Day by day the element who wished to compromise and end the strike grew stronger, brought more and more pressure on the leaders. These people were subsidized, Antonelli declared, by the capitalists. . . .

CHAPTER XVIII

1

A MORE serious atmosphere pervaded Headquarters, where it was realized that the issue hung in the balance. And more proclamations, à la Napoleon, were issued to sustain and hearten those who were finding bread and onions meagre fare, to shame the hesitating, the wavering. As has been said, it was Rolfe who, because of his popular literary gift, composed these appeals for the consideration of the Committee, dictating them to Janet as he paced up and down the *bibliothèque*, inhaling innumerable cigarettes and flinging down the ends on the floor. A famous one was headed: "*Shall Wool and Cotton Kings Rule the Nation?*" "We are winning!" it declared. "The World is with us! Forced by the unshaken solidarity of tens of thousands, the manufacturers offer bribes to end the reign of terror they have inaugurated. . . . Inhuman treatment and oppressive toil have brought all nationalities together into one great army to fight against a brutal system of exploitation. In years and years of excessive labour we have produced millions for a class of idle parasites, who enjoy all the luxuries of life while our wives have to leave their firesides and our children their schools to eke out a miserable existence." And this for the militia: "The lowest aim of life is to be a soldier! The 'good' soldier never tries to distinguish right from wrong, he never thinks, he never reasons, he only obeys —"

"But," Janet was tempted to say, "your syndicalism declares that none of us should think or reason. We should

373

only feel." She was beginning to detect Rolfe's inconsistencies, yet she refrained from interrupting the inspirational flow.

"The soldier is a blind, heartless, soulless, murderous machine." Rolfe was fond of adjectives. "All that is human in him, all that is divine has been sworn away when he took the enlistment oath. No man can fall lower than a soldier. It is a depth beyond which we cannot go."

"All that is human, all that is divine," wrote Janet, and thrilled a little at the words. Why was it that mere words, and their arrangement in certain sequences, gave one a delicious, creepy feeling up and down the spine? Her attitude toward him had become more and more critical, she had avoided him when she could, but when he was in this ecstatic mood she responded, forgot his red lips, his contradictions, lost herself in a medium she did not comprehend. Perhaps it was because, in his absorption in the task, he forgot her, forgot himself. She, too, despised the soldiers, fervently believed they had sold themselves to the oppressors of mankind. And Rolfe, when in the throes of creation, had the manner of speaking to the soldiers themselves, as though these were present in the lane just below the window; as though he were on the tribune. At such times he spoke with such rapidity that, quick though she was, she could scarcely keep up with him. "Most of you, Soldiers, are workingmen!" he cried. "Yesterday you were slaving in the mills yourselves. You will profit by our victory. Why should you wish to crush us? Be human!"

Pale, excited, he sank down into the chair by her side and lit another cigarette.

"They ought to listen to that!" he exclaimed. "It's the best one I've done yet."

Night had come. Czernowitz sat in the other room, talking to Jastro, a buzz of voices came from the hall through the thin pine panels of the door. All day long a sixty-mile gale had twisted the snow of the lane into whirling, fantastic columns and rattled the windows of Franco-Belgian Hall. But now the wind had fallen. . . . Presently, as his self-made music ceased to vibrate within him, Rolfe began to watch the girl as she sat motionless, with parted lips and eyes alight, staring at the reflection of the lamp in the blue-black window.

"Is that the end?" she asked, at length.

"Yes," he replied sensitively. "Can't you see it's a climax? Don't you think it's a good one?"

She looked at him, puzzled.

"Why, yes," she said, "I think it's fine. You see, I have to take it down so fast I can't always follow it as I'd like to."

"When you feel, you can do anything," he exclaimed. "It is necessary to feel."

"It is necessary to know," she told him.

"I do not understand you," he cried, leaning toward her. "Sometimes you are a flame — a wonderful, scarlet flame — I can express it in no other way. Or again, you are like the Madonna of our new faith, and I wish I were a del Sarto to paint you. And then again you seem as cold as your New England snow, you have no feeling, you are an Anglo-Saxon — a Puritan."

She smiled, though she felt a pang of reminiscence at the word. Ditmar had called her so, too.

"I can't help what I am," she said.

"It is that which inhibits you," he declared. "That Puritanism. It must be eradicated before you can develop, and then — and then you will be completely wonderful. When this strike is over, when we have time, I will teach you many things — develop you. We will read Sorel together — he is beautiful, like poetry — and the great poets, Dante and Petrarch and Tasso — yes, and d'Annunzio. We shall live."

"We are living, now," she answered. The look with which she surveyed him he found enigmatic. And then, abruptly, she rose and went to her typewriter.

"You don't believe what I say!" he reproached her.

But she was cool. "I'm not sure that I believe all of it. I want to think it out for myself — to talk to others, too."

"What others?"

"Nobody in particular — everybody," she replied, as she set her notebook on the rack.

"There is some one else!" he exclaimed, rising.

"There is every one else," she said.

As was his habit when agitated, he began to smoke feverishly, glancing at her from time to time as she fingered the keys. Experience had led him to believe that he who finds a woman in revolt and gives her a religion inevitably becomes her possessor. But more than a month had passed, he had not become her possessor — and now for the first time there entered his mind a doubt as to having given her a religion! The obvious inference was that of another man, of another influence in opposition to his own; characteristically, however, he shrank from accepting this, since he was of those who believe what they wish to believe. The sudden fear of losing her — intruding itself immediately upon an ecstatic, creative mood — unnerved him, yet he strove to appear confident as he stood over her.

"When you've finished typewriting that, we'll go out to supper," he told her.

But she shook her head.

"Why not?"

"I don't want to," she replied — and then, to soften her refusal, she added, "I can't, to-night."

"But you never will come with me any more. Why is it?"

"I'm very tired at night. I don't feel like going out." She sought to temporize.

"You've changed!" he accused her. "You're not the same as you were at first — you avoid me."

The swift gesture with which she flung over the carriage of her machine might have warned him.

"I don't like that Hampton Hotel," she flashed back. "I'm —I'm not a vagabond — yet."

"A vagabond!" he repeated.

She went on savagely with her work..

"You have two natures," he exclaimed. "You are still a bourgeoise, a Puritan. You will not be yourself, you will not be free until you get over that."

"I'm not sure I want to get over it."

He leaned nearer to her.

"But now that I have found you, Janet, I will not let you go."

"You've no rights over me," she cried, in sudden alarm and anger. "I'm not doing this work, I'm not wearing myself out here for you."

"Then — why are you doing it?" His suspicions rose again, and made him reckless.

"To help the strikers," she said. . . . He could get no more out of her, and presently, when Anna Mower entered the room, he left it. . . .

2

More than once since her first visit to the soup kitchen in Dey Street Janet had returned to it. The universe rocked, but here was equilibrium. The streets were filled with soldiers, with marching strikers, terrible things were constantly happening; the tension at Headquarters never seemed to relax. Out in the world and within her own soul were strife and suffering, and sometimes fear; the work in which she sought to lose herself no longer sufficed to keep her from thinking, and the spectacle — when she returned home — of her mother's increasing apathy grew more and more appalling. But in Dey Street she gained calmness, was able to renew something of that sense of proportion the lack of which, in the chaos in which she was engulfed, often brought her to the verge of madness. At first she had had a certain hesitation about going back, and on the occasion of her second visit had walked twice around the block before venturing to enter. She had no claim on this man. He was merely a chance acquaintance, a stranger — and yet he seemed nearer to her, to understand her better than any one else she knew in the world. This was queer, because she had not explained herself; nor had he asked her for any confidences. She would have liked to confide in him — some things: he gave her the impression of comprehending life; of having, as his specialty, humanity itself; he should, she reflected, have been a minister, and smiled at the thought: ministers, at any rate, ought to be like *him*, and then one might embrace Christianity — the religion of her forefathers that Rolfe ridiculed. But there was about Insall nothing of religion as she had grown up to apprehend the term.

Now that she had taken her courage in her hands and renewed her visits, they seemed to be the most natural proceedings in the world. On that second occasion, when she had opened the door and palpitatingly climbed to the loft, the second batch of children were finishing their midday meal, — rather more joyously, she thought, than before, — and Insall himself was stooping over a small boy whom he had taken away from the table. He did not notice her at once, and Janet watched them. The child had a cough, his extreme thinness was emphasized by the coat he wore, several sizes too large for him.

"You come along with me, Marcus, I guess I can fit you out," Insall was saying, when he looked up and saw Janet.

"Why, if it isn't Miss Bumpus! I thought you'd forgotten us."

"Oh no," she protested. "I wanted to come."

"Then why didn't you?"

"Well, I have come," she said, with a little sigh, and he did not press her further. And she refrained from offering any conventional excuse, such as that of being interested in the children. She had come to see him, and such was the faith with which he inspired her — now that she was once more in his presence — that she made no attempt to hide the fact.

"You've never seen my clothing store, have you?" he asked. And with the child's hand in his he led the way into a room at the rear of the loft. A kit of carpenter's tools was on the floor, and one wall was lined with box-like compartments made of new wood, each with its label in neat lettering indicating the articles contained therein. "Shoes?" he repeated, as he ran his eye down the labels and suddenly opened a drawer. "Here we are, Marcus. Sit down there on the bench, and take off the shoes you have on."

The boy had one of those long faces of the higher Jewish type, intelligent, wistful. He seemed dazed by Insall's kindness. The shoes he wore were those of an adult, but cracked and split, revealing the cotton stocking and here and there the skin. His little blue hands fumbled with the knotted strings that served for lacings until Insall, producing a pocket knife, deftly cut the strings.

"Those are summer shoes, Marcus — well ventilated."

"They're by me since August," said the boy.

"And now the stockings," prompted Insall. The old ones, wet, discoloured, and torn, were stripped off, and thick, woollen ones substituted. Insall, casting his eye over the open drawer, chose a pair of shoes that had been worn, but which were stout and serviceable, and taking one

in his hand knelt down before the child. "Let's see how
good a guesser I am," he said, loosening the strings and
turning back the tongue, imitating good-humouredly the
deferential manner of a salesman of footwear as he slipped on
the shoe. "Why, it fits as if it were made for you! Now
for the other one. Yes, your feet *are* mates — I know a
man who wears a whole size larger on his left foot." The
dazed expression remained on the boy's face. The experience was beyond him. "That's better," said Insall,
as he finished the lacing. "Keep out of the snow, Marcus,
all you can. Wet feet aren't good for a cough, you know.
And when you come in to supper a nice doctor will be here,
and we'll see if we can't get rid of the cough."

The boy nodded. He got to his feet, stared down at
the shoes, and walked slowly toward the door, where he
turned.

"Thank you, Mister Insall," he said.

And Insall, still sitting on his heels, waved his hand.

"It is not to mention it," he replied. "Perhaps you
may have a clothing store of your own some day — who
knows!" He looked up at Janet amusedly and then, with
a spring, stood upright, his easy, unconscious pose betoken-
ing command of soul and body. "I ought to have kept a
store," he observed. "I missed my vocation."

"It seems to me that you missed a great many vocations,"
she replied. Commonplaces alone seemed possible, adequate. "I suppose you made all those drawers yourself."

He bowed in acknowledgment of her implied tribute.
With his fine nose and keen eyes — set at a slightly downward angle, creased at the corners — with his thick, greying
hair, despite his comparative youth he had the look one
associates with portraits of earlier, patriarchal Americans. . . .
These calls of Janet's were never of long duration. She had
fallen into the habit of taking her lunch between one and

two, and usually arrived when the last installment of young-
sters were finishing their meal; sometimes they were filing
out, stopping to form a group around Insall, who always
managed to say something amusing — something pertinent
and good-naturedly personal. For he knew most of them
by name, and had acquired a knowledge of certain individual
propensities and idiosyncrasies that delighted their companions.

"What's the trouble, Stépan — swallowed your spoon?"
Stépan was known to be greedy. Or he would suddenly
seize an unusually solemn boy from behind and tickle him
until the child screamed with laughter. It was, indeed,
something of an achievement to get on terms of confidence
with these alien children of the tenements and the streets
who from their earliest years had been forced to shift for
themselves, and many of whom had acquired a precocious
suspicion of Greeks bearing gifts. Insall himself had used
the phrase, and explained it to Janet. That sense of *caveat
donor* was perhaps their most pathetic characteristic. But
he broke it down; broke down, too, the shyness accompanying it, the shyness and solemnity emphasized in them by
contact with hardship and poverty, with the stark side of
life they faced at home. He had made them — Mrs. Maturin
once illuminatingly remarked — more like *children*. Sometimes he went to see their parents, — as in the case of Marcus
— to suggest certain hygienic precautions in his humorous
way; and his accounts of these visits, too, were always
humorous. Yet through that humour ran a strain of pathos
that clutched — despite her smile — at Janet's heartstrings.
This gift of emphasizing and heightening tragedy while
apparently dealing in comedy she never ceased to wonder at.
She, too, knew that tragedy of the tenements, of the poor,
its sordidness and cruelty. All her days she had lived precariously near it, and lately she had visited these people,

had been torn by the sight of what they endured. But Insall's jokes, while they stripped it of sentimentality — of which she had an instinctive dislike — made it for her even more poignant. One would have thought, to have such an insight into it, that he too must have lived it, must have been brought up in some dirty alley of a street. That gift, of course, must be a writer's gift.

When she saw the waifs trooping after him down the stairs, Mrs. Maturin called him the Pied Piper of Hampton.

As time went on, Janet sometimes wondered over the quiet manner in which these two people, Insall and Mrs. Maturin, took her visits as though they were matters of course, and gave her their friendship. There was, really, no obvious excuse for her coming, not even that of the waifs for food — and yet she came to be fed. The sustenance they gave her would have been hard to define; it flowed not so much from what they said, as from what they were; it was in the atmosphere surrounding them. Sometimes she looked at Mrs. Maturin to ask herself what this lady would say if she knew her history, her relationship with Ditmar — which had been her real reason for entering the ranks of the strikers. And was it fair for her, Janet, to permit Mrs. Maturin to bestow her friendship without revealing this? She could not make up her mind as to what this lady would say. Janet had had no difficulty in placing Ditmar; not much trouble, after her first surprise was over, in classifying Rolfe and the itinerant band of syndicalists who had descended upon her restricted world. But Insall and Mrs. Maturin were not to be ticketed. What chiefly surprised her, in addition to their kindliness, to their taking her on faith without the formality of any recommendation or introduction, was their lack of intellectual narrowness. She did not, of course, so express it. But she sensed, in their presence, from references casually let fall in their conversation, a wider culture of which they were in possession, a culture at once puzzling and exciting, one that she despaired of acquiring for herself. Though it came from reading, it did not seem "literary," according to the notion she had conceived of the term. Her speculations concerning it must be focussed and interpreted. It was a culture, in the first place, not harnessed to an obvious Cause: something like that struck her. It was a culture that contained tolerance and charity, that did not label a portion of mankind as its enemy, but seemed, by understanding all, to forgive all. It had no prejudices; nor did it boast, as the Syndicalists boasted, of its absence of convention. And little by little Janet connected it with Silliston.

"It must be wonderful to live in such a place as that," she exclaimed, when the Academy was mentioned. On this occasion Insall had left for a moment, and she was in the little room he called his "store," alone with Mrs. Maturin, helping to sort out a batch of garments just received.

"It was there you first met Brooks, wasn't it?" She always spoke of him as Brooks. "He told me about it, how you walked out there and asked him about a place to lunch." Mrs. Maturin laughed. "You didn't know what to make of him, did you?"

"I thought he was a carpenter!" said Janet. "I — I never should have taken him for an author. But of course I don't know any other authors."

"Well, he's not like any of them, he's just like himself. You can't put a tag on people who are really big."

Janet considered this. "I never thought of that. I suppose not," she agreed.

Mrs. Maturin glanced at her. "So you liked Silliston," she said.

"I liked it better than any place I ever saw. I haven't seen many places, but I'm sure that few can be nicer."

"What did you like about it, Janet?" Mrs. Maturin was interested.

"It's hard to say," Janet replied, after a moment. "It gave me such a feeling of peace — of having come home, although I lived in Hampton. I can't express it."

"I think you're expressing it rather well," said Mrs. Maturin.

"It was so beautiful in the spring," Janet continued, dropping the coat she held into the drawer. "And it wasn't just the trees and the grass with the yellow dandelions, it was the houses, too — I've often wondered why those houses pleased me so much. I wanted to *live* in every one of them. Do you know that feeling?" Mrs. Maturin nodded. "They didn't hurt your eyes when you looked at them, and they seemed to be so much at home there, even the new ones. The new ones were like the children of the old."

"I'll tell the architect. He'll be pleased," said Mrs. Maturin.

Janet flushed.

"Am I being silly?" she asked.

"No, my dear," Mrs. Maturin replied. "You've expressed what I feel about Silliston. What do you intend to do when the strike is over?"

"I hadn't thought." Janet started at the question, but Mrs. Maturin did not seem to notice the dismay in her tone. "You don't intend to — to travel around with the I. W. W. people, do you?"

"I — I hadn't thought," Janet faltered. It was the first time Mrs. Maturin had spoken of her connection with Syndicalism. And she surprised herself by adding: "I don't see how I could. They can get stenographers anywhere, and that's all I'm good for." And the question occurred to her — did she really wish to?

"What I was going to suggest," continued Mrs. Maturin, quietly, "was that you might try Silliston. There's a chance for a good stenographer there, and I'm sure you are a good one. So many of the professors send to Boston."

Janet stood stock still. Then she said: "But you don't know anything about me, Mrs. Maturin."

Kindliness burned in the lady's eyes as she replied: "I know more now — since you've told me I know nothing. Of course there's much I don't know, how you, a stenographer, became involved in this strike and joined the I. W. W. But you shall tell me or not, as you wish, when we become better friends."

Janet felt the blood beating in her throat, and an impulse to confess everything almost mastered her. From the first she had felt drawn toward Mrs. Maturin, who seemed to hold out to her the promise of a woman's friendship — for which she had felt a life-long need: a woman friend who would understand the insatiate yearning in her that gave her no rest in her search for a glittering essence never found, that had led her only to new depths of bitterness and despair. It would destroy her, if indeed it had not already done so. Mrs. Maturin, Insall, seemed to possess the secret that would bring her peace — and yet, in spite of something urging her to speak, she feared the risk of losing them. Perhaps, after all, they would not understand! perhaps it was too late!

"You do not believe in the Industrial Workers of the World," was what she said.

Mrs. Maturin herself, who had been moved and excited as she gazed at Janet, was taken by surprise. A few moments elapsed before she could gather herself to reply, and then she managed to smile.

2 c

"I do not believe that wisdom will die with them, my dear. Their — their doctrine is too simple, it does not seem as if life, the social order is to be so easily solved."

"But you must sympathize with them, with the strikers." Janet's gesture implied that the soup kitchen was proof of this.

"Ah," replied Mrs. Maturin, gently, "that is different — to understand them. There is one philosophy for the lamb, and another for the wolf."

"You mean," said Janet, trembling, "that what happens to us makes us inclined to believe certain things?"

"Precisely," agreed Mrs. Maturin, in admiration. "But I must be honest with you, it was Brooks who made me see it."

"But — he never said that to me. And I asked him once, almost the same question."

"He never said it to me, either," Mrs. Maturin confessed. "He doesn't tell you what he believes; I simply gathered that this is his idea. And apparently the workers can only improve their condition by strikes, by suffering — it seems to be the only manner in which they can convince the employers that the conditions *are* bad. It isn't the employers' fault."

"Not their fault!" Janet repeated.

"Not in a large sense," said Mrs. Maturin. "When people grow up to look at life in a certain way, from a certain viewpoint, it is difficult, almost impossible to change them. It's — it's their religion. They are convinced that if the world doesn't go on in their way, according to their principles, everything will be destroyed. They aren't inhuman. Within limits everybody is more than willing to help the world along, if only they can be convinced that what they are asked to do will help."

Janet breathed deeply. She was thinking of Ditmar.

And Mrs. Maturin, regarding her, tactfully changed the subject.

"I didn't intend to give you a lecture on sociology or psychology, my dear," she said. "I know nothing about them, although we have a professor who does. Think over what I've said about coming to Silliston. It will do you good — you are working too hard here. I know you would enjoy Silliston. And Brooks takes such an interest in you," she added impulsively. "It is quite a compliment."

"But why?" Janet demanded, bewildered.

"Perhaps it's because you have — possibilities. You may be typewriting his manuscripts. And then, I am a widow, and often rather lonely — you could come in and read to me occasionally."

"But — I've never read anything."

"How fortunate!" said Insall, who had entered the doorway in time to hear Janet's exclamation. "More than half of modern culture depends on what one shouldn't read."

Mrs. Maturin laughed. But Insall waved his hand deprecatingly.

"That isn't my own," he confessed. "I cribbed it from a clever Englishman. But I believe it's true."

3

"I think I'll adopt her," said Mrs. Maturin to Insall, when she had repeated to him the conversation. "I know — you are always convicting me of enthusiasms, Brooks, and I suppose I do get enthusiastic."

"Well, you adopt her — and I'll marry her," replied Insall, with a smile, as he cut the string from the last bundle of clothing.

"You might do worse. It would be a joke if you did!"

His friend paused to consider this preposterous possibility. "One never can tell whom a man like you, an artist, will marry."

"We've no business to marry at all," said Insall, laughing. "I often wonder where that romantic streak will land you, Augusta. But you do have a delightful time!"

"Don't begrudge it me, it makes life so much more interesting," Mrs. Maturin begged, returning his smile. "I haven't the faintest idea that you will marry her or any one else. But I insist on saying she's your type — she's the kind of a person artists do dig up and marry — only better than most of them, far better."

"Dig up?" said Insall.

"Well, you know I'm not a snob — I only mean that she seems to be one of the surprising anomalies that sometimes occur in — what shall I say? — in the working-classes. I do feel like a snob when I say that. But what is it? Where does that spark come from? Is it in our modern air, that discontent, that desire, that thrusting forth toward a new light — something as yet unformulated, but which we all feel, even at small institutions of learning like Silliston?"

"Now you're getting beyond me."

"Oh no, I'm not," Mrs. Maturin retorted confidently. "If you won't talk about it, I will, I have no shame. And this girl has it — this thing I'm trying to express. She's modern to her finger tips, and yet she's extraordinarily American — in spite of her modernity, she embodies in some queer way our tradition. She loves our old houses at Silliston — they make her feel at home — that's her own expression."

"Did she say that?"

"Exactly. And I know she's of New England ancestry, she told me so. What I can't make out is, why she joined the I.W.W. That seems so contradictory."

"Perhaps she was searching for light there," Insall hazarded. "Why don't you ask her?"

"I don't know," replied Mrs. Maturin, thoughtfully. "I want to, my curiosity almost burns me alive, and yet I don't. She isn't the kind you can ask personal questions of — that's part of her charm, part of her individuality. One is a little afraid to intrude. And yet she keeps coming here — of course *you* are a sufficient attraction, Brooks. But I must give her the credit of not flirting with you."

"I've noticed that, too," said Insall, comically.

"She's searching for light," Mrs. Maturin went on, struck by the phrase. "She has an instinct we can give it to her, because we come from an institution of learning. I felt something of the kind when I suggested her establishing herself in Silliston. Well, she's more than worth while experimenting on, she must have lived and breathed what you call the 'movie atmosphere' all her life, and yet she never seems to have read and absorbed any sentimental literature or cheap religion. She doesn't suggest the tawdry. That part of her, the intellectual part, is a clear page to be written upon."

"There's my chance," said Insall.

"No, it's *my* chance — since you're so cynical."

"I'm not cynical," he protested.

"I don't believe you really are. And if you are, there may be a judgment upon you," she added playfully. "I tell you she's the kind of woman artists go mad about. She has what sentimentalists call temperament, and after all we haven't any better word to express dynamic desires. She'd keep you stirred up, stimulated, and you could educate her."

"No, thanks, I'll leave that to you. He who educates a woman is lost. But how about Syndicalism and all the mysticism that goes with it? There's an intellectual over at Headquarters who's been talking to her about Bergson, the life-force, and the World-We-Ourselves-Create."

Mrs. Maturin laughed.

"Well, we go wrong when we don't go right. That's just it, we must go some way. And I'm sure, from what I gather, that she isn't wholly satisfied with Syndicalism."

"What *is* right?" demanded Insall.

"Oh, I don't intend to turn her over to Mr. Worrall and make a sociologist and a militant suffragette out of her. She isn't that kind, anyhow. But I could give her good literature to read — yours, for instance," she added maliciously.

"You're preposterous, Augusta," Insall exclaimed.

"I may be, but you've got to indulge me. I've taken this fancy to her — of course I mean to see more of her. But — you know how hard it is for me, sometimes, since I've been left alone."

Insall laid his hand affectionately on her shoulder.

"I remember what you said the first day I saw her, that the strike was in *her*," Mrs. Maturin continued. "Well, I see now that she does express and typify it — and I don't mean the 'labour movement' alone, or this strike in Hampton, which is symptomatic, but crude. I mean something bigger — and I suppose you do — the protest, the revolt, the struggle for self-realization that is beginning to be felt all over the nation, all over the world to-day, that is not yet focussed and self-conscious, but groping its way, clothing itself in any philosophy that seems to fit it. I can imagine myself how such a strike as this might appeal to a girl with a sense of rebellion against sordidness and lack of opportunity — especially if she has had a tragic experience. And sometimes I suspect she has had one."

"Well, it's an interesting theory," Insall admitted indulgently.

"I'm merely amplifying your suggestions, only you won't admit that they are yours. And she was your protégée."

"And you are going to take her off my hands."

"I'm not so sure," said Mrs. Maturin.

CHAPTER XIX

1

THE Hampton strike had reached the state of grim dead-lock characteristic of all stubborn wars. There were aggressions, retaliations on both sides, the antagonism grew more intense. The older labour unions were accused by the strikers of playing the employers' game, and thus grew to be hated even more than the "capitalists." These organizations of the skilled had entered but half-heartedly into a struggle that now began to threaten, indeed, their very existence, and when it was charged that the Textile Workers had been attempting to secure recruits from the ranks of the strikers, and had secretly offered the mill-owners a scale of demands in the hope that a sufficient number of operatives would return to work, and so break the strike, a serious riot was barely averted. "Scab-hunting agencies," the unions were called. One morning when it was learned that the loom-fixers, almost to a man, had gone back to the mills, a streetcar was stopped near the power house at the end of Faber Street, and in a twinkling, before the militia or police could interfere, motorman, conductor, and passengers were dragged from it and the trolley pole removed. This and a number of similar aggressive acts aroused the mill-owners and their agents to appeal with renewed vigour to the public through the newspapers, which it was claimed they owned or subsidized. Then followed a series of arraignments of the strike leaders calculated to stir the wildest prejudices and fears of the citizens of Hampton. Antonelli and Jastro — so rumour had it — in various nightly speeches had advised their followers to "sleep in the daytime and prowl like wild animals at night"; urged the power house employees to desert and leave the city in darkness; made the declaration, "We will win if we raise scaffolds on every street!" insisted that the strikers, too, should have "gun permits," since the police hirelings carried arms. And the fact that the mill-owners replied with pamphlets whose object was proclaimed to be one of discrediting their leaders in the eyes of the public still further infuriated the strikers. Such charges, of course, had to be vehemently refuted, the motives behind them made clear, and counter-accusations laid at the door of the mill-owners.

The atmosphere at Headquarters daily grew more tense. At any moment the spark might be supplied to precipitate an explosion that would shake the earth. The hungry, made more desperate by their own sufferings or the spectacle of starving families, were increasingly difficult to control: many wished to return to work, others clamoured for violence, nor were these wholly discouraged by a portion of the leaders. A riot seemed imminent — a riot Antonelli feared and firmly opposed, since it would alienate the sympathy of that wider public in the country on which the success of the strike depended. Watchful, yet apparently unconcerned, unmoved by the quarrels, the fierce demands for "action," he sat on the little stage, smoking his cigars and reading his newspapers.

Janet's nerves were taut. There had been times during the past weeks when she had been aware of new and vaguely disquieting portents. Inexperience had led her to belittle them, and the absorbing nature of her work, the excitement due to the strange life of conflict, of new ideas, into which she had so unreservedly flung herself, the

resentment that galvanized her — all these had diverted
her from worry. At night, hers had been the oblivious
slumber of the weary. . . . And then, as a desperate
wayfarer, pressing on, feels a heavy drop of rain and
glances up to perceive the clouds that have long been
gathering, she awoke in the black morning hours, and fear
descended upon her. Suddenly her brain became hideously
active as she lay, dry-lipped, staring into the darkness,
striving to convince herself that it could not be. But the
thing had its advocate, also, to summon ingeniously, in
cumulative array, those omens she had ignored : to cause
her to piece together, in this moment of torture, portions
of the knowledge of sexual facts that prudery banishes from
education, a smattering of which reaches the ears of such
young women as Janet in devious, roundabout ways. Several
times, in the month just past, she had had unwonted attacks
of dizziness, of faintness, and on one occasion Anna Mower,
alarmed, had opened the window of the *bibliothèque* and
thrust her into the cold air. Now, with a pang of fear
she recalled what Anna had said : —

"You're working too hard — you hadn't ought to stay
here nights. If it was some girls I've met, I'd know what
to think."

Strange that the significance of this sentence had failed
to penetrate her consciousness until now ! *"If it was some
girls I've met, I'd know what to think!"* It had come into
her mind abruptly ; and always, when she sought to reassure
herself, to declare her terror absurd, it returned to confront her. Heat waves pulsed through her, she grew in-
tolerably warm, perspiration started from her pores, and
she flung off the blankets. The rain from the roofs was
splashing on the bricks of the passage. . . . What would
Mr. Insall say, if he knew ? and Mrs. Maturin ? She could
never see them again. Now there was no one to whom to

turn, she was cut off, utterly, from humanity, an outcast. Like Lise! And only a little while ago she and Lise had lain in that bed together! Was there not somebody — God? Other people believed in God, prayed to him. She tried to say, "Oh God, deliver me from this thing!" but the words seemed a mockery. After all, it was mechanical, it had either happened or it hadn't happened. A life-long experience in an environment where only unpleasant things occurred, where miracles were unknown, had effaced a fleeting, childhood belief in miracles. Cause and effect were the rule. And if there were a God who did interfere, why hadn't he interfered before this thing happened? Then would have been the logical time. Why hadn't he informed her that in attempting to escape from the treadmill in which he had placed her, in seeking happiness, she had been courting destruction? Why had he destroyed Lise? And if there were a God, would he comfort her now, convey to her some message of his sympathy and love? No such message, alas, seemed to come to her through the darkness.

After a while — a seemingly interminable while — the siren shrieked, the bells jangled loudly in the wet air, another day had come. Could she face it — even the murky grey light of this that revealed the ashes and litter of the back yard under the downpour? The act of dressing brought a slight relief; and then, at breakfast, a numbness stole over her — suggested and conveyed, perchance, by the apathy of her mother. Something had killed suffering in Hannah; perhaps she herself would mercifully lose the power to suffer! But the thought made her shudder. She could not, like her mother, find a silly refuge in shining dishes, in cleaning pots and pans, or sit idle, vacant-minded, for long hours in a spotless kitchen. What would happen to her? . . . Howbeit, the ache that had tortured her became a dull, leaden pain, like that she had known at another time — how long ago ! — when the suffering caused by Ditmar's deception had dulled, when she had sat in the train on her way back to Hampton from Boston, after seeing Lise. The pain would throb again, unsupportably, and she would wake, and this time it would drive her — she knew not where.

She was certain, now, that the presage of the night was true. . . .

She reached Franco-Belgian Hall to find it in an uproar. Anna Mower ran up to her with the news that dynamite had been discovered by the police in certain tenements of the Syrian quarter, that the tenants had been arrested and taken to the police station where, bewildered and terrified, they had denied any knowledge of the explosive. Dynamite had also been found under the power house, and in the mills — the sources of Hampton's prosperity. And Hampton believed, of course, that this was the inevitable result of the anarchistic preaching of such enemies of society as Jastro and Antonelli — if these, indeed, had not incited the Syrians to the deed. But it was a plot of the mill-owners, Anna insisted — they themselves had planted the explosive, adroitly started the rumours, told the police where the dynamite was to be found. Such was the view that prevailed at Headquarters, pervaded the angrily buzzing crowd that stood outside — heedless of the rain — and animated the stormy conferences in the *Salle de Réunion*.

The day wore on. In the middle of the afternoon, as she was staring out of the window, Anna Mower returned with more news. Dynamite had been discovered in Hawthorne Street, and it was rumoured that Antonelli and Jastro were to be arrested.

"You ought to go home and rest, Janet," she said kindly.

Janet shook her head.

"Rolfe's back," Anna informed her, after a moment. "He's talking to Antonelli about another proclamation to let people know who's to blame for this dynamite business. I guess he'll be in here in a minute to dictate the draft. Say, hadn't you better let Minnie take it, and go home?"

"I'm not sick," Janet repeated, and Anna reluctantly left her.

Rolfe had been absent for a week, in New York, consulting with some of the I.W.W. leaders; with Lockhart, the chief protagonist of Syndicalism in America, just returned from Colorado, to whom he had given a detailed account of the Hampton strike. And Lockhart, next week, was coming to Hampton to make a great speech and look over the ground for himself. All this Rolfe told Janet eagerly when he entered the *bibliothèque*. He was glad to get back; he had missed her.

"But you are pale!" he exclaimed, as he seized her hand, "and how your eyes burn! You do not take care of yourself when I am not here to watch you." His air of solicitude, his assumption of a peculiar right to ask, might formerly have troubled and offended her. Now she was scarcely aware of his presence. "You feel too much — that is it — you are like a torch that consumes itself in burning. But this will soon be over, we shall have them on their knees, the capitalists, before very long, when it is known what they have done to-day. It is too much — they have overreached themselves with this plot of the dynamite. . . . You have missed me, a little?"

"I have been busy," she said, releasing her hand and sitting down at her desk and taking up her notebook.

"You are not well," he insisted.

"I'm all right," she replied.

He lit a cigarette and began to pace the room — his customary manner of preparing himself for the creative mood. After a while he began to dictate — but haltingly. He had come here from Antonelli all primed with fervour and indignation, but it was evident that this feeling had ebbed, that his mind refused to concentrate on what he was saying. Despite the magnificent opportunity to flay the capitalists which their most recent tactics afforded him, he paused, repeated himself, and began again, glancing from time to time reproachfully, almost resentfully at Janet. Usually, on these occasions, he was transported, almost inebriated by his own eloquence; but now he chafed at her listlessness, he was at a loss to account for the withdrawal of the enthusiasm he had formerly been able to arouse. Lacking the feminine stimulus, his genius limped. For Rolfe there had been a woman in every strike — sometimes two. What had happened, during his absence, to alienate the most promising of all neophytes he had ever encountered?

"The eyes of the world are fixed on the workers of Hampton! They must be true to the trust their fellows have placed in them! To-day the mill-owners, the masters, are at the end of their tether. Always unscrupulous, they have descended to the most despicable of tactics in order to deceive the public. But truth will prevail! . . ." Rolfe lit another cigarette, began a new sentence and broke it off. Suddenly he stood over her. "It's you!" he said. "You don't feel it, you don't help me, you're not in sympathy."

He bent over her, his red lips gleaming through his beard, a terrible hunger in his lustrous eyes — the eyes of a soul to which self-denial was unknown. His voice was thick with uncontrolled passion, his hand was cold.

"Janet, what has happened? I love you, you must love me — I cannot believe that you do not. Come with me. We shall work together for the workers — it is all nothing without you."

For a moment she sat still, and then a pain shot through her, a pain as sharp as a dagger thrust. She drew her hand away.

"I can't love — I can only hate," she said.

"But you do not hate me!" Rolfe repudiated so gross a fact. His voice caught as in a sob. "I, who love you, who have taught you!"

She dismissed this — what he had taught her — with a gesture which, though slight, was all-expressive. He drew back from her.

"Shall I tell you who has planned and carried out this plot?" he cried. "It is Ditmar. He is the one, and he used Janes, the livery stable keeper, the politician who brought the dynamite to Hampton, as his tool. Half an hour before Janes got to the station in Boston he was seen by a friend of ours talking to Ditmar in front of the Chippering offices, and Janes had the satchel with him then. Ditmar walked to the corner with him."

Janet, too, had risen.

"I don't believe it," she said.

"Ah, I thought you wouldn't! But we have the proof that dynamite was in the satchel, we've found the contractor from whom it was bought. I was a fool — I might have known that you loved Ditmar."

"I hate him!" said Janet.

"It is the same thing," said Rolfe.

She did not answer. . . . He watched her in silence as she put on her hat and coat and left the room.

2

The early dusk was gathering when she left the hall and made her way toward the city. The huge bottle-shaped chimneys of the power plant injected heavy black smoke into the wet air. In Faber Street the once brilliant signs above the "ten-foot" buildings seemed dulled, the telegraph poles starker, nakeder than ever, their wires scarcely discernible against the smeared sky. The pedestrians were sombrely garbed, and went about in "rubbers" — the most depressing of all articles worn by man. Sodden piles of snow still hid the curb and gutters, but the pavements were trailed with mud that gleamed in the light from the shop windows. And Janet, lingering unconsciously in front of that very emporium where Lise had been incarcerated, the *Bagatelle*, stared at the finery displayed there, at the blue tulle dress that might be purchased, she read, for $22.99. She found herself repeating, in meaningless, subdued tones, the words, "twenty-two ninety-nine." She even tried — just to see if it were possible — to concentrate her mind on that dress, on the fur muffs and tippets in the next window; to act as if this were just an ordinary, sad February afternoon, and she herself once more just an ordinary stenographer leading a monotonous, uneventful existence. But she knew that this was not true, because, later on, she was going to do something — to commit some act. She didn't know what this act would be. Her head was hot, her temples throbbed. . . .

Night had fallen, the electric arcs burned blue overhead, she was in another street — was it Stanley? Sounds of music reached her, the rumble of marching feet; dark, massed figures were in the distance swimming toward her along the glistening line of the car tracks, and she heard the shrill whistling of the doffer boys, who acted as a sort of fife corps in these parades — which by this time had become familiar to the citizens of Hampton. And Janet remembered when the little red book that contained the songs had arrived at Headquarters from the west and had been distributed by thousands among the strikers. She recalled the words of this song, though the procession was as yet too far away for her to distinguish them : —

> "The People's flag is deepest red,
> It shrouded oft our martyred dead,
> And ere their limbs grew stiff and cold,
> Their life-blood dyed its every fold."

The song ceased, and she stood still, waiting for the procession to reach her. A group of heavy Belgian women were marching together. Suddenly, as by a simultaneous impulse, their voices rang out in the Internationale — the terrible Marseillaise of the workers : —

> "Arise, ye prisoners of starvation !
> Arise, ye wretched of the earth !"

And the refrain was taken up by hundreds of throats : —

> "'Tis the final conflict,
> Let each stand in his place !" . . .

The walls of the street flung it back. On the sidewalk, pressed against the houses, men and women heard it with white faces. But Janet was carried on. . . . The scene changed, now she was gazing at a mass of human beings hemmed in by a line of soldiers. Behind the crowd was a row of old-fashioned brick houses, on the walls of which were patterned, by the cold electric light, the branches of the bare elms ranged along the sidewalk. People leaned out of the windows, like theatregoers at a play. The light illuminated the red and white bars of the ensign, upheld by the standard bearer of the regiment, the smaller flags flaunted by the strikers — each side clinging hardily to the emblem of human liberty. The light fell, too, harshly and brilliantly, on the workers in the front rank confronting the bayonets, and these seemed strangely indifferent, as though waiting for the flash of a photograph. A little farther on

2 D

a group of boys, hands in pockets, stared at the soldiers
with bravado. From the rear came that indescribable
"booing" which those who have heard never forget, mingled
with curses and cries : –

"*Vive la grève!*"

"To hell with the Cossacks!"

"Kahm on — shoot!"

The backs of the soldiers, determined, unyielding, were
covered with heavy brown capes that fell below the waist.
As Janet's glance wandered down the line it was arrested
by the face of a man in a visored woollen cap — a face that
was almost sepia, in which large white eyeballs struck a
note of hatred. And what she seemed to see in it, confronting her, were the hatred and despair of her own soul!
The man might have been a Hungarian or a Pole; the breadth
of his chin was accentuated by a wide, black moustache, his
attitude was tense, — that of a maddened beast ready to
spring at the soldier in front of him. He was plainly one
of those who had reached the mental limit of endurance.

In contrast with this foreigner, confronting him, a young
lieutenant stood motionless, his head cocked on one side,
his hand grasping the club held a little behind him, his
glance meeting the other's squarely, but with a different
quality of defiance. All his faculties were on the alert.
He wore no overcoat, and the uniform fitting close to his
figure, the broad-brimmed campaign hat of felt served to
bring into relief the physical characteristics of the American
Anglo-Saxon, of the individualist who became the fighting
pioneer. But Janet, save to register the presence of the
intense antagonism between the two, scarcely noticed her
fellow countryman. . . . Every moment she expected to
see the black man spring, — and yet movement would have
marred the drama of that consuming hatred. . . .

Then, by one of those bewildering, kaleidoscopic shifts

to which crowds are subject, the scene changed, more troops arrived, little by little the people were dispersed to drift together again by chance — in smaller numbers — several blocks away. Perhaps a hundred and fifty were scattered over the space formed by the intersection of two streets, where three or four special policemen with night sticks urged them on. Not a riot, or anything approaching it. The police were jeered, but the groups, apparently, had already begun to scatter, when from the triangular vestibule of a saloon on the corner darted a flame followed by an echoing report, a woman bundled up in a shawl screamed and sank on the snow. For an instant the little French-Canadian policeman whom the shot had missed gazed stupidly down at her. . . .

3

As Janet ran along the dark pavements the sound of the shot and of the woman's shriek continued to ring in her ears. At last she stopped in front of the warehouse beyond Mr. Tiernan's shop, staring at the darkened windows of the flat—of the front room in which her mother now slept alone. For a minute she stood looking at these windows, as though hypnotized by some message they conveyed — the answer to a question suggested by the incident that had aroused and terrified her. They drew her, as in a trance, across the street, she opened the glass-panelled door, remembering mechanically the trick it had of not quite closing, turned and pushed it to and climbed the stairs. In the dining-room the metal lamp, brightly polished, was burning as usual, its light falling on the chequered red table-cloth, on her father's empty chair, on that somewhat battered heirloom, the horsehair sofa. All was so familiar, and yet so amazingly unfamiliar, so silent! At this time Edward should be reading the *Banner*, her mother bustling in and out, setting the table for supper. But not a dish was set. The ticking of the ancient clock only served to intensify the silence. Janet entered, almost on tiptoe, made her way to the kitchen door, and looked in. The stove was polished, the pans bright upon the wall, and Hannah was seated in a corner, her hands folded across a spotless apron. Her scant hair was now pure white, her dress seemed to have fallen away from her wasted neck, which was like a trefoil column.

"Is that you, Janet? You hain't seen anything of your father?"

The night before Janet had heard this question, and she had been puzzled as to its meaning — whether in the course of the day she had seen her father, or whether Hannah thought he was coming home.

"He's at the mill, mother. You know he has to stay there."

"I know," replied Hannah, in a tone faintly reminiscent of the old aspersion. "But I've got everything ready for him in case he should come — any time — if the strikers hain't killed him."

"But he's safe where he is."

"I presume they will try to kill him, before they get through," Hannah continued evenly. "But in case he should come at any time, and I'm not here, you tell him all those Bumpus papers are put away in the drawer of that old chest, in the corner. I can't think what he'd do without those papers. That is," she added, "if you're here yourself."

"Why shouldn't *you* be here?" asked Janet, rather sharply.

"I dunno, I seem to have got through." She glanced helplessly around the kitchen. "There don't seem to be much left to keep me alive. . . . I guess you'll be wanting your supper, won't you? You hain't often home these days — whatever it is you're doing. I didn't expect you."

Janet did not answer at once.

"I — I have to go out again, mother," she said.

Hannah accepted the answer as she had accepted every other negative in life, great and small.

"Well, I guessed you would."

Janet made a step toward her.

"Mother!" she said, but Hannah gazed at her uncomprehendingly. Janet stooped convulsively, and kissed her. Straightening up, she stood looking down at her mother for a few moments, and went out of the room, pausing in the dining-room, to listen, but Hannah apparently had not stirred. She took the box of matches from its accustomed place on the shelf beside the clock, entered the dark bedroom in the front of the flat, closing the door softly behind her. The ghostly blue light from a distant arc came slanting in at the window, glinting on the brass knobs of the chest of drawers — another Bumpus heirloom. She remembered that chest from early childhood; it was one of the few pieces that, following them in all their changes of residence, had been faithful to the end: she knew everything in it, and the place for everything. Drawing a match from the box, she was about to turn on the gas — but the light from the arc would suffice. As she made her way around the walnut bed she had a premonition of poignant anguish as yet unrealized, of anguish being held at bay by a stronger, fiercer, more imperative emotion now demanding expression, refusing at last to be denied. She opened the top drawer of the chest, the drawer in which Hannah, breaking tradition, had put the Bumpus genealogy. Edward had never kept it there. Would the other things be in place? Groping with her hands in the left-hand corner, her fingers clasped exultantly something heavy, something wrapped carefully in layers of flannel. She had feared her father might have taken it to the mill! She drew it out, unwound the flannel, and held to the light an old-fashioned revolver, the grease glistening along its barrel. She remembered, too, that the cartridges had lain beside it, and thrusting her hand once more into the drawer found the box, extracting several, and replacing the rest, closed the drawer, and crept through the dining-room to her bedroom, where she lit the gas in order to examine the weapon — finally contriving, more by accident than skill, to break it. The cartridges, of course, fitted into the empty cylinder. But before inserting them she closed the pistol once more, cocked it, and held it out. Her arm trembled violently as she pulled the trigger. Could she do it? As though to refute this doubt of her ability to carry out an act determined upon, she broke the weapon once more, loaded and closed it, and thrust it in the pocket of her coat. Then, washing the grease from her hands, she put on her gloves, and was about to turn out the light when she saw reflected in the glass the red button of the I.W.W. still pinned on her coat. This she tore off, and flung on the bureau.

When she had kissed her mother, when she had stood hesitatingly in the darkness of the familiar front bedroom in the presence of unsummoned memories of a home she had believed herself to resent and despise, she had nearly faltered. But once in the street, this weakness suddenly vanished, was replaced by a sense of wrong that now took complete and furious possession of her, driving her like a gale at her back. She scarcely felt on her face the fine rain that had begun to fall once more. Her feet were accustomed to the way. When she had turned down West Street and almost gained the canal, it was with a shock of surprise that she found herself confronted by a man in a long cape who held a rifle and barred her path. She stared at him as at an apparition.

"You can't get by here," he said. "Don't you know that?"

She did not reply. He continued to look at her, and presently asked, in a gentler tone: —

"Where did you wish to go, lady?"

"Into the mill," she replied, "to the offices."

"But there can't anybody go through here unless they have a pass. I'm sorry, but that's the order."

Her answer came so readily as to surprise her.

"I was Mr. Ditmar's private stenographer. I have to see him."

The sentry hesitated, and then addressed another soldier, who was near the bridge.

"Hi, sergeant!" he called. The sergeant came up — a conscientious Boston clerk who had joined the militia from a sense of duty and a need for exercise. While the sentry explained the matter he gazed at Janet. Then he said politely: —

"I'm sorry, Miss, but I can't disobey orders."

"But can't you send word to Mr. Ditmar, and tell him I want to see him?" she asked.

"Why, I guess so," he answered, after a moment. "What name shall I say?"

"Miss Bumpus."

"Bumpus," he repeated. "That's the gatekeeper's name."

"I'm his daughter — but I want to see Mr. Ditmar."

"Well," said the sergeant, "I'm sure it's all right, but I'll have to send in anyway. Orders are orders. You understand?"

She nodded as he departed. She saw him cross the bridge like a ghost through the white mist rising from the canal. And through the mist she could make out the fortress-like mass of the mill itself, and the blurred, distorted lights in the paymaster's offices smeared on the white curtain of the vapour.

"Nasty weather," the sentry remarked, in friendly fashion. He appeared now, despite his uniform, as a good-natured, ungainly youth.

Janet nodded.

"You'd ought to have brought an umbrella," he said. "I guess it'll rain harder, before it gets through. But it's better than ten below zero, anyhow."

She nodded again, but he did not seem to resent her silence. He talked about the hardship of patrolling in winter, until the sergeant came back.

"It's all right, Miss Bumpus," he said, and touched his hat as he escorted her to the bridge. She crossed the canal and went through the vestibule without replying to the greeting of the night-watchman, or noticing his curious glance; she climbed the steel-clad stairway, passed the paymaster's offices and Mr. Orcutt's, and gained the outer office where she had worked as a stenographer. It was dark, but sufficient light came through Ditmar's open door to guide her beside the rail. He had heard her step, and as she entered his room he had put his hands heavily on his desk, in the act of rising from his chair.

"Janet!" he said, and started toward her, but got no farther than the corner of the desk. The sight of her heaving breast, of the peculiar light that flashed from beneath her lashes stopped him suddenly. Her hands were in her pockets. "What is it?" he demanded stupidly.

But she continued to stand there, breathing so heavily that she could not speak. It was then that he became aware of an acute danger. He did not flinch.

"What is it?" he repeated.

Still she was silent. One hand was thrust deeper into its pocket, he saw a shudder run through her, and suddenly she burst into hysterical weeping, sinking into a chair. He stood for some moments helplessly regarding her before he gained the presence of mind to go to the door and lock it, returning to bend over her.

"Don't touch me!" she said, shrinking from him.

"For God's sake tell me what's the matter," he begged.

She looked up at him and tried to speak, struggling against the sobs that shook her.

"I — I came here to — to kill you — only I can't do it."

"To kill me!" he said, after a pause. In spite of the fact that he had half divined her intention, the words shocked him. Whatever else may be said of him, he did not lack courage, his alarm was not of a physical nature. Mingled with it were emotions he himself did not understand, caused by the unwonted sight of her loss of self-control, of her anger, and despair. "Why did you want to kill me?"

And again he had to wait for an answer.

"Because you've spoiled my life — because I'm going to have a child!"

"What do you mean? Are you?... it can't be possible."

"It is possible, it's true — it's true. I've waited and waited, I've suffered, I've almost gone crazy — and now I know. And I said I'd kill you if it were so, I'd kill myself — only I can't. I'm a coward." Her voice was drowned again by weeping.

A child! He had never imagined such a contingency! And as he leaned back against the desk, his emotions became chaotic. The sight of her, even as she appeared crazed by anger, had set his passion aflame — for the intensity and fierceness of her nature had always made a strong appeal to dominant qualities in Ditmar's nature. And then — this announcement! Momentarily it turned his heart to water. Now that he was confronted by an exigency that had once vicariously yet deeply disturbed him in a similar affair of a friend of his, the code and habit of a lifetime gained an immediate ascendency — since then he had insisted that this particular situation was to be avoided above all others. And his mind leaped to possibilities. She had wished to kill him — would she remain desperate enough to ruin him? Even though he were not at a crisis in his affairs, a scandal of this kind would be fatal.

"I didn't know," he said desperately, "I couldn't guess. Do you think I would have had this thing happen to you? I was carried away — we were both carried away —"

"You planned it!" she replied vehemently, without looking up. "You didn't care for me, you only — wanted me."

"That isn't so — I swear that isn't so. I loved you — I love you."

"Oh, do you think I believe that?" she exclaimed.

"I swear it — I'll prove it!" he protested. Still under the influence of an acute anxiety, he was finding it difficult to gather his wits, to present his case. "When you left me that day the strike began — when you left me without giving me a chance — you'll never know how that hurt me."

"You'll never know how it hurt me!" she interrupted.

"Then why, in God's name, did you do it? I wasn't myself, then, you ought to have seen that. And when I heard from Caldwell here that you'd joined those anarchists —"

"They're no worse than you are — they only want what you've got," she said.

He waved this aside. "I couldn't believe it — I wouldn't believe it until somebody saw you walking with one of them to their Headquarters. Why did you do it?"

"Because I know how they feel, I sympathize with the strikers, I want them to win — against you!" She lifted her head and looked at him, and in spite of the state of his feelings he felt a twinge of admiration at her defiance.

"Because you love me!" he said.

"Because I hate you," she answered.

And yet a spark of exultation leaped within him at the thought that love had caused this apostasy. He had had that suspicion before, though it was a poor consolation when he could not reach her. Now she had made it vivid. A woman's logic, or lack of logic — *her* logic.

"Listen!" he pleaded. "I tried to forget you — I tried to keep myself going all the time that I mightn't think of you, but I couldn't help thinking of you, wanting you, longing for you. I never knew why you left me, except that you seemed to believe I was unkind to you, and that something had happened. It wasn't my fault —" he pulled himself up abruptly.

"I found out what men were like," she said. "A man made my sister a woman of the streets — that's what you've done to me."

He winced. And the calmness she had regained, which was so characteristic of her, struck him with a new fear.

"I'm not that kind of a man," he said.

But she did not answer. His predicament became more trying.

"I'll take care of you," he assured her, after a moment. "If you'll only trust me, if you'll only come to me I'll see that no harm comes to you."

She regarded him with a sort of wonder — a look that put a fine edge of dignity and scorn to her words when they came.

"I told you I didn't want to be taken care of — I wanted to kill you, and kill myself. I don't know why I can't — what prevents me." She rose. "But I'm not going to trouble you any more — you'll never hear of me again."

She would not trouble him, she was going away, he would never hear of her again! Suddenly, with the surge of relief he experienced, came a pang. He could not let her go — it was impossible. It seemed that he had never understood his need of her, his love for her, until now that he had brought her to this supreme test of self-revelation. She had wanted to kill him, yes, to kill herself — but how could he ever have believed that she would stoop to another method of retaliation? As she stood before him the light in her eyes — still wet with tears — transfigured her.

"I love you, Janet," he said. "I want you to marry me."

"You don't understand," she answered. "You never did. If I had married you, I'd feel just the same — but it isn't really as bad as if we had been married."

"Not as bad!" he exclaimed.

"If we were married, you'd think you had rights over me," she explained, slowly. "Now you haven't any, I can go away. I couldn't live with you. I know what happened to me, I've thought it all out, I wanted to get away from the life I was leading — I hated it so, I was crazy to have a chance, to see the world, to get nearer some of the beautiful things I knew were there, but couldn't reach. . . . And you came along. I did love you, I would have done anything for you — it was only when I saw that you didn't really love me that I began to hate you, that I wanted to get away from you, when I saw that you only wanted me until you should get tired of me. That's your nature, you can't help it. And it would have been the same if we were married, only worse, I couldn't have stood it any more than I can now — I'd have left you. You say you'll marry me now, but that's because you're sorry for me — since I've said I'm not going to trouble you any more. You'll be glad I've gone. You may — want me now, but that isn't love. When you say you love me, I can't believe you."

"You must believe me! And the child, Janet, — our child!"

"If the world was right," she said, "I could have this child and nobody would say anything. I could support it — I guess I can anyway. And when I'm not half crazy I want it. Maybe that's the reason I couldn't do what I tried to do just now. It's natural for a woman to want a child — especially a woman like me, who hasn't anybody or anything."

Ditmar's state of mind was too complicated to be wholly described. As the fact had been gradually brought home to him that she had not come as a supplicant, that even in her misery she was free, and he helpless, there revived in him wild memories of her body, of the kisses he had wrung from her — and yet this physical desire was accompanied by a realization of her personality never before achieved. And because he had hitherto failed to achieve it, she had escaped him. This belated, surpassing glimpse of what she essentially was, and the thought of the child — *their* child — permeating his passion, transformed it into a feeling hitherto unexperienced and unimagined. He hovered over her, pitifully, his hands feeling for her, yet not daring to touch her.

"Can't you see that I love you?" he cried, "that I'm ready to marry you now, to-night. You must love me, I won't believe that you don't after — after all we have been to each other."

But even then she could not believe. Something in her, made hard by the intensity of her suffering, refused to melt. And her head was throbbing, and she scarcely heard him.

"I can't stay any longer," she said, getting to her feet. "I can't bear it."

"Janet, I swear I'll care for you as no woman was ever cared for. For God's sake listen to me, give me a chance, forgive me!" He seized her arm; she struggled, gently but persistently, to free herself from his hold.

"Let me go, please." All the passionate anger had gone out of her, and she spoke in a monotone, as one under hypnosis, dominated by a resolution which, for the present at least, he was powerless to shake.

"But to-morrow?" he pleaded. "You'll let me see you to-morrow, when you've had time to think it over, when you realize that I love you and want you, that I haven't meant to be cruel — that you've misjudged me — thought I was a different kind of a man. I don't blame you for that, I guess something happened to make you believe it. I've got enemies. For the sake of the child, Janet, if for nothing else, you'll come back to me! You're — you're tired to-night, you're not yourself. I don't wonder, after all you've been through. If you'd only come to me before! God knows what I've suffered, too!"

"Let me go, please," she repeated, and this time, despairingly, he obeyed her, a conviction of her incommunicability overwhelming him. He turned and, fumbling with the key, unlocked the door and opened it. "I'll see you to-morrow," he faltered once more, and watched her as she went through the darkened outer room until she gained the lighted hallway beyond and disappeared. Her footsteps died away into silence. He was trembling. For several minutes he stood where she had left him, tortured by a sense of his inability to act, to cope with this, the great crisis of his life, when suddenly the real significance of that strange last look in her eyes was borne home to him. And he had allowed her to go out into the streets alone! Seizing his hat and coat, he fairly ran out of the office and down the stairs and across the bridge.

"Which way did that young lady go?" he demanded of the sergeant.

"Why — up West Street, Mr. Ditmar."

He remembered where Fillmore Street was; he had,

indeed, sought it out one evening in the hope of meeting her. He hurried toward it now, his glance strained ahead to catch sight of her figure under a lamp. But he reached Fillmore Street without overtaking her, and in the rain he stood gazing at the mean houses there, wondering in which of them she lived, and whether she had as yet come home. . . .

4

After leaving Ditmar Janet, probably from force of habit, had indeed gone through West Street, and after that she walked on aimlessly. It was better to walk than to sit alone in torment, to be gnawed by that Thing from which she had so desperately attempted to escape, and failed. She tried to think why she had failed. . . . Though the rain fell on her cheeks, her mouth was parched; and this dryness of her palate, this physical sense of lightness, almost of dizziness, were intimately yet incomprehensibly part and parcel of the fantastic moods into which she floated. It was as though, in trying to solve a problem, she caught herself from time to time falling off to sleep. In her waking moments she was terror-stricken. Scarce an hour had passed since, in a terrible exaltation at having found a solution, she had gone to Ditmar's office in the mill. What had happened to stay her? It was when she tried to find the cause of the weakness that so abruptly had overtaken her, or to cast about for a plan to fit the new predicament to which her failure had sentenced her, that the fantasies intruded. She heard Ditmar speaking, the arguments were curiously familiar — but they were not Ditmar's! They were her father's, and now it was Edward's voice to which she listened, he was telling her how eminently proper it was that she should marry Ditmar, because of her Bumpus blood. And this made her laugh. . . . Again, Ditmar was kissing her hair. He had often praised it. She had taken it down and combed it out for him; it was like a cloud, he said — so fine; its odour made him faint — and then the odour changed, became that of the detested perfume of Miss Lottie Myers! Even that made Janet smile! But Ditmar was strong, he was powerful, he was a Fact, why not go back to him and let him absorb and destroy her? That annihilation would be joy. . . .

It could not have been much later than seven o'clock when she found herself opposite the familiar, mulberry-shingled Protestant church. The light from its vestibule made a gleaming square on the wet sidewalk, and into this area, from the surrounding darkness, came silhouetted figures of men and women holding up umbrellas; some paused for a moment's chat, their voices subdued by an awareness of the tabernacle. At the sight of this tiny congregation something stirred within her. She experienced a twinge of surprise at the discovery that other people in the world, in Hampton, were still leading tranquil, untormented existences. They were contented, prosperous, stupid, beyond any need of help from God, and yet they were going to prayer-meeting to ask something! He refused to find her in the dark streets. Would she find Him if she went in there? and would He help her?

The bell in the tower began to clang, with heavy, relentless strokes — like physical blows from which she flinched — each stirring her reluctant, drowsy soul to a quicker agony. From the outer blackness through which she fled she gazed into bright rooms of homes whose blinds were left undrawn, as though to taunt and mock the wanderer. She was an outcast! Who henceforth would receive her save those, unconformed and unconformable, sentenced to sin in this realm of blackness? Henceforth from all warmth and love she was banished. . . . In the middle of the Stanley

Street bridge she stopped to lean against the wet rail; the mill lights were scattered, dancing points of fire over the invisible swift waters, and she raised her eyes presently to the lights themselves, seeking one unconsciously — Ditmar's! Yes, it was his she sought; though it was so distant, sometimes it seemed to burn like a red star, and then to flicker and disappear. She could not be sure. . . . Something chill and steely was in the pocket of her coat — it made a heavy splash in the water when she dropped it. The river could not be so very cold! She wished she could go down like that into forgetfulness. But she couldn't. . . . Where was Lise now? . . . It would be so easy just to drop over that parapet and be whirled away, and down and down. Why couldn't she? Well, it was because — because — she was going to have a child. Well, if she had a child to take care of, she would not be so lonely — she would have something to love. She loved it now, as though she felt it quickening within her, she wanted it, to lavish on it all of a starved affection. She seemed actually to feel in her arms its soft little body pressed against her. Claude Ditmar's child! And she suddenly recalled, as an incident of the remote past, that she had told him she wanted it!

This tense craving for it she felt now was somehow the answer to an expressed wish which had astonished her. Perhaps that was the reason why she had failed to do what she had tried to do, to shoot Ditmar and herself! It was Ditmar's child, Ditmar's and hers! He had loved her, long ago, and just now — was it just now? — he had said he loved her still, he had wanted to marry her. Then why had she run away from him? Why had she taken the child into outer darkness, to be born without a father, — when she loved Ditmar? Wasn't that one reason why she wanted the child? why, even in her moments of passionate hatred she recalled having been surprised by some such yearning as now came

2 E

over her? And for an interval, a brief interval, she viewed him with startling clarity. Not because he embodied any ideal did she love him, but because he was what he was, because he had overcome her will, dominated and possessed her, left his mark upon her indelibly. He had been cruel to her, willing to sacrifice her to his way of life, to his own desires, but he loved her, for she had seen, if not heeded in his eyes the look that a woman never mistakes! She remembered it now, and the light in his window glowed again, like a star to guide her back to him. It was drawing her, irresistibly. . . .

The sentry recognized her as she came along the canal.

"Mr. Ditmar's gone," he told her.

"Gone!" she repeated. "Gone!"

"Why, yes, about five minutes after you left he was looking for you — he asked the sergeant about you."

"And — he won't be back?"

"I guess not," answered the man, sympathetically. "He said good-night."

She turned away dully. The strength and hope with which she had been so unexpectedly infused while gazing from the bridge at his window had suddenly ebbed; her legs ached, her feet were wet, and she shivered, though her forehead burned. The world became distorted, people flitted past her like weird figures of a dream, the myriad lights of Faber Street were blurred and whirled in company with the electric signs. Seeking to escape from their confusion she entered a side street leading north, only to be forcibly seized by some one who darted after her from the sidewalk.

"Excuse me, but you didn't see that automobile," he said, as he released her.

Shaken, she went on through several streets to find herself at length confronted by a pair of shabby doors that looked familiar, and pushing one of them open, halted at the bottom of a stairway to listen. The sound of cheerful voices came to her from above; she started to climb—even with the help of the rail it seemed as if she would never reach the top of that stairway. But at last she stood in a loft where long tables were set, and at the end of one of these, sorting out spoons and dishes, three women and a man were chatting and laughing together. Janet was troubled because she could not remember who the man was, although she recognized his bold profile, his voice and gestures. . . . At length one of the women said something in a low tone, and he looked around quickly and crossed the room.

"Why, it's you!" he said, and suddenly she recalled his name.

"Mr. Insall!"

But his swift glance had noticed the expression in her eyes, the sagged condition of her clothes, the attitude that proclaimed exhaustion. He took her by the arm and led her to the little storeroom, turning on the light and placing her in a chair. Darkness descended on her. . . .

Mrs. Maturin, returning from an errand, paused for an instant in the doorway, and ran forward and bent over Janet.

"Oh, Brooks, what is it — what's happened to her?"

"I don't know," he replied, "I didn't have a chance to ask her. I'm going for a doctor."

"Leave her to me, and call Miss Hay."   Mrs. Maturin was instantly competent. . . . And when Insall came back from the drug store where he had telephoned she met him at the head of the stairs. "We've done everything we can, Edith Hay has given her brandy, and gone off for dry clothes, and we've taken all the children's things out of the drawers and laid her on the floor, but she hasn't come to. Poor child,— what can have happened to her? Is the doctor coming?"

"Right away," said Insall, and Mrs. Maturin went back into the storeroom. Miss Hay brought the dry clothes before the physician arrived.

"It's probably pneumonia," he explained to Insall a little later. "She must go to the hospital — but the trouble is all our hospitals are pretty full, owing to the sickness caused by the strike." He hesitated. "Of course, if she has friends, she could have better care in a private institution just now."

"Oh, she has friends," said Mrs. Maturin. "Couldn't we take her to our little hospital at Silliston, doctor? It's only four miles — that isn't much in an automobile, and the roads are good now."

"Well, the risk isn't much greater, if you have a closed car, and she would, of course, be better looked after," the physician consented.

"I'll see to it at once," said Insall. . . .

CHAPTER XX

1

THE Martha Wootton Memorial Hospital was the hobby
of an angel alumnus of Silliston. It was situated in Hovey's
Lane, but from the window of the white-enameled room in
which she lay Janet could see the bare branches of the
Common elms quivering to the spring gusts, could watch,
day by day, the grass changing from yellow-brown to vivid
green in the white sunlight. In the morning, when the
nurse opened the blinds, that sunlight swept radiantly
into the room, lavish with its caresses; always spending,
always giving, the symbol of a loving care that had been
poured out on her, unasked and unsought. It was sweet
to rest, to sleep. And instead of the stringent monster-
cry of the siren, of the discordant clamour of the mill bells,
it was sweet yet strange to be awakened by silver-toned
chimes proclaiming peaceful hours. At first she surrendered
to the spell, and had no thought of the future. For a little
while every day, Mrs. Maturin read aloud, usually from
books of poetry. And knowing many of the verses by
heart, she would watch Janet's face, framed in the soft
dark hair that fell in two long plaits over her shoulders.
For Janet little guessed the thought that went into the choosing of these books, nor could she know of the hours spent
by this lady pondering over library shelves or consulting
eagerly with Brooks Insall. Sometimes Augusta Maturin
thought of Janet as a wildflower — one of the rare, shy ones,
hiding under its leaves; sprung up in Hampton, of all places,

crushed by a heedless foot, yet miraculously not destroyed, and already pushing forth new and eager tendrils. And she had transplanted it. To find the proper nourishment, to give it a chance to grow in a native, congenial soil, — such was her breathless task. And so she had selected "The Child's Garden of Verses."

> "I should like to rise and go
> Where the golden apples grow" . . .

When she laid down her book it was to talk, perhaps, of Silliston. Established here before the birth of the Republic, its roots were bedded in the soil of a racial empire, to a larger vision of which Augusta Maturin clung: an empire of Anglo-Saxon tradition which, despite disagreements and conflicts — nay, through them — developed imperceptibly toward a sublimer union, founded not on dominion, but on justice and right. She spoke of the England she had visited on her wedding journey, of the landmarks and literature that also through generations have been American birthrights; and of that righteous self-assertion and independence which, by protest and even by war, America had contributed to the democracy of the future. Silliston, indifferent to cults and cataclysms, undisturbed by the dark tides flung westward to gather in deposits in other parts of the land, had held fast to the old tradition, stood ready to do her share to transform it into something even nobler when the time should come. Simplicity and worth and beauty — these elements at least of the older Republic should not perish, but in the end prevail.

She spoke simply of these things, connecting them with a Silliston whose spirit appealed to all that was inherent and abiding in the girl. All was not chaos: here at least a beacon burned with a bright and steady flame. And she spoke of Andrew Silliston, the sturdy colonial prototype of the American culture, who had fought against his King, who had spent his modest fortune to found this seat of learning, believing as he did that education is the corner-stone of republics; divining that lasting unity is possible alone by the transformation of the individual into the citizen through voluntary bestowal of service and the fruits of labour. Samuel Wootton, the Boston merchant who had given the hospital, was Andrew's true descendant, imbued with the same half-conscious intuition that builds even better that it recks. And Andrew, could he have returned to earth in his laced coat and long silk waistcoat, would still recognize his own soul in Silliston Academy, the soul of his creed and race.

> "Away down the river,
> A hundred miles or more,
> Other little children
> Shall bring my boats ashore." . . .

Janet drew in a great breath, involuntarily. These were moments when it seemed that she could scarcely contain what she felt of beauty and significance, when the ecstasy and pain were not to be borne. And sometimes, as she listened to Mrs. Maturin's voice, she wept in silence. Again a strange peace descended on her, the peace of an exile come home; if not to remain, at least to know her own land and people before faring forth. She would not think of that faring yet awhile, but strive to live and taste the present — and yet as life flowed back into her veins that past arose to haunt her, she yearned to pour it out to her new friend, to confess all that had happened to her. Why couldn't she? But she was grateful because Mrs. Maturin betrayed no curiosity. Janet often lay watching her, puzzled, under the spell of a frankness, an ingenuousness, a simplicity she had least expected to find in one who belonged

to such a learned place as that of Silliston. But even learning, she was discovering, could be amazingly simple. Freely
and naturally Mrs. Maturin dwelt on her own past, on the
little girl of six taken from her the year after her husband
died, on her husband himself, once a professor here, and who,
just before his last illness, had published a brilliant book
on Russian literature which resulted in his being called to
Harvard. They had gone to Switzerland instead, and
Augusta Maturin had come back to Silliston. She told
Janet of the loon-haunted lake, hemmed in by the Lauren-
tian hills, besieged by forests, where she had spent her girl-
hood summers with her father, Professor Wishart, of the
University of Toronto. There, in search of health, Gifford
Maturin had come at her father's suggestion to camp.

Janet, of course, could not know all of that romance,
though she tried to picture it from what her friend told
her. Augusta Wishart, at six and twenty, had been one of
those magnificent Canadian women who are most at home
in the open; she could have carried Gifford Maturin out of
the wilderness on her back. She was five feet seven, mod-
elled in proportion, endowed by some Celtic ancestor with
that dark chestnut hair which, because of its abundance,
she wore braided and caught up in a heavy knot behind her
head. Tanned by the northern sun, kneeling upright in a
canoe, she might at a little distance have been mistaken for
one of the race to which the forests and waters had once
belonged. The instinct of mothering was strong in her,
and from the beginning she had taken the shy and delicate
student under her wing, recognizing in him one of the physically helpless dedicated to a supreme function. He was
forever catching colds, his food disagreed with him, and on
her own initiative she discharged his habitant cook and supplied him with one of her own choosing. When overtaken
by one of his indispositions she paddled him about the lake

with lusty strokes, first placing a blanket over his knees, and he submitted : he had no pride of that sort, he was utterly indifferent to the figure he cut beside his Amazon. His gentleness of disposition, his brilliant conversations with those whom, like her father, he knew and trusted, captivated Augusta. At this period of her life she was awakening to the glories of literature and taking a special course in that branch. He talked to her of Gogol, Turgenief, and Dostoievsky, and seated on the log piazza read in excellent French "Dead Souls," "Pères et Enfants," and "The Brothers Karamazoff." At the end of August he went homeward almost gaily, quite ignorant of the arrow in his heart, until he began to miss Augusta Wishart's ministrations — and Augusta Wishart herself. . . .   Then had followed that too brief period of intensive happiness. . . .

The idea of remarriage had never occurred to her. At eight and thirty, though tragedy had left its mark, it had been powerless to destroy the sweetness of a nature of such vitality as hers. The innate necessity of loving remained, and as time went on had grown more wistful and insistent. Insall and her Silliston neighbours were wont, indeed, gently to rally her on her enthusiams, while understanding and sympathizing with this need in her. A creature of intuition, Janet had appealed to her from the beginning, arousing first her curiosity, and then the maternal instinct that craved a mind to mould, a soul to respond to her touch. . . .

Mrs. Maturin often talked to Janet of Insall, who had, in a way, long been connected with Silliston. In his early wandering days, when tramping over New England, he used unexpectedly to turn up at Dr. Ledyard's, the principal's, remain for several weeks and disappear again. Even then he had been a sort of institution, a professor emeritus in botany, bird lore, and woodcraft, taking the boys on long walks through the neighbouring hills ; and suddenly he had surprised everybody by fancying the tumble-down farm-house in Judith's Lane, which he had restored with his own hands into the quaintest of old world dwellings. Behind it he had made a dam in the brook, and put in a water wheel that ran his workshop. In play hours the place was usually overrun by boys. . . . But sometimes the old craving for tramping would overtake him, one day his friends would find the house shut up, and he would be absent for a fort-night, perhaps for a month — one never knew when he was going, or when he would return. He went, like his hero, Silas Simpkins, through the byways of New England, stop-ping at night at the farm-houses, or often sleeping out under the stars. And then, perhaps, he would write another book. He wrote only when he felt like writing.

It was this book of Insall's, "The Travels of Silas Simp-kins," rather than his "Epworth Green" or "The Hermit of Blue Mountain," that Mrs. Maturin chose to read to Janet. Unlike the sage of Walden, than whom he was more gre-garious, instead of a log house for his castle Silas Simpkins chose a cart, which he drove in a most leisurely manner from the sea to the mountains, penetrating even to hamlets beside the silent lakes on the Canadian border, and then went back to the sea again. Two chunky grey horses with wide fore-heads and sagacious eyes propelled him at the rate of three miles an hour; for these, as their master, had learned the lesson that if life is to be fully savoured it is not to be bolted. Silas cooked and ate, and sometimes read under the maples beside the stone walls: usually he slept in the cart in the midst of the assortment of goods that proclaimed him, to the astute, an expert in applied psychology. At first you might have thought Silas merely a peddler, but if you knew your Thoreau you would presently begin to perceive that peddling was the paltry price he paid for liberty. Silas was in a way a sage — but such a human sage! He never intruded with theories, he never even hinted at the folly of the mortals who bought or despised his goods, or with whom he chatted by the wayside, though he may have had his ideas on the subject: it is certain that presently one began to have one's own: nor did he exclaim with George Sand, " *Il n'y a rien de plus bêtement méchant que l'habitant des petites villes !*" Somehow the meannesses and jealousies were accounted for, if not excused. To understand is to pardon.

It was so like Insall, this book, in its whimsicality, in its feeling of space and freedom, in its hidden wisdom that gradually revealed itself as one thought it over before falling off to sleep! New England in the early summer! Here, beside the tender greens of the Ipswich downs was the sparkling cobalt of the sea, and she could almost smell its cool salt breath mingling with the warm odours of hay and the pungent scents of roadside flowers. Weathered grey cottages were scattered over the landscape, and dark copses of cedars, while oceanward the eye was caught by the gleam of a lighthouse or a lonely sail.

Even in that sandy plain, covered with sickly, stunted pines and burned patches, stretching westward from the Merrimac, Silas saw beauty and colour, life in the once prosperous houses not yet abandoned. . . . Presently the hills, all hyacinth blue, rise up against the sunset, and the horses' feet are on the "Boston Road" — or *rud*, according to the authorized pronunciation of that land. Hardly, indeed, in many places, a "rud" to-day, reverting picturesquely into the forest trail over which the early inland settlers rode their horses or drove their oxen with up-country produce to the sea. They were not a people who sought the easiest way, and the Boston Road reflects their characters: few valleys are deep enough to turn it aside, few mountains can appal it: railroads have given it a wide berth. Here and there the forest opens out to reveal, on a knoll or "flat," a forgotten village or tavern-stand. Over the high shelf of Washington Town it runs where the air is keen and the lakes are blue, where long-stemmed wild flowers nod on its sunny banks, to reach at length the rounded, classic hills and sentinel mountain that mark the sheep country of the Connecticut. . . .

2

It was before Janet's convalescence began that Mrs. Maturin had consulted Insall concerning her proposed experiment in literature. Afterwards he had left Silliston for a lumber camp on a remote river in northern Maine, abruptly to reappear, on a mild afternoon late in April, in Augusta Maturin's garden. The crocuses and tulips were in bloom, and his friend, in a gardening apron, was on her knees, trowel in hand, assisting a hired man to set out marigolds and snapdragons.

"Well, it's time you were home again," she exclaimed, as she rose to greet him and led him to a chair on the little flagged terrace beside the windows of her library. "I've got so much to tell you about our invalid."

"Our invalid!" Insall retorted.

"Of course. I look to you to divide the responsibility with me, and you've shirked by running off to Maine. You found her, you know — and she's really remarkable."

"Now see here, Augusta, you can't expect me to share the guardianship of an attractive and — well, a dynamic young woman. If she affects you this way, what will she do to me? I'm much too susceptible."

"Susceptible!" she scoffed. "But you can't get out of it. I need you. I've never been so interested and so perplexed in my life."

"How is she?" Insall asked.

"Frankly, I'm worried," said Mrs. Maturin. "At first she seemed to be getting along beautifully. I read to her, a little every day, and it was wonderful how she responded to it. I'll tell you about that — I've got so much to tell you! Young Dr. Trent is puzzled, too, it seems there are symptoms in the case for which he cannot account. Some three weeks ago he asked me what I made out of her, and I can't make anything — that's the trouble, except that she seems pathetically grateful, and that I've grown absurdly fond of her. But she isn't improving as fast as she should, and Dr. Trent doesn't know whether or not to suspect functional complications. Her constitution seems excellent, her vitality unusual. Trent's impressed by her, he inclines to the theory that she has something on her mind, and if this is so she should get rid of it, tell it to somebody — in short, tell it to me. I know she's fond of me, but she's so maddeningly self-contained, and at moments when I look at her she baffles me, she makes me feel like an atom. Twenty times at least I've almost screwed up my courage to ask her, but when it comes to the point, I simply can't do it."

"You ought to be able to get at it, if any one can," said Insall.

"I've a notion it may be connected with the strike," Augusta Maturin continued. "I never could account for her being mixed up in that, plunging into Syndicalism. It seemed so foreign to her nature. I wish I'd waited a little longer before telling her about the strike, but one day she asked me how it had come out — and she seemed to be getting along so nicely I didn't see any reason for not telling her. I said that the strike was over, that the mill-owners had accepted the I.W.W. terms, but that Antonelli and Jastro had been sent to jail and were awaiting trial

because they had been accused of instigating the murder of
a woman who was shot by a striker aiming at a policeman. It seems that she had seen that! She told me so
quite casually. But she was interested, and I went on to
mention how greatly the strikers were stirred by the arrests,
how they paraded in front of the jail, singing, and how the
feeling was mostly directed against Mr. Ditmar, because he
was accused of instigating the placing of dynamite in the
tenements."

"And you spoke of Mr. Ditmar's death?" Insall inquired.

"Why yes, I told her how he had been shot in Dover
Street by a demented Italian, and if it hadn't been proved
that the Italian was insane and not a mill worker, the result
of the strike might have been different."

"How did she take it?"

"Well, she was shocked, of course. She sat up in bed,
staring at me, and then leaned back on the pillows again.
I pretended not to notice it — but I was sorry I'd said anything about it."

"She didn't say anything?"

"Not a word."

"Didn't you know that, before the strike, she was Ditmar's private stenographer?"

"No!" Augusta Maturin exclaimed. "Why didn't you
tell me?"

"It never occurred to me to tell you," Insall replied.

"That must have something to do with it!" said Mrs.
Maturin.

Insall got up and walked to the end of the terrace, gazing at a bluebird on the edge of the lawn.

"Well, not necessarily," he said, after a while. "Did you
ever find out anything about her family?"

"Oh, yes, I met the father once, he's been out two or
three times, on Sunday, and came over here to thank me

for what I'd done.   The mother doesn't come — she has some trouble, I don't know exactly what.   Brooks, I wish you could see the father, he's so typically unique — if one may use the expression.   A gatekeeper at the Chippering Mills!"

"A gatekeeper?"

"Yes, and I'm quite sure he doesn't understand to this day how he became one, or why.   He's delightfully naïve on the subject of genealogy, and I had the Bumpus family by heart before he left.   That's the form his remnant of the intellectual curiosity of his ancestors takes.   He was born in Dolton, which was settled by the original Bumpus, back in the Plymouth Colony days, and if he were rich he'd have a library stuffed with gritty, yellow-backed books and be a leading light in the Historical Society.   He speaks with that nicety of pronunciation of the old New Englander, never slurring his syllables, and he has a really fine face, the kind of face one doesn't often see nowadays.   I kept looking at it, wondering what was the matter with it, and at last I realized what it lacked — will, desire, ambition, — it was what a second-rate sculptor might have made of Bradford, for instance.   But there is a remnant of fire in him.   Once, when he spoke of the strike, of the foreigners, he grew quite indignant."

"He didn't tell you why his daughter had joined the strikers?" Insall asked.

"He was just as much at sea about that as you and I are.   Of course I didn't ask him — he asked me if I knew. It's only another proof of her amazing reticence.   And I can imagine an utter absence of sympathy between them. He accounts for her, of course; he's probably the unconscious transmitter of qualities the Puritans possessed and tried to smother.   Certainly the fires are alight in her, and yet it's almost incredible that he should have conveyed them. Of course I haven't seen the mother."

"It's curious he didn't mention her having been Ditmar's stenographer," Insall put in. "Was that reticence?"

"I hardly think so," Augusta Maturin replied. "It may have been, but the impression I got was of an incapacity to feel the present. All his emotions are in the past, most of his conversation was about Bumpuses who are dead and buried, and his pride in Janet — for he has a pride — seems to exist because she is *their* representative. It's extraordinary, but he sees her present situation, her future, with extraordinary optimism; he apparently regards her coming to Silliston, even in the condition in which we found her, as a piece of deserved fortune for which she has to thank some virtue inherited from her ancestors! Well, perhaps he's right. If she were not unique, I shouldn't want to keep her here. It's pure selfishness. I told Mr. Bumpus I expected to find work for her."

Mrs. Maturin returned Insall's smile. "I suppose you're too polite to say that I'm carried away by my enthusiasms. But you will at least do me the justice to admit that they are rare and — discriminating, as a connoisseur's should be. I think even you will approve of her."

"Oh, I have approved of her — that's the trouble."

Mrs. Maturin regarded him for a moment in silence.

"I wish you could have seen her when I began to read those verses of Stevenson's. It was an inspiration, your thinking of them."

"Did I think of them?"

"You know you did. You can't escape your responsibility. Well, I felt like — like a gambler, as though I were staking everything on a throw. And, after I began, as if I were playing on some rare instrument. She lay there, listening, without uttering a word, but somehow she seemed to be interpreting them for me, giving them a meaning and a beauty I hadn't imagined. Another time I told her about

Silliston, and how this little community for over a century
and a half had tried to keep its standard flying, to carry
on the work begun by old Andrew, and I thought of those
lines,

> 'Other little children
> Shall bring my boats ashore.'

That particular application just suddenly occurred to me,
but she inspired it."

"You're a born schoolma'am," Insall laughed.

"I'm much too radical for a schoolma'am," she declared.
"No board of trustees would put up with me — not even
Silliston's! We've kept the faith, but we do move slowly,
Brooks. Even tradition grows, and sometimes our blindness
here to changes, to modern, scientific facts, fairly maddens
me. I read her that poem of Moody's — you know it : —

> 'Here, where the moors stretch free
> In the high blue afternoon,
> Are the marching sun and the talking sea.'

and those last lines : —

> 'But thou, vast outbound ship of souls,
> What harbour town for thee?
> What shapes, when thy arriving tolls,
> Shall crowd the banks to see?
> Shall all the happy shipmates then
> Stand singing brotherly?
> Or shall a haggard, ruthless few
> Warp her over and bring her to,
> While the many broken souls of me
> Fester down in the slaver's pen,
> And nothing to say or do?'

I was sorry afterwards, I could see that she was tremen-
dously excited. And she made me feel as if I, too, had been
battened down in that hold and bruised and almost strangled.
I often wonder whether she *has* got out of it into the light
— whether we can rescue her." Mrs. Maturin paused.

2 F

"What do you mean?" Insall asked.

"Well, it's difficult to describe, what I feel — she's such a perplexing mixture of old New England and modernity, of a fatalism, and an aliveness that fairly vibrates. At first, when she began to recover, I was conscious only of the vitality — but lately I feel the other quality. It isn't exactly the old Puritan fatalism, or even the Greek, it's oddly modern, too, almost agnostic, I should say, — a calm acceptance of the hazards of life, of nature, of sun and rain and storm alike — very different from the cheap optimism one finds everywhere now. She isn't exactly resigned — I don't say that — I know she can be rebellious. And she's grateful for the sun, yet she seems to have a conviction that the clouds will gather again. . . .   The doctor says she may leave the hospital on Monday, and I'm going to bring her over here for awhile. Then," she added insinuatingly, "we can collaborate."

"I think I'll go back to Maine," Insall exclaimed.

"If you desert me, I shall never speak to you again," said Mrs. Maturin.

3

"Janet," said Mrs. Maturin the next day, as she laid down the book from which she was reading, "do you remember that I spoke to you once in Hampton of coming here to Silliston? Well, now we've got you here, we don't want to lose you. I've been making inquiries; quite a number of the professors have typewriting to be done, and they will be glad to give their manuscripts to you instead of sending them to Boston. And there's Brooks Insall too — if he ever takes it into his head to write another book. You wouldn't have any trouble reading his manuscript, it's like script. Of course it has to be copied. You can board with Mrs. Case — I've arranged that, too. But on Monday I'm going to take you to my house, and keep you until you're strong enough to walk."

Janet's eyes were suddenly bright with tears.

"You'll stay?"

"I can't," answered Janet. "I couldn't."

"But why not? Have you any other plans?"

"No, I haven't any plans, but — I haven't the right to stay here." Presently she raised her face to her friend. "Oh Mrs. Maturin, I'm so sorry! I didn't want to bring any sadness here — it's all so bright and beautiful! And now I've made you sad!"

It was a moment before Augusta Maturin could answer her.

"What are friends for, Janet," she asked, "if not to share sorrow with? And do you suppose there's any place, however bright, where sorrow has not come? Do you think I've not known it, too? And Janet, I haven't sat here all these days with you without guessing that something worries you. I've been waiting, all this time, for you to tell me, in order that I might help you."

"I wanted to," said Janet, "every day I wanted to, but I couldn't. I couldn't bear to trouble you with it, I didn't mean ever to tell you. And then — it's so terrible, I don't know what you'll think."

"I think I know you, Janet," answered Mrs. Maturin. "Nothing human, nothing natural is terrible, in the sense you mean. At least I'm one of those who believe so."

Presently Janet said, "I'm going to have a child."

Mrs. Maturin sat very still. Something closed in her throat, preventing her immediate reply.

"I, too, had a child, my dear," she answered. "I lost her." She felt the girl's clasp tighten on her fingers.

"But you — you had a right to it — you were married."

"Children are sacred things," said Augusta Maturin.

Sacred! Could it be that a woman like Mrs. Maturin thought that this child which was coming to her was sacred, too?

"However they come?" asked Janet. "Oh, I tried to believe that, too! At first — at first I didn't want it, and when I knew it was coming I was driven almost crazy. And then, all at once, when I was walking in the rain, I knew I wanted it to have — to keep all to myself. You understand?"

Augusta Maturin inclined her head.

"But the father?" she managed to ask, after a moment. "I don't wish to pry, my dear, but does he — does he realize? Can't he help you?"

"It was Mr. Ditmar."

"Perhaps it will help you to tell me about it, Janet."

"I'd — I'd like to. I've been so unhappy since you told me he was dead — and I felt like a cheat. You see, he promised to marry me, and I know now that he loved me, that he really wanted to marry me, but something happened to make me believe he wasn't going to, I saw — another girl who'd got into trouble, and then I thought he'd only been playing with me, and I couldn't stand it. I joined the strikers — I just had to do something."

Augusta Maturin nodded, and waited.

"I was only a stenographer, and we were very poor, and he was rich and lived in a big house, the most important man in Hampton. It seemed too good to be true — I suppose I never really thought it could happen. Please don't think I'm putting all the blame on him, Mrs. Maturin — it was my fault just as much as his. I ought to have gone away from Hampton, but I didn't have the strength. And I shouldn't have —" Janet stopped.

"But — you loved him?"

"Yes, I did. For a long time, after I left him, I thought I didn't, I thought I hated him, and when I found out what had happened to me — that night I came to you — I got my father's pistol and went to the mill to shoot him. I was going to shoot myself, too."

"Oh!" Mrs. Maturin gasped. She gave a quick glance of sheer amazement at Janet, who did not seem to notice it; who was speaking objectively, apparently with no sense of the drama in her announcement.

"But I couldn't," she went on. "At the time I didn't know why I couldn't, but when I went out I understood it was because I wanted the child, because it was his child. And though he was almost out of his head, he seemed so glad because I'd come back to him, and said he'd marry me right away."

"And you refused!" exclaimed Mrs. Maturin.

"Well, you see, I was out of my head, too, I still thought I hated him — but I'd loved him all the time. It was funny! He had lots of faults, and he didn't seem to understand or care much about how poor people feel, though he was kind to them in the mills. He might have come to understand — I don't know — it wasn't because he didn't want to, but because he was so separated from them, I guess, and he was so interested in what he was doing. He had ambition, he thought everything of that mill, he'd made it. I don't know why I loved him, it wasn't because he was fine, like Mr. Insall, but he was strong and brave, and he needed me and just took me."

"One never knows!" Augusta Maturin murmured.

"I went back that night to tell him I'd marry him — and he'd gone. Then I came to you, to the soup kitchen. I didn't mean to bother you, I've never quite understood how I got there. I don't care so much what happens to me, now that I've told you," Janet added. "It was mean, not to tell you, but I'd never had anything like this — what you were giving me — and I wanted all I could get."

"I'm thankful you did come to us!" Augusta Maturin managed to reply.

"You mean —?" Janet exclaimed.

"I mean, that we who have been more — fortunate don't look at these things quite as we used to, that the world is less censorious, is growing to understand situations it formerly condemned. And — I don't know what kind of a monster you supposed me to be, Janet."

"Oh, Mrs. Maturin!"

"I mean that I'm a woman, too, my dear, although my life has been sheltered. Otherwise, what has happened to you might have happened to me. And besides, I am what is called unconventional, I have little theories of my own about life, and now that you have told me everything I understand you and love you even more than I did before."

Save that her breath came fast, Janet lay still against the cushions of the armchair. She was striving to grasp the momentous and unlooked-for fact of her friend's unchanged attitude. Then she asked : —

"Mrs. Maturin, do you believe in God?"

Augusta Maturin was startled by the question. "I like to think of Him as light, Janet, and that we are plants seeking to grow toward Him — no matter from what dark crevice we may spring. Even in our mistakes and sins we are seeking Him, for these are ignorances, and as the world learns more, we shall know Him better and better. It is natural to long for happiness, and happiness is self-realization, and self-realization is knowledge and light."

"That is beautiful," said Janet at length.

"It is all we can know about God," said Mrs. Maturin, "but it is enough." She had been thinking rapidly. "And now," she went on, "we shall have to consider what is to be done. I don't pretend that the future will be easy, but it will not be nearly as hard for you as it might have been,

since I am your friend, and I do not intend to desert you.
I'm sure you will not let it crush you. In the first place,
you will have something to go on with — mental resources,
I mean, for which you have a natural craving, books and
art and nature, the best thoughts and the best interpretations.
We can give you these. And you will have your child, and
work to do, for I'm sure you're industrious. And of course
I'll keep your secret, my dear."

"But — how?" Janet exclaimed.

"I've arranged it all. You'll stay here this spring, you'll
come to my house on Monday, just as we planned, and later
on you may go to Mrs. Case's, if it will make you feel more
independent, and do typewriting until the spring term is
over. I've told you about my little camp away up in
Canada, in the heart of the wilderness, where I go in summer. We'll stay there until the autumn, until your baby
comes, and, after that, I know it won't be difficult to get you
a position in the west, where you can gain your living and
have your child. I have a good friend in California who I'm
sure will help you. And even if your secret should eventually
be discovered — which is not probable — you will have
earned respect, and society is not as stern as it used to be.
And you will always have me for a friend. There, that's
the bright side of it. Of course it isn't a bed of roses, but
I've lived long enough to observe that the people who lie on
roses don't always have the happiest lives. Whenever you
want help and advice, I shall always be here, and from
time to time I'll be seeing you. Isn't that sensible?"

"Oh, Mrs. Maturin — if you really want me — still?"

"I do want you, Janet, even more than I did — before,
because you need me more," Mrs. Maturin replied, with a
sincerity that could not fail to bring conviction. . . .

CHAPTER XXI

1

As the spring progressed, Janet grew stronger, became well again, and through the kindness of Dr. Ledyard, the principal, was presently installed with a typewriter in a little room in an old building belonging to the Academy in what was called Bramble Street, and not far from the Common. Here, during the day, she industriously copied manuscripts or, from her notebook, letters dictated by various members of the faculty. And she was pleased when they exclaimed delightedly at the flawless copies and failed to suspect her of frequent pilgrimages to the dictionary in the library in order to familiarize herself with the meaning and manner of spelling various academic words. At first it was almost bewildering to find herself in some degree thus sharing the Silliston community life; and an unpremeditated attitude toward these learned ones, high priests of the muses she had so long ignorantly worshipped, accounted perhaps for a great deal in their attitude toward her. Her fervour, repressed yet palpable, was like a flame burning before their altars — a flattery to which the learned, being human, are quick to respond. Besides, something of her history was known, and she was of a type to incite a certain amount of interest amongst these discerning ones. Often, after she had taken their dictation, or brought their manuscripts home, they detained her in conversation. In short, Silliston gave its approval to this particular experiment of Augusta Maturin. As for Mrs. Maturin herself, her feeling was one of controlled pride not unmixed with concern, always conscious as she was of the hidden element of tragedy in the play she had so lovingly staged. Not that she had any compunction in keeping Janet's secret, even from Insall; but sometimes as she contemplated it the strings of her heart grew tight. Silliston was so obviously where Janet belonged, she could not bear the thought of the girl going out again from this sheltered spot into a chaotic world of smoke and struggle.

Janet's own feelings were a medley. It was not, of course, contentment she knew continually, nor even peace, although there were moments when these stole over her. There were moments, despite her incredible good fortune, of apprehension when she shrank from the future, when fear assailed her; moments of intense sadness at the thought of leaving her friends, of leaving this enchanted place now that miraculously she had found it; moments of stimulation, of exaltation, when she forgot. Her prevailing sense, as she found herself again, was of thankfulness and gratitude, of determination to take advantage of, to drink in all of this wonderful experience, lest any precious memory be lost.

Like a jewel gleaming with many facets, each sunny day was stored and treasured. As she went from Mrs. Case's boarding-house forth to her work, the sweet, sharp air of these spring mornings was filled with delicious smells of new things, of new flowers and new grass and tender, new leaves of myriad shades, bronze and crimson, fuzzy white, primrose, and emerald green. And sometimes it seemed as though the pink and white clouds of the little orchards were wafted into swooning scents. She loved best the moment when the Common came in view, when through the rows of elms the lineaments of those old houses rose before her, lineaments seemingly long familiar, as of old and trusted friends, and yet ever stirring new harmonies and new visions. Here, in their midst, she belonged, and here, had the world been otherwise ordained, she might have lived on in one continuous, shining spring. At the corner of the Common, foursquare, ample, painted a straw colour trimmed with white, with its high chimneys and fan-shaped stairway window, its balustraded terrace porch open to the sky, was the eighteenth century mansion occupied by Dr. Ledyard. What was the secret of its flavour? And how account for the sense of harmony inspired by another dwelling, built during the term of the second Adams, set in a frame of maples and shining white in the morning sun? Its curved portico was capped by a wrought-iron railing, its long windows were touched with purple, and its low garret — set like a deckhouse on the wide roof — suggested hidden secrets of the past. Here a Motley or a Longfellow might have dwelt, a Bryant penned his "Thanatopsis." Farther on, chequered by shade, stood the quaint brick row of professors' houses, with sloping eaves and recessed entrances of granite — a subject for an old English print. . . . Along the border of the Common were interspersed among the ancient dormitories and halls the new and dignified buildings of plum-coloured brick that still preserved the soul of Silliston. And to it the soul of Janet responded.

In the late afternoon, when her tasks were finished, Janet would cross the Common to Mrs. Maturin's — a dwelling typical of the New England of the past, with the dimensions of a cottage and something of the dignity of a mansion. Fluted white pilasters adorned the corners, the windows were protected by tiny eaves, the roof was guarded by a rail; the classically porched entrance was approached by a path between high clipped hedges of hemlock; and through the library, on the right, you reached the flagged terrace beside a garden, rioting in the carnival colours of spring. By September it would have changed. For there is one glory of the hyacinth, of the tulip and narcissus and the jonquil, and another of the Michaelmas daisy and the aster.

Insall was often there, and on Saturdays and Sundays he took Mrs. Maturin and Janet on long walks into the country. There were afternoons when the world was flooded with silver light, when the fields were lucent in the sun; and afternoons stained with blue, — the landscape like a tapestry woven in delicate greens on a ground of indigo. The arbutus, all aglow and fragrant beneath its leaves, the purple fringed polygala were past, but they found the pale gold lily of the bellwort, the rust-red bloom of the ginger. In the open spaces under the sky were clouds of bluets, wild violets, and white strawberry flowers clustering beside the star moss all ashimmer with new green. The Canada Mayflower spread a carpet under the pines; and in the hollows where the mists settled, where the brooks flowed, where the air was heavy with the damp, ineffable odour of growing things, they gathered drooping adder's-tongues, white-starred bloodroots and foam-flowers. From Insall's quick eye nothing seemed to escape. He would point out to them the humming-bird that hovered, a bright blur, above the columbine, the woodpecker glued to the trunk of a maple high above their heads, the red gleam of a tanager flashing through sunlit foliage, the oriole and vireo where they hid. And his was the ear that first caught the exquisite, distant note of the hermit. Once he stopped them, startled, to listen to the cock partridge drumming to its mate. . . .

Sometimes, of an evening, when Janet was helping Mrs. Maturin in her planting or weeding, Insall would join them, rolling up the sleeves of his flannel shirt and kneeling beside them in the garden paths. Mrs. Maturin was forever asking his advice, though she did not always follow it.

"Now, Brooks," she would say, "you've just got to suggest something to put in that border to replace the hyacinths.

I had larkspur last year — you remember — and it looked like a chromo in a railroad folder."

"Let me see — did I advise larkspur?" he would ask.

"Oh, I'm sure you must have — I always do what you tell me. It seems to me I've thought of every possible flower in the catalogue. You *know*, too, only you're so afraid of committing yourself."

Insall's comic spirit, betrayed by his expressions, by the quizzical intonations of his voice, never failed to fill Janet with joy, while it was somehow suggestive, too, of the vast fund of his resource. Mrs. Maturin was right, he could have solved many of her questions offhand if he had so wished, but he had his own method of dealing with appeals. His head tilted on one side, apparently in deep thought over the problem, he never answered outright, but by some process of suggestion unfathomable to Janet, and by eliminating, not too deprecatingly, Mrs. Maturin's impatient proposals, brought her to a point where she blurted out the solution herself.

"Oriental poppies! How stupid of me not to think of them!"

"How stupid of *me!*" Insall echoed — and Janet, bending over her weeding, made sure they had been in his mind all the while.

Augusta Maturin's chief extravagance was books; she could not bear to await her turn at the library, and if she liked a book she wished to own it. Subscribing to several reviews, three English and one American, she scanned them eagerly every week and sent in orders to her Boston bookseller. As a consequence the carved walnut racks on her library table were constantly being strained. A good book, she declared, ought to be read aloud, and discussed even during its perusal. And thus Janet, after an elementary and decidedly unique introduction to worth-while literature in the hospital, was suddenly plunged into the vortex of modern thought. The dictum Insall quoted, that modern culture depended largely upon what one had not read, was applied to her; a child of the new environment fallen into skilful hands, she was spared the boredom of wading through the so-called classics which, though useful as milestones, as landmarks for future reference, are largely mere reminders of an absolute universe now vanished. The arrival of a novel, play, or treatise by one of that small but growing nucleus of twentieth century seers was an event, and often a volume begun in the afternoon was taken up again after supper. While Mrs. Maturin sat sewing on the other side of the lamp, Janet had her turn at reading. From the first she had been quick to note Mrs. Maturin's inflections, and the relics of a high-school manner were rapidly eliminated. The essence of latter-day realism and pragmatism, its courageous determination to tear away a veil of which she had always been dimly aware, to look the facts of human nature in the face, refreshed her : an increasing portion of it she understood ; and she was constantly under the spell of the excitement that partially grasps, that hovers on the verge of inspiring discoveries. This excitement, whenever Insall chanced to be present, was intensified, as she sat a silent but often quivering listener to his amusing and pungent comments on these new ideas. His method of discussion never failed to illuminate and delight her, and often, when she sat at her typewriter the next day, she would recall one of his quaint remarks that suddenly threw a bright light on some matter hitherto obscure. . . . Occasionally a novel or a play was the subject of their talk, and then they took a delight in drawing her out, in appealing to a spontaneous judgment unhampered by pedagogically implanted preconceptions. Janet would grow hot from shyness.

"Say what you think, my dear," Mrs. Maturin would urge her. "And remember that your own opinion is worth more than Shakespeare's or Napoleon's!"

Insall would escort her home to Mrs. Case's boarding house. . . .

2

One afternoon early in June Janet sat in her little room working at her letters when Brooks Insall came in. "I don't mean to intrude in business hours, but I wanted to ask if you would do a little copying for me," he said, and he laid on her desk a parcel bound with characteristic neatness.

"Something you've written?" she exclaimed, blushing with pleasure and surprise. He was actually confiding to her one of his manuscripts!

"Well — yes," he replied comically, eyeing her.

"I'll be very careful with it. I'll do it right away."

"There's no particular hurry," he assured her. "The editor's waited six months for it — another month or so won't matter."

"Another month or so!" she ejaculated, — but he was gone. Of course she couldn't have expected him to remain and talk about it; but this unexpected exhibition of shyness concerning his work — so admired by the world's choicer spirits — thrilled yet amused her, and made her glow with a new understanding. With eager fingers she undid the string and sat staring at the regular script without taking in, at first, the meaning of a single sentence. It was a comparatively short sketch entitled "The Exile," in which shining, winged truths and elusive beauties flitted continually against a dark background of Puritan oppression; the story of one Basil Grelott, a dreamer of Milton's day, Oxford nurtured, who, casting off the shackles of dogma and man-made decrees, sailed with his books to the New England wilderness across the sea. There he lived, among the savages, in peace and freedom until the arrival of Winthrop and his devotees, to encounter persecution from those who themselves had fled from it. The Lord's Brethren, he averred, were worse than the Lord's Bishops — Blackstone's phrase. Janet, of course, had never heard of Blackstone, some of whose experiences Insall had evidently used. And the Puritans dealt with Grelott even as they would have served the author of "Paradise Lost" himself, especially if he had voiced among them the opinions set forth in his pamphlet on divorce. A portrait of a stern divine with his infallible Book gave Janet a vivid conception of the character of her ancestors; and early Boston, with yellow candlelight gleaming from the lantern-like windows of the wooden, Elizabethan houses, was unforgettably etched. There was an inquisition in a freezing barn of a church, and Basil Grelott banished to perish amid the forest in his renewed quest for freedom. . . . After reading the manuscript, Janet sat typewriting into the night, taking it home with her and placing it beside her bed, lest it be lost to posterity. By five the next evening she had finished the copy.

A gentle rain had fallen during the day, but had ceased as she made her way toward Insall's house. The place was familiar now: she had been there to supper with Mrs. Maturin, a supper cooked and served by Martha Vesey, an elderly, efficient and appallingly neat widow, whom Insall had discovered somewhere in his travels and installed as his housekeeper. Janet paused with her hand on the gate latch to gaze around her, at the picket fence on which he had been working when she had walked hither the year before. It was primly painted now, its posts crowned with the carved pineapples; behind the fence old-fashioned flowers were in bloom, lupins and false indigo; and the retaining wall of blue-grey slaty stone, which he had laid that spring, was finished. A wind stirred the maple, releasing a shower of heavy drops, and she opened the gate and went up the path and knocked at the door. There was no response — even Martha must be absent, in the village! Janet was disappointed, she had looked forward to seeing him, to telling him how great had been her pleasure in the story he had written, at the same time doubting her courage to do so. She had never been able to speak to him about his work — and what did her opinion matter to him? As she turned away the stillness was broken by a humming sound gradually rising to a crescendo, so she ventured slowly around the house and into the orchard of gnarled apple trees on the slope until she came in sight of a little white building beside the brook. The weathervane perched on the gable, and veering in the wet breeze, seemed like a live fish swimming in its own element; and through the open window she saw Insall bending over a lathe, from which the chips were flying. She hesitated. Then he looked up, and seeing her, reached above his head to pull the lever that shut off the power.

"Come in," he called out, and met her at the doorway. He was dressed in a white duck shirt, open at the neck, and a pair of faded corduroy trousers. "I wasn't looking for this honour," he told her, with a gesture of self-deprecation, "or I'd have put on a dinner coat."

And, despite her eagerness and excitement, she laughed.

"I didn't dare to leave this in the house," she explained. "Mrs. Vesey wasn't home. And I thought you might be here."

"You haven't made the copy already!"

"Oh, I loved doing it!" she replied, and paused, flushing. She might have known that it would be simply impossible to talk to him about it! So she laid it down on the work-bench, and, overcome by a sudden shyness, retreated toward the door.

"You're not going!" he exclaimed.

"I must — and you're busy."

"Not at all," he declared, "not at all, I was just killing time until supper. Sit down!" And he waved her to a magisterial-looking chair of Jacobean design, with turned legs, sandpapered and immaculate, that stood in the middle of the shop.

"Oh, not in that!" Janet protested. "And besides, I'd spoil it — I'm sure my skirt is wet."

But he insisted, thrusting it under her. "You've come along just in time, I wanted a woman to test it — men are no judges of chairs. There's a vacuum behind the small of your back, isn't there? Augusta will have to put a cushion in it."

"Did you make it for Mrs. Maturin? She will be pleased!" exclaimed Janet, as she sat down. "I don't think it's uncomfortable."

"I copied it from an old one in the Boston Art Museum. Augusta saw it there, and said she wouldn't be happy until she had one like it. But don't tell her."

"Not for anything!" Janet got to her feet again. "I really must be going."

"Going where?"

"I told Mrs. Maturin I'd read that new book to her. I couldn't go yesterday — I didn't want to go," she added, fearing he might think his work had kept her.

"Well, I'll walk over with you. She asked me to make a little design for a fountain, you know, and I'll have to get some measurements."

As they emerged from the shop and climbed the slope Janet tried to fight off the sadness that began to invade her. Soon she would have to be leaving all this! Her glance

2 G

lingered wistfully on the old farmhouse with its great centre chimney from which the smoke was curling, with its diamond-paned casements Insall had put into the tiny frames.

"What queer windows!" she said. "But they seem to go with the house, beautifully."

"You think so?" His tone surprised her; it had a touch more of earnestness than she had ever before detected. "They belong to that type of house — the old settlers brought the leaded glass with them. Some people think they're cold, but I've arranged to make them fairly tight. You see, I've tried to restore it as it must have been when it was built."

"And these?" she asked, pointing to the millstones of different diameters that made the steps leading down to the garden.

"Oh, that's an old custom, but they are nice," he agreed. "I'll just put this precious manuscript inside and get my foot rule," he added, opening the door, and she stood awaiting him on the threshold, confronted by the steep little staircase that disappeared into the wall half way up. At her left was the room where he worked, and which once had been the farmhouse kitchen. She took a few steps into it, and while he was searching in the table drawer she halted before the great chimney over which, against the panel, an old bell-mouthed musket hung. Insall came over beside her.

"Those were trees!" he said. "That panel's over four feet across, I measured it once. I dare say the pine it was cut from grew right where we are standing, before the land was cleared to build the house."

"But the gun?" she questioned. "You didn't have it the night we came to supper."

"No, I ran across it at a sale in Boston. The old settler

must have owned one like that.   I like to think of him, away off here in the wilderness in those early days."

She thought of how Insall had made those early days live for her, in his story of Basil Grelott.   But to save her soul, even with such an opening, she could not speak of it.

"He had to work pretty hard, of course," Insall continued, "but I dare say he had a fairly happy life, no movies, no Sunday supplements, no automobiles or gypsy moths.   His only excitement was to trudge ten miles to Dorset and listen to a three hour sermon on everlasting fire and brimstone by a man who was supposed to know.   No wonder he slept soundly and lived to be over ninety!"

Insall was standing with his head thrown back, his eyes still seemingly fixed on the musket that had suggested his remark — a pose eloquent, she thought, of the mental and physical balance of the man.   She wondered what belief gave him the free mastery of soul and body he possessed. Some firm conviction, she was sure, must energize him — yet she respected him the more for concealing it.

"It's hard to understand such a terrible religion!" she cried.   "I don't see how those old settlers could believe in it, when there are such beautiful things in the world, if we only open our eyes and look for them.   Oh Mr. Insall, I wish I could tell you how I felt when I read your story, and when Mrs. Maturin read me those other books of yours!"

She stopped breathlessly, aghast at her boldness — and then, suddenly, a barrier between them seemed to break down, and for the first time since she had known him she felt near to him.   He could not doubt the sincerity of her tribute.

"You like them as much as that, Janet?" he said, looking at her.

"I can't tell you how much, I can't express myself.   And I want to tell you something else, Mr. Insall, while I have

the chance — how just being with you and Mrs. Maturin
has changed me. I can face life now, you have shown me
so much in it I never saw before."

"While you have the chance?" he repeated.

"Yes." She strove to go on cheerfully, "Now I've
said it, I feel better, I promise not to mention it again.
I knew — you didn't think me ungrateful. It's funny,"
she added, "the more people have done for you — when
they've given you everything, life and hope, — the harder
it is to thank them." She turned her face away, lest he
might see that her eyes were wet. "Mrs. Maturin will be
expecting us."

"Not yet," she heard him say, and felt his hand on her
arm. "You haven't thought of what you're doing for me."

"What I'm doing for you!" she echoed. "What hurts
me most, when I think about it, is that I'll never be able to
do anything."

"Why do you say that?" he asked.

"If I only could believe that some day I might be able to
help you — just a little — I should be happier. All I have,
all I am I owe to you and Mrs. Maturin."

"No, Janet," he answered. "What you are is *you*, —
and it's more real than anything we could have put into you.
What you have to give is — yourself." His fingers trembled
on her arm, but she saw him smile a little before he spoke
again. "Augusta Maturin was right when she said that
you were the woman I needed. I didn't realize it then —
perhaps she didn't — but now I'm sure of it. Will you
come to me?"

She stood staring at him, as in terror, suddenly penetrated by a dismay that sapped her strength, and she leaned
heavily against the fireplace, clutching the mantel-shelf.

"Don't!" she pleaded. "Please don't — I can't."

"You can't! . . . Perhaps, after a while, you may

come to feel differently — I didn't mean to startle you,"
she heard him reply gently. This humility, in him, was
unbearable.

"Oh, it isn't that — it isn't that! If I could, I'd be willing to serve you all my life — I wouldn't ask for anything
more. I never thought that this would happen. I oughtn't
to have stayed in Silliston."

"You didn't suspect that I loved you?"

"How could I? Oh, I might have loved you, if I'd been
fortunate — if I'd deserved it. But I never thought, I
always looked up to you — you are so far above me!"
She lifted her face to him in agony. "I'm sorry — I'm
sorry for you — I'll never forgive myself!"

"It's — some one else?" he asked.

"I was — going to be married to — to Mr. Ditmar," she
said slowly, despairingly.

"But even then —" Insall began.

"You don't understand!" she cried. "What will you
think of me? — Mrs. Maturin was to have told you, after
I'd gone. It's — it's the same as if I were married to him
— only worse."

"Worse!" Insall repeated uncomprehendingly. . . .
And then she was aware that he had left her side. He was
standing by the window.

A thrush began to sing in the maple. She stole silently
toward the door, and paused to look back at him, once —
to meet his glance. He had turned.

"I can't — I can't let you go like this!" she heard him
say, but she fled from him, out of the gate and toward
the Common. . . .

3

When Janet appeared, Augusta Maturin was in her garden. With an instant perception that something was

wrong, she went to the girl and led her to the sofa in the library. There the confession was made.

"I never guessed it," Janet sobbed. "Oh, Mrs. Maturin, you'll believe me — won't you?"

"Of course I believe you, Janet," Augusta Maturin replied, trying to hide her pity, her own profound concern and perplexity. "I didn't suspect it either. If I had —"

"You wouldn't have brought me here, you wouldn't have asked me to stay with you. But I was to blame, I oughtn't to have stayed, I knew all along that something would happen — something terrible — that I hadn't any right to stay."

"Who could have foreseen it!" her friend exclaimed helplessly. "Brooks isn't like any other man I've ever known — one can never tell what he has in mind. Not that I'm surprised as I look back upon it all!"

"I've hurt him!"

Augusta Maturin was silent awhile. "Remember, my dear," she begged, "you haven't only yourself to think about, from now on."

But comfort was out of the question, the task of calming the girl impossible. Finally the doctor was sent for, and she was put to bed. . . .

Augusta Maturin spent an agonized, sleepless night, a prey of many emotions; of self-reproach, seeing now that she had been wrong in not telling Brooks Insall of the girl's secret; of sorrow and sympathy for him; of tenderness toward the girl, despite the suffering she had brought; of unwonted rebellion against a world that cheated her of this cherished human tie for which she had longed — the first that had come into her life since her husband and child had gone. And there was her own responsibility for Insall's unhappiness — when she recalled with a pang her innocent sayings that Janet was the kind of woman he, an artist, should marry! And it was true — if he must marry. He himself had seen it. Did Janet love him? or did she still remember Ditmar? Again and again, during the summer that followed, this query was on her lips, but remained unspoken. . . .

The next day Insall disappeared. No one knew where he had gone, but his friends in Silliston believed he had been seized by one of his sudden, capricious fancies for wandering. For many months his name was not mentioned between Augusta Maturin and Janet. By the middle of June they had gone to Canada. . . .

4

In order to reach the camp on Lac du Sablier from the tiny railroad station at Saint Hubert, a trip of some eight miles up the *décharge* was necessary. The day had been when Augusta Maturin had done her share of paddling and poling, with an habitant guide in the bow. She had foreseen all the needs of this occasion, warm clothes for Janet, who was wrapped in blankets and placed on cushions in the middle of a canoe, while she herself followed in a second, from time to time exclaiming, in a reassuring voice, that one had nothing to fear in the hands of Delphin and Hervé, whom she had known intimately for more than twenty years. It was indeed a wonderful, exciting, and at moments seemingly perilous journey up the forested aisle of the river : at sight of the first roaring reach of rapids Janet held her breath — so incredible did it appear that any human power could impel and guide a boat up the white stairway between the boulders! Was it not courting destruction? Yet she felt a strange, wild delight in the sense of danger, of amazement at the woodsman's eye that found and followed the crystal paths through the waste of foam. . . . There were long, quiet stretches, hemmed in by alders, where the canoes, dodging the fallen trees, glided through the still water. No such silent, exhilarating motion Janet had ever known. Even the dipping paddles made no noise, though sometimes there was a gurgle, as though a fish had broken the water behind them; sometimes, in the shining pools ahead, she saw the trout leap out. At every startling flop Delphin would exclaim: *"Un gros!"* From an upper branch of a spruce a kingfisher darted like an arrow into the water, making a splash like a falling stone. Once, after they had passed through the breach of a beaver dam, Hervé nodded his head toward a mound of twigs by the bank and muttered something. Augusta Maturin laughed.

"Cabane de castor, he says — a beaver cabin. And the beavers made the dam we just passed. Did you notice, Janet, how beautifully clean those logs had been cut by their sharp teeth?"

At moments she conversed rapidly with Delphin in the same patois Janet had heard on the streets of Hampton. How long ago that seemed!

On two occasions, when the falls were sheer, they had to disembark and walk along little portages through the green raspberry bushes. The prints of great hooves in the black silt betrayed where wild animals had paused to drink. They stopped for lunch on a warm rock beside a singing waterfall, and at last they turned an elbow in the stream and with suddenly widened vision beheld the lake's sapphire expanse and the distant circle of hills. *"Les montagnes,"* Hervé called them as he flung out his pipe, and this Janet could translate for herself. Eastward they lay lucent in the afternoon light; westward, behind the generous log camp standing on a natural terrace above the landing, they were in shadow. Here indeed seemed peace, if remoteness, if nature herself might bestow it.

Janet little suspected that special preparations had been

made for her comfort. Early in April, while the wilderness
was still in the grip of winter, Delphin had been summoned
from a far-away lumber camp to Saint Hubert, where several
packing-cases and two rolls of lead pipe from Montreal lay
in a shed beside the railroad siding. He had superintended
the transportation of these, on dog sledges, up the frozen
décharge, accompanied on his last trip by a plumber of sorts
from Beaupré, thirty miles down the line; and between
them they had improvised a bathroom, and attached a
boiler to the range! Only a week before the arrival of
Madame the spring on the hillside above the camp had been
tapped, and the pipe laid securely underground. Besides
this unheard-of luxury for the Lac du Sablier there were
iron beds and mattresses and little wood stoves to go in the
four bedrooms, which were more securely chinked with
moss. The traditions of that camp had been hospitable.
In Professor Wishart's day many guests had come and
gone, or pitched their tents nearby; and Augusta Maturin,
until this summer, had rarely been here alone, although she
had no fears of the wilderness, and Delphin brought his
daughter Delphine to do the housework and cooking. The
land for miles round about was owned by a Toronto capitalist who had been a friend of her father, and who could
afford as a hobby the sparing of the forest. By his permission a few sportsmen came to fish or shoot, and occasionally
their campfires could be seen across the water, starlike
glows in the darkness of the night, at morning and evening
little blue threads of smoke that rose against the forest;
"*bocane,*" Delphin called it, and Janet found a sweet,
strange magic in these words of the pioneer.

The lake was a large one, shaped like an hourglass, as its
name implied, and Augusta Maturin sometimes paddled
Janet through the wide, shallow channel to the northern
end, even as she had once paddled Gifford. Her genius was

for the helpless.   One day, when the waters were high, and the portages could be dispensed with, they made an excursion through the Rivière des Pères to the lake of that name, the next in the chain above.   For luncheon they ate the trout Augusta caught; and in the afternoon, when they returned to the mouth of the outlet, Hervé, softly checking the canoe with his paddle, whispered the word *"Arignal!"* Thigh deep in the lush grasses of the swamp was an animal with a huge grey head, like a donkey's, staring foolishly in their direction — a cow moose.   With a tremendous commotion that awoke echoes in the forest she tore herself from the mud and disappeared, followed by her panic-stricken offspring, a caricature of herself. . . .

By September the purple fireweed that springs up beside old camps, and in the *bois brulé*, had bloomed and scattered its myriad, impalpable thistledowns over crystal floors. Autumn came to the Laurentians.   In the morning the lake lay like a quicksilver pool under the rising mists, through which the sun struck blinding flashes of light.   A little later, when the veil had lifted, it became a mirror for the hills and crags, the blue reaches of the sky.   The stinging air was spiced with balsam.   Revealed was the incredible brilliance of another day, — the arsenic-green of the spruce, the red and gold of the maples, the yellow of the alders bathing in the shallows, of the birches, whose white limbs could be seen gleaming in the twilight of the thickets. Early, too early, the sun fell down behind the serrated forest-edge of the western hill, a ball of orange fire. . . .   One evening Delphin and Hervé, followed by two other canoes, paddled up to the landing.   New visitors had arrived, Dr. McLeod, who had long been an intimate of the Wishart family, and with him a buxom, fresh-complexioned Canadian woman, a trained nurse whom he had brought from Toronto. There, in nature's wilderness, Janet knew the supreme experience of women, the agony, the renewal and joy symbolic of nature herself. When the child was bathed and dressed in the clothes Augusta Maturin herself had made for it, she brought it into the room to the mother.

"It's a daughter," she announced.

Janet regarded the child wistfully. "I hoped it would be a boy," she said. "He would have had — a better chance." But she raised her arms, and the child was laid in the bed beside her.

"We'll see that she has a chance, my dear," Augusta Maturin replied, as she kissed her.

5

Ten days went by, Dr. McLeod lingered at Lac du Sablier, and Janet was still in bed. Even in this life-giving air she did not seem to grow stronger. Sometimes, when the child was sleeping in its basket on the sunny porch, Mrs. Maturin read to her; but often when she was supposed to rest, she lay gazing out of the open window into silver space listening to the mocking laughter of the loons, watching the ducks flying across the sky; or, as evening drew on, marking in the waters a steely angle that grew and grew — the wake of a beaver swimming homeward in the twilight. In the cold nights the timbers cracked to the frost, she heard the owls calling to one another from the fastnesses of the forest, and thought of life's inscrutable mystery. Then the child would be brought to her. It was a strange, unimagined happiness she knew when she felt it clutching at her breasts, at her heart, a happiness not unmixed with yearning, with sadness as she pressed it to her. Why could it not remain there always, to comfort her, to be nearer her than any living thing? Reluctantly she gave it back to the nurse, wistfully her eyes followed it. . . .

Twice a week, now, Delphin and Hervé made the journey to Saint Hubert, and one evening, after Janet had watched them paddling across the little bay that separated the camp from the outlet's mouth, Mrs. Maturin appeared, with an envelope in her hand.

"I've got a letter from Brooks Insall, Janet," she said, with a well-disguised effort to speak naturally. "It's not the first one he's sent me, but I haven't mentioned the others. He's in Silliston — and I wrote him about the daughter."

"Yes," said Janet.

"Well — he wants to come up here, to see you, before we go away. He asks me to telegraph your permission."

"Oh no, he mustn't, Mrs. Maturin!"

"You don't care to see him?"

"It isn't that. I'd like to see him if things had been different. But now that I've disappointed him — hurt him, I couldn't stand it. I know it's only his kindness."

After a moment Augusta Maturin handed Janet a sealed envelope she held in her hand.

"He asked me to give you this," she said, and left the room. Janet read it, and let it fall on the bedspread, where it was still lying when her friend returned and began tidying the room. From the direction of the guide's cabin, on the point, came the sounds of talk and laughter, broken by snatches of habitant songs. Augusta Maturin smiled. She pretended not to notice the tears in Janet's eyes, and strove to keep back her own.

"Delphin and Hervé saw a moose in the *décharge*," she explained. "Of course it was a big one, it always is! They're telling the doctor about it."

"Mrs. Maturin," said Janet, "I'd like to talk to you. I think I ought to tell you what Mr. Insall says."

"Yes, my dear," her friend replied, a little faintly, sitting down on the bed.

"He asks me to believe what — I've done makes no difference to him. Of course he doesn't put it in so many words, but he says he doesn't care anything about conventions," Janet continued slowly. "What I told him when he asked me to marry him in Silliston was a shock to him, it was so — so unexpected. He went away, to Maine, but as soon as he began to think it all over he wanted to come and tell me that he loved me in spite of it, but he felt he couldn't, under the circumstances, that he had to wait until — now. Although I didn't give him any explanation, he wants me to know that he trusts me, he understands — it's because, he says, I am what I am. He still wishes to marry me, to take care of me and the child. We could live in California, at first — he's always been anxious to go there, he says."

"Well, my dear?" Augusta Maturin forced herself to say at last.

"It's so generous — so like him!" Janet exclaimed. "But of course I couldn't accept such a sacrifice, even if —" She paused. "Oh, it's made me so sad all summer to think that he's unhappy because of me!"

"I know, Janet, but you should realize, as I told you in Silliston, that it isn't by any deliberate act of your own, it's just one of those things that occur in this world and that can't be foreseen or avoided." Augusta Maturin spoke with an effort. In spite of Janet's apparent calm, she had never been more acutely aware of the girl's inner suffering.

"I know," said Janet. "But it's terrible to think that those things we unintentionally do, perhaps because of faults we have previously committed, should have the same effect as acts that are intentional."

"The world is very stupid. All suffering, I think, is brought about by stupidity. If we only could learn to look at ourselves as we are! It's a stupid, unenlightened society that metes out most of our punishments and usually de-

mands a senseless expiation." Augusta Maturin waited,
and presently Janet spoke again.

"I've been thinking all summer, Mrs. Maturin. There
was so much I wanted to talk about with you, but I wanted
to be sure of myself first. And now, since the baby came,
and I know I'm not going to get well, I seem to see things
much more clearly."

"Why do you say you're not going to get well, Janet?
In this air, and with the child to live for!"

"I know it. Dr. McLeod knows it, or he wouldn't be
staying here, and you've both been too kind to tell me.
You've been so kind, Mrs. Maturin — I can't talk about it.
But I'm sure I'm going to die, I've really known it ever
since we left Silliston. Something's gone out of me, the
thing that drove me, that made me want to live — I can't
express what I mean any other way. Perhaps it's this child,
the new life — perhaps I've just been broken, I don't know.
You did your best to mend me, and that's one thing that
makes me sad. And the thought of Mr. Insall's another.
In some ways it would have been worse to live — I couldn't
have ruined his life. And even if things had been different,
I hadn't come to love him, in *that* way — it's queer, because
he's such a wonderful person. I'd like to live for the child,
if only I had the strength, the will left in me — but that's
gone. And maybe I could save her from — what I've been
through."

Augusta Maturin took Janet's hand in hers.

"Janet," she said, "I've been a lonely woman, as you
know, with nothing to look forward to. I've always wanted
a child since my little Edith went. I wanted you, my dear,
I want your child, your daughter — as I want nothing else in
the world. I will take her, I will try to bring her up in the
light, and Brooks Insall will help me. . . ."

THE END

Printed in the United States of America.

A Far Country

By WINSTON CHURCHILL

Author of " The Inside of the Cup," etc.

Illustrated, $1.50

"No one can afford to miss reading 'A Far Country,' or reading it can fail to be interested. The themes Mr. Churchill handles are the big themes confronting all America and in the fortunes and misfortunes of his characters he indicates energies and developments that are nation-wide. It touches on what is vital . . . and it will help in no small degree to broaden our thought and clarify our vision. Many people read 'The Inside of the Cup,' but 'A Far Country' should reach a wider audience." — *New York Times.*

"A powerfully written story, displaying wonderful scope and clarity of vision. Presents a wonderful study of American emotions." — *Boston Globe.*

"A story worthily complete . . . vastly encouraging. The kind of a book that points to a hope and a right road." — *New York World.*

"Mr. Churchill has done a difficult thing well. . . . We congratulate him on an achievement well worth while." — *Chicago Post.*

"A great piece of art, comprising admirable humanization, plot and sympathy, diverse as intrinsic . . . and many interesting side issues. Any author might well be proud of such an achievement." — *Chicago Herald.*

"'A Far Country'" is a strong story that is vital and compelling. . . . Adds one more leaf to Mr. Churchill's literary laurels." — *Philadelphia Ledger.*

THE MACMILLAN COMPANY

Publishers   64-66 Fifth Avenue   New York

The Crossing
Illustrated, $1.50

"A thoroughly interesting book, packed with exciting adventure and sentimental incident, yet faithful to historical fact both in detail and in spirit." — *The Dial*.

"Mr. Churchill's novel is a vigorous and absorbing love story." — *The Seattle Times*.

"Deals with one of the most fascinating dramas in the history of the world. It is brimming with interest." — *Brooklyn Eagle*.

"So widespread is Winston Churchill's popularity, so breathless the public interest excited by each anxiously awaited new novel from his pen, that one is perforce compelled to pay him the compliment of early reading and thorough consideration. But his achievement is noteworthy. . . .

"'The Crossing' is, moreover, far in advance of 'The Crisis.' It is more real, more genuine, more spontaneous, more vigorous, a clearer and more coherent picture of its times. It contains no little humor." — *Boston Transcript*.

The Crisis
Illustrated, $1.50

"A charming love story that never loses its interest. . . . The intense political bitterness, the intense patriotism of both parties, are shown understandingly." — *Evening Telegraph*, Philadelphia.

"In some respects 'Richard Carvel' was a new thing; by comparison 'The Crisis' is something that has been done often before, but never done so well. The vivacity, variety and spirit of the old Southern social life have never been so well suggested, not even in 'Red Rock.' The women are altogether delightful — Mr. Churchill's forte is fascinating and spirited patrician women." — *Boston Herald*.

"There have been many novels built upon the interests aroused and stilled by the Civil War, but there has been none surpassing this in truth and power." — *Argonaut*, San Francisco.

"It is a high office to give a new generation of Americans their first vivid conception of the struggle in which the Nation was reborn." — *The Review of Reviews*.

THE MACMILLAN COMPANY
Publishers   **64-66 Fifth Avenue**   **New York**